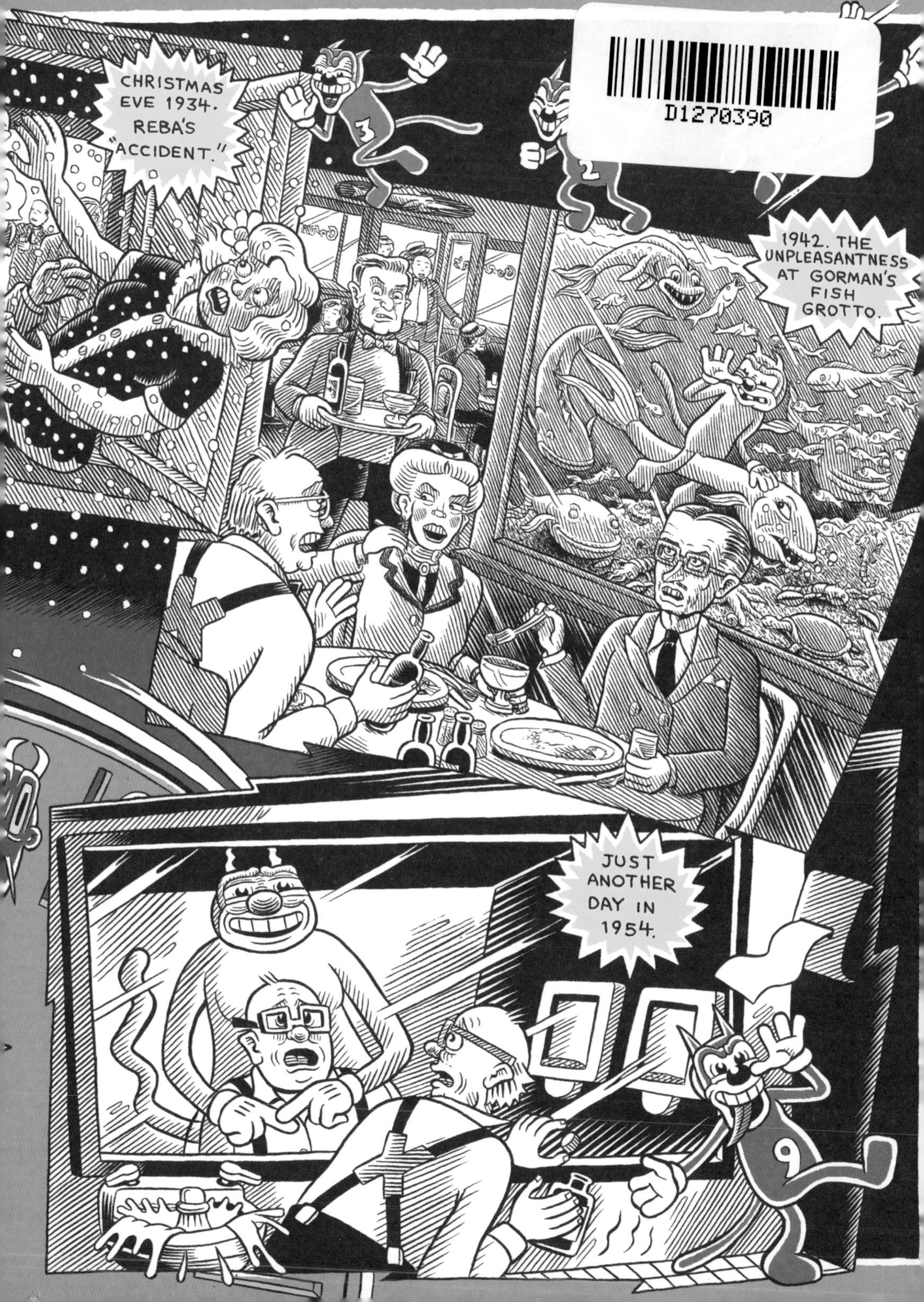
CHRISTMAS EVE 1934. REBA'S "ACCIDENT."
1942. THE UNPLEASANTNESS AT GORMAN'S FISH GROTTO.
JUST ANOTHER DAY IN 1954.

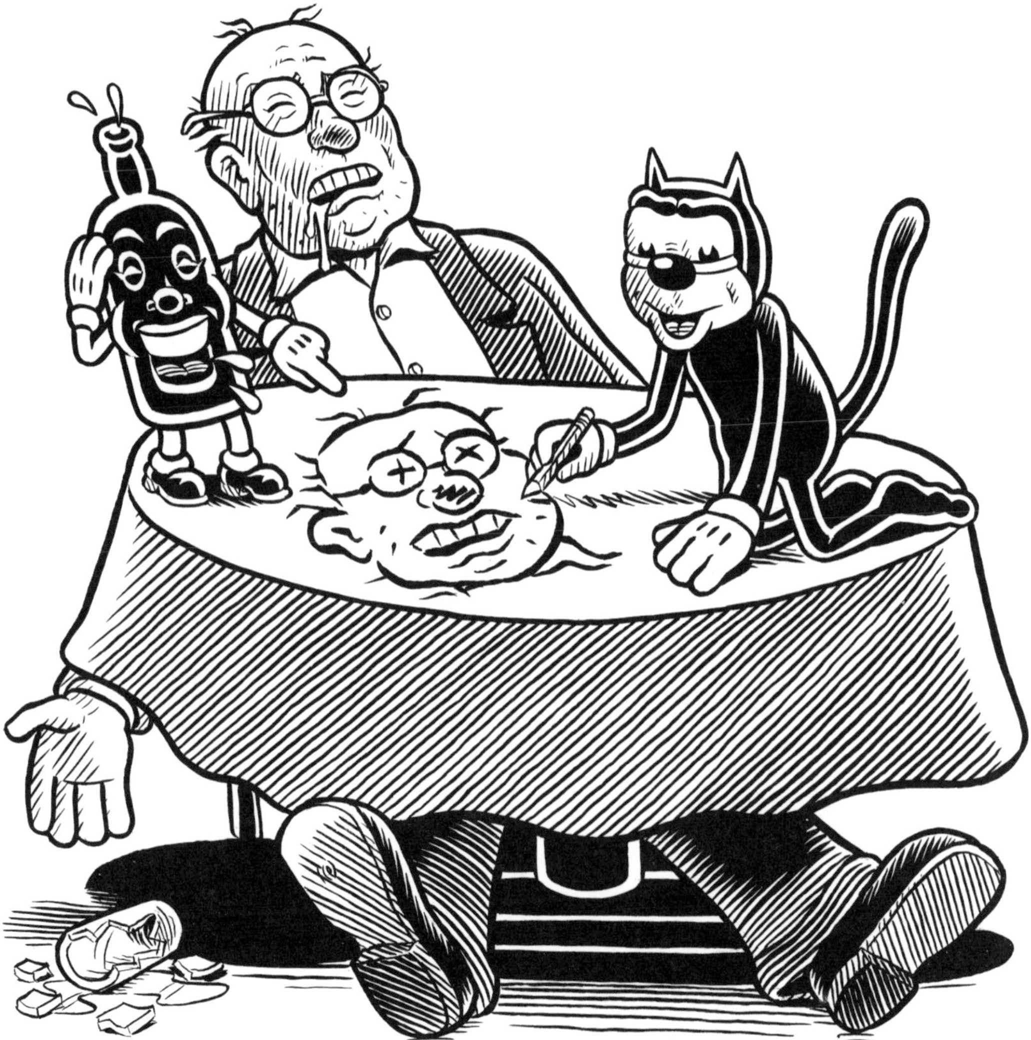

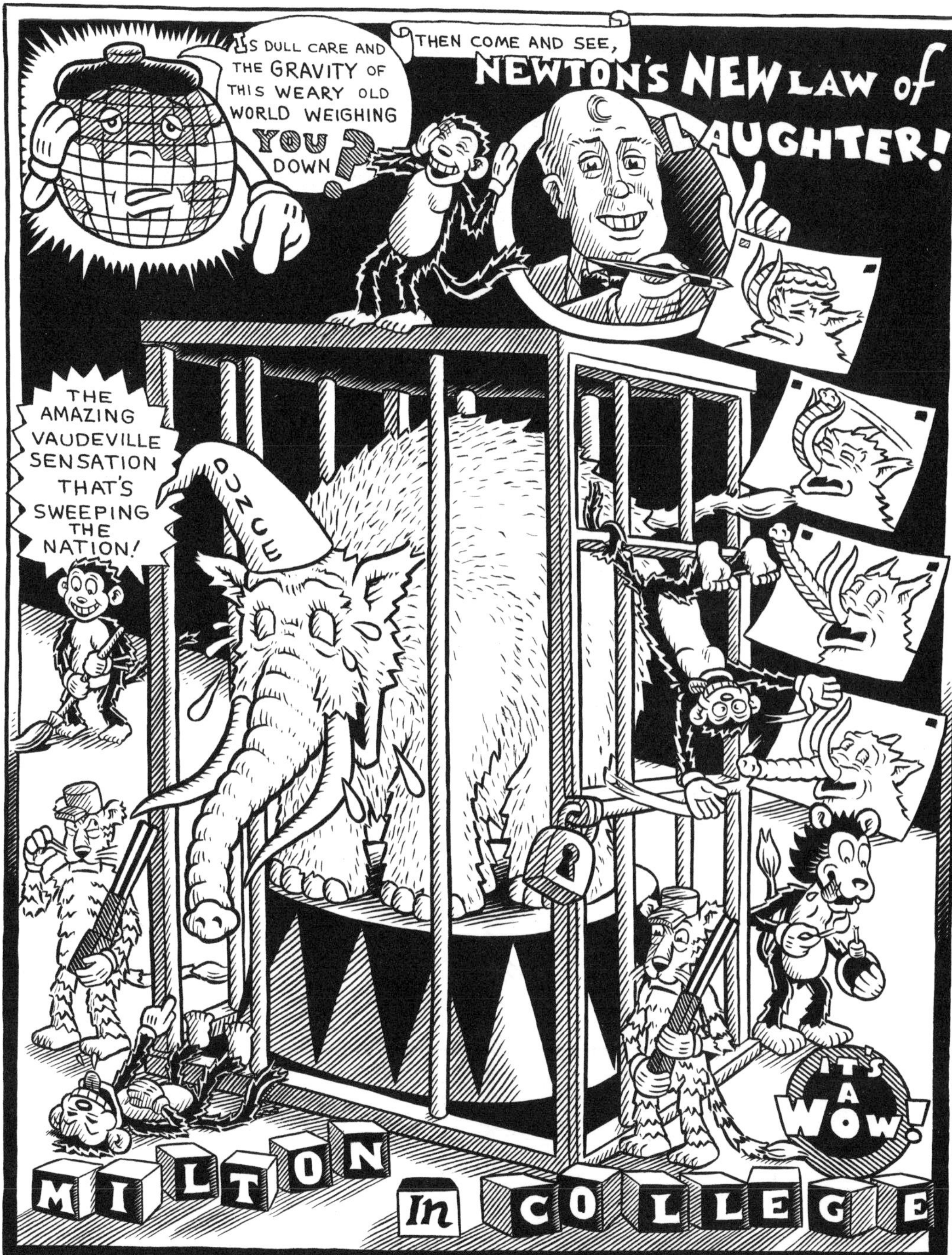
IS DULL CARE AND THE GRAVITY OF THIS WEARY OLD WORLD WEIGHING YOU DOWN?
THEN COME AND SEE,
NEWTON'S NEW LAW of LAUGHTER!
THE AMAZING VAUDEVILLE SENSATION THAT'S SWEEPING THE NATION!
DUNCE
IT'S A WOW!
MILTON In COLLEGE

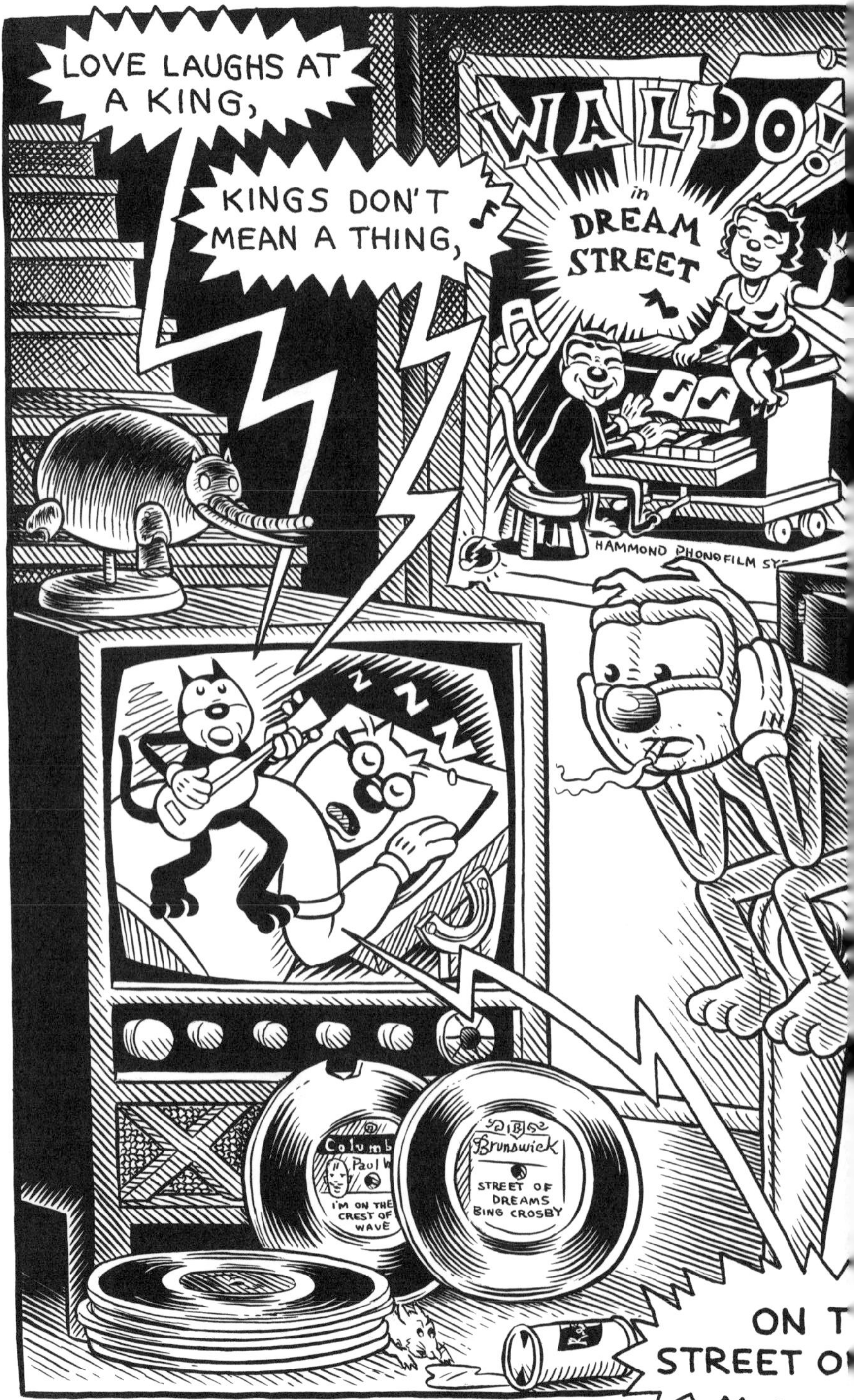
LOVE LAUGHS AT A KING,
KINGS DON'T MEAN A THING,
WALDO
in DREAM STREET
HAMMOND PHONOFILM SYS
Columbia
Paul W
I'M ON THE CREST OF A WAVE
Brunswick
STREET OF DREAMS BING CROSBY
ON T
STREET O

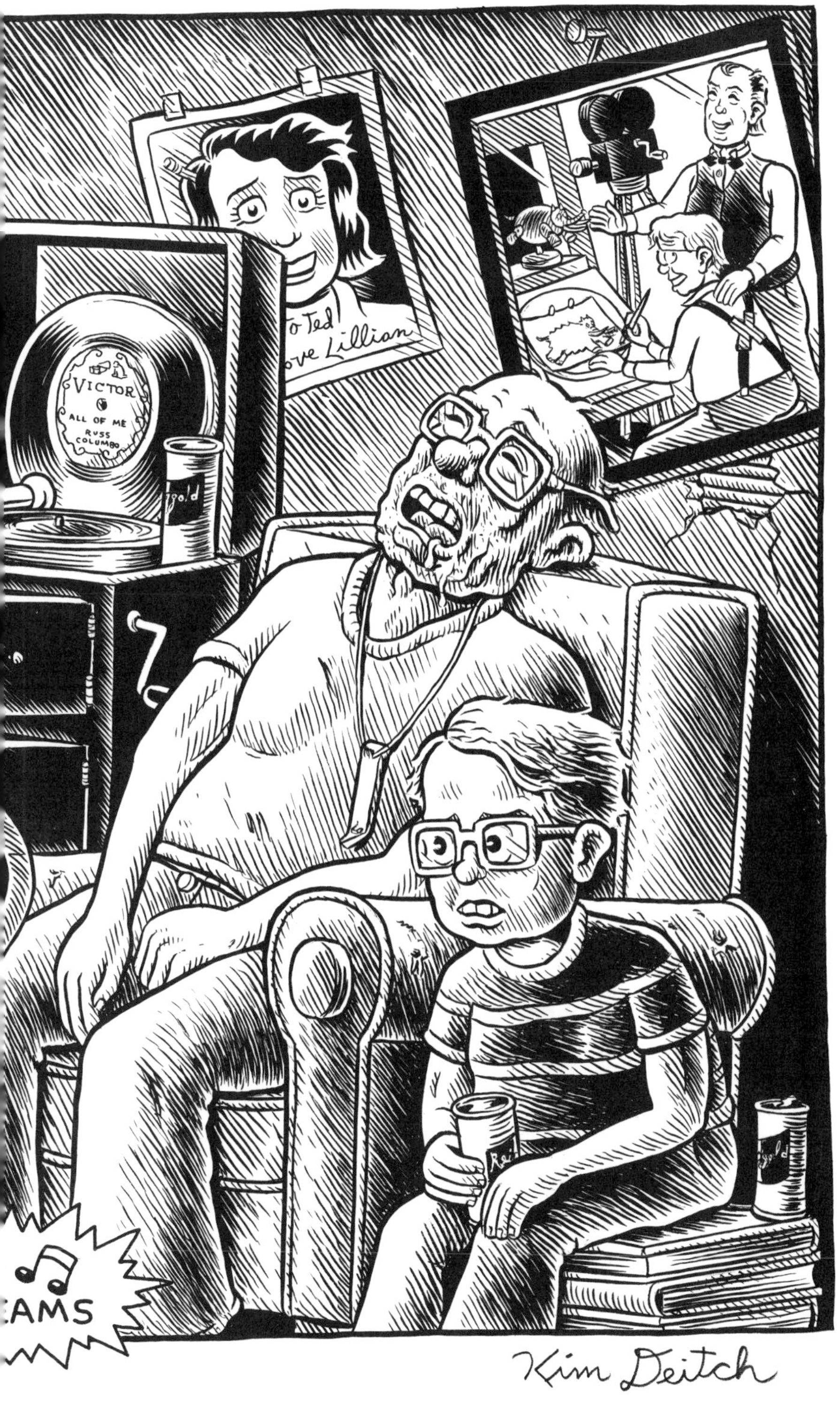
To Ted
ove Lillian
VICTOR
ALL OF ME
RUSS COLUMBO
AMS
Kim Deitch

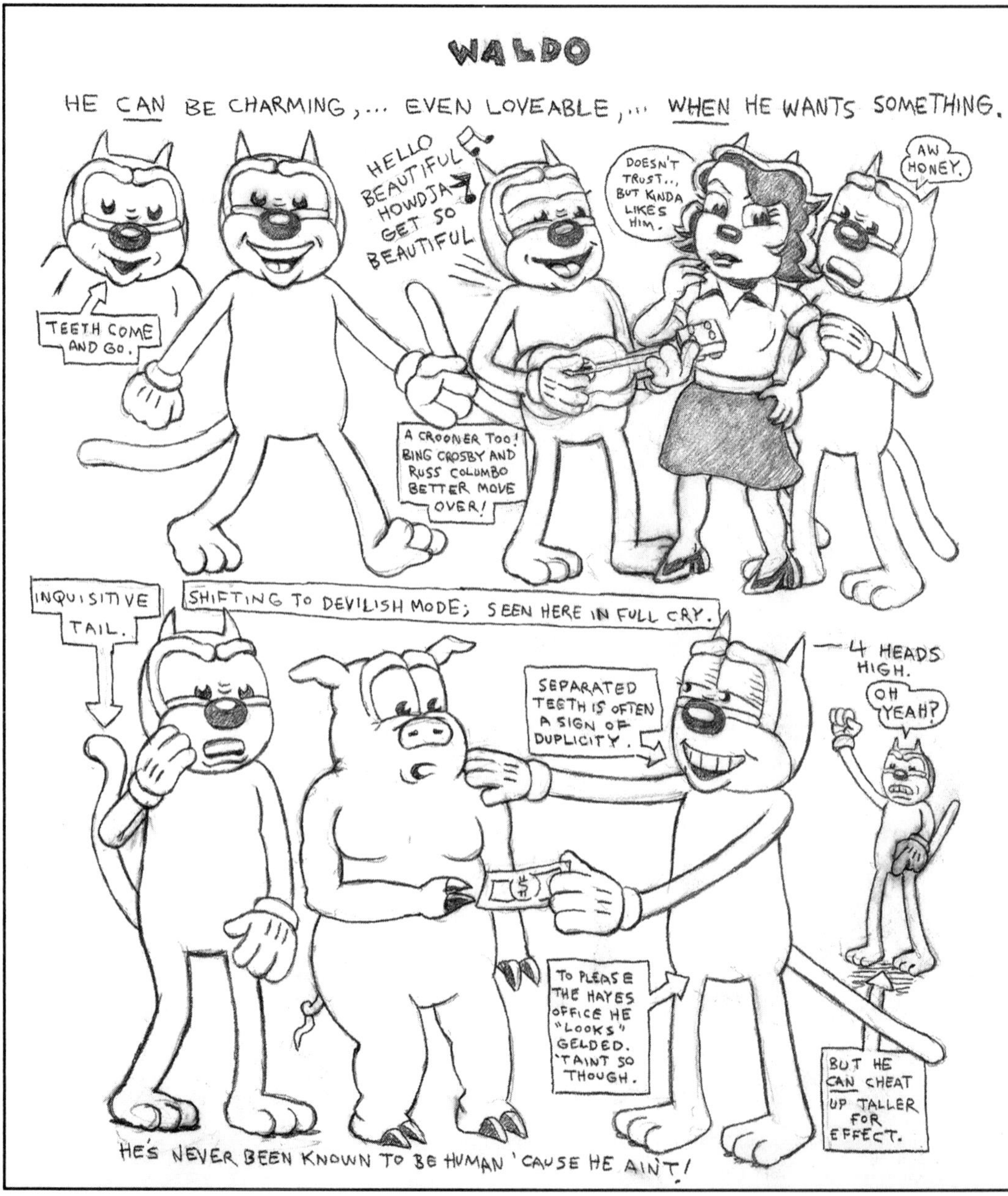
WALDO
HE CAN BE CHARMING,... EVEN LOVEABLE,... WHEN HE WANTS SOMETHING.
TEETH COME AND GO.
HELLO BEAUTIFUL HOWDJA GET SO BEAUTIFUL
A CROONER TOO! BING CROSBY AND RUSS COLUMBO BETTER MOVE OVER!
DOESN'T TRUST.., BUT KINDA LIKES HIM.
AW HONEY.
INQUISITIVE TAIL.
SHIFTING TO DEVILISH MODE; SEEN HERE IN FULL CRY.
SEPARATED TEETH IS OFTEN A SIGN OF DUPLICITY.
— 4 HEADS HIGH.
OH YEAH?
TO PLEASE THE HAYES OFFICE HE "LOOKS" GELDED. 'TAINT SO THOUGH.
BUT HE CAN CHEAT UP TALLER FOR EFFECT.
HE'S NEVER BEEN KNOWN TO BE HUMAN 'CAUSE HE AIN'T!

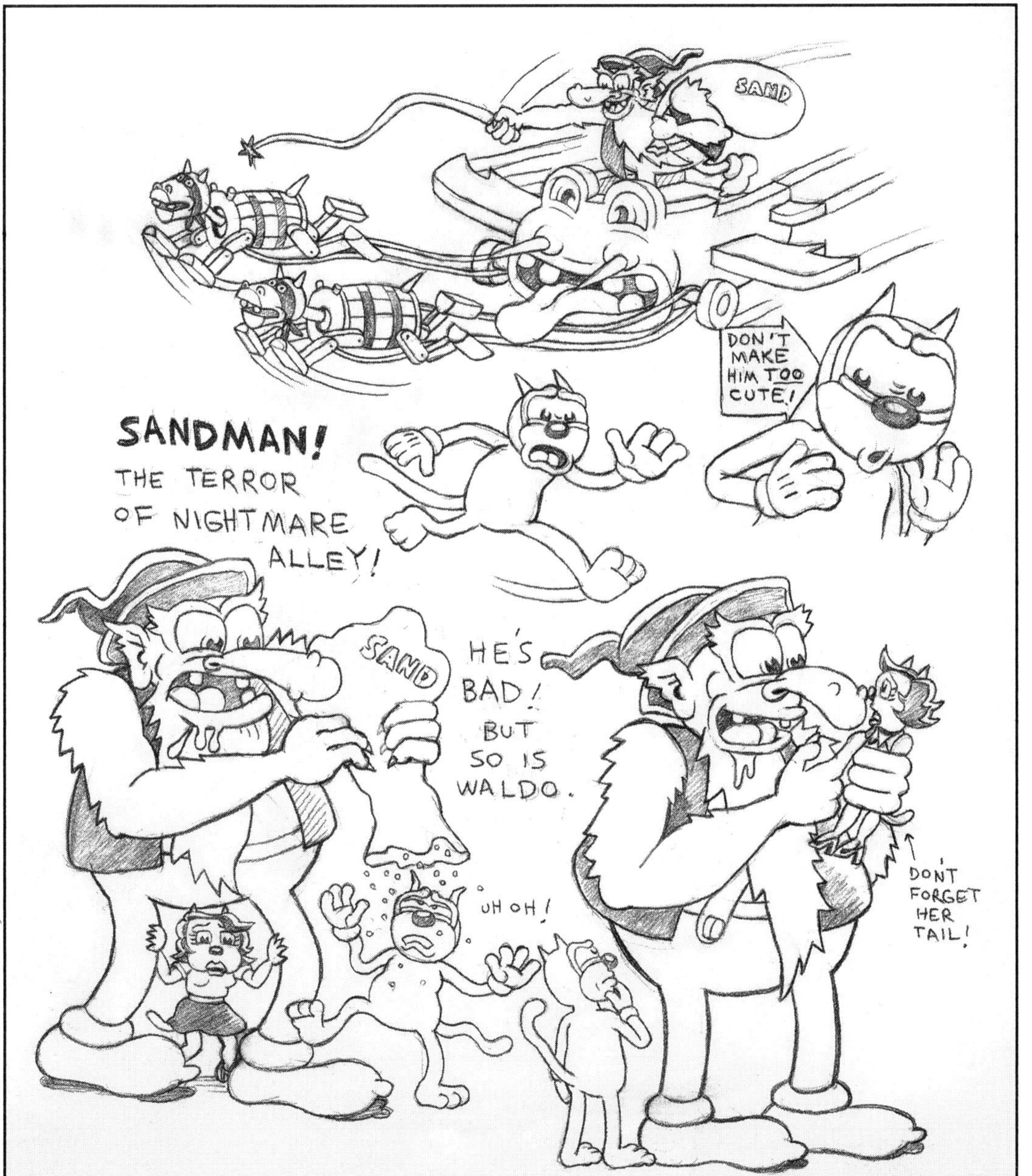
SAND
DON'T MAKE HIM TOO CUTE!
SANDMAN! THE TERROR OF NIGHTMARE ALLEY!
SAND
HE'S BAD! BUT SO IS WALDO.
UH OH!
DON'T FORGET HER TAIL!

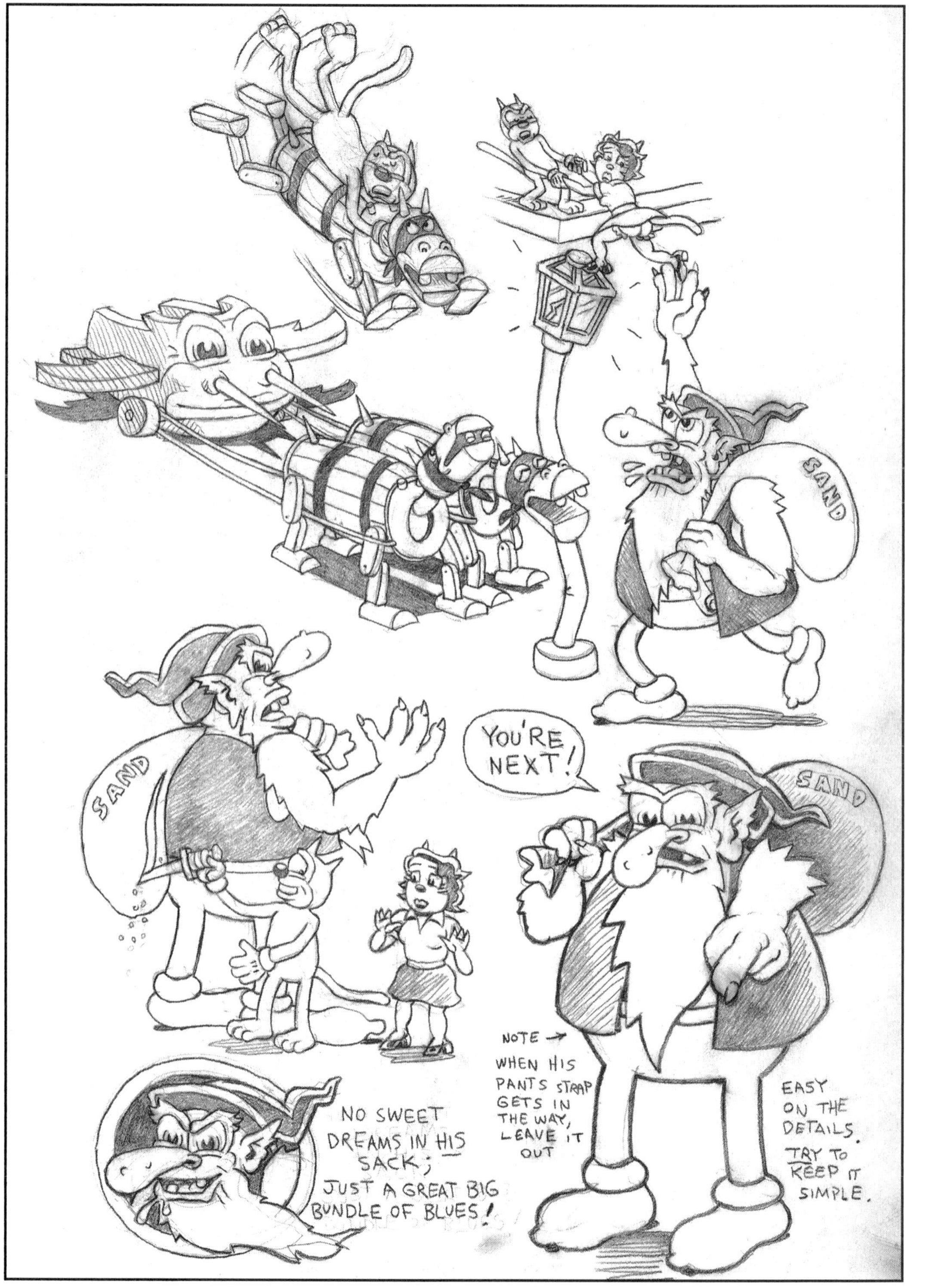
SAND
YOU'RE NEXT!
SAND
SAND
NOTE →
WHEN HIS PANTS STRAP GETS IN THE WAY, LEAVE IT OUT
EASY ON THE DETAILS. TRY TO KEEP IT SIMPLE.
NO SWEET DREAMS IN HIS SACK; JUST A GREAT BIG BUNDLE OF BLUES!

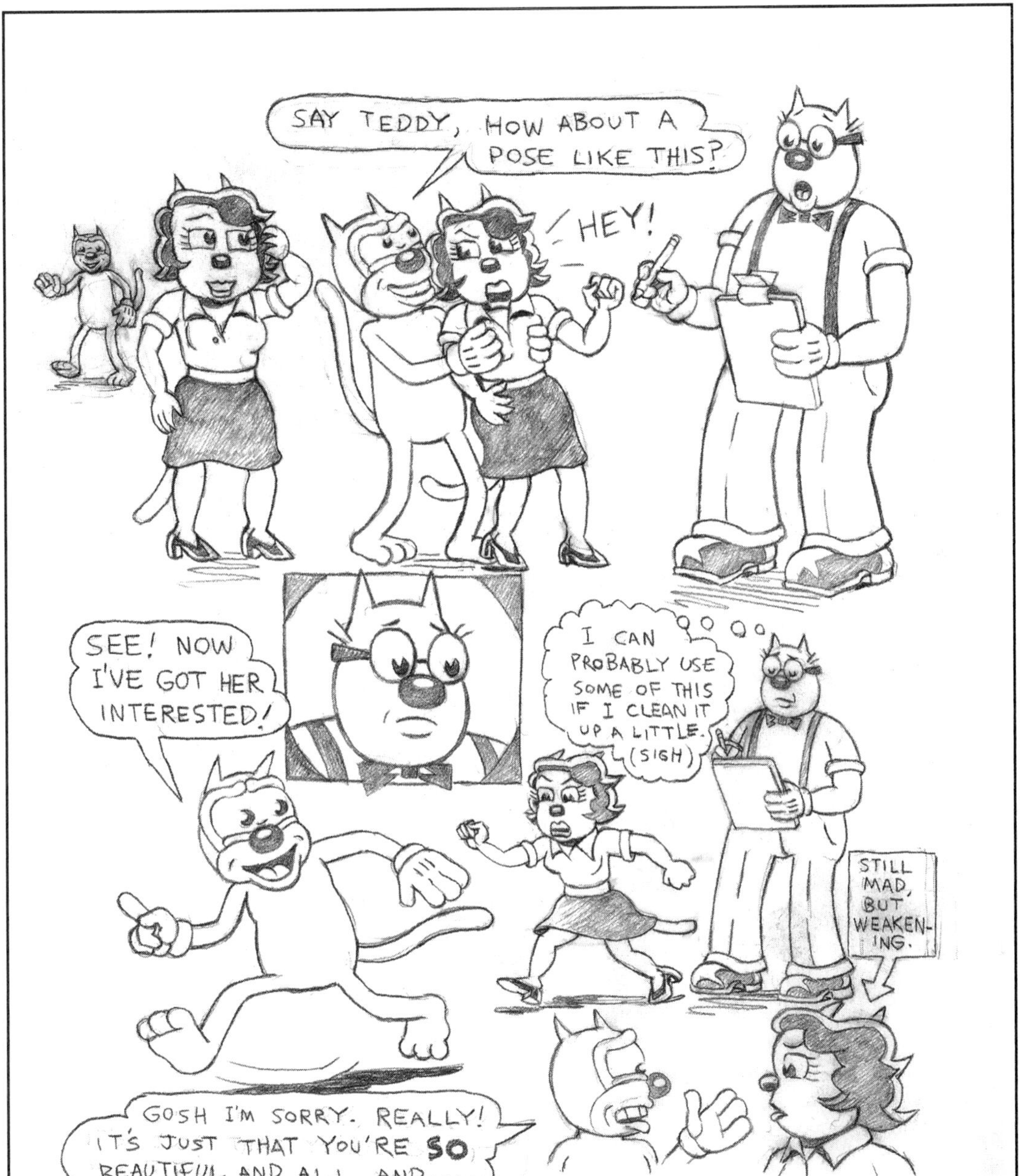
SAY TEDDY, HOW ABOUT A POSE LIKE THIS?
HEY!
SEE! NOW I'VE GOT HER INTERESTED!
I CAN PROBABLY USE SOME OF THIS IF I CLEAN IT UP A LITTLE. (SIGH)
STILL MAD, BUT WEAKEN-ING.
GOSH I'M SORRY. REALLY! IT'S JUST THAT YOU'RE SO BEAUTIFUL AND ALL, AND....

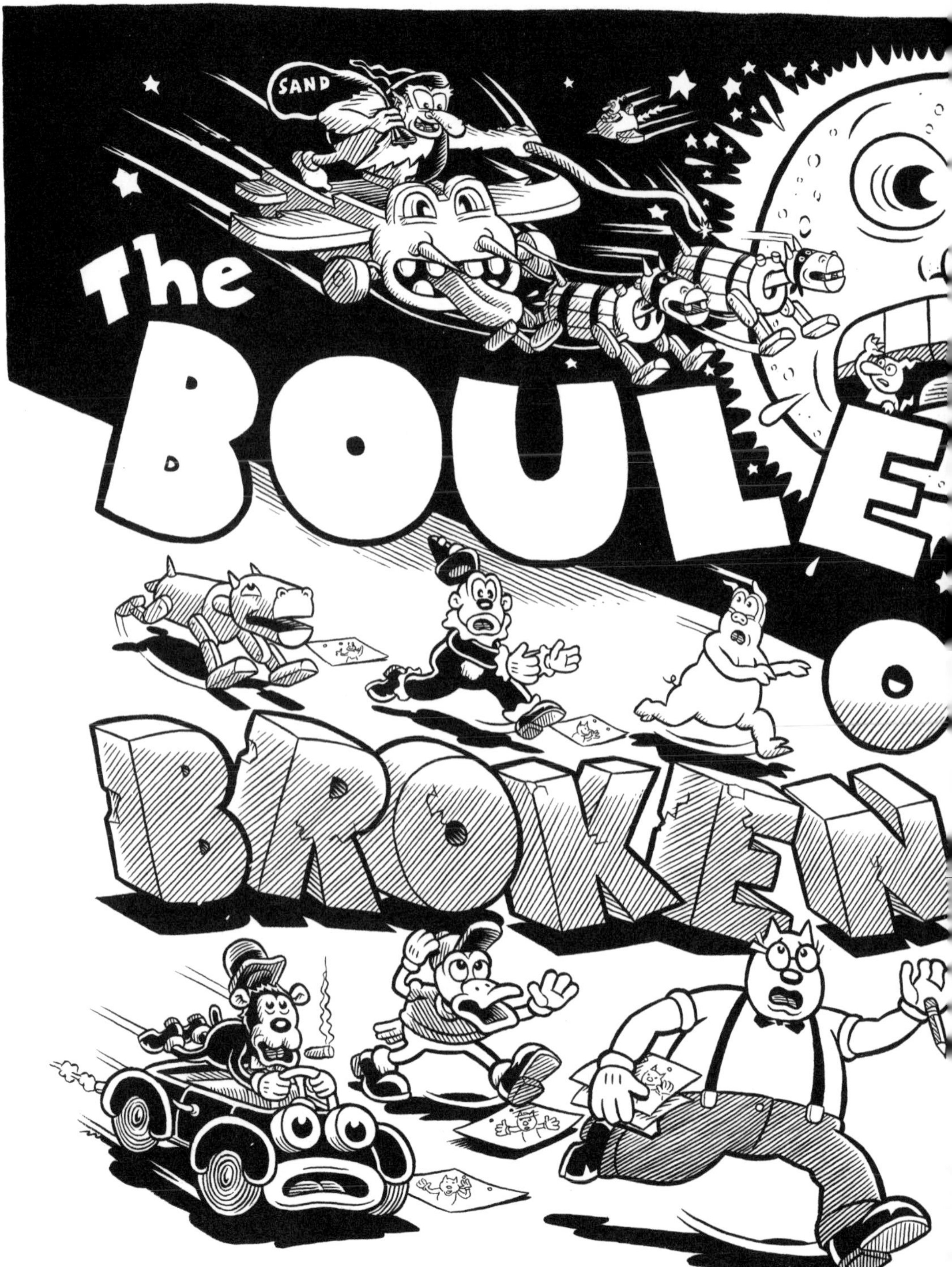
SAND
The
BOULE
O
BROKEN

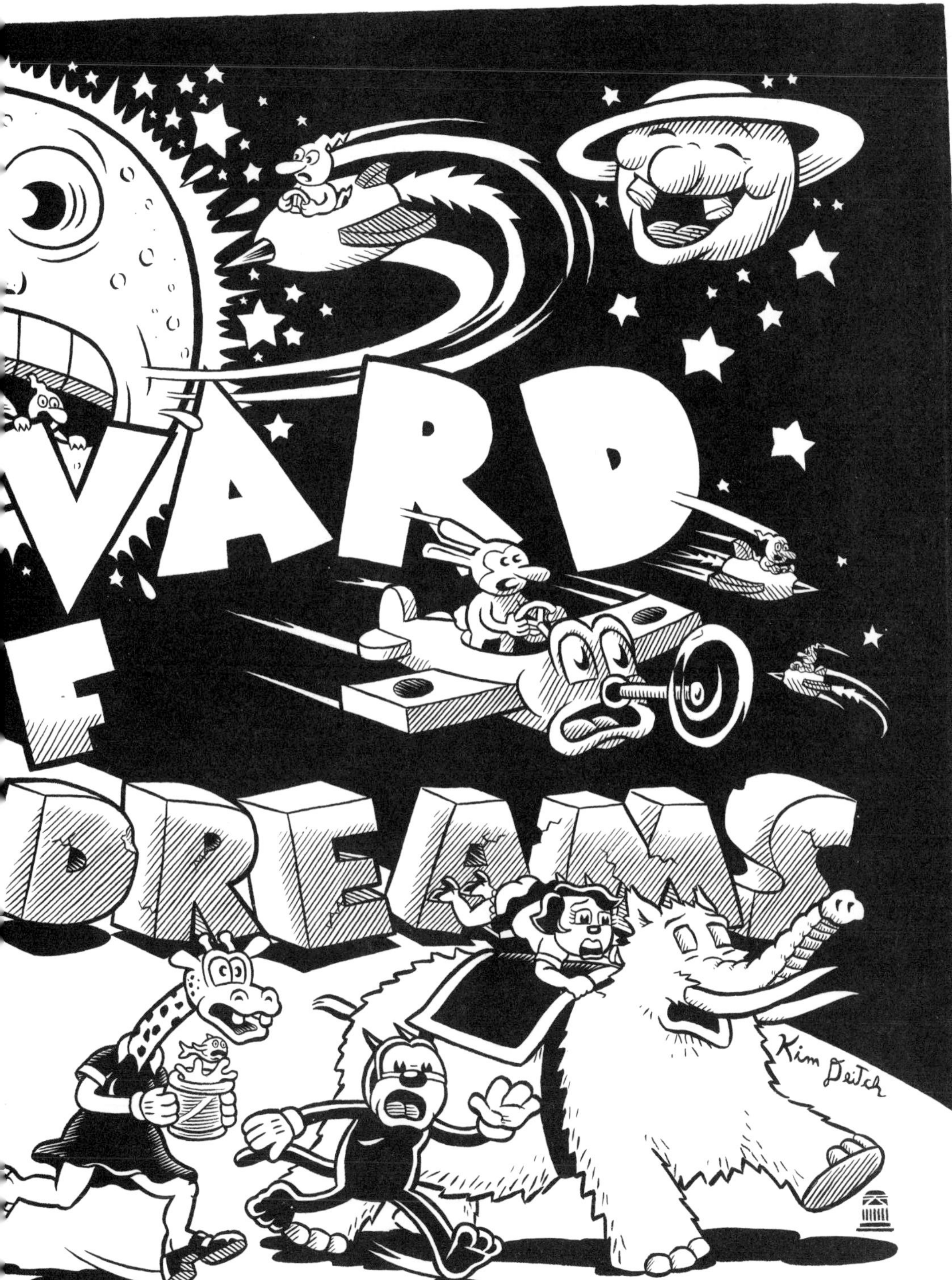
VARD
F
DREAMS
Kim Deitch

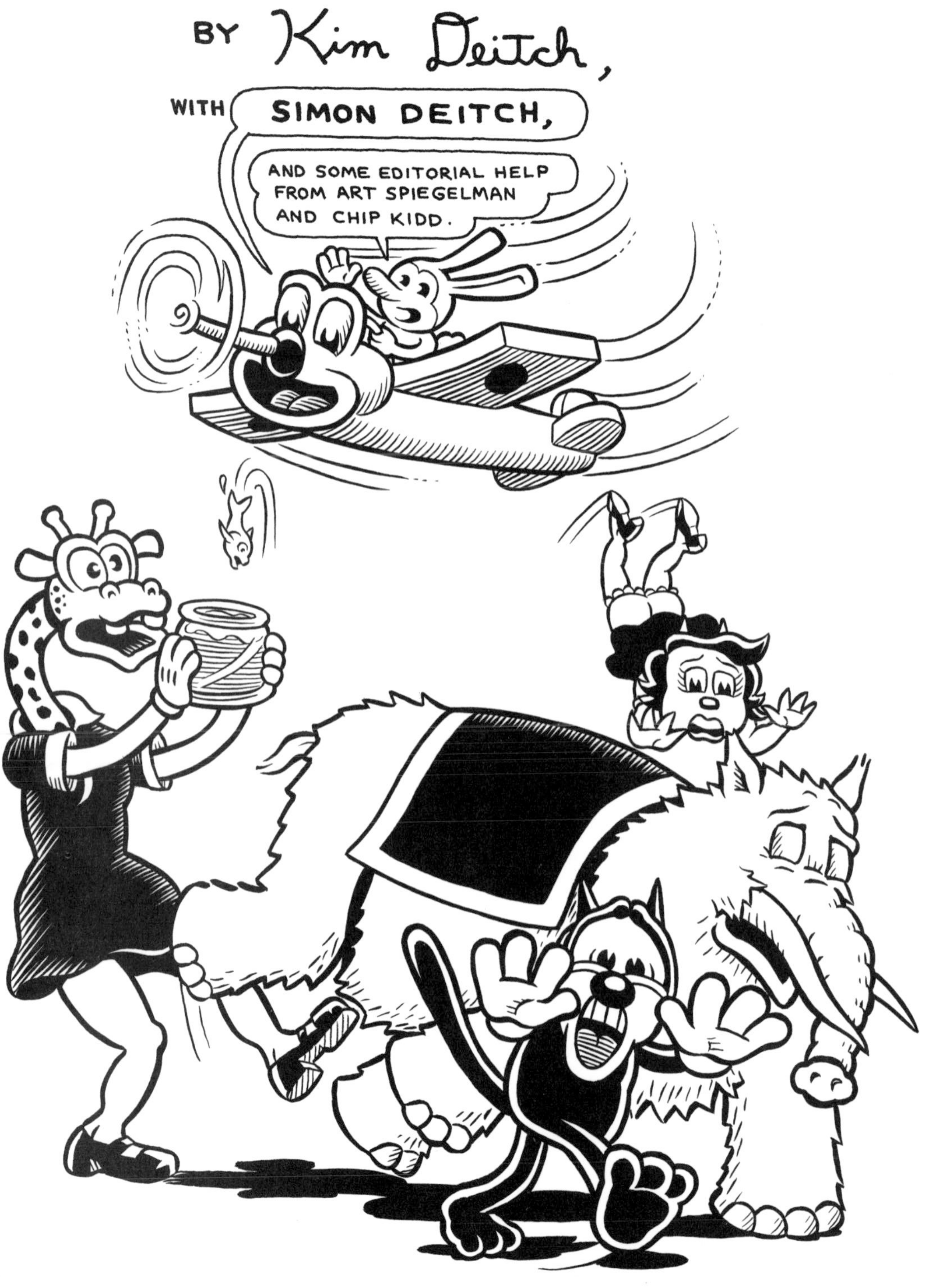
BY Kim Deitch,
WITH SIMON DEITCH,
AND SOME EDITORIAL HELP FROM ART SPIEGELMAN AND CHIP KIDD.

PUBLISHED IN THE UNITED STATES BY PANTHEON BOOKS, A DIVISION OF RANDOM HOUSE, Inc., NEW YORK, AND SIMULTANEOUSLY IN CANADA BY RANDOM HOUSE OF CANADA LIMITED, TORONTO.

PORTIONS OF THIS BOOK WERE PREVIOUSLY PUBLISHED IN RAW MAGAZINE.

LIBRARY OF CONGRESS CATALOGING-IN-PUBLICATION DATA
DEITCH, KIM
THE BOULEVARD OF BROKEN DREAMS / KIM DEITCH.
P. CM.
ISBN 0-375-42191-2
I. TITLE.
PN6727.D383 B68 2002 741.5'973--dc21 2002022484

www.pantheonbooks.com
BOOK DESIGN BY KIM DEITCH
PRINTED IN THE UNITED STATES OF AMERICA
FIRST EDITION
9 8 7 6 5 4 3 2 1

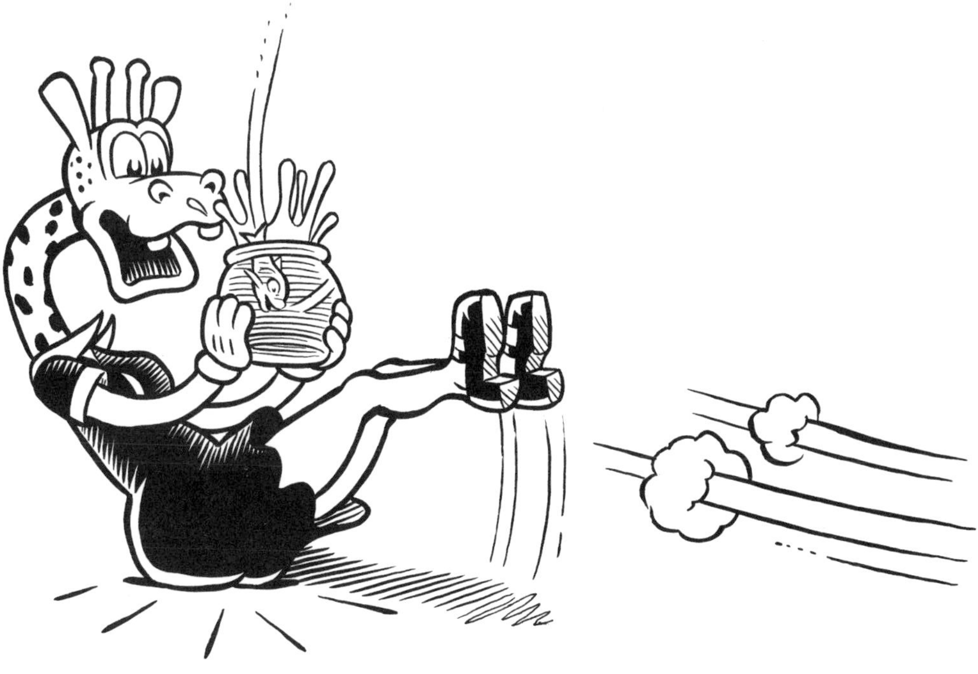

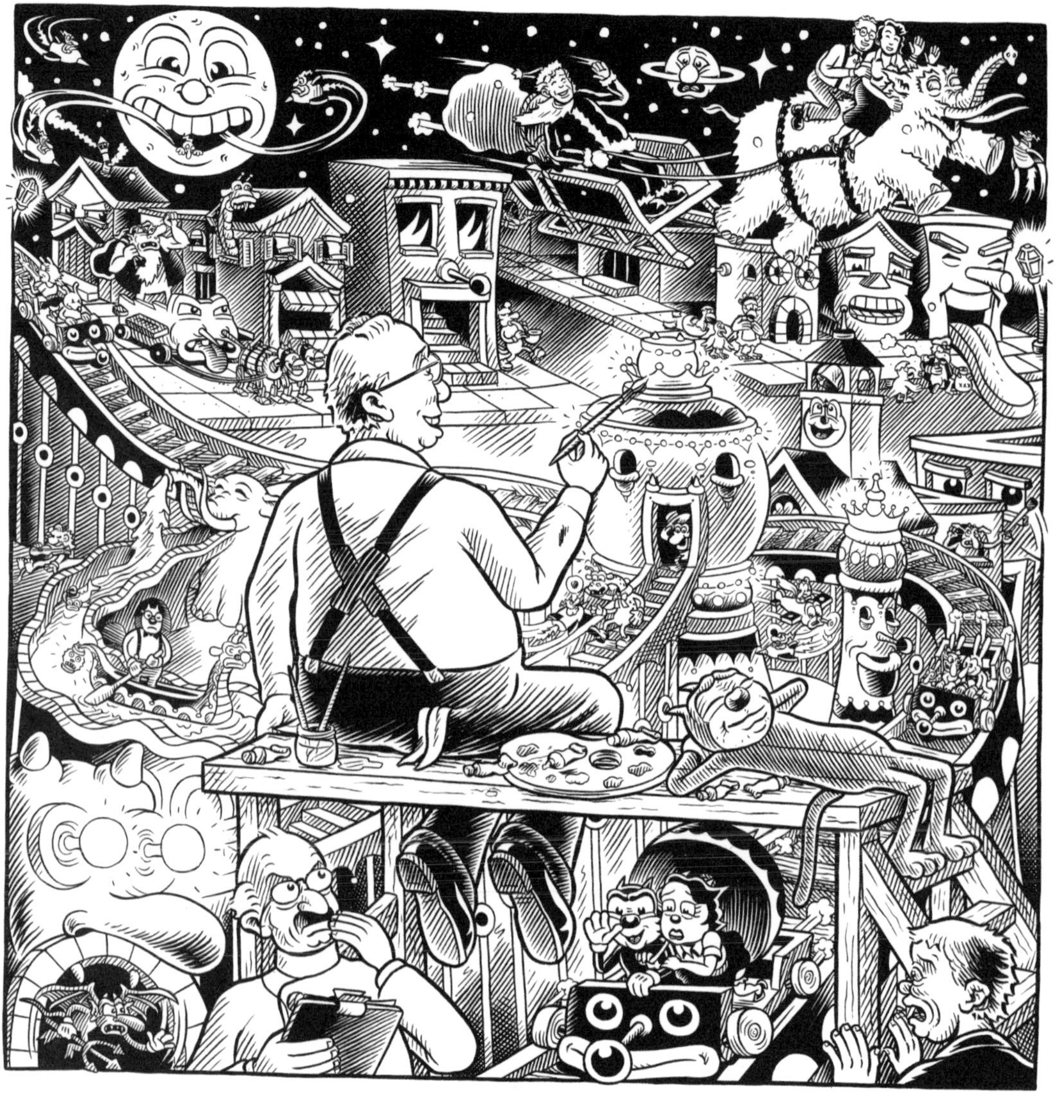

Kim Deitch

THIS BOOK IS DEDICATED TO MY MOTHER, MY FATHER, BOTH OF MY BROTHERS, ART SPIEGELMAN, CHRIS WARE, CHIP KIDD, AND MOST OF ALL, TO MY LOVELY WIFE PAM.

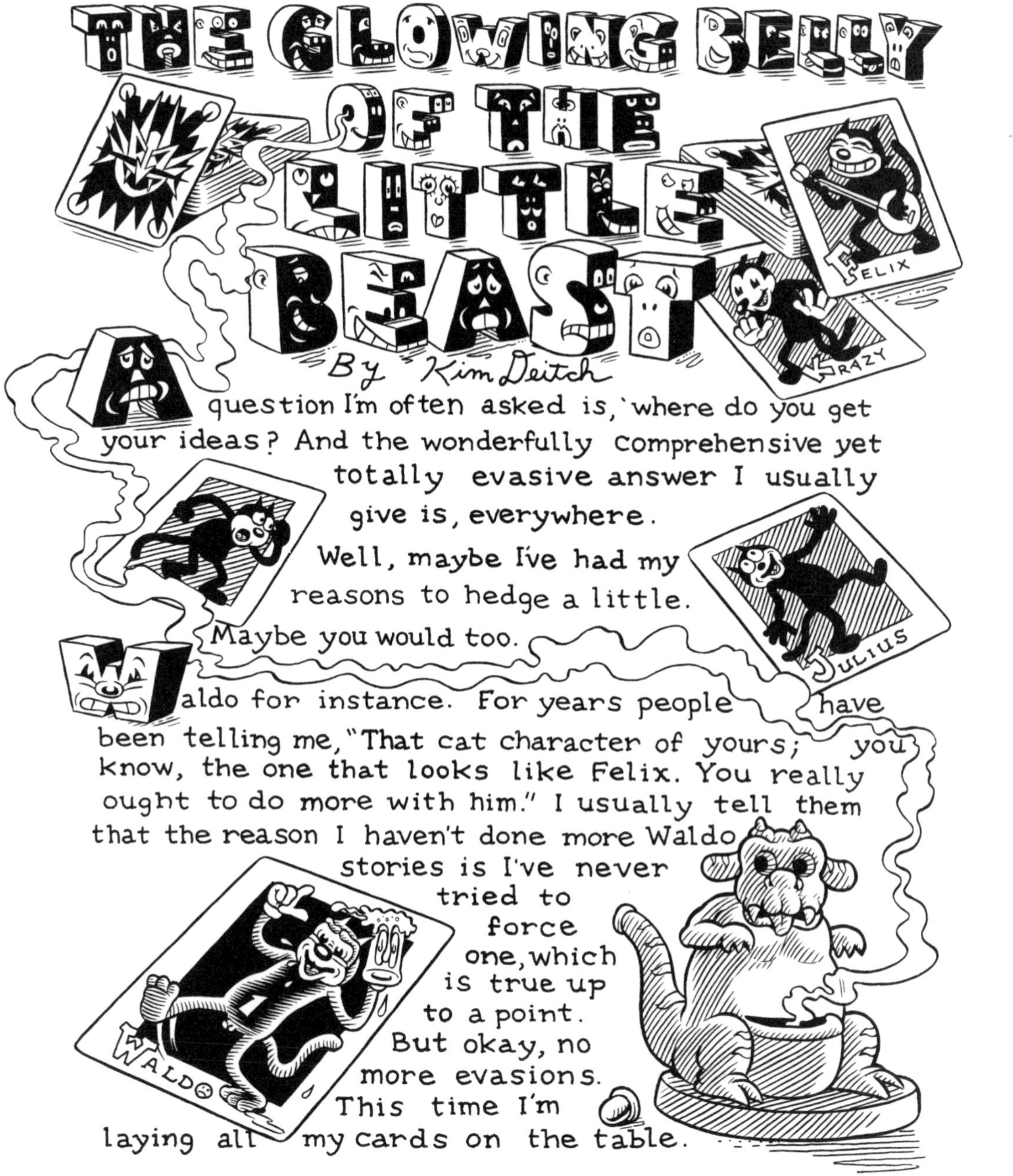
THE GLOWING BELLY OF THE LITTLE BEAST
By Kim Deitch
FELIX
KRAZY
A question I'm often asked is, `where do you get your ideas? And the wonderfully comprehensive yet totally evasive answer I usually give is, everywhere.
Well, maybe I've had my reasons to hedge a little.
Maybe you would too.
JULIUS
Waldo for instance. For years people have been telling me, "That cat character of yours; you know, the one that looks like Felix. You really ought to do more with him." I usually tell them that the reason I haven't done more Waldo stories is I've never tried to force one, which is true up to a point.
But okay, no more evasions.
WALDO
This time I'm laying all my cards on the table.

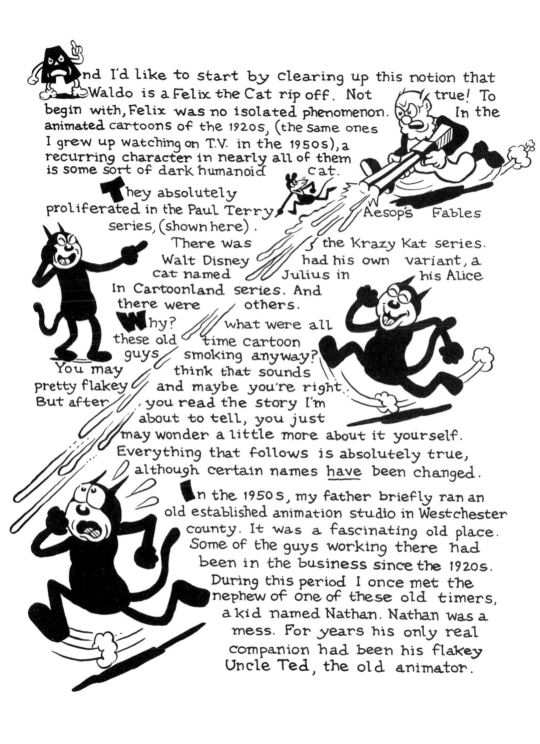

And I'd like to start by clearing up this notion that Waldo is a Felix the Cat rip off. Not true! To begin with, Felix was no isolated phenomenon. In the animated cartoons of the 1920s, (the same ones I grew up watching on T.V. in the 1950s), a recurring character in nearly all of them is some sort of dark humanoid cat.

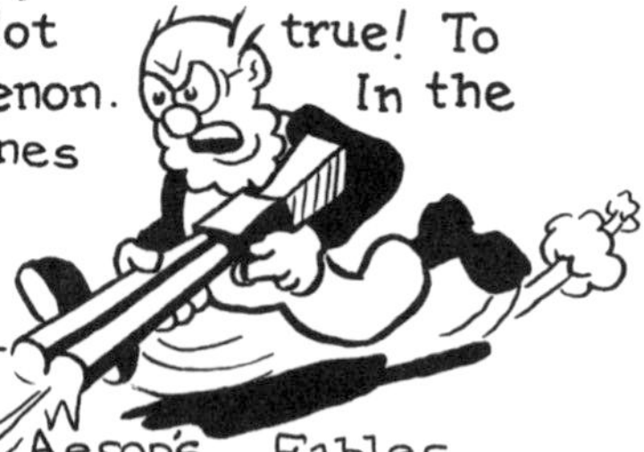

They absolutely proliferated in the Paul Terry Aesop's Fables series, (shown here). There was the Krazy Kat series. Walt Disney had his own variant, a cat named Julius in his Alice In Cartoonland series. And there were others.

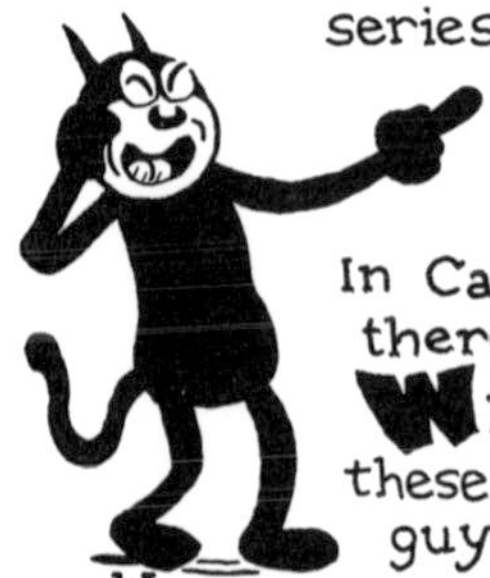

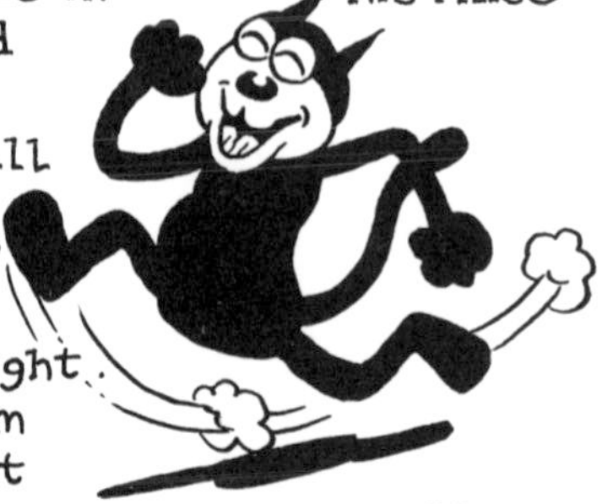

Why? what were all these old time cartoon guys smoking anyway? You may think that sounds pretty flakey and maybe you're right. But after you read the story I'm about to tell, you just may wonder a little more about it yourself. Everything that follows is absolutely true, although certain names have been changed.

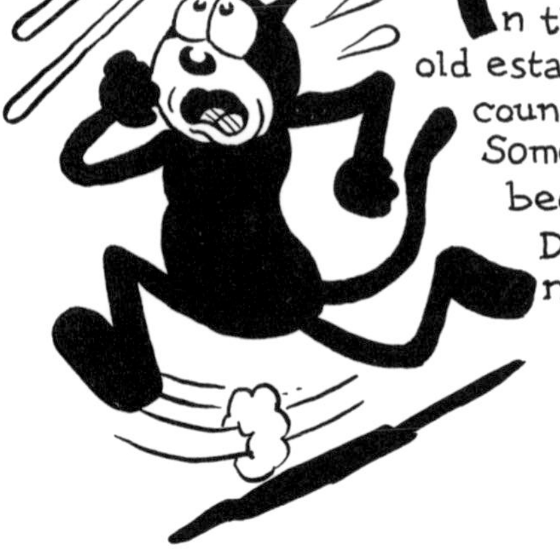

In the 1950s, my father briefly ran an old established animation studio in Westchester county. It was a fascinating old place. Some of the guys working there had been in the business since the 1920s. During this period I once met the nephew of one of these old timers, a kid named Nathan. Nathan was a mess. For years his only real companion had been his flakey Uncle Ted, the old animator.

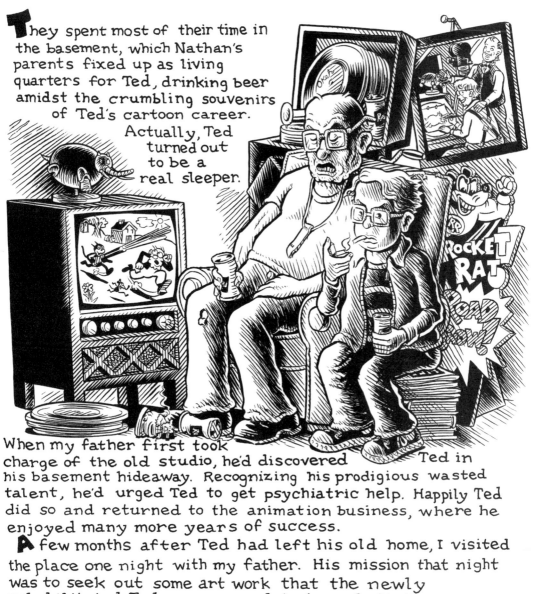

They spent most of their time in the basement, which Nathan's parents fixed up as living quarters for Ted, drinking beer amidst the crumbling souvenirs of Ted's cartoon career.

Actually, Ted turned out to be a real sleeper.

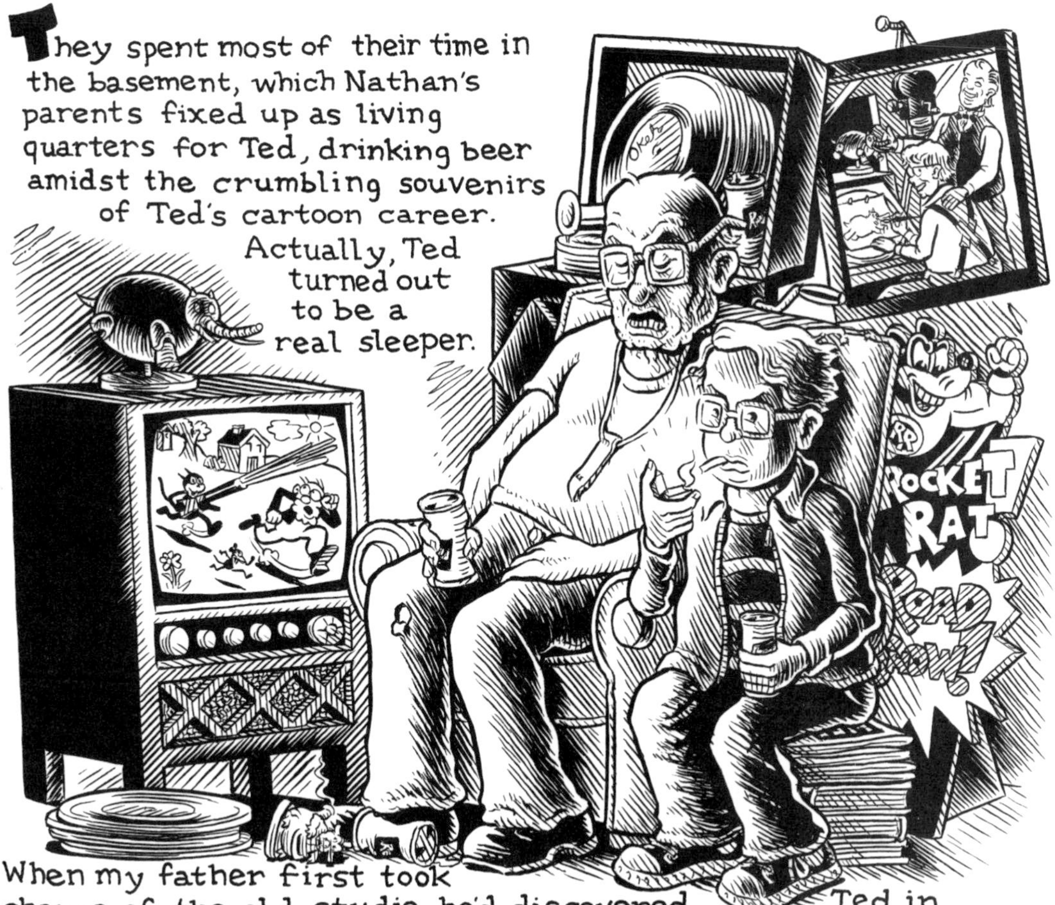
ROCKET RAT

When my father first took charge of the old studio, he'd discovered Ted in his basement hideaway. Recognizing his prodigious wasted talent, he'd urged Ted to get psychiatric help. Happily Ted did so and returned to the animation business, where he enjoyed many more years of success.

A few months after Ted had left his old home, I visited the place one night with my father. His mission that night was to seek out some art work that the newly rehabilitated Ted was supposed to have left there.

I'd gone along because even at age thirteen, I was interested in the lore of animation. This visit to a veteran animator's old haunt seemed full of interesting potential, and I was not disappointed.

After interminable knocking, Nathan's mother opened her front door and peered out at us. She was obviously drunk and didn't want to let us in. She didn't know what the hell my father was talking about when we finally did get in.

However, gradually, she seemed to take a fuzzily amorous interest in my father, and poured him a large drink of gin.

My father, never a big drinker, took a polite sip and tried valiantly to get through what seemed to be quickly developing into a big fiasco.

It was about then that Nathan's mother really focused in on me for the first time.

Abruptly she half dragged me to the threshold of her basement. Down its dark stairs

she bellowed, "Nathan! I'm sending a boy for you to play with!" Then, half pushing me, she cooed, "Go play with Nathan dear, while I talk with your father."

I'm not sure who was more uncomfortable, my father upstairs with this drunk maniac woman or me, half way down a dark flight of stairs heading for God knows what!

Nathan was about sixteen and not particularly friendly. After much interminable silence, he picked up a strange little figurine. It looked like some sort of demon with a kangaroo-like pouch and a fat tail. When Nathan removed a brass tip on its tail, I saw that it was some kind of pipe.

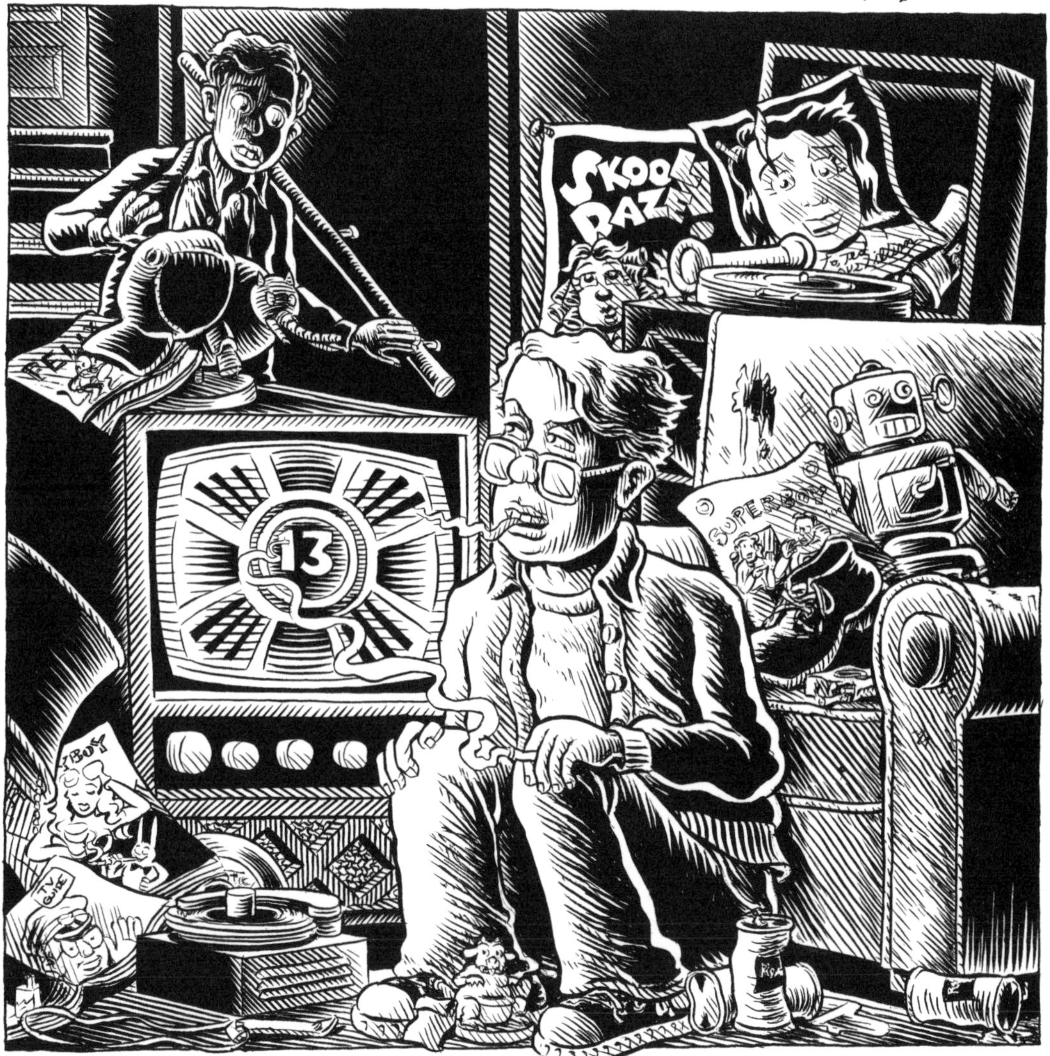
13

He put some green flakey stuff into the odd pipe and shoved it at me. Perhaps it was marijuana though no marijuana that I ever smoked later affected me this way.

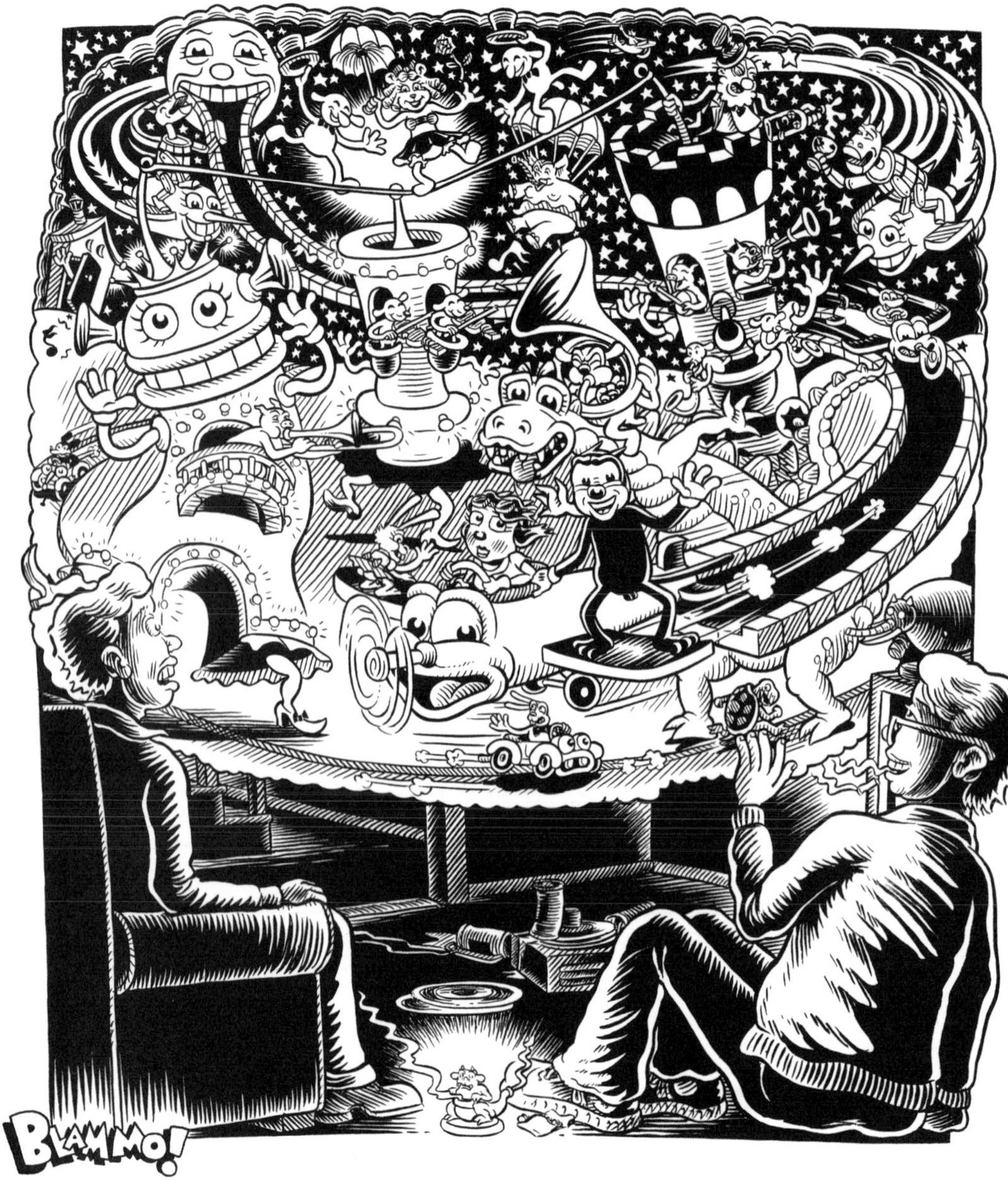
BLAMMO!

A few minutes later, Nathan and I were sitting paralyzed! while the greatest visions in the world danced before us. In many ways they resembled old cartoons I'd seen on T.V. except that these visions were in 3-D and in full blazing color!

It was like the most wonderful, cosmic, colorful cartoon vaudeville show ever! And the master of ceremonies was an irreverent cartoon cat named Waldo.

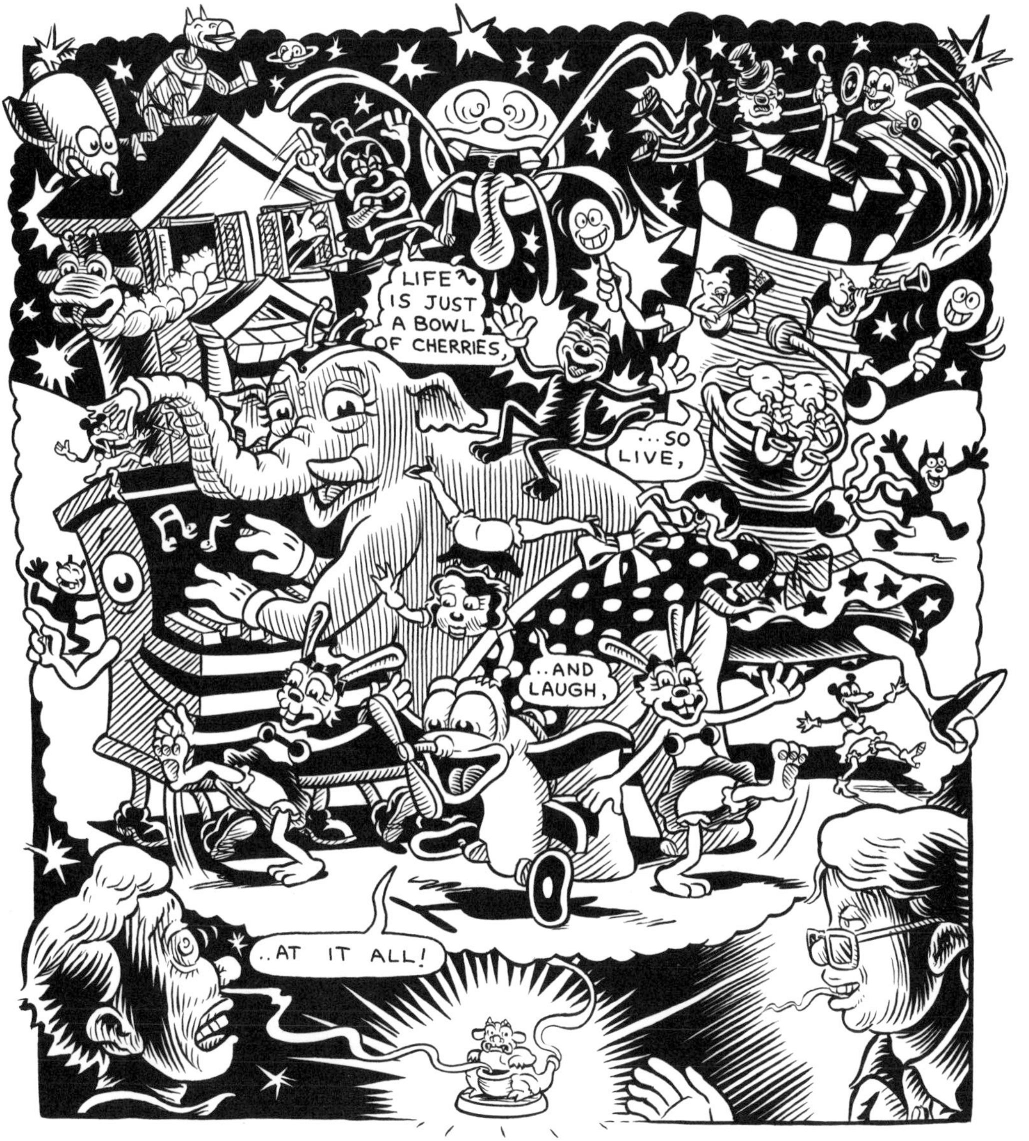

LIFE IS JUST A BOWL OF CHERRIES,
...SO LIVE,
..AND LAUGH,
..AT IT ALL!

The only real piece of information I got out of Nathan was that the odd pipe was apparently something that had belonged to his uncle Ted.

The visions seemed to go on for hours, but apparently this wasn't true. For the next thing I remember was my father shaking me out of a sound sleep! Not even half an hour had passed since we'd arrived there! I looked back as I groggily trudged upstairs. Nathan was still asleep, with the strange figurine clutched in his hand. I never saw him again, but later heard he'd been committed to a mental hospital.

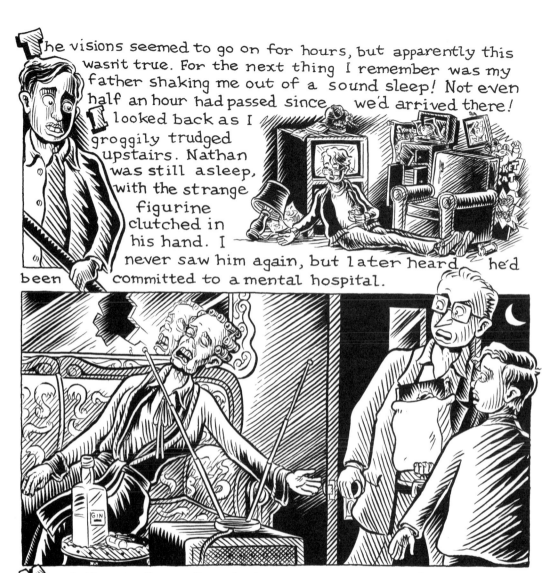

My father had not found the cartoon art he'd been looking for. All he was coming away with was a small painting which Nathan's mother had stuffed into a paper bag. As we let ourselves out, she too was passed out.

On the ride home I'd just about convinced myself that everything I thought I'd seen in the basement had all been a dream, when I idly slipped the small painting out of the paper bag. It took everything in me to keep from crying out in shock!

It was a murky thing, apparently painted by Nathan's uncle Ted. In some ways it reminded me of one of those mysterious decaying canvases of Albert Pinkham Ryder. It had a similar torturously over worked quality, as if the painter had strained terrifically to get it exactly right without succeeding.

One of its figures was an ugly blue thing that looked uncanilly like a horror version of the blue cat I may or may not have seen in Nathan's basement. This creature was taunting a cowering figure that looked a lot like Nathan's uncle Ted. The title, scrawled on the back in burnt sienna was, "Waldo Demon From Hell!" What a night! And as it became isolated in memory, as years went by, I came to even wonder whether it had ever actually happened![*]

[*] Indeed these doubts were further fed in later years by my father, who for reasons known only to himself, has consistantly denied that any such incident ever occured. When I recently showed him the strange painting, he denied ever having seen it before. Strange to say the least!

That is until one night in 1966. My brother Simon and I were coming home from a party in Brooklyn. We weren't exactly sober and soon it was pretty obvious we were lost. We'd gone blocks without seeing a soul, when we spotted a black man sitting on a stoop. He was chuckling to himself and seemed to be looking at something in his hands.

Ordinarily I never would have spoken to him, but we'd been blocks without seeing any kind of subway or recognizable street. So I asked him how to get to the nearest subway. He looked up and slowly replied, "cross my palm with five dollahs, and the urn of Chondra be yours."

There in his hand was the very pipe I last saw Nathan holding years before, right down to the brass tip covering its tail.

"Burn incense in the mystic urn of Chondra", he said, pointing at the opening in the figure's belly, "and mighty mysteries shall be revealed."

Then, not even waiting for me to reply, he placed the figurine in my hand. As he slowly walked away he said, "Incense in the glowing belly of the little beast. any kind at all will do."

We stared after him; and in a twinkling, he was gone!

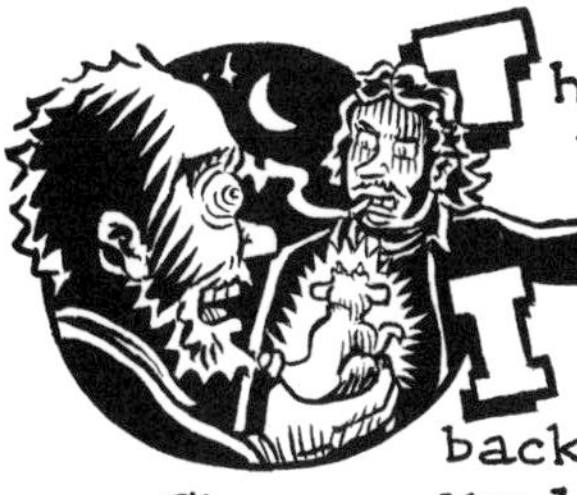

Then Simon pointed to something at the end of the street we'd missed seeing before. Not half a block away, was a subway stop! I don't even remember the ride home.

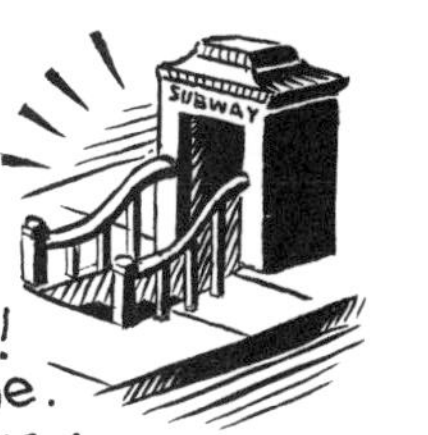
SUBWAY

I do remember just staring at that thing back at our place, for the longest time, when Simon walked in with some beers and a bag of incense he'd dug up somewhere. While I sipped beer he loaded incense into Chondra's belly and lit it. Well I was never much on incense and it wasn't making a big impression now. But after Simon conked out a while later, a weirdly familiar feeling gradually came over me. My mind began to be filled with vague half visions of a strange cartoony cat-like being.

It wasn't as if I could actually see him standing there, but my mind was full of the idea of him. Before I knew it, I was at my drawing board. And that night, in a feverish all night session, I produced the very first Waldo comic page! What all this really means, I honestly cannot say.

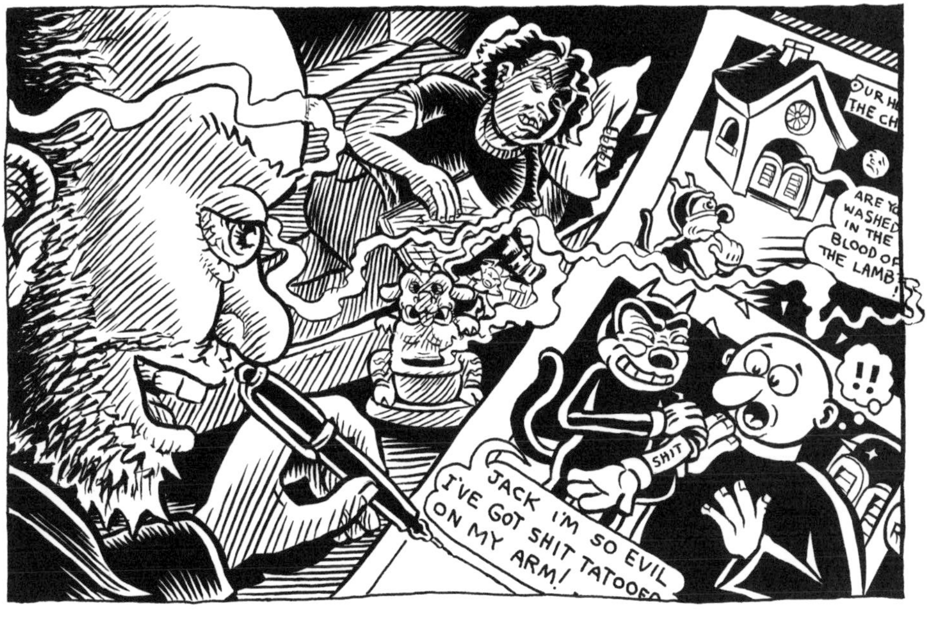
ARE YO WASHED IN THE BLOOD OF THE LAMB!
!!
SHIT
JACK I'M SO EVIL I'VE GOT SHIT TATOOED ON MY ARM!

But I will now reiterate my earlier claim that I have never forced a Waldo story. They have always come as if inspired by something beyond myself, and always when the belly of Chondra glows bright.

And there you have it. Perhaps its just my over-active imagination. I'm willing to accept that possibility. But maybe, just maybe it's some form of demonic or even divine channeling.

I don't know.

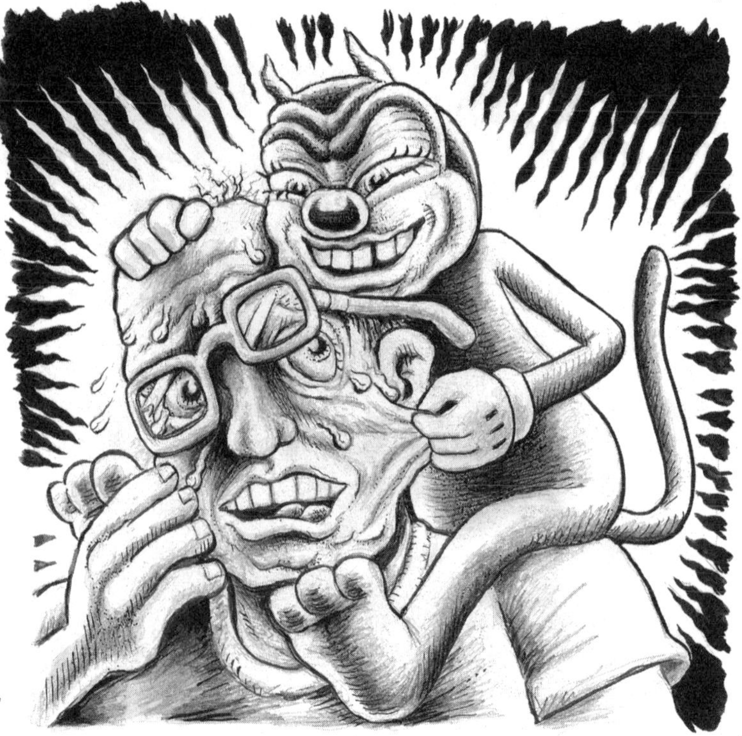

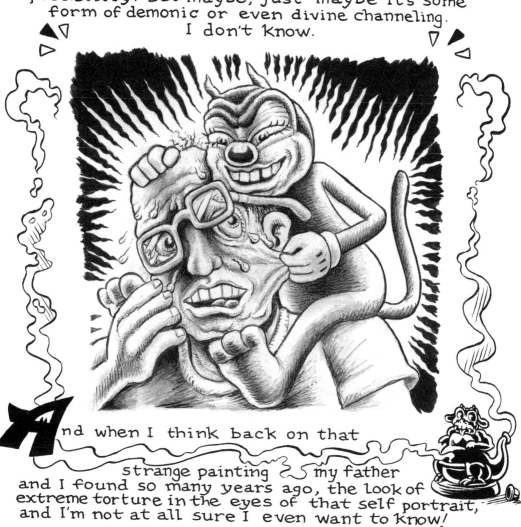

And when I think back on that strange painting my father and I found so many years ago, the look of extreme torture in the eyes of that self portrait, and I'm not at all sure I even want to know!

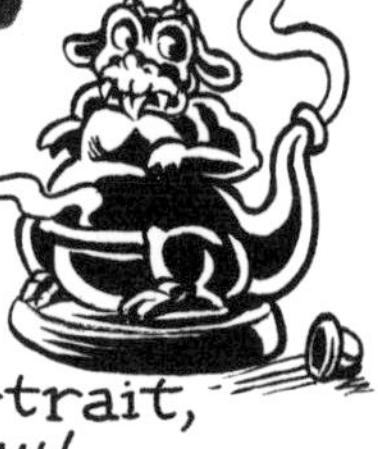

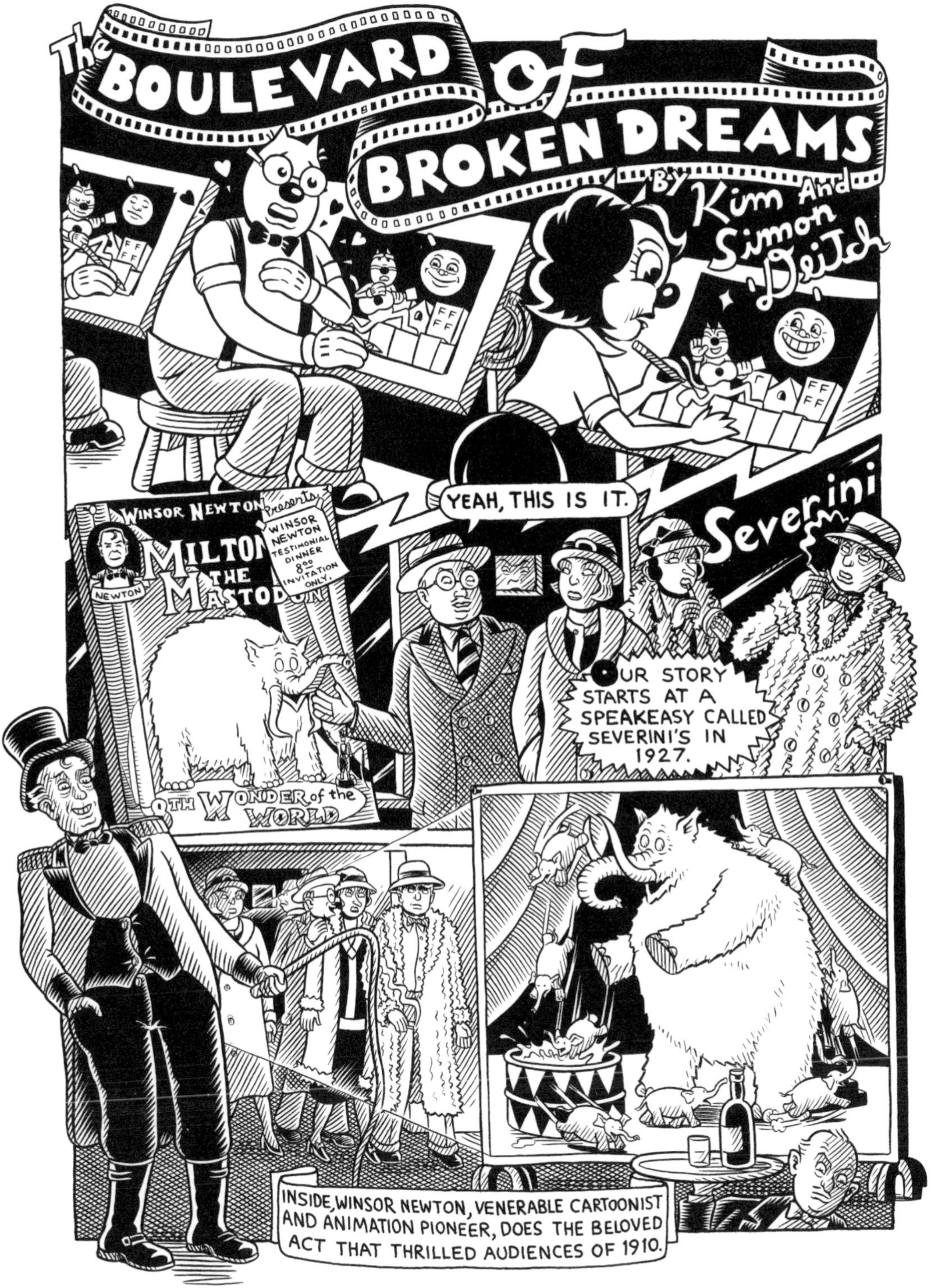

The BOULEVARD OF BROKEN DREAMS
By Kim And Simon Deitch
YEAH, THIS IS IT.
Severini
WINSOR NEWTON
Presents
WINSOR NEWTON TESTIMONIAL DINNER 8OO INVITATION ONLY.
MILTON THE MASTODON
NEWTON
9TH WONDER of the WORLD
OUR STORY STARTS AT A SPEAKEASY CALLED SEVERINI'S IN 1927.
INSIDE, WINSOR NEWTON, VENERABLE CARTOONIST AND ANIMATION PIONEER, DOES THE BELOVED ACT THAT THRILLED AUDIENCES OF 1910.

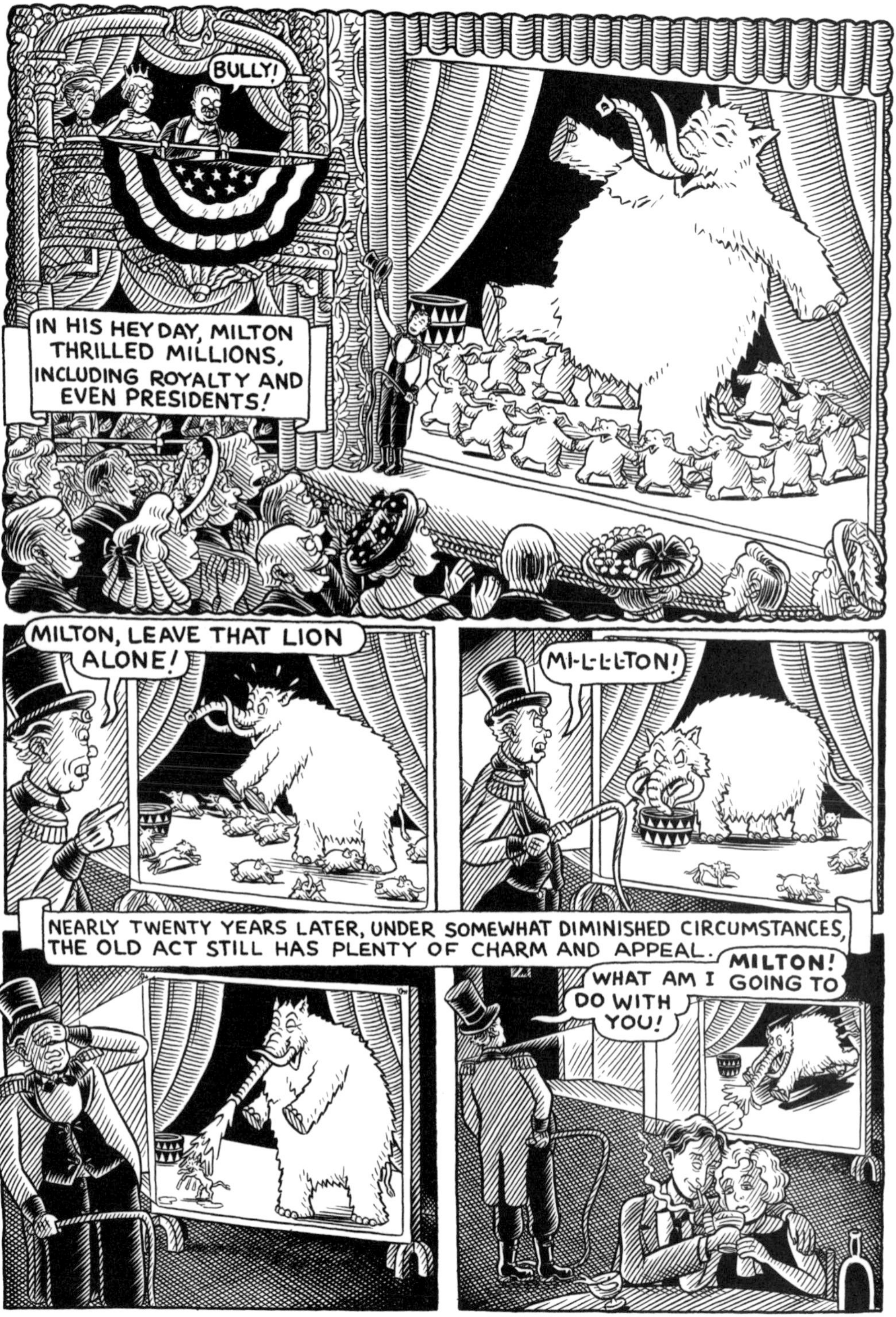

BULLY!
IN HIS HEY DAY, MILTON THRILLED MILLIONS, INCLUDING ROYALTY AND EVEN PRESIDENTS!
MILTON, LEAVE THAT LION ALONE!
MI-L-L-L-TON!
NEARLY TWENTY YEARS LATER, UNDER SOMEWHAT DIMINISHED CIRCUMSTANCES, THE OLD ACT STILL HAS PLENTY OF CHARM AND APPEAL.
MILTON! WHAT AM I GOING TO DO WITH YOU!

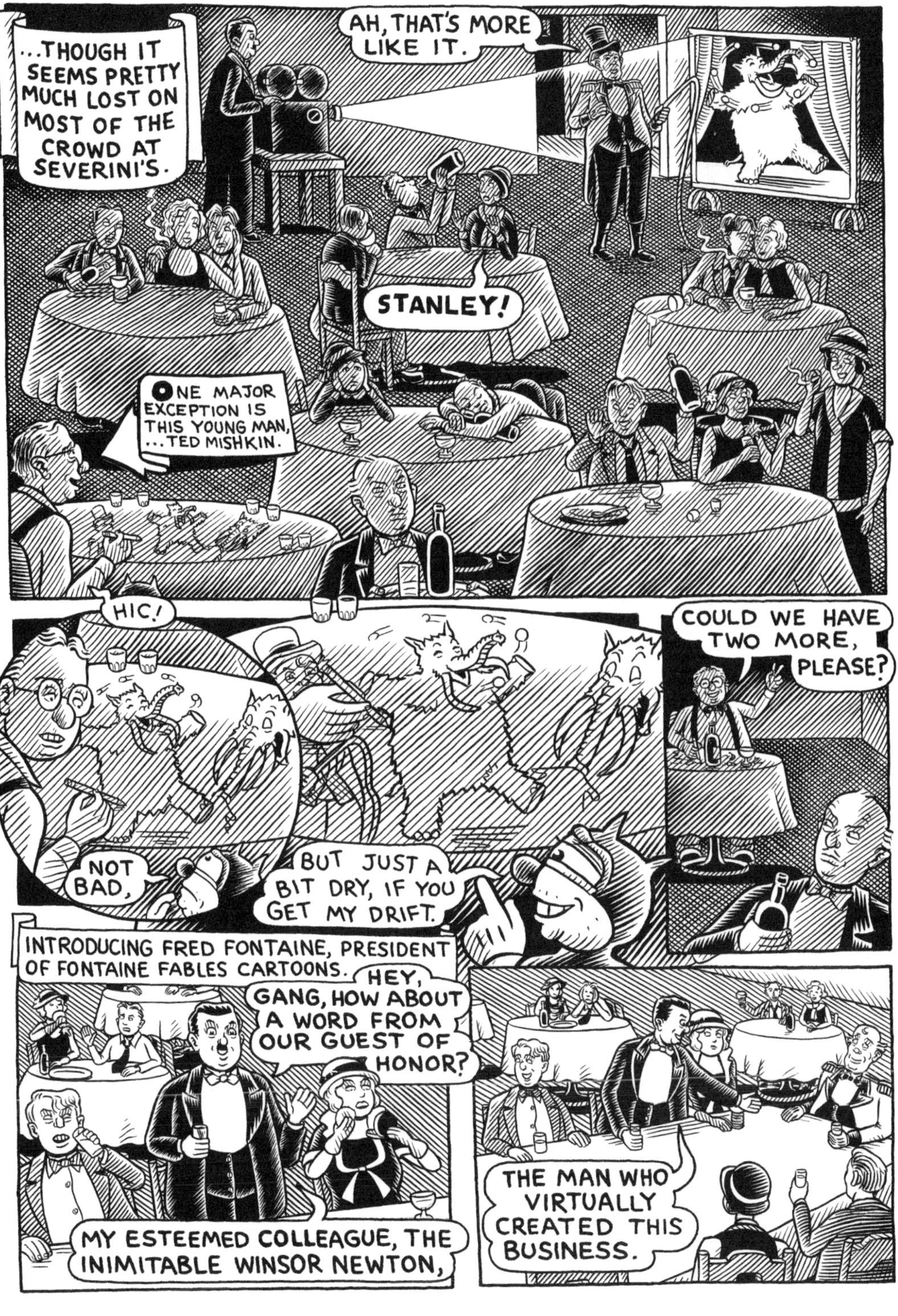

...THOUGH IT SEEMS PRETTY MUCH LOST ON MOST OF THE CROWD AT SEVERINI'S.
AH, THAT'S MORE LIKE IT.
STANLEY!
ONE MAJOR EXCEPTION IS THIS YOUNG MAN, ...TED MISHKIN.
HIC!
COULD WE HAVE TWO MORE, PLEASE?
NOT BAD,
BUT JUST A BIT DRY, IF YOU GET MY DRIFT.
INTRODUCING FRED FONTAINE, PRESIDENT OF FONTAINE FABLES CARTOONS.
HEY, GANG, HOW ABOUT A WORD FROM OUR GUEST OF HONOR?
MY ESTEEMED COLLEAGUE, THE INIMITABLE WINSOR NEWTON,
THE MAN WHO VIRTUALLY CREATED THIS BUSINESS.

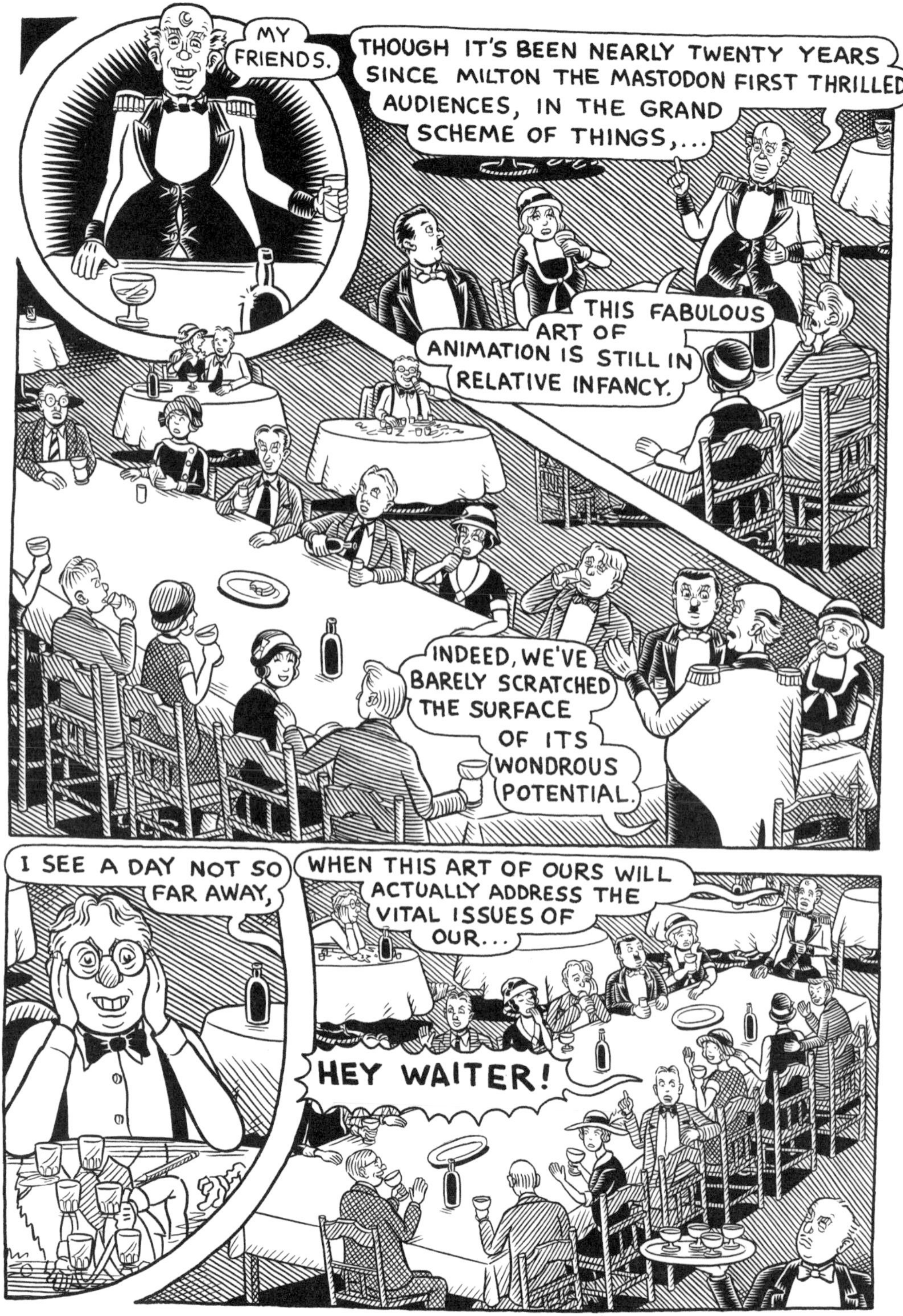
MY FRIENDS.
THOUGH IT'S BEEN NEARLY TWENTY YEARS SINCE MILTON THE MASTODON FIRST THRILLED AUDIENCES, IN THE GRAND SCHEME OF THINGS,...
THIS FABULOUS ART OF ANIMATION IS STILL IN RELATIVE INFANCY.
INDEED, WE'VE BARELY SCRATCHED THE SURFACE OF ITS WONDROUS POTENTIAL.
I SEE A DAY NOT SO FAR AWAY,
WHEN THIS ART OF OURS WILL ACTUALLY ADDRESS THE VITAL ISSUES OF OUR...
HEY WAITER!

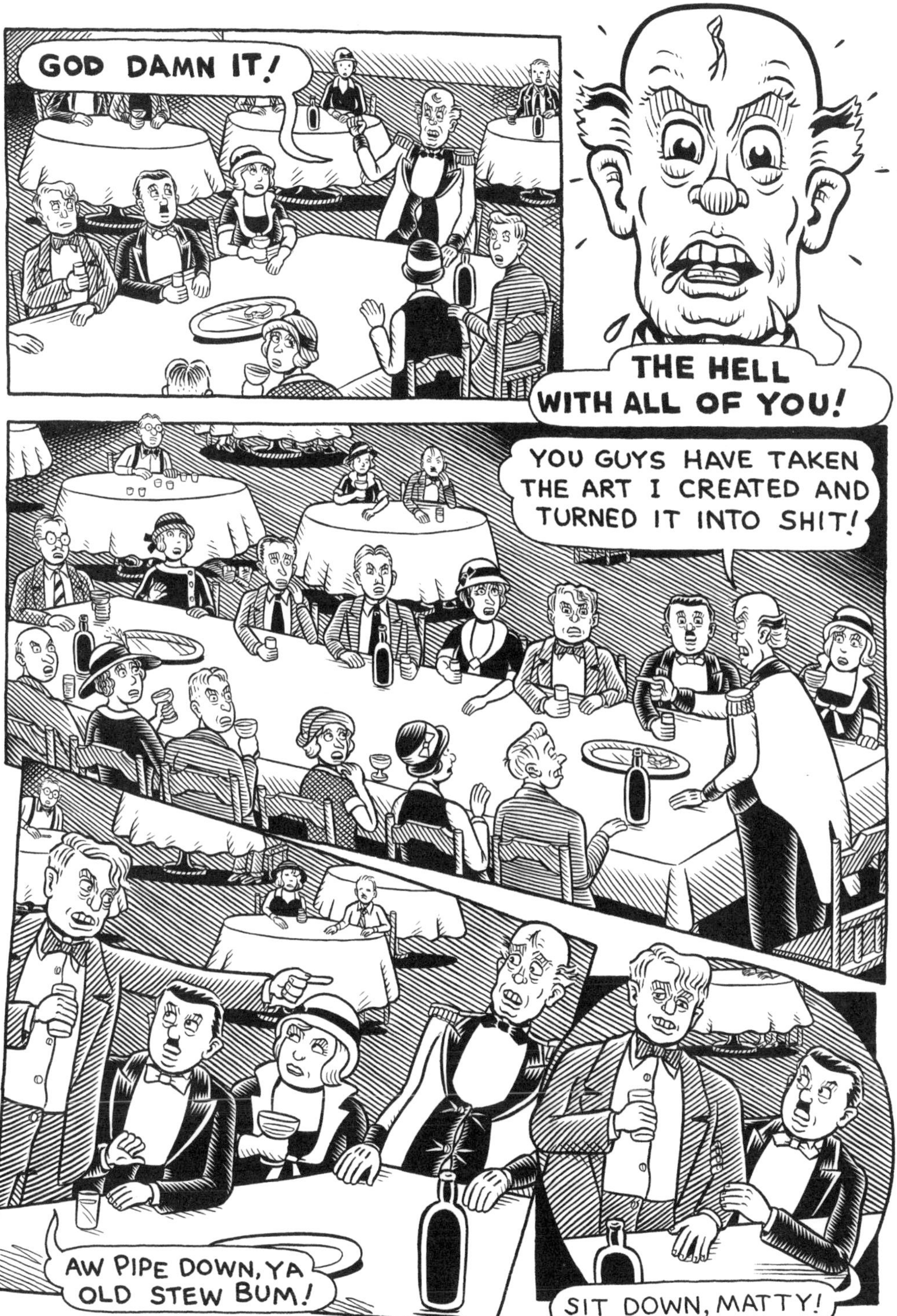
GOD DAMN IT!
THE HELL WITH ALL OF YOU!
YOU GUYS HAVE TAKEN THE ART I CREATED AND TURNED IT INTO SHIT!
AW PIPE DOWN, YA OLD STEW BUM!
SIT DOWN, MATTY!

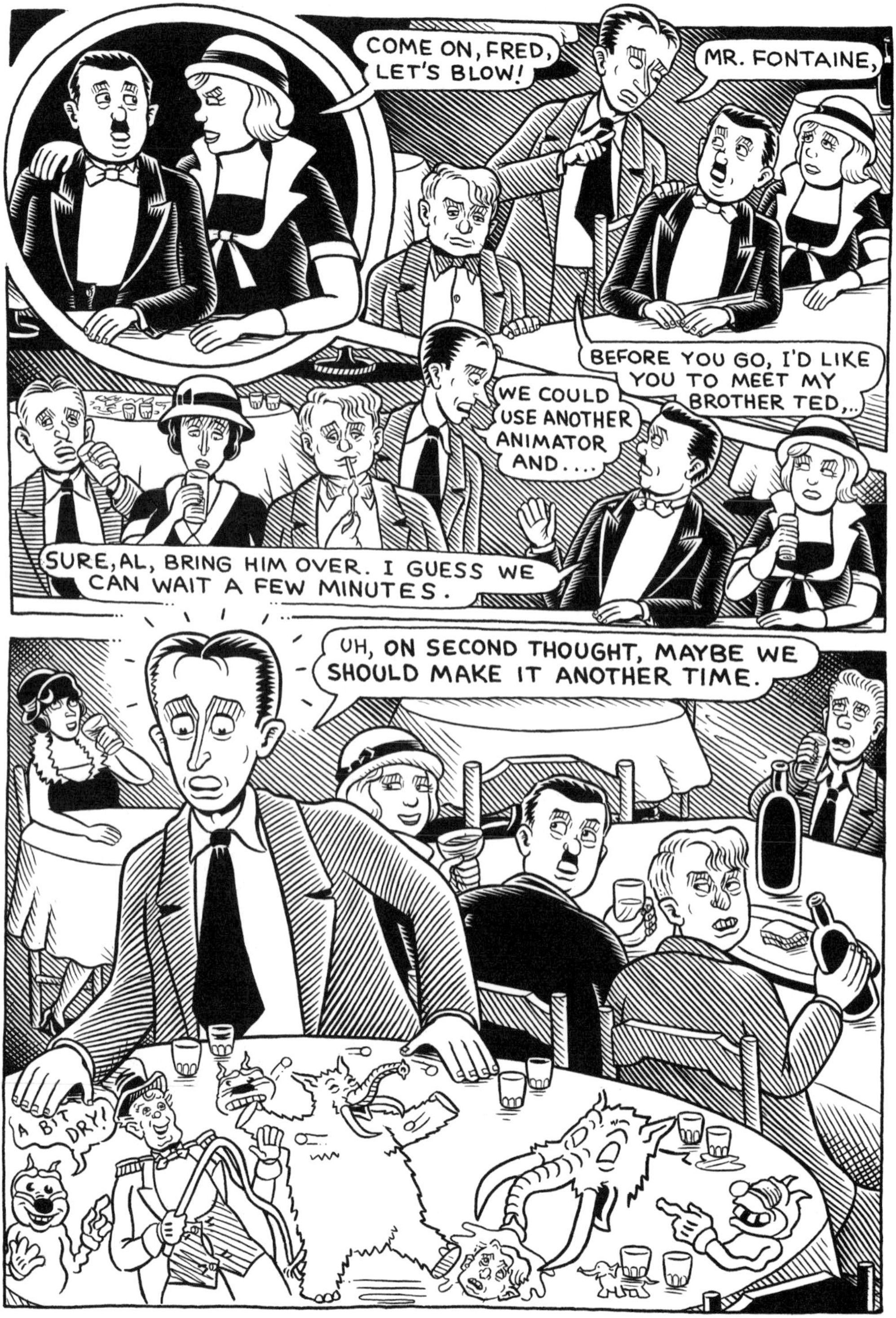
COME ON, FRED, LET'S BLOW!
MR. FONTAINE,
BEFORE YOU GO, I'D LIKE YOU TO MEET MY BROTHER TED,..
WE COULD USE ANOTHER ANIMATOR AND....
SURE, AL, BRING HIM OVER. I GUESS WE CAN WAIT A FEW MINUTES.
UH, ON SECOND THOUGHT, MAYBE WE SHOULD MAKE IT ANOTHER TIME.
A BIT DRY!

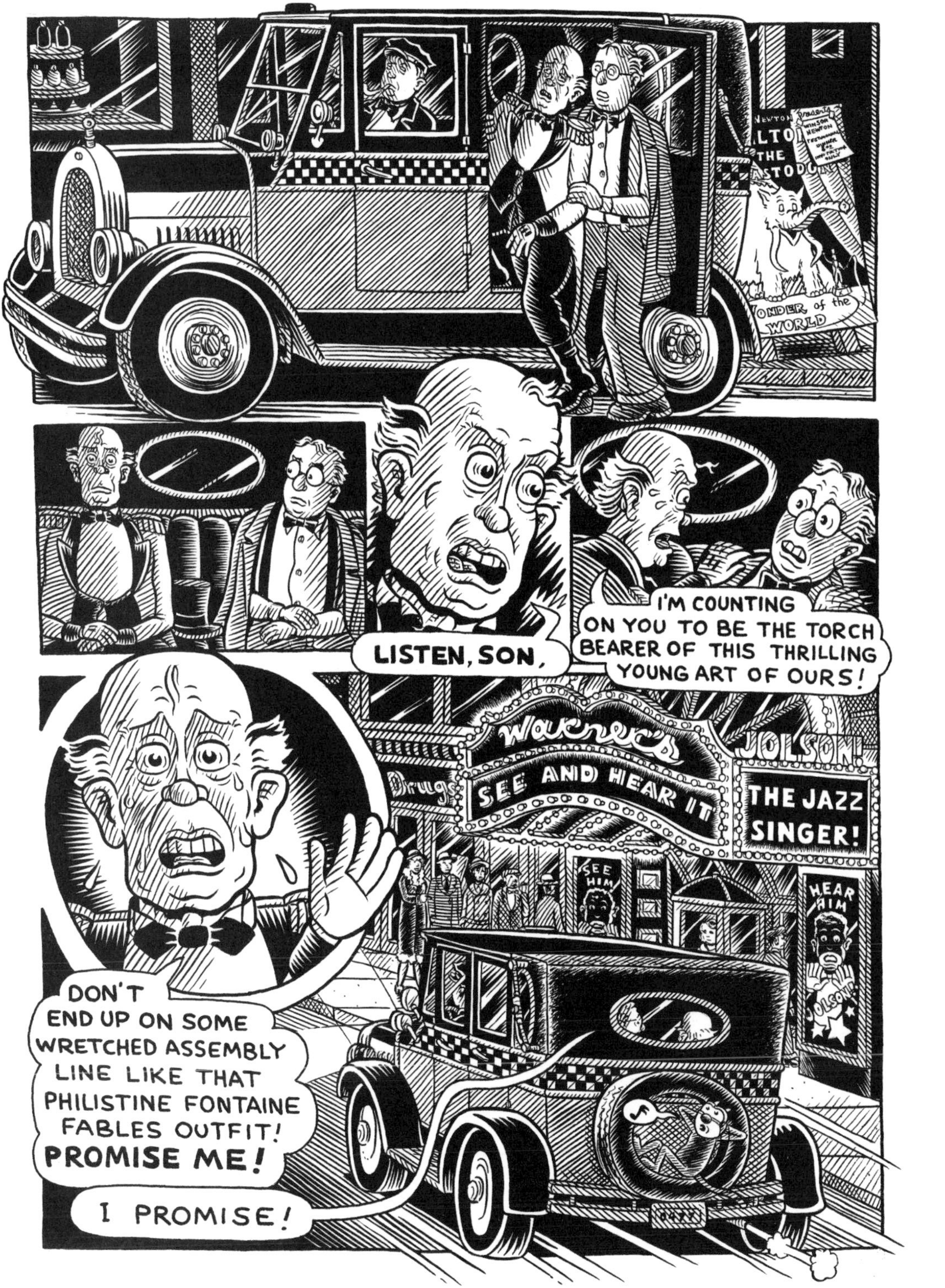
NEWTON
LTO
THE
ASTODO
Presents
WINSOR NEWTON
ONDER of the WORLD
LISTEN, SON,
I'M COUNTING ON YOU TO BE THE TORCH BEARER OF THIS THRILLING YOUNG ART OF OURS!
Warner's
SEE AND HEAR IT
JOLSON!
THE JAZZ SINGER!
Drugs
SEE HIM
HEAR HIM
JOLSON
DON'T END UP ON SOME WRETCHED ASSEMBLY LINE LIKE THAT PHILISTINE FONTAINE FABLES OUTFIT! PROMISE ME!
I PROMISE!

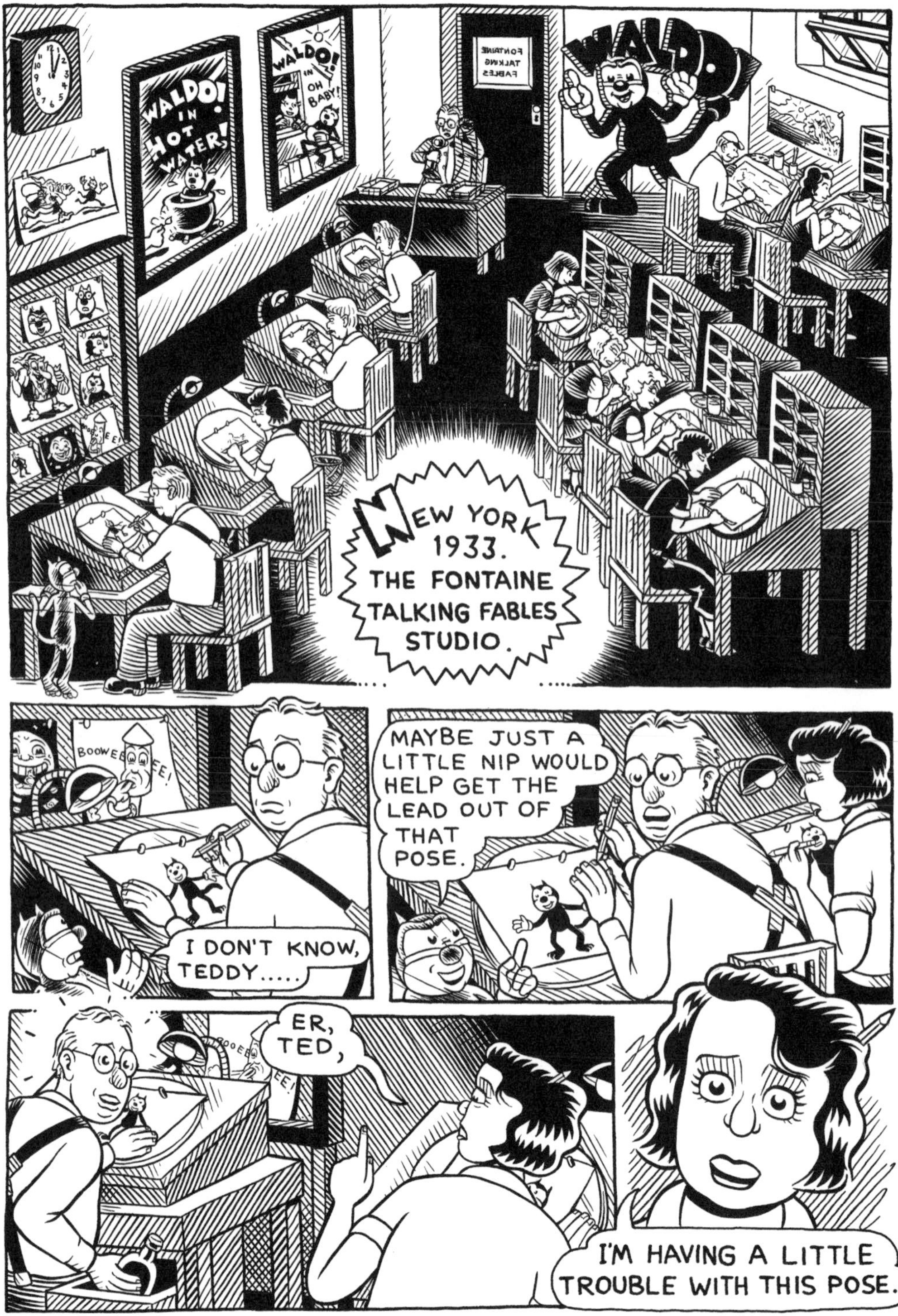

WALDO! IN HOT WATER!
WALDO! IN OH BABY!
FONTAINE TALKING FABLES
WALDO!
NEW YORK 1933. THE FONTAINE TALKING FABLES STUDIO.
BOOWEE EE!
I DON'T KNOW, TEDDY.....
MAYBE JUST A LITTLE NIP WOULD HELP GET THE LEAD OUT OF THAT POSE.
ER, TED,
I'M HAVING A LITTLE TROUBLE WITH THIS POSE.

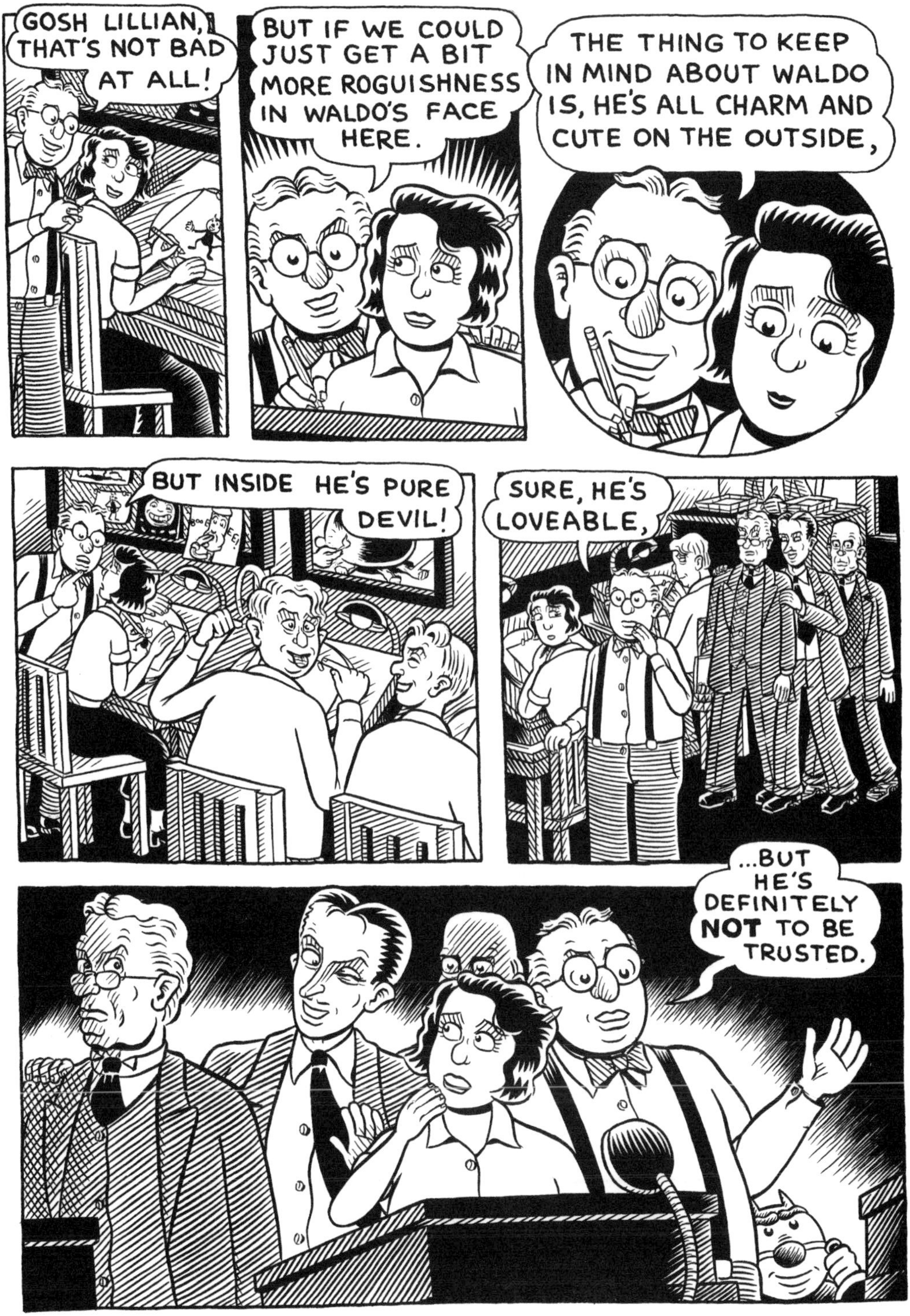
GOSH LILLIAN, THAT'S NOT BAD AT ALL!
BUT IF WE COULD JUST GET A BIT MORE ROGUISHNESS IN WALDO'S FACE HERE.
THE THING TO KEEP IN MIND ABOUT WALDO IS, HE'S ALL CHARM AND CUTE ON THE OUTSIDE,
BUT INSIDE HE'S PURE DEVIL!
SURE, HE'S LOVEABLE,
...BUT HE'S DEFINITELY **NOT** TO BE TRUSTED.

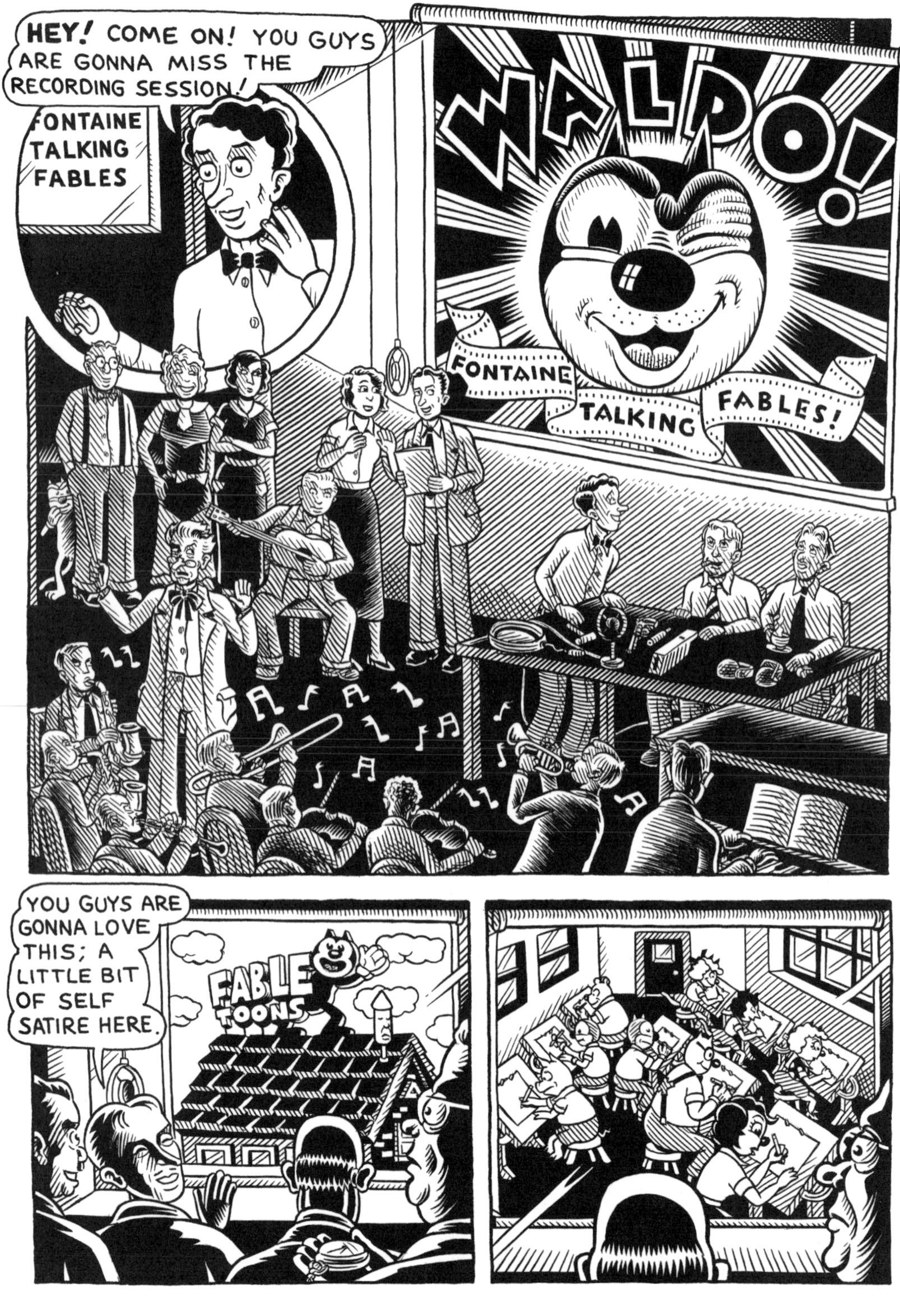
HEY! COME ON! YOU GUYS ARE GONNA MISS THE RECORDING SESSION!
FONTAINE TALKING FABLES
WALDO!
FONTAINE TALKING FABLES!
YOU GUYS ARE GONNA LOVE THIS; A LITTLE BIT OF SELF SATIRE HERE.
FABLE TOONS

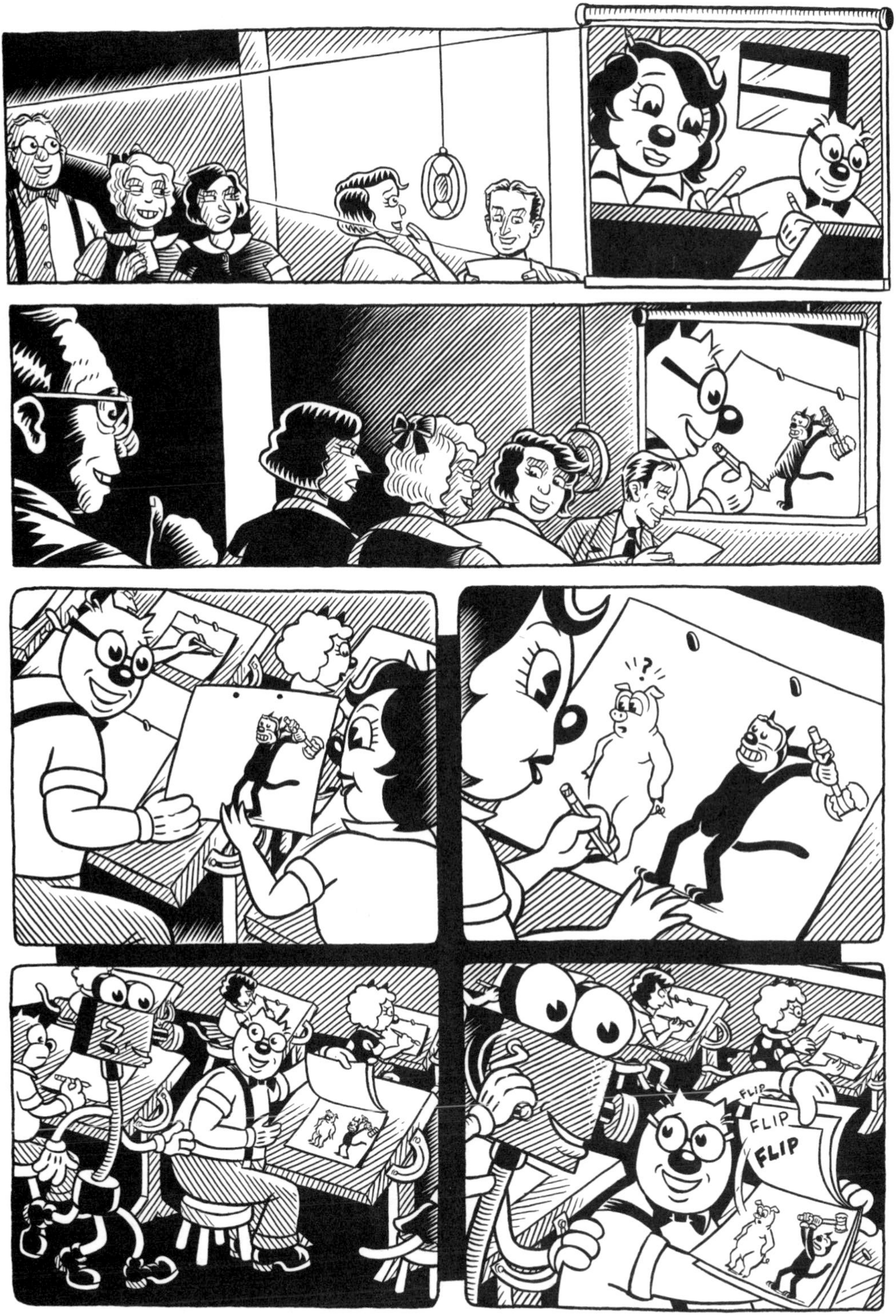

?
FLIP
FLIP
FLIP

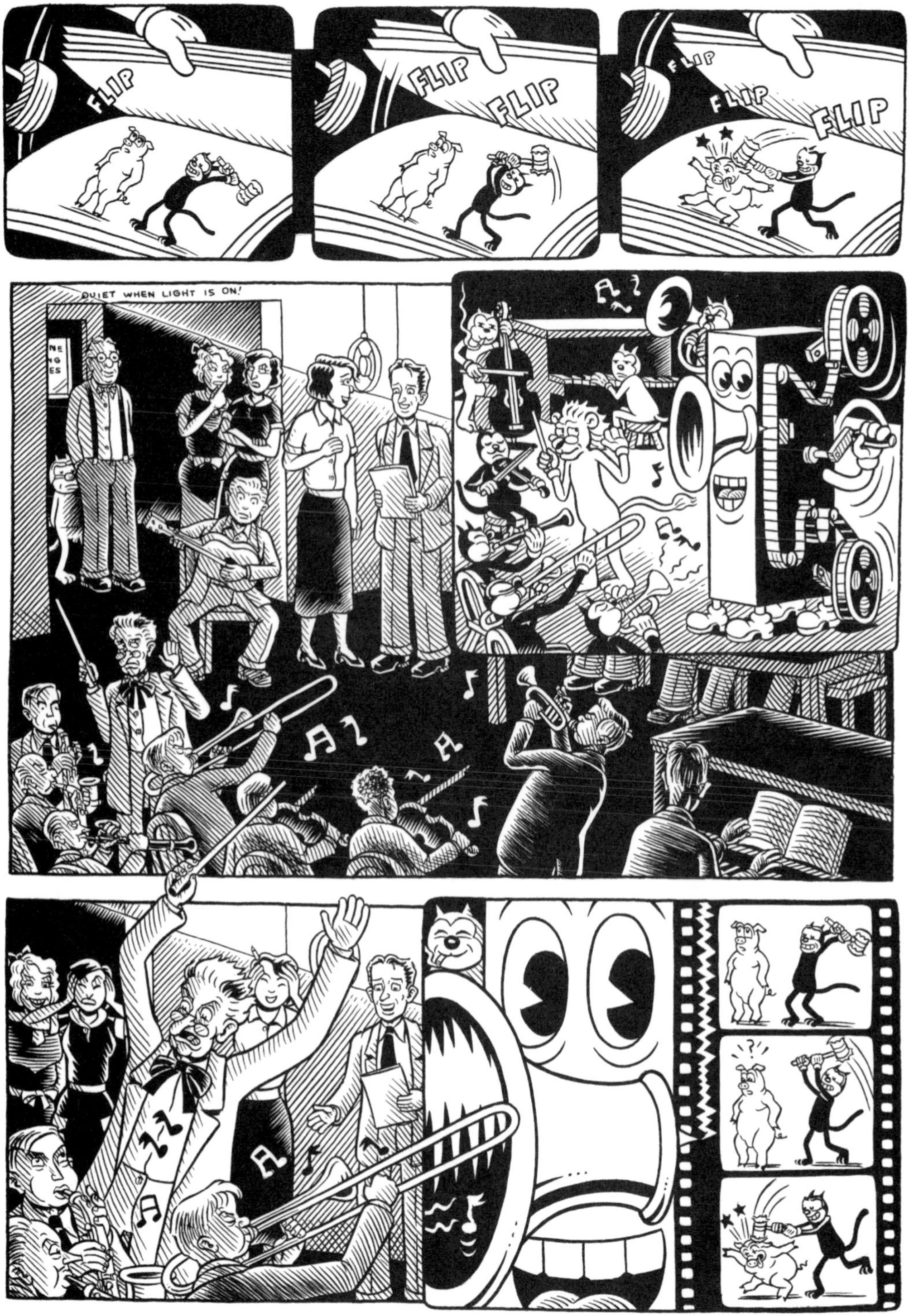
FLIP
FLIP
FLIP
FLIP
FLIP
FLIP
QUIET WHEN LIGHT IS ON!

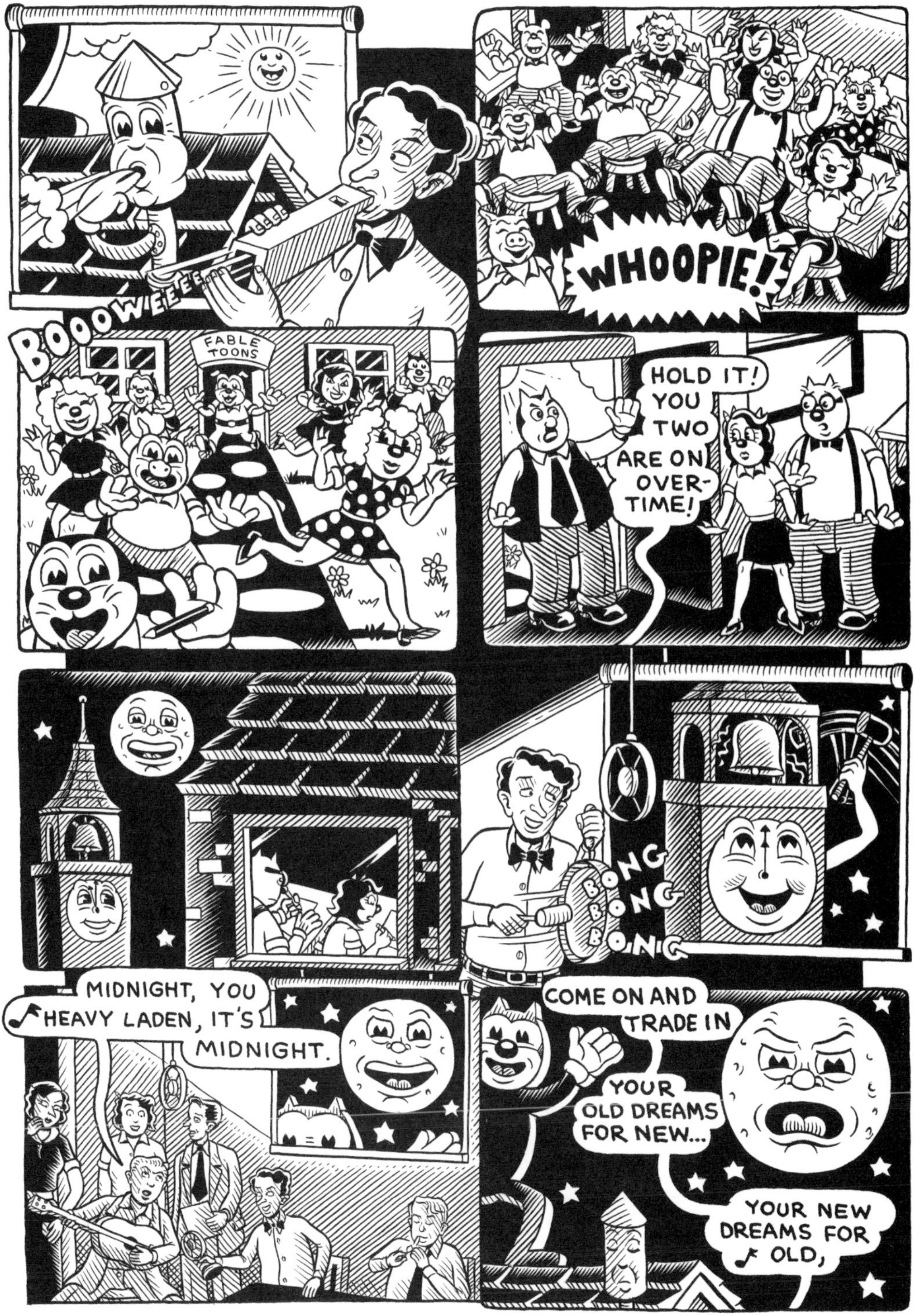
BOOOWEEEEE
WHOOPIE!
FABLE TOONS
HOLD IT! YOU TWO ARE ON OVER-TIME!
BONG BONG BONG BONG
MIDNIGHT, YOU HEAVY LADEN, IT'S MIDNIGHT.
COME ON AND TRADE IN
YOUR OLD DREAMS FOR NEW...
YOUR NEW DREAMS FOR OLD,

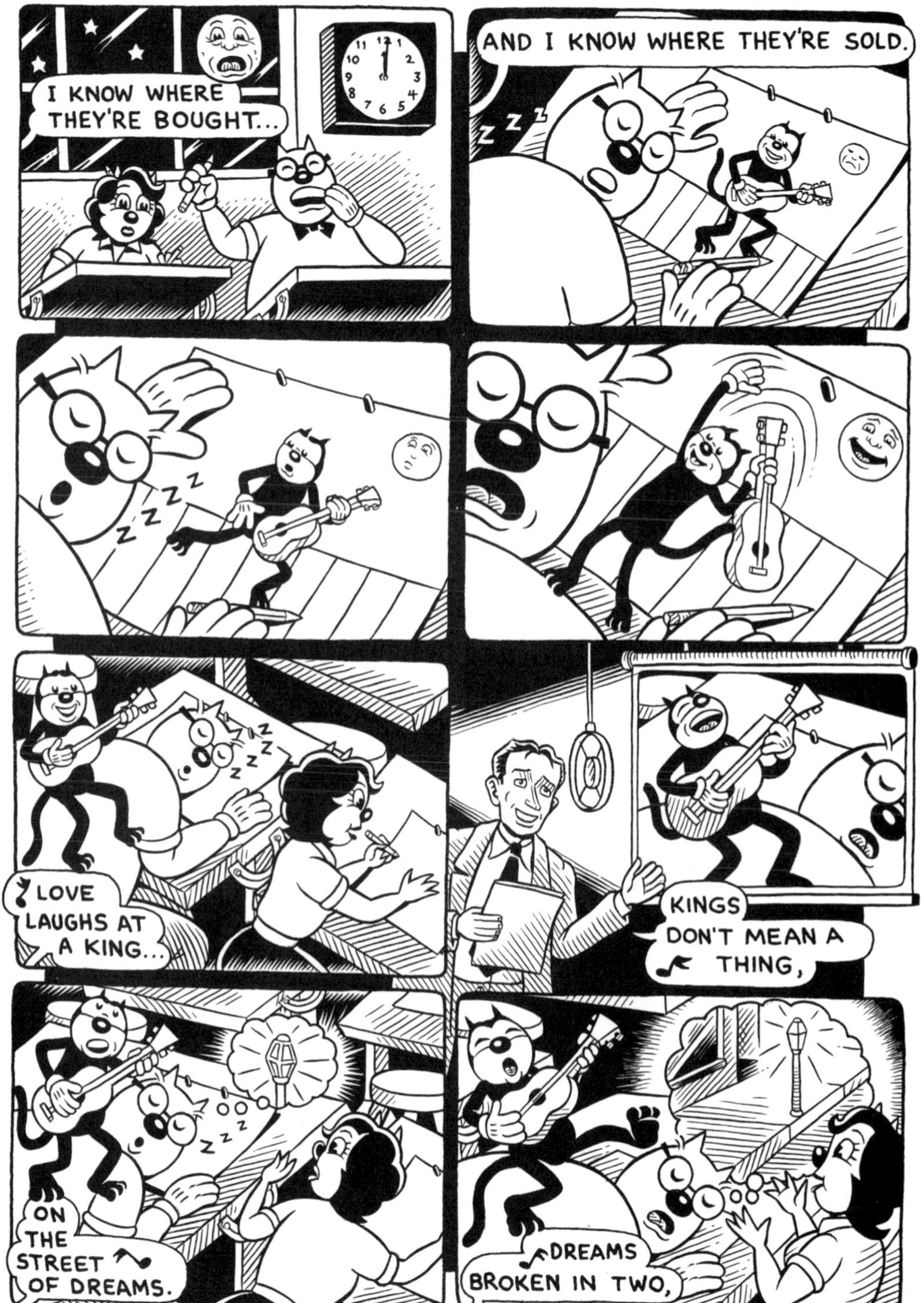
I KNOW WHERE THEY'RE BOUGHT...
AND I KNOW WHERE THEY'RE SOLD.
LOVE LAUGHS AT A KING...
KINGS DON'T MEAN A THING,
ON THE STREET OF DREAMS.
DREAMS BROKEN IN TWO,

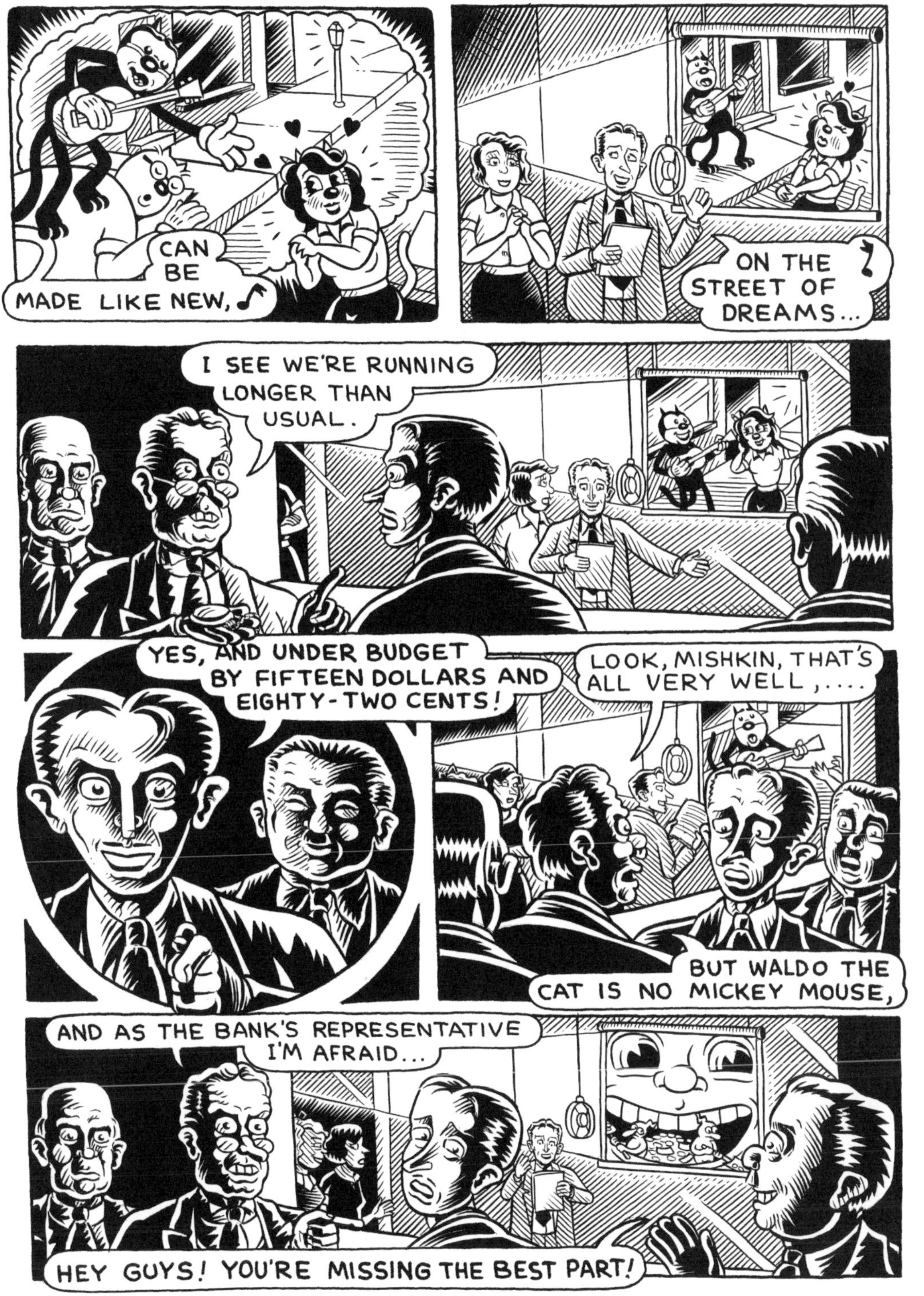
CAN BE
MADE LIKE NEW,
ON THE STREET OF DREAMS...
I SEE WE'RE RUNNING LONGER THAN USUAL.
YES, AND UNDER BUDGET BY FIFTEEN DOLLARS AND EIGHTY-TWO CENTS!
LOOK, MISHKIN, THAT'S ALL VERY WELL,....
BUT WALDO THE CAT IS NO MICKEY MOUSE,
AND AS THE BANK'S REPRESENTATIVE I'M AFRAID...
HEY GUYS! YOU'RE MISSING THE BEST PART!

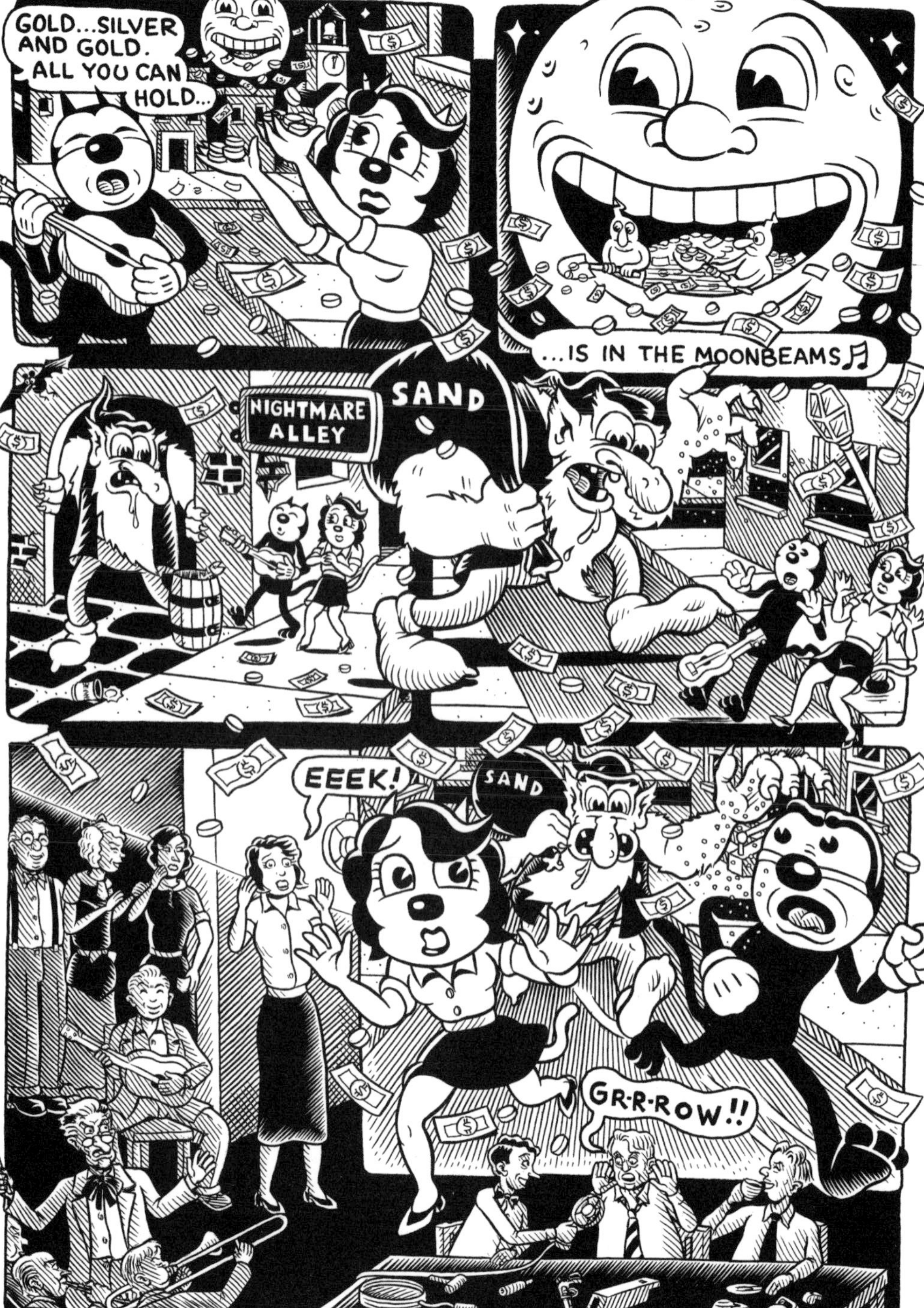
GOLD...SILVER AND GOLD. ALL YOU CAN HOLD...
...IS IN THE MOONBEAMS♫
NIGHTMARE ALLEY
SAND
EEEK!
SAND
GR-R-ROW!!

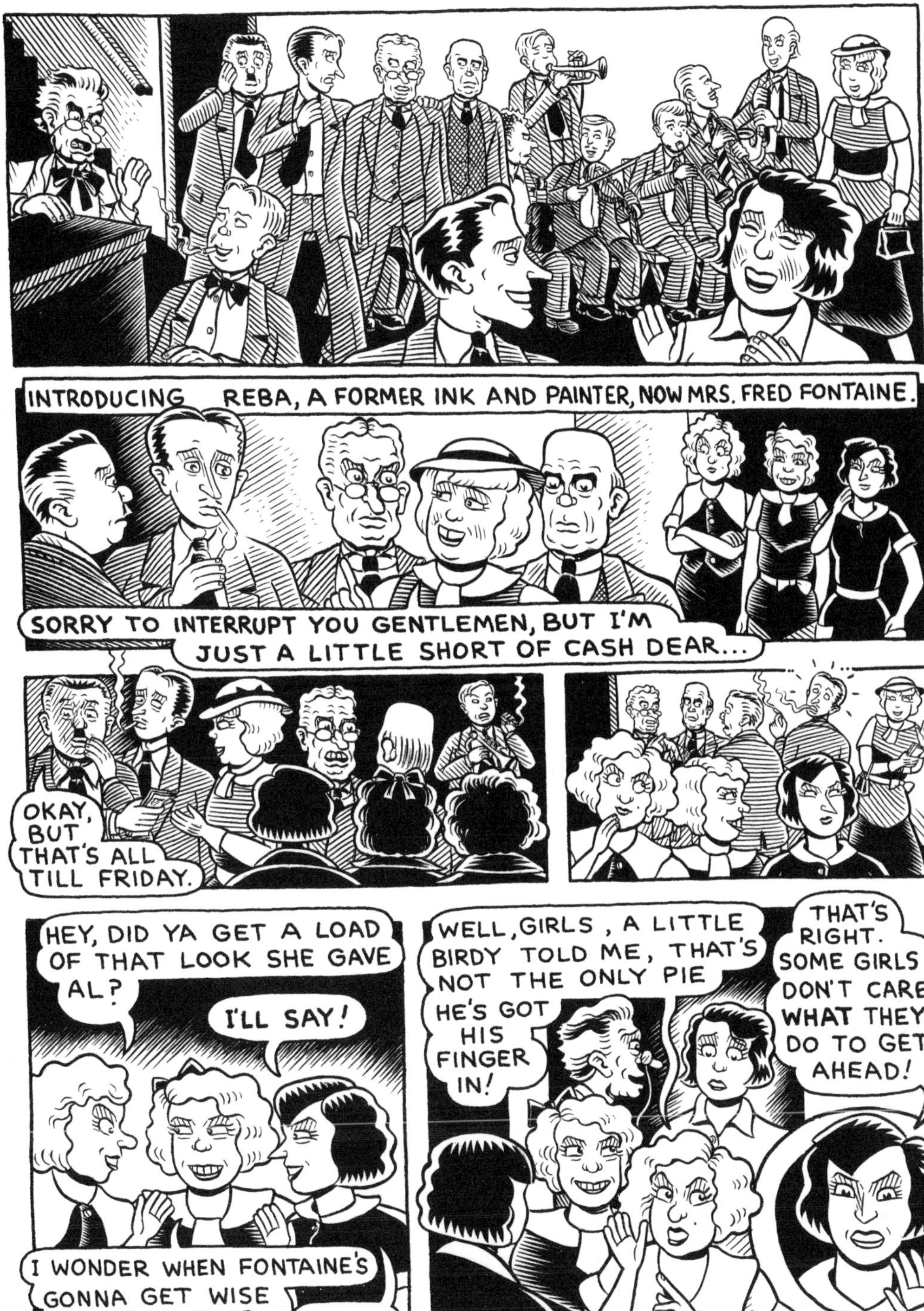

INTRODUCING REBA, A FORMER INK AND PAINTER, NOW MRS. FRED FONTAINE.
SORRY TO INTERRUPT YOU GENTLEMEN, BUT I'M JUST A LITTLE SHORT OF CASH DEAR...
OKAY, BUT THAT'S ALL TILL FRIDAY.
HEY, DID YA GET A LOAD OF THAT LOOK SHE GAVE AL?
I'LL SAY!
I WONDER WHEN FONTAINE'S GONNA GET WISE TO THOSE TWO?
YEAH!
WELL, GIRLS, A LITTLE BIRDY TOLD ME, THAT'S NOT THE ONLY PIE
HE'S GOT HIS FINGER IN!
THAT'S RIGHT. SOME GIRLS DON'T CARE WHAT THEY DO TO GET AHEAD!

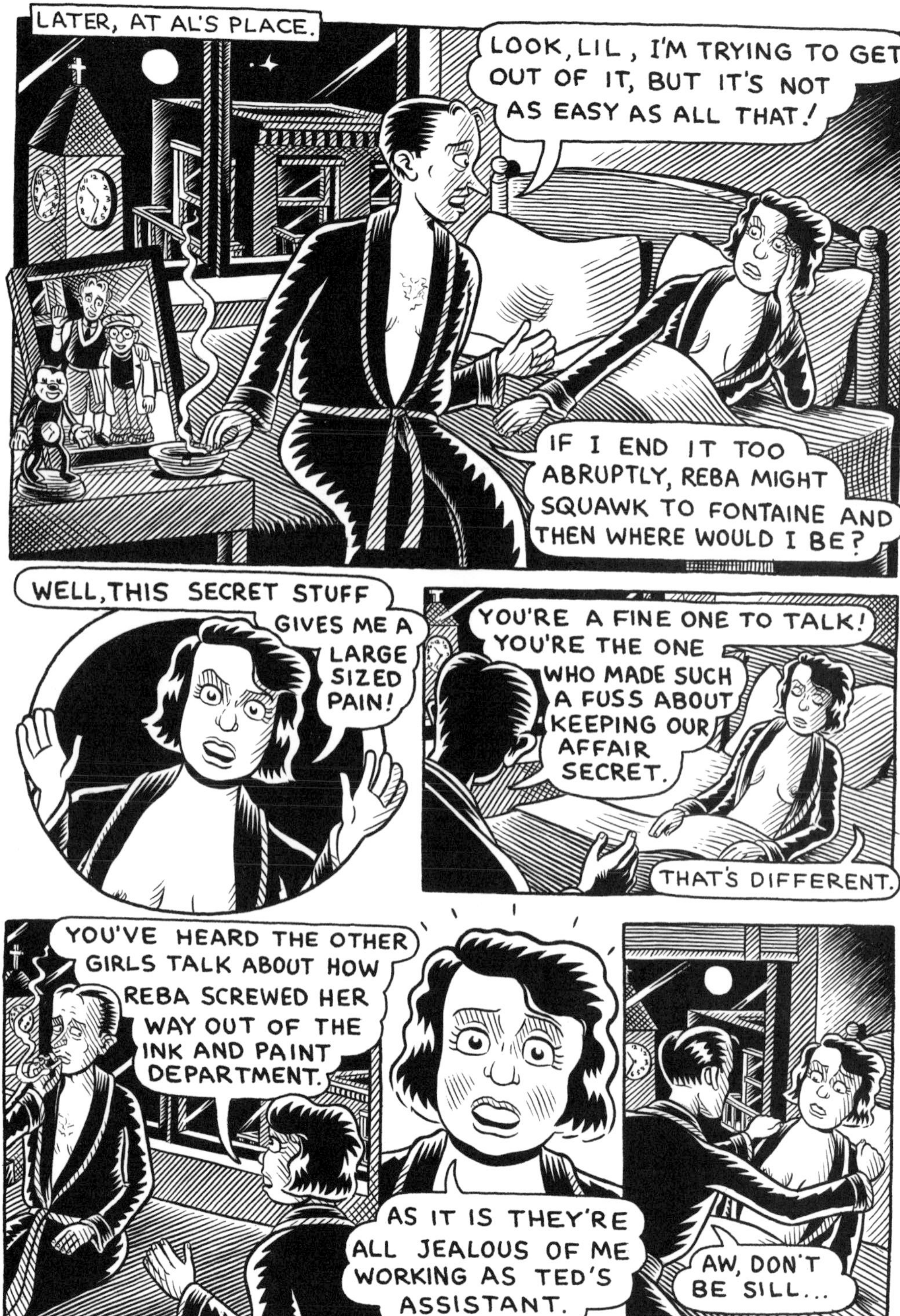
LATER, AT AL'S PLACE.
LOOK, LIL, I'M TRYING TO GET OUT OF IT, BUT IT'S NOT AS EASY AS ALL THAT!
IF I END IT TOO ABRUPTLY, REBA MIGHT SQUAWK TO FONTAINE AND THEN WHERE WOULD I BE?
WELL, THIS SECRET STUFF GIVES ME A LARGE SIZED PAIN!
YOU'RE A FINE ONE TO TALK! YOU'RE THE ONE WHO MADE SUCH A FUSS ABOUT KEEPING OUR AFFAIR SECRET.
THAT'S DIFFERENT.
YOU'VE HEARD THE OTHER GIRLS TALK ABOUT HOW REBA SCREWED HER WAY OUT OF THE INK AND PAINT DEPARTMENT.
AS IT IS THEY'RE ALL JEALOUS OF ME WORKING AS TED'S ASSISTANT.
AW, DON'T BE SILL...

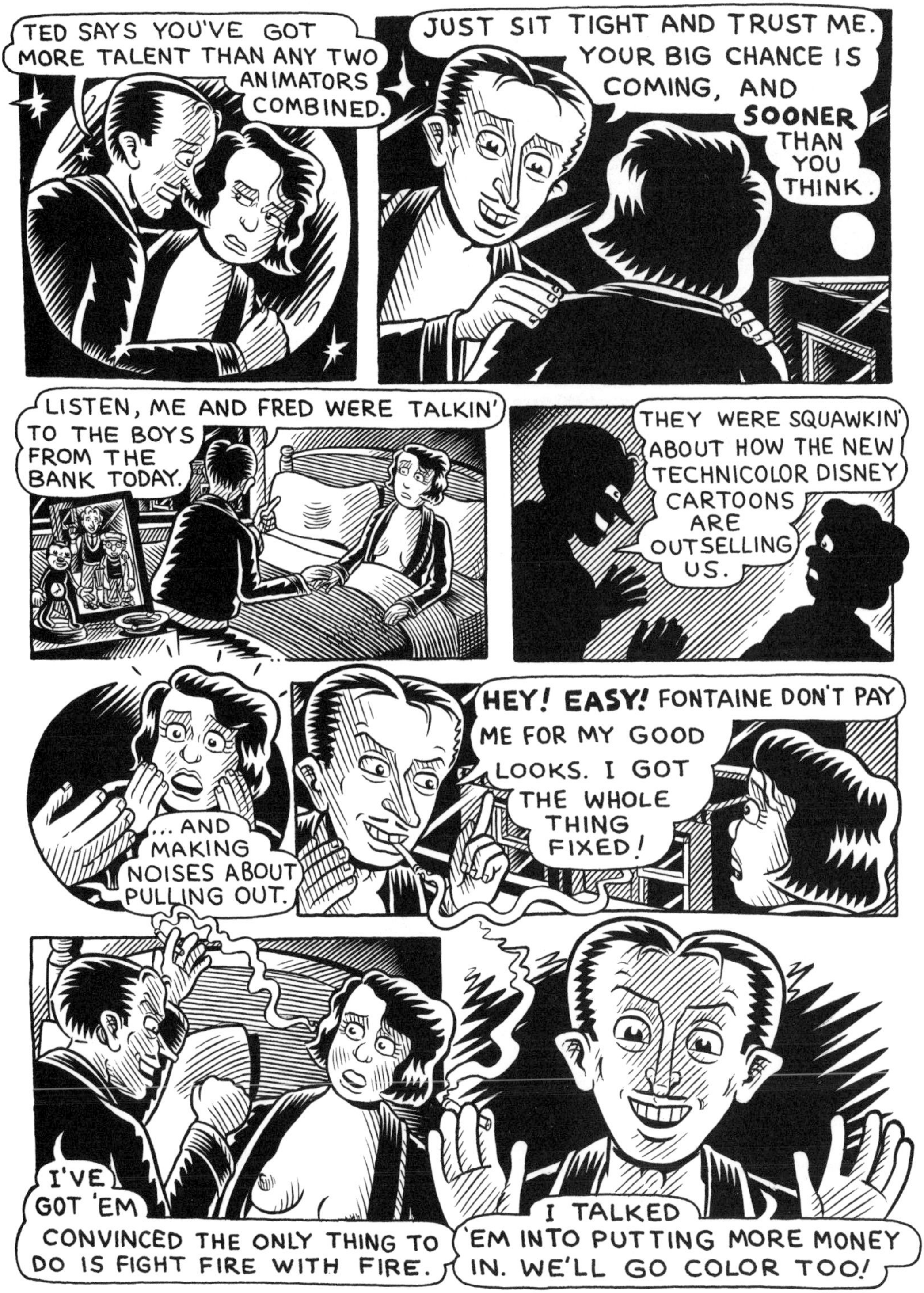
TED SAYS YOU'VE GOT MORE TALENT THAN ANY TWO ANIMATORS COMBINED.
JUST SIT TIGHT AND TRUST ME. YOUR BIG CHANCE IS COMING, AND **SOONER** THAN YOU THINK.
LISTEN, ME AND FRED WERE TALKIN' TO THE BOYS FROM THE BANK TODAY.
THEY WERE SQUAWKIN' ABOUT HOW THE NEW TECHNICOLOR DISNEY CARTOONS ARE OUTSELLING US.
...AND MAKING NOISES ABOUT PULLING OUT.
HEY! EASY! FONTAINE DON'T PAY ME FOR MY GOOD LOOKS. I GOT THE WHOLE THING FIXED!
I'VE GOT 'EM CONVINCED THE ONLY THING TO DO IS FIGHT FIRE WITH FIRE.
I TALKED 'EM INTO PUTTING MORE MONEY IN. WE'LL GO COLOR TOO!

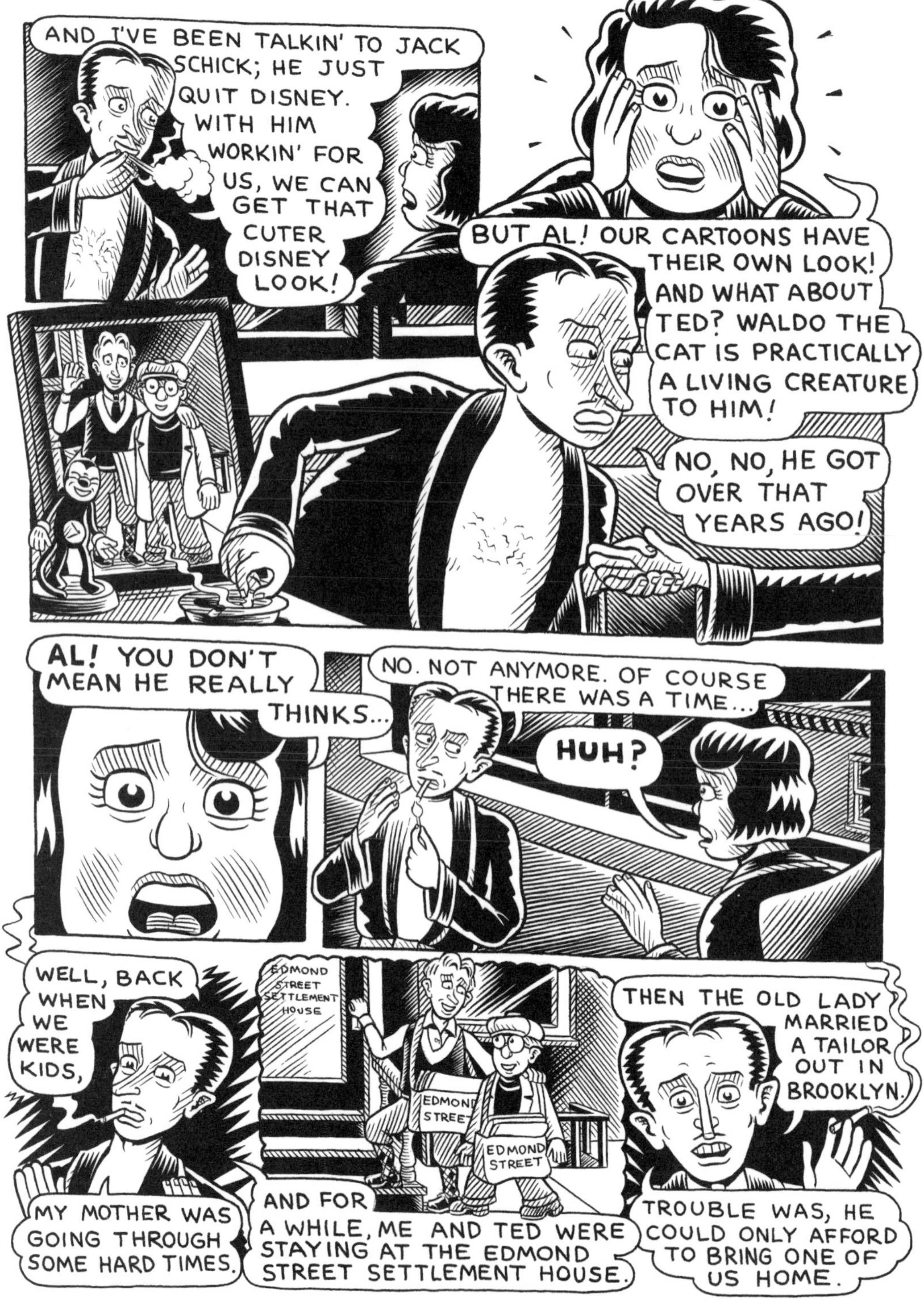
AND I'VE BEEN TALKIN' TO JACK SCHICK; HE JUST QUIT DISNEY. WITH HIM WORKIN' FOR US, WE CAN GET THAT CUTER DISNEY LOOK!
BUT AL! OUR CARTOONS HAVE THEIR OWN LOOK! AND WHAT ABOUT TED? WALDO THE CAT IS PRACTICALLY A LIVING CREATURE TO HIM!
NO, NO, HE GOT OVER THAT YEARS AGO!
AL! YOU DON'T MEAN HE REALLY THINKS...
NO. NOT ANYMORE. OF COURSE THERE WAS A TIME...
HUH?
WELL, BACK WHEN WE WERE KIDS,
MY MOTHER WAS GOING THROUGH SOME HARD TIMES.
EDMOND STREET SETTLEMENT HOUSE
EDMOND STREET
EDMOND STREET
AND FOR A WHILE, ME AND TED WERE STAYING AT THE EDMOND STREET SETTLEMENT HOUSE.
THEN THE OLD LADY MARRIED A TAILOR OUT IN BROOKLYN.
TROUBLE WAS, HE COULD ONLY AFFORD TO BRING ONE OF US HOME.

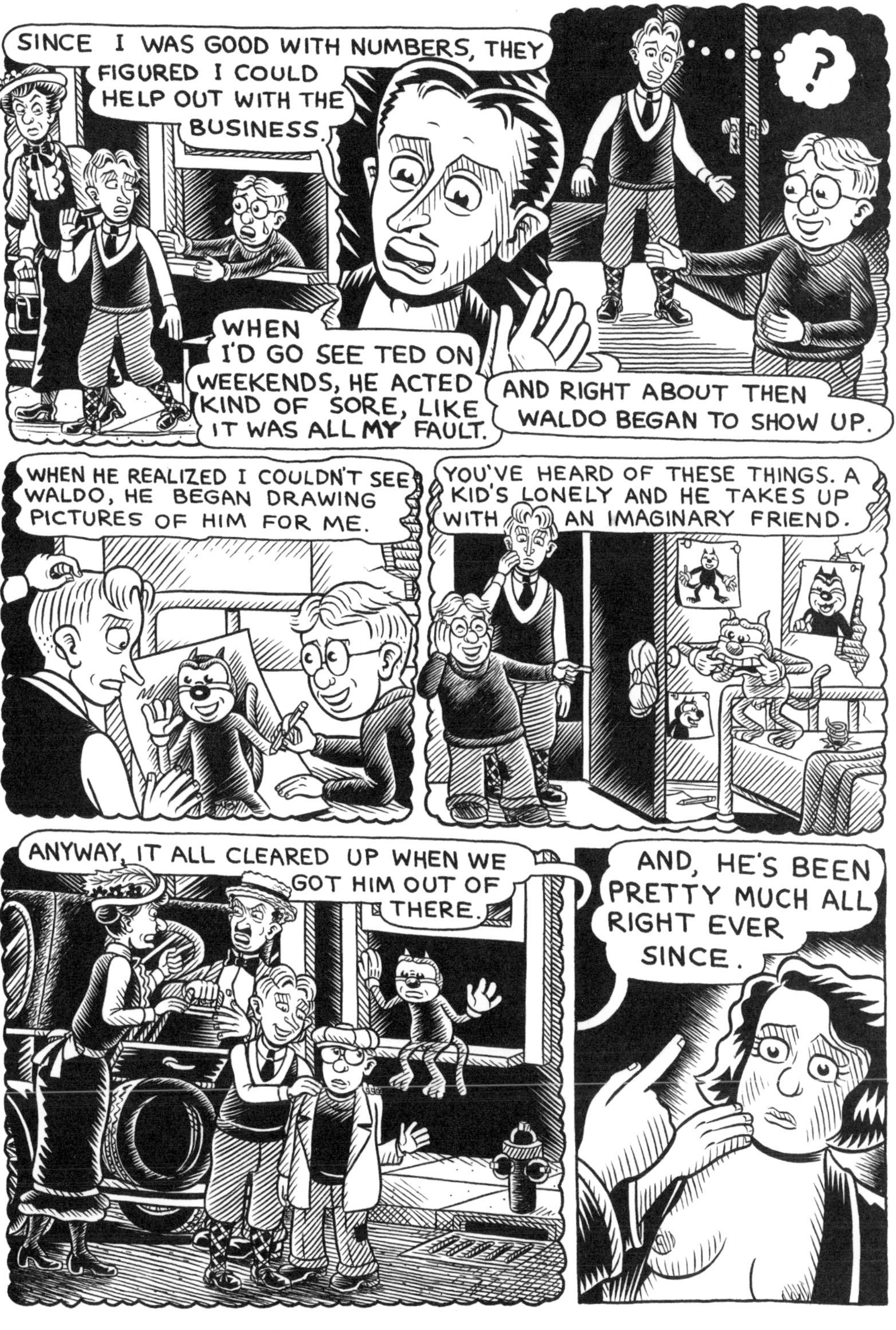

SINCE I WAS GOOD WITH NUMBERS, THEY FIGURED I COULD HELP OUT WITH THE BUSINESS.
WHEN I'D GO SEE TED ON WEEKENDS, HE ACTED KIND OF SORE, LIKE IT WAS ALL MY FAULT.
?
AND RIGHT ABOUT THEN WALDO BEGAN TO SHOW UP.
WHEN HE REALIZED I COULDN'T SEE WALDO, HE BEGAN DRAWING PICTURES OF HIM FOR ME.
YOU'VE HEARD OF THESE THINGS. A KID'S LONELY AND HE TAKES UP WITH AN IMAGINARY FRIEND.
ANYWAY, IT ALL CLEARED UP WHEN WE GOT HIM OUT OF THERE.
AND, HE'S BEEN PRETTY MUCH ALL RIGHT EVER SINCE.

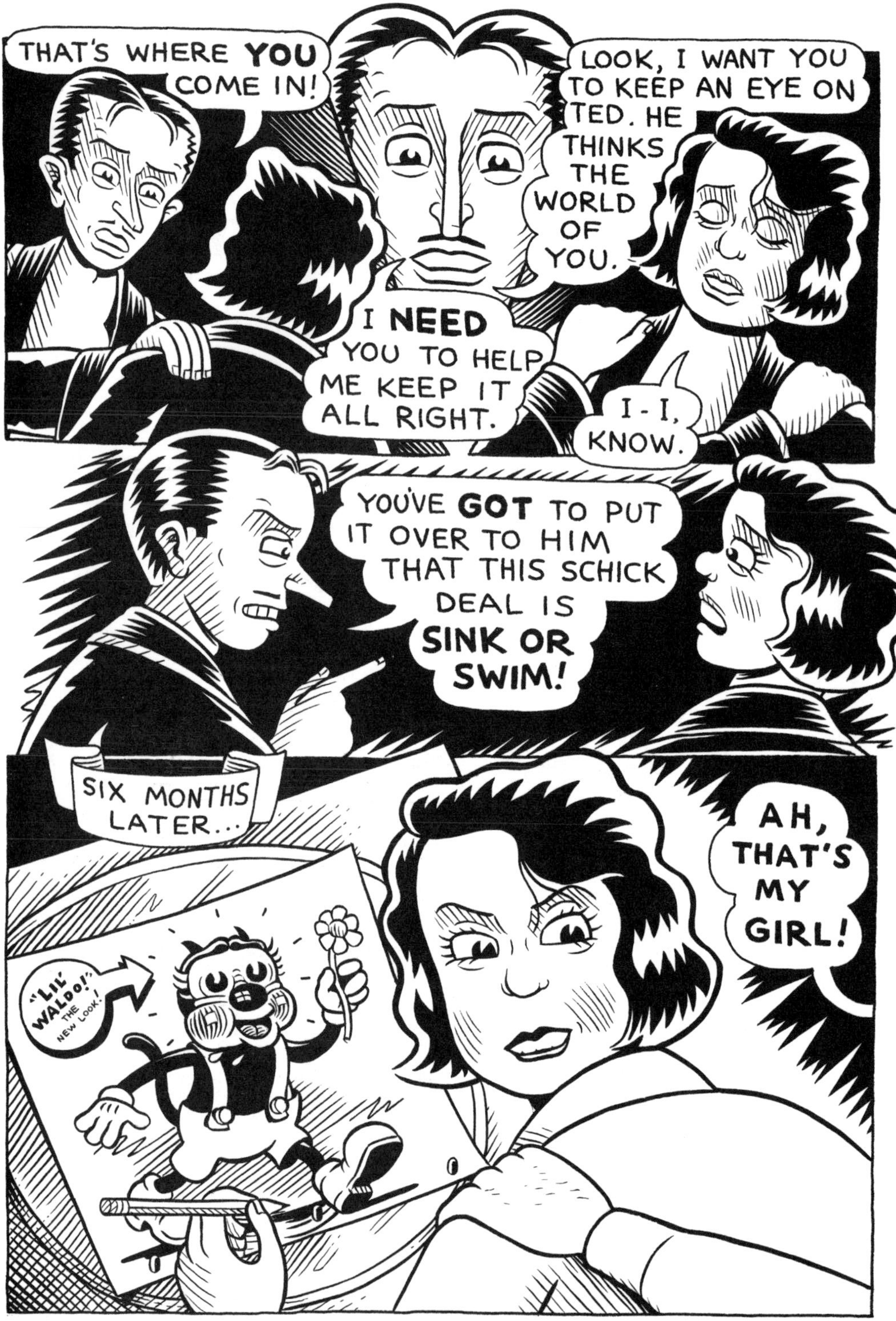

THAT'S WHERE YOU COME IN!
LOOK, I WANT YOU TO KEEP AN EYE ON TED. HE THINKS THE WORLD OF YOU.
I NEED YOU TO HELP ME KEEP IT ALL RIGHT.
I - I, KNOW.
YOU'VE GOT TO PUT IT OVER TO HIM THAT THIS SCHICK DEAL IS SINK OR SWIM!
SIX MONTHS LATER...
"LIL' WALDO!" THE NEW LOOK!
AH, THAT'S MY GIRL!

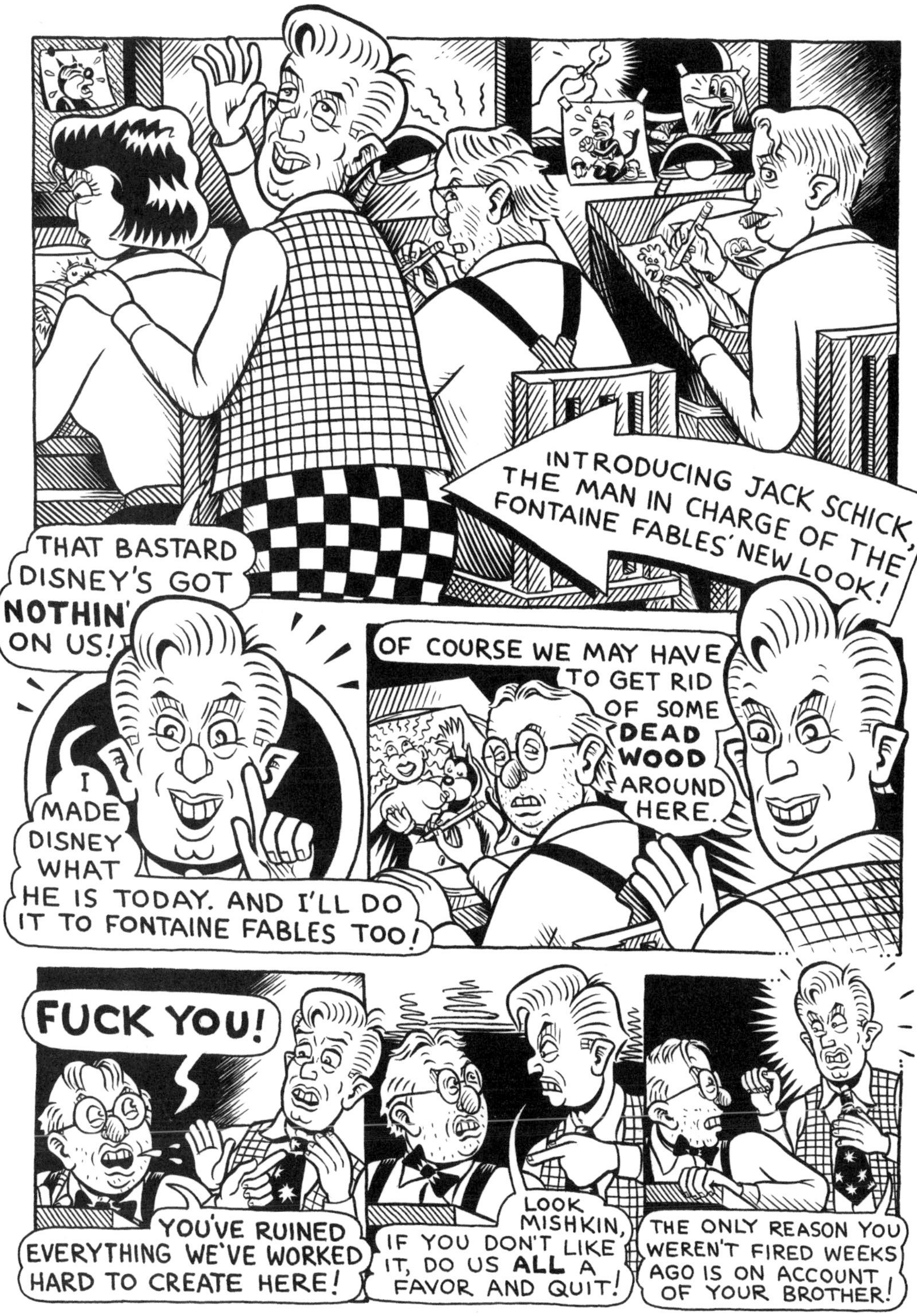
INTRODUCING JACK SCHICK, THE MAN IN CHARGE OF THE FONTAINE FABLES' NEW LOOK!
THAT BASTARD DISNEY'S GOT **NOTHIN'** ON US!
I MADE DISNEY WHAT HE IS TODAY. AND I'LL DO IT TO FONTAINE FABLES TOO!
OF COURSE WE MAY HAVE TO GET RID OF SOME **DEAD WOOD** AROUND HERE.
FUCK YOU!
YOU'VE RUINED EVERYTHING WE'VE WORKED HARD TO CREATE HERE!
LOOK MISHKIN, IF YOU DON'T LIKE IT, DO US **ALL** A FAVOR AND QUIT!
THE ONLY REASON YOU WEREN'T FIRED WEEKS AGO IS ON ACCOUNT OF YOUR BROTHER!

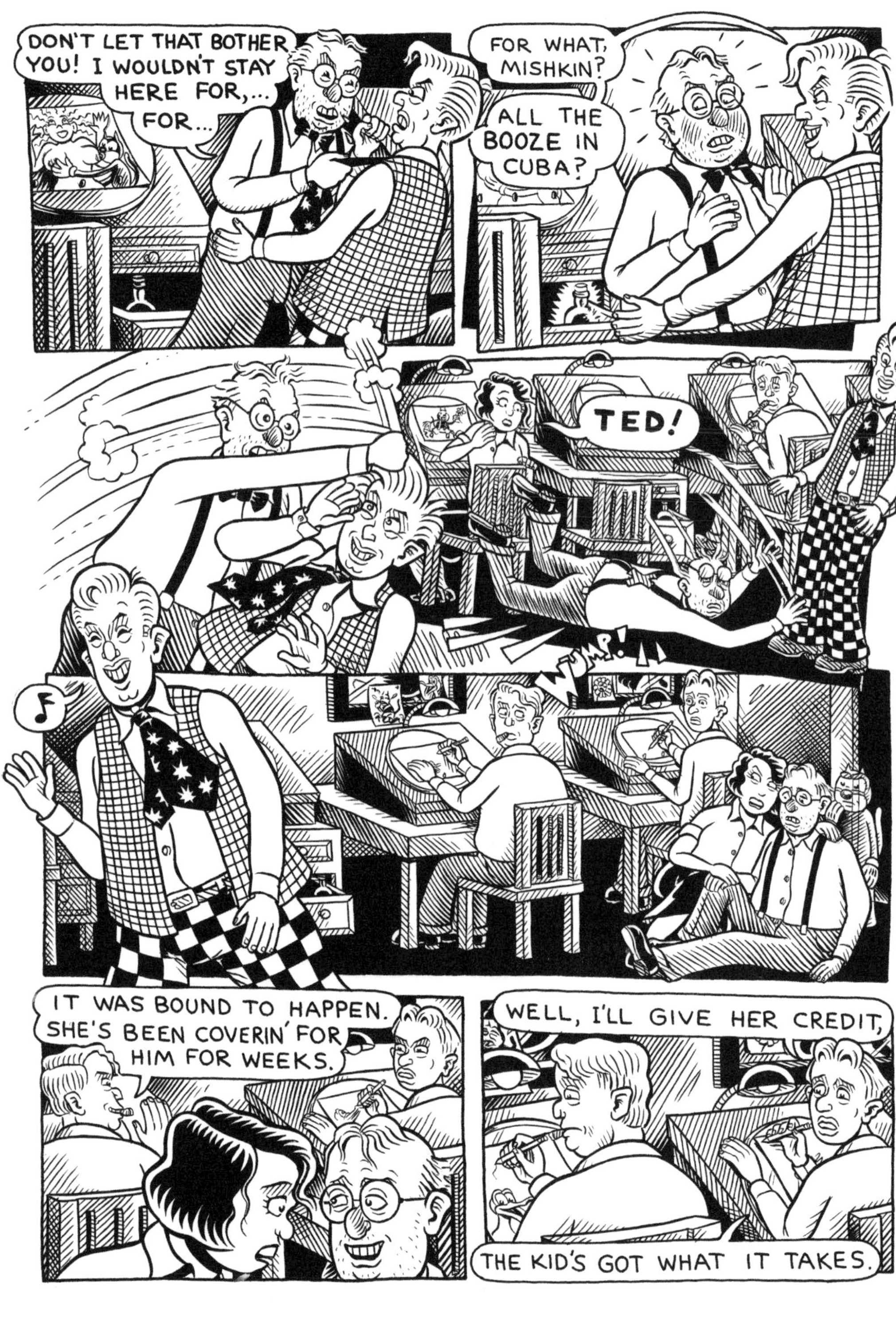
DON'T LET THAT BOTHER YOU! I WOULDN'T STAY HERE FOR,... FOR...
FOR WHAT, MISHKIN?
ALL THE BOOZE IN CUBA?
TED!
WUMP!
IT WAS BOUND TO HAPPEN. SHE'S BEEN COVERIN' FOR HIM FOR WEEKS.
WELL, I'LL GIVE HER CREDIT,
THE KID'S GOT WHAT IT TAKES.

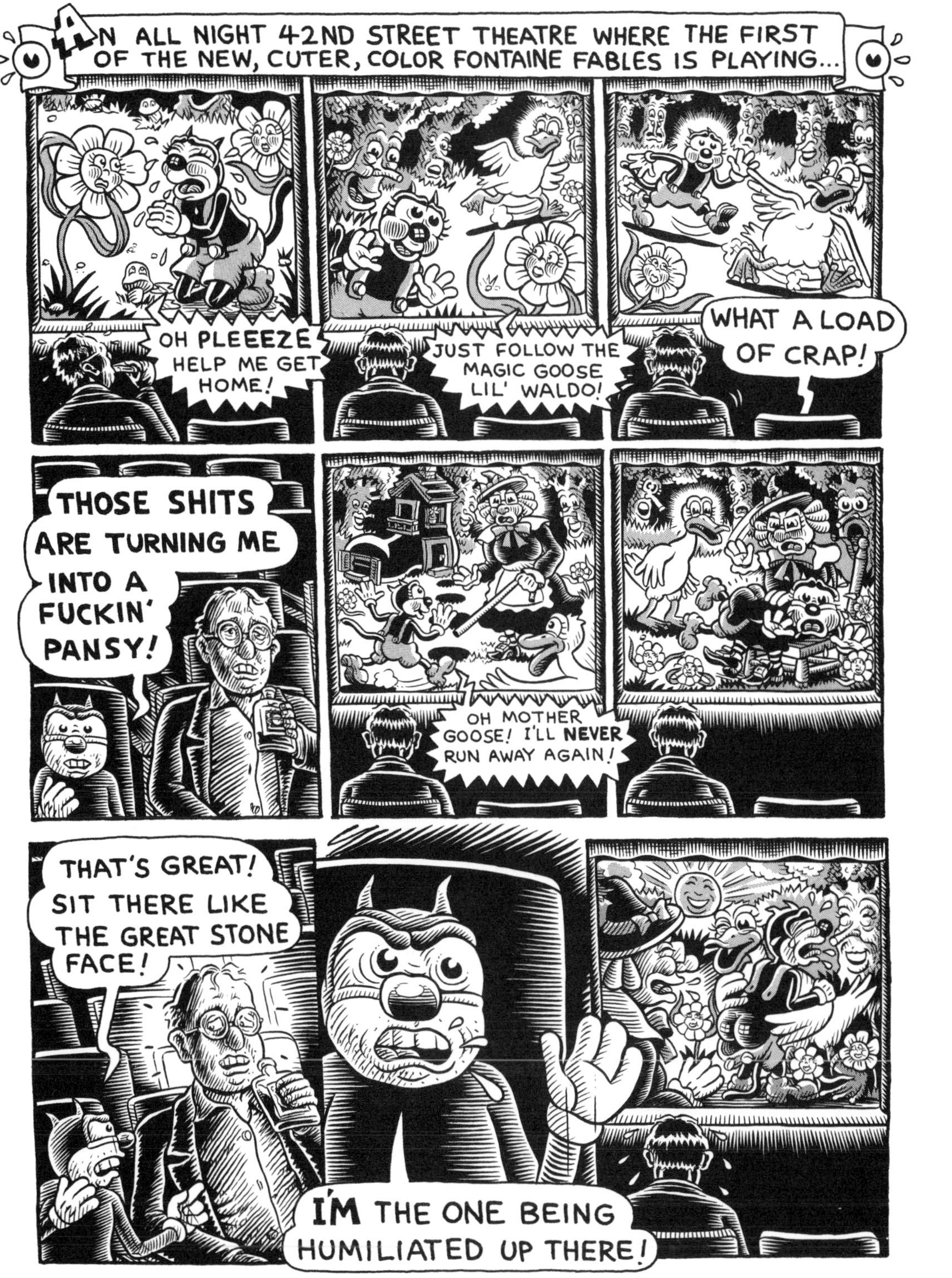
AN ALL NIGHT 42ND STREET THEATRE WHERE THE FIRST OF THE NEW, CUTER, COLOR FONTAINE FABLES IS PLAYING...
OH PLEEEZE HELP ME GET HOME!
JUST FOLLOW THE MAGIC GOOSE LIL' WALDO!
WHAT A LOAD OF CRAP!
THOSE SHITS ARE TURNING ME INTO A FUCKIN' PANSY!
OH MOTHER GOOSE! I'LL NEVER RUN AWAY AGAIN!
THAT'S GREAT! SIT THERE LIKE THE GREAT STONE FACE!
I'M THE ONE BEING HUMILIATED UP THERE!

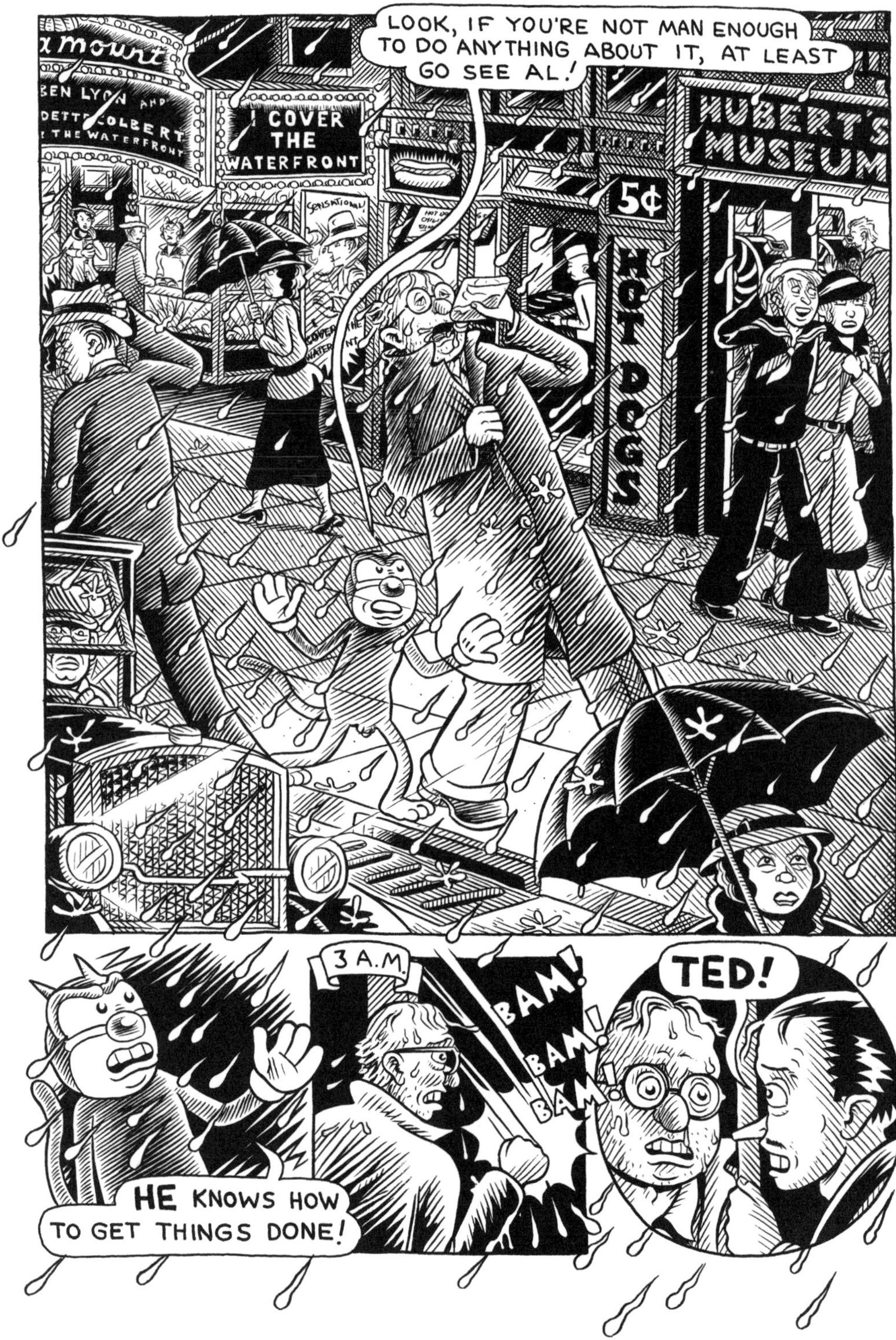
LOOK, IF YOU'RE NOT MAN ENOUGH TO DO ANYTHING ABOUT IT, AT LEAST GO SEE AL!
I COVER THE WATERFRONT
HUBERT'S MUSEUM
5¢
HOT DOGS
HE KNOWS HOW TO GET THINGS DONE!
3 A.M.
BAM!
BAM!
BAM!
TED!

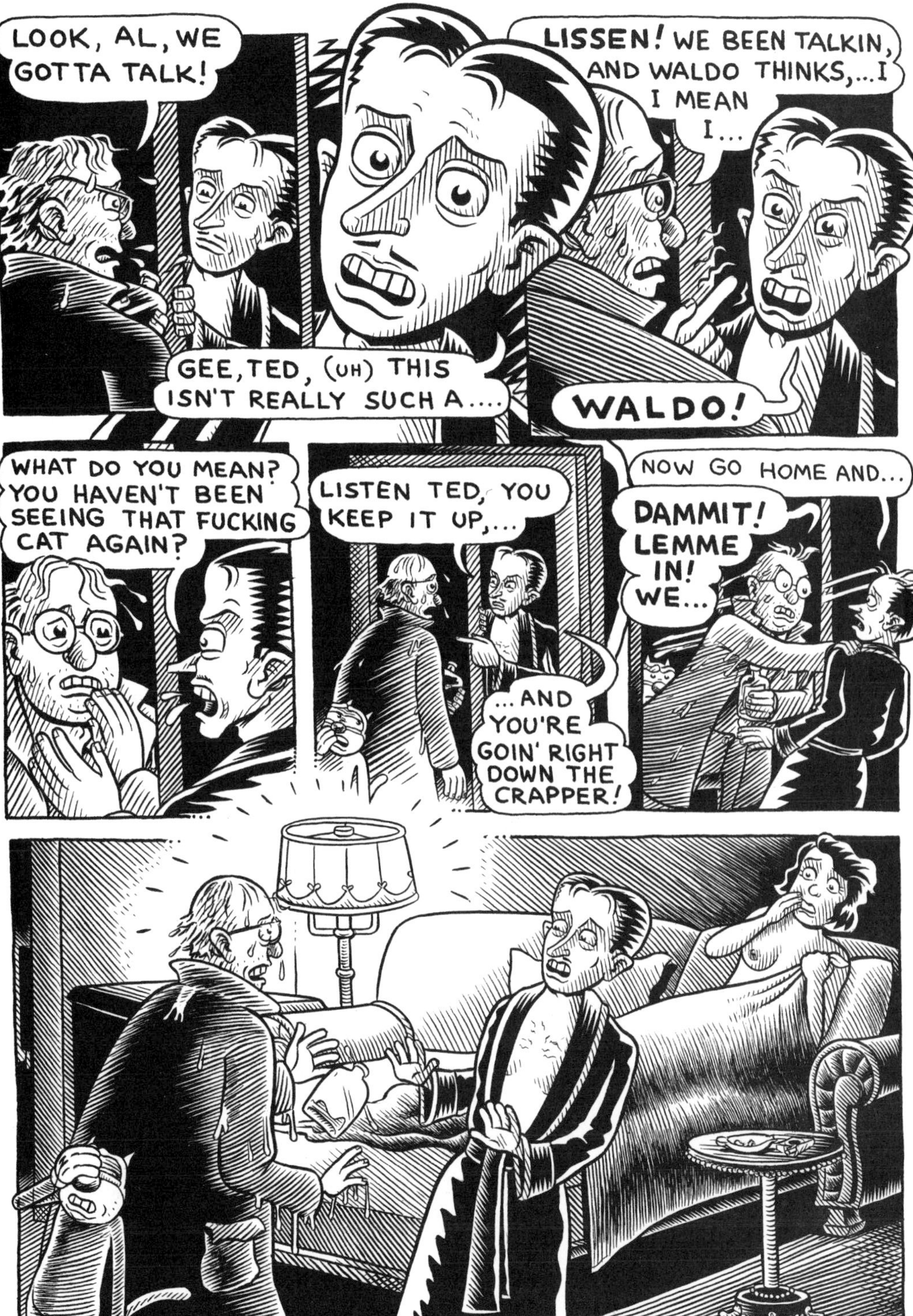
LOOK, AL, WE GOTTA TALK!
GEE, TED, (UH) THIS ISN'T REALLY SUCH A....
LISSEN! WE BEEN TALKIN, AND WALDO THINKS,...I I MEAN I...
WALDO!
WHAT DO YOU MEAN? YOU HAVEN'T BEEN SEEING THAT FUCKING CAT AGAIN?
LISTEN TED, YOU KEEP IT UP,...
...AND YOU'RE GOIN' RIGHT DOWN THE CRAPPER!
NOW GO HOME AND...
DAMMIT! LEMME IN! WE...

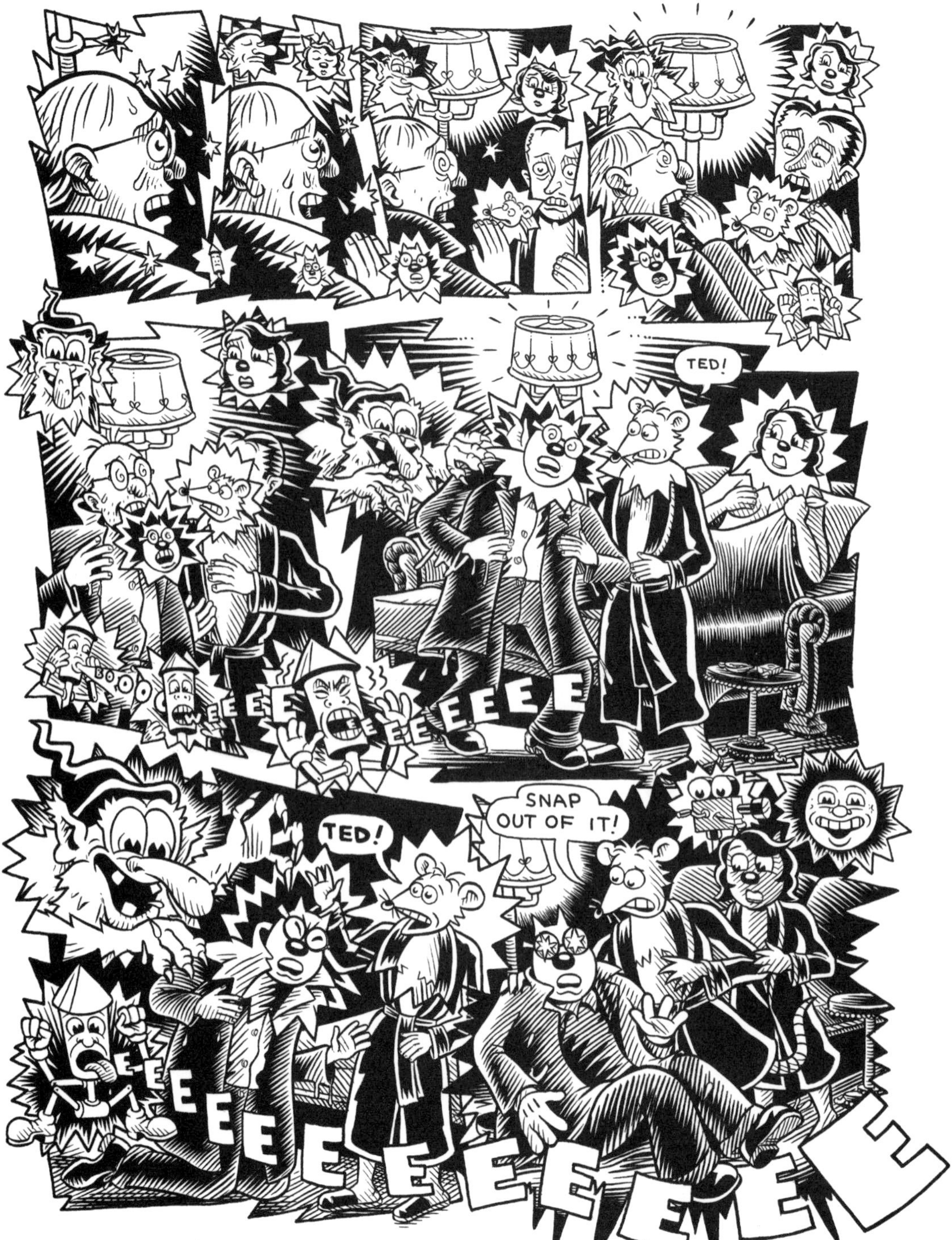
TED!
BOOO
WEEEE
EEEEEEEE
TED!
SNAP OUT OF IT!
EEEEEEEEEEEEE

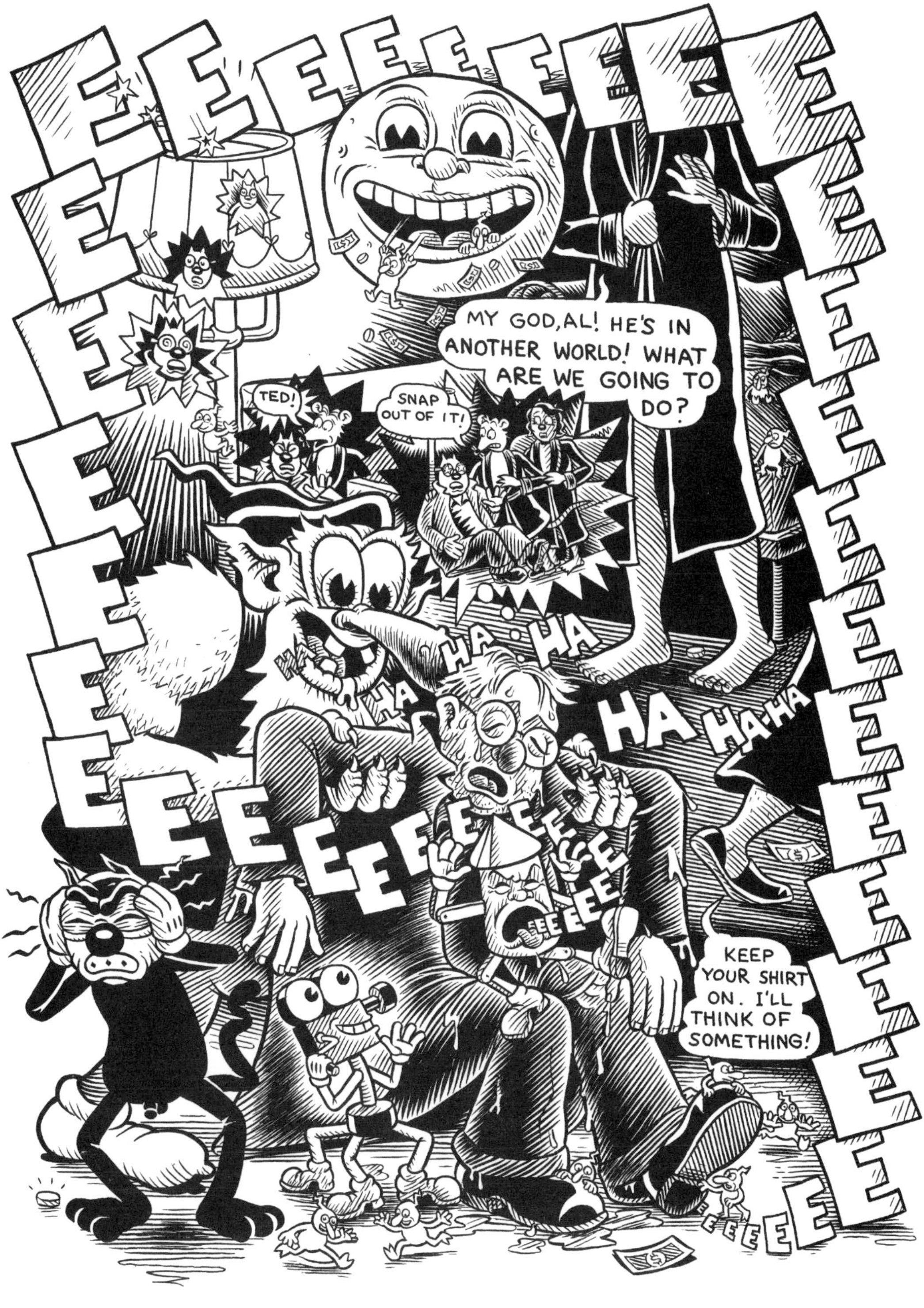
EEEEEEEEEEEEEEEEEEEEEEEEEEEEEEEEEEEEEEEEEEEEEE
MY GOD, AL! HE'S IN ANOTHER WORLD! WHAT ARE WE GOING TO DO?
TED!
SNAP OUT OF IT!
HA HA HA HA
HA HA-HA
KEEP YOUR SHIRT ON. I'LL THINK OF SOMETHING!

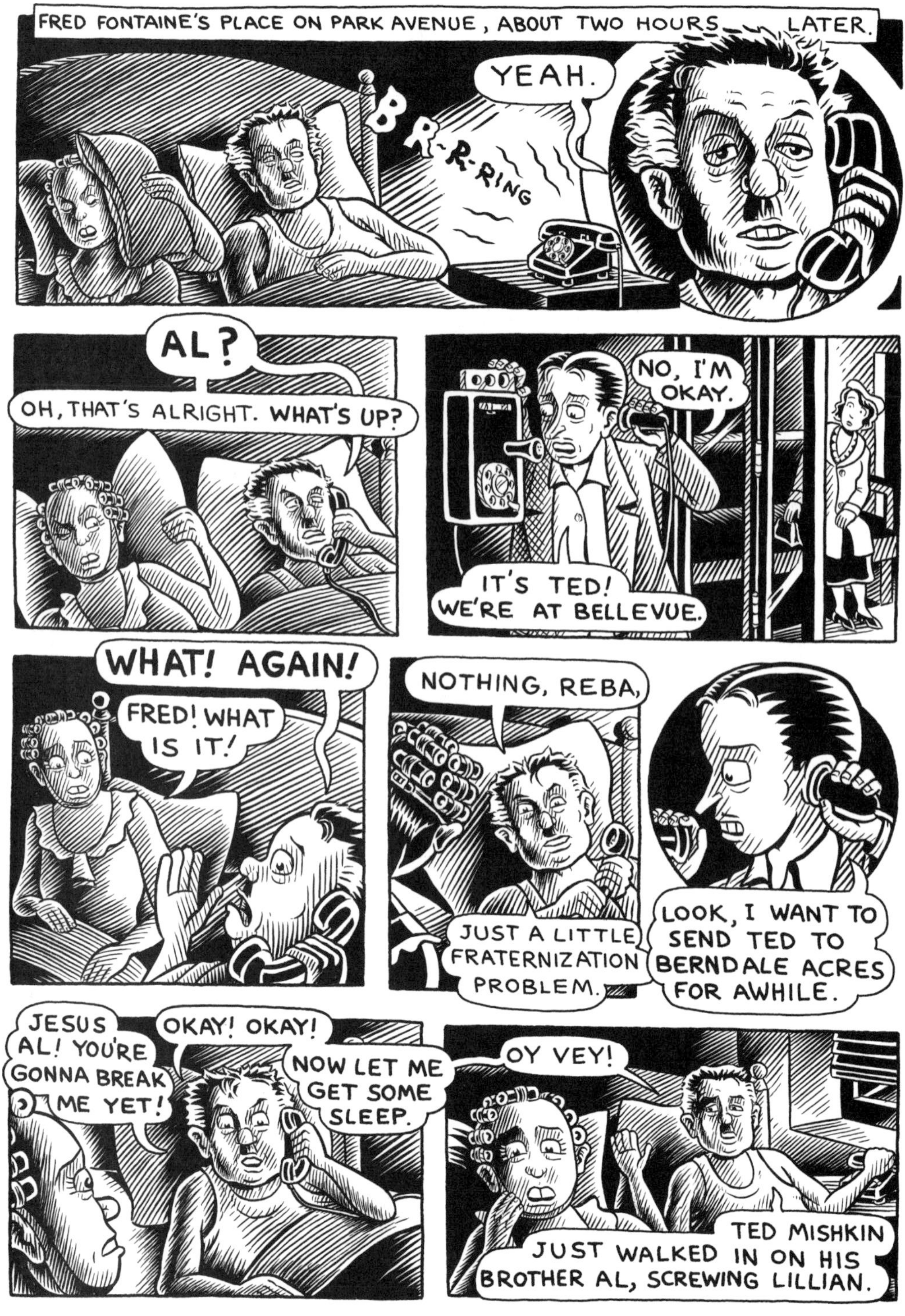
FRED FONTAINE'S PLACE ON PARK AVENUE, ABOUT TWO HOURS LATER.
B-R-R-RING
YEAH.
AL?
OH, THAT'S ALRIGHT. WHAT'S UP?
NO, I'M OKAY.
IT'S TED! WE'RE AT BELLEVUE.
WHAT! AGAIN!
FRED! WHAT IS IT!
NOTHING, REBA,
JUST A LITTLE FRATERNIZATION PROBLEM.
LOOK, I WANT TO SEND TED TO BERNDALE ACRES FOR AWHILE.
JESUS AL! YOU'RE GONNA BREAK ME YET!
OKAY! OKAY!
NOW LET ME GET SOME SLEEP.
OY VEY!
TED MISHKIN JUST WALKED IN ON HIS BROTHER AL, SCREWING LILLIAN.

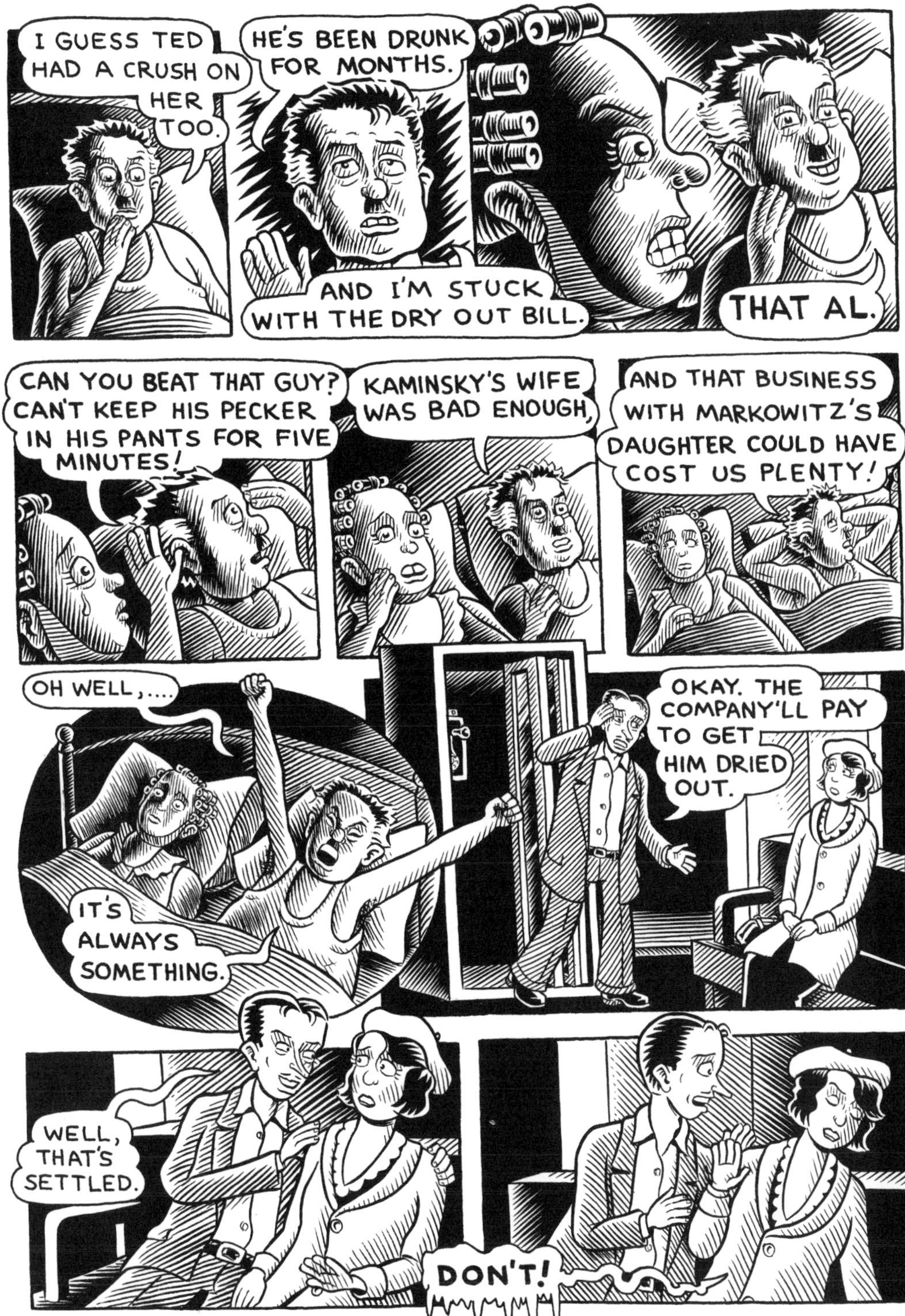
I GUESS TED HAD A CRUSH ON HER TOO.
HE'S BEEN DRUNK FOR MONTHS.
AND I'M STUCK WITH THE DRY OUT BILL.
THAT AL.
CAN YOU BEAT THAT GUY? CAN'T KEEP HIS PECKER IN HIS PANTS FOR FIVE MINUTES!
KAMINSKY'S WIFE WAS BAD ENOUGH,
AND THAT BUSINESS WITH MARKOWITZ'S DAUGHTER COULD HAVE COST US PLENTY!
OH WELL,....
IT'S ALWAYS SOMETHING.
OKAY. THE COMPANY'LL PAY TO GET HIM DRIED OUT.
WELL, THAT'S SETTLED.
DON'T!

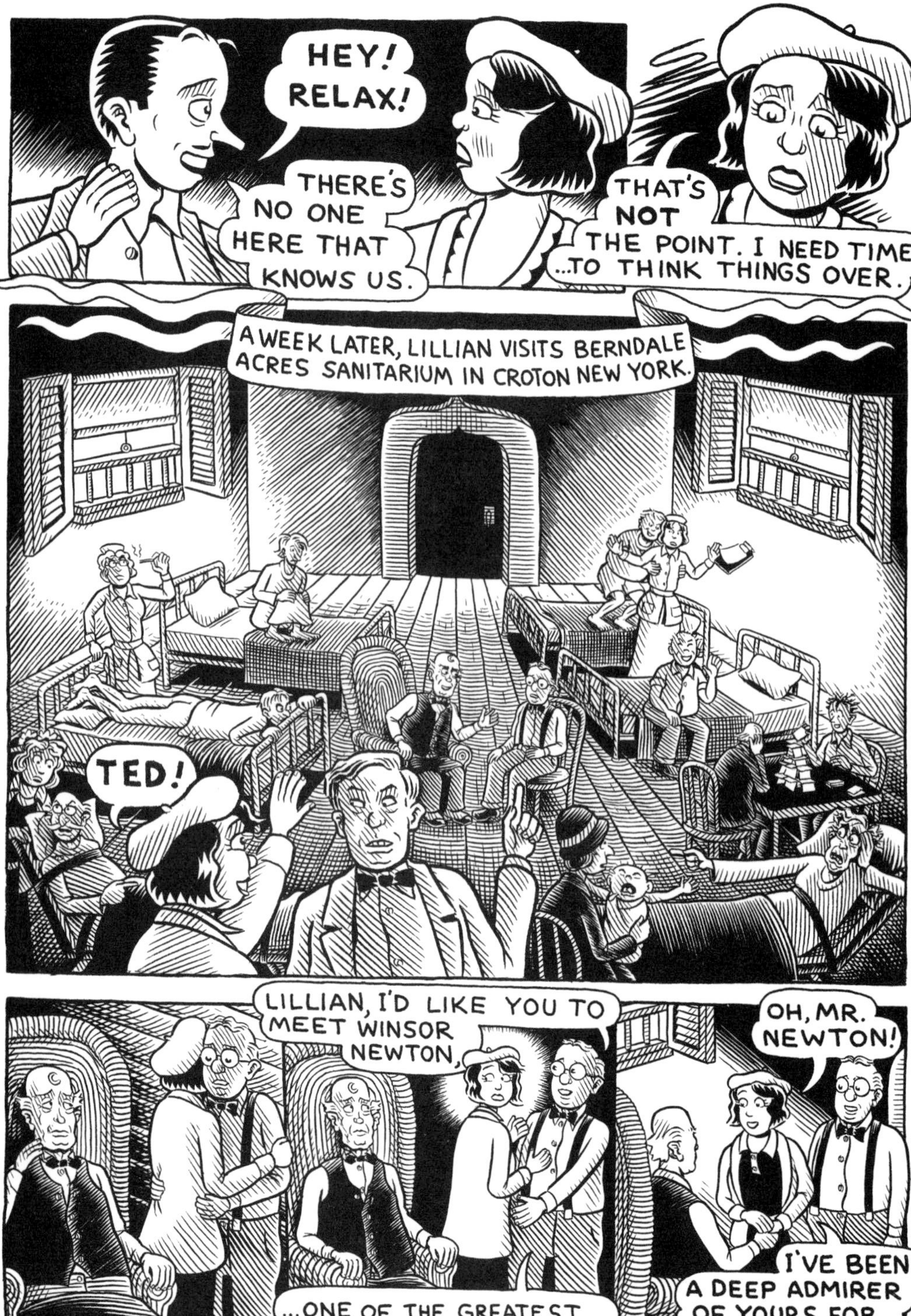

HEY! RELAX!
THERE'S NO ONE HERE THAT KNOWS US.
THAT'S NOT THE POINT. I NEED TIME, ...TO THINK THINGS OVER.
A WEEK LATER, LILLIAN VISITS BERNDALE ACRES SANITARIUM IN CROTON NEW YORK.
TED!
LILLIAN, I'D LIKE YOU TO MEET WINSOR NEWTON,
...ONE OF THE GREATEST...
OH, MR. NEWTON!
I'VE BEEN A DEEP ADMIRER OF YOURS FOR...

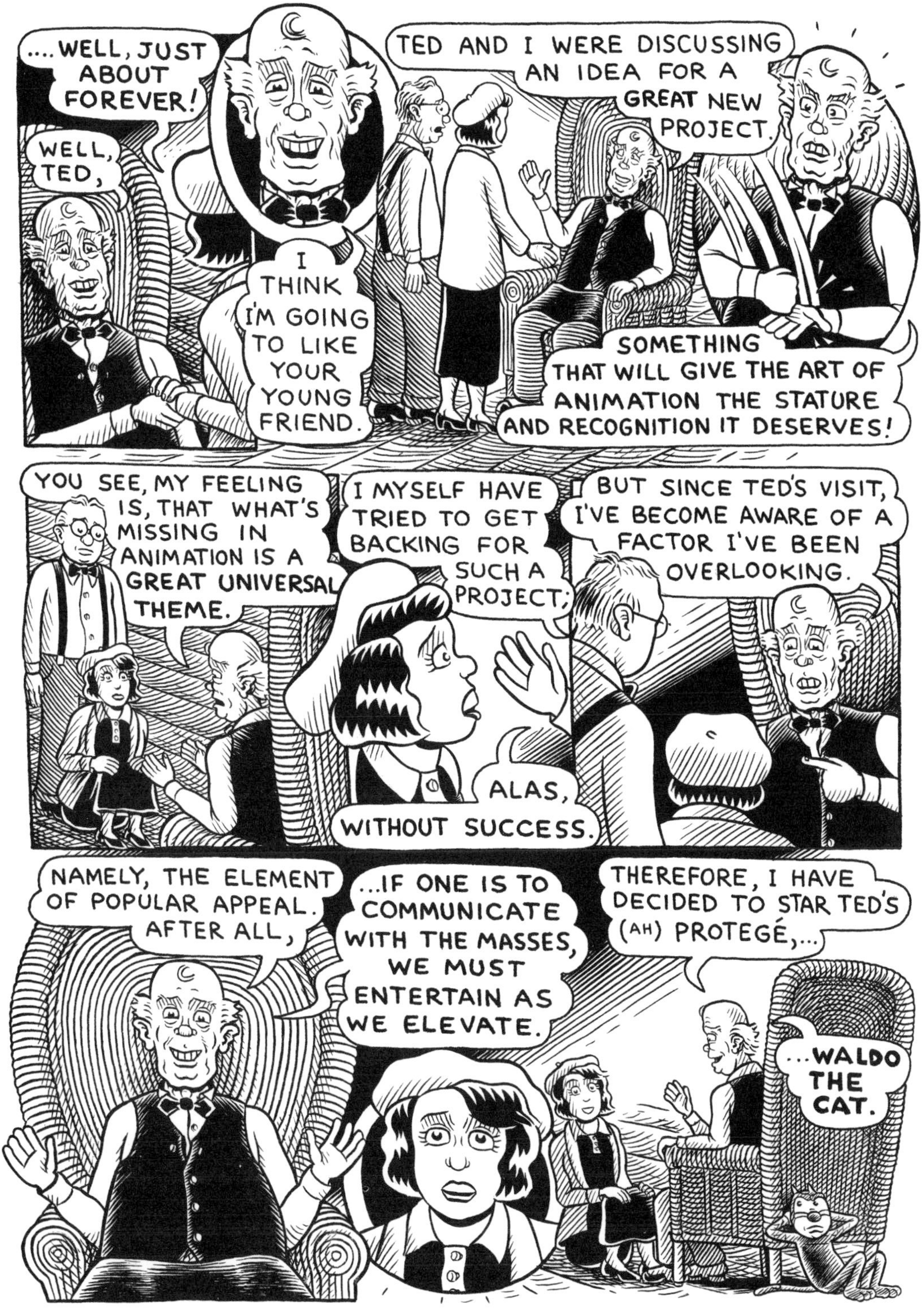
....WELL, JUST ABOUT FOREVER!
WELL, TED,
I THINK I'M GOING TO LIKE YOUR YOUNG FRIEND.
TED AND I WERE DISCUSSING AN IDEA FOR A GREAT NEW PROJECT,
SOMETHING THAT WILL GIVE THE ART OF ANIMATION THE STATURE AND RECOGNITION IT DESERVES!
YOU SEE, MY FEELING IS, THAT WHAT'S MISSING IN ANIMATION IS A GREAT UNIVERSAL THEME.
I MYSELF HAVE TRIED TO GET BACKING FOR SUCH A PROJECT;
ALAS, WITHOUT SUCCESS.
BUT SINCE TED'S VISIT, I'VE BECOME AWARE OF A FACTOR I'VE BEEN OVERLOOKING.
NAMELY, THE ELEMENT OF POPULAR APPEAL. AFTER ALL,
...IF ONE IS TO COMMUNICATE WITH THE MASSES, WE MUST ENTERTAIN AS WE ELEVATE.
THEREFORE, I HAVE DECIDED TO STAR TED'S (AH) PROTEGÉ,...
...WALDO THE CAT.

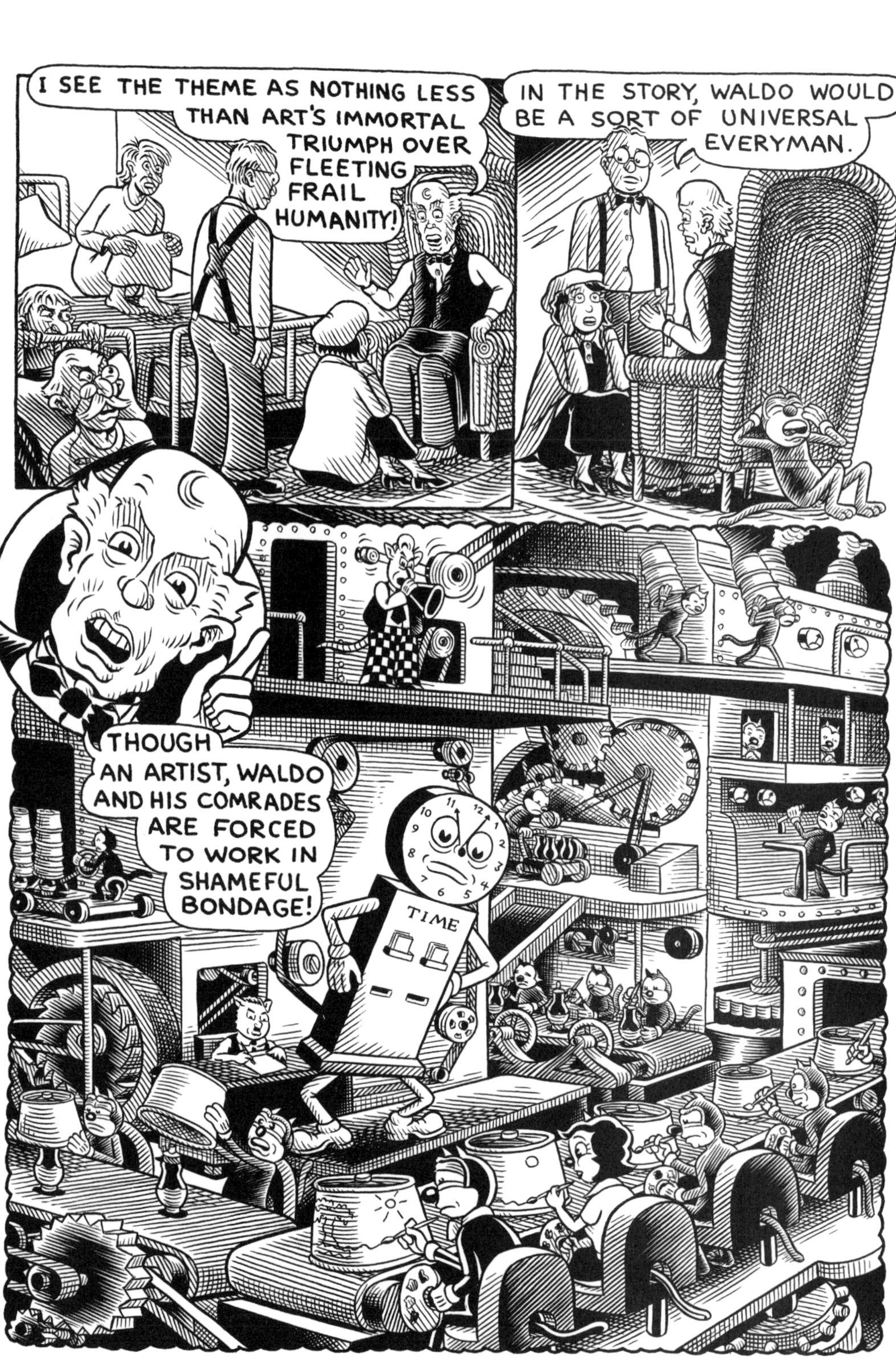
I SEE THE THEME AS NOTHING LESS THAN ART'S IMMORTAL TRIUMPH OVER FLEETING FRAIL HUMANITY!
IN THE STORY, WALDO WOULD BE A SORT OF UNIVERSAL EVERYMAN.
THOUGH AN ARTIST, WALDO AND HIS COMRADES ARE FORCED TO WORK IN SHAMEFUL BONDAGE!
TIME

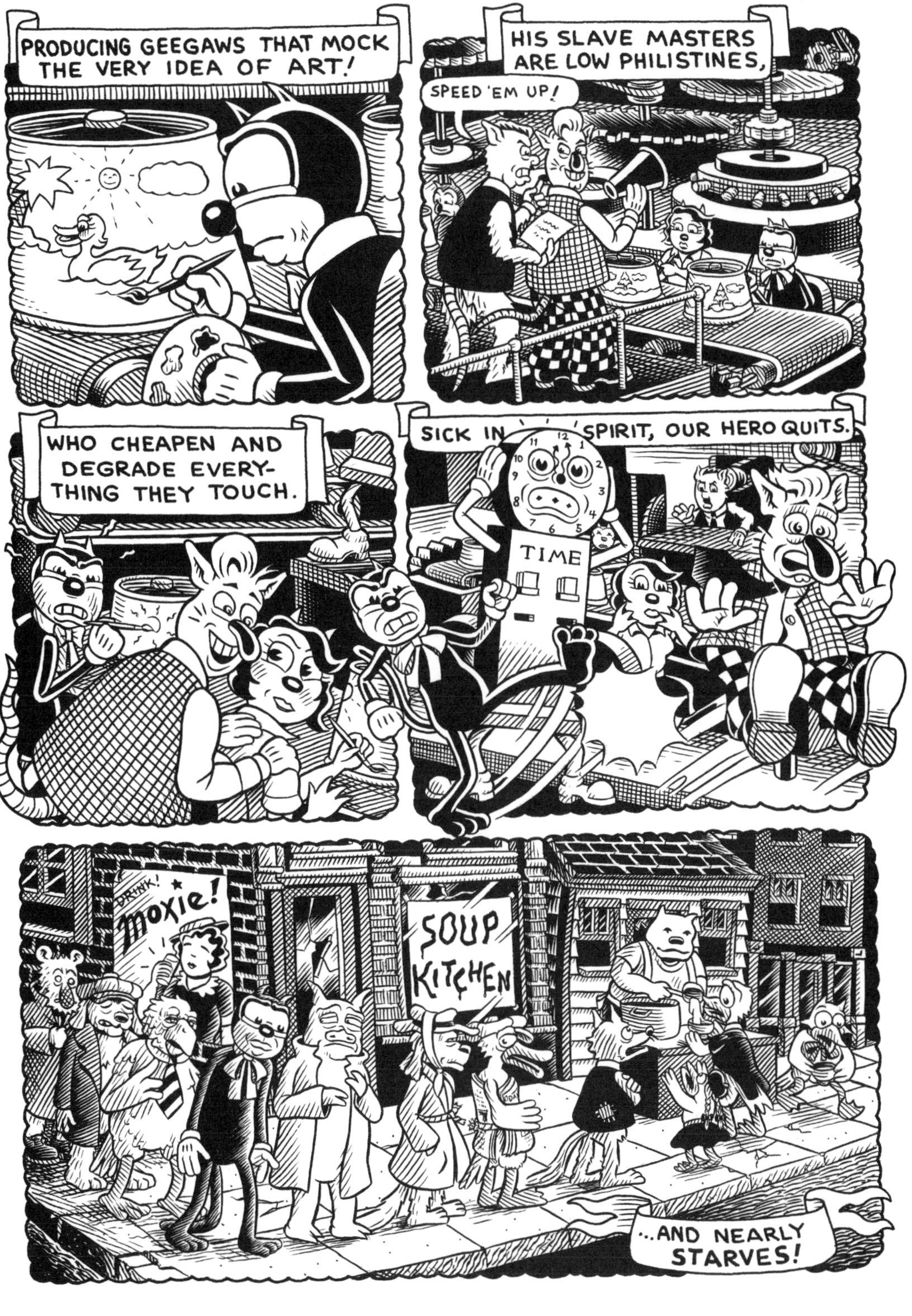
PRODUCING GEEGAWS THAT MOCK THE VERY IDEA OF ART!
HIS SLAVE MASTERS ARE LOW PHILISTINES,
SPEED 'EM UP!
WHO CHEAPEN AND DEGRADE EVERY-THING THEY TOUCH.
SICK IN SPIRIT, OUR HERO QUITS.
TIME
DRINK! moxie!
SOUP KITCHEN
...AND NEARLY STARVES!

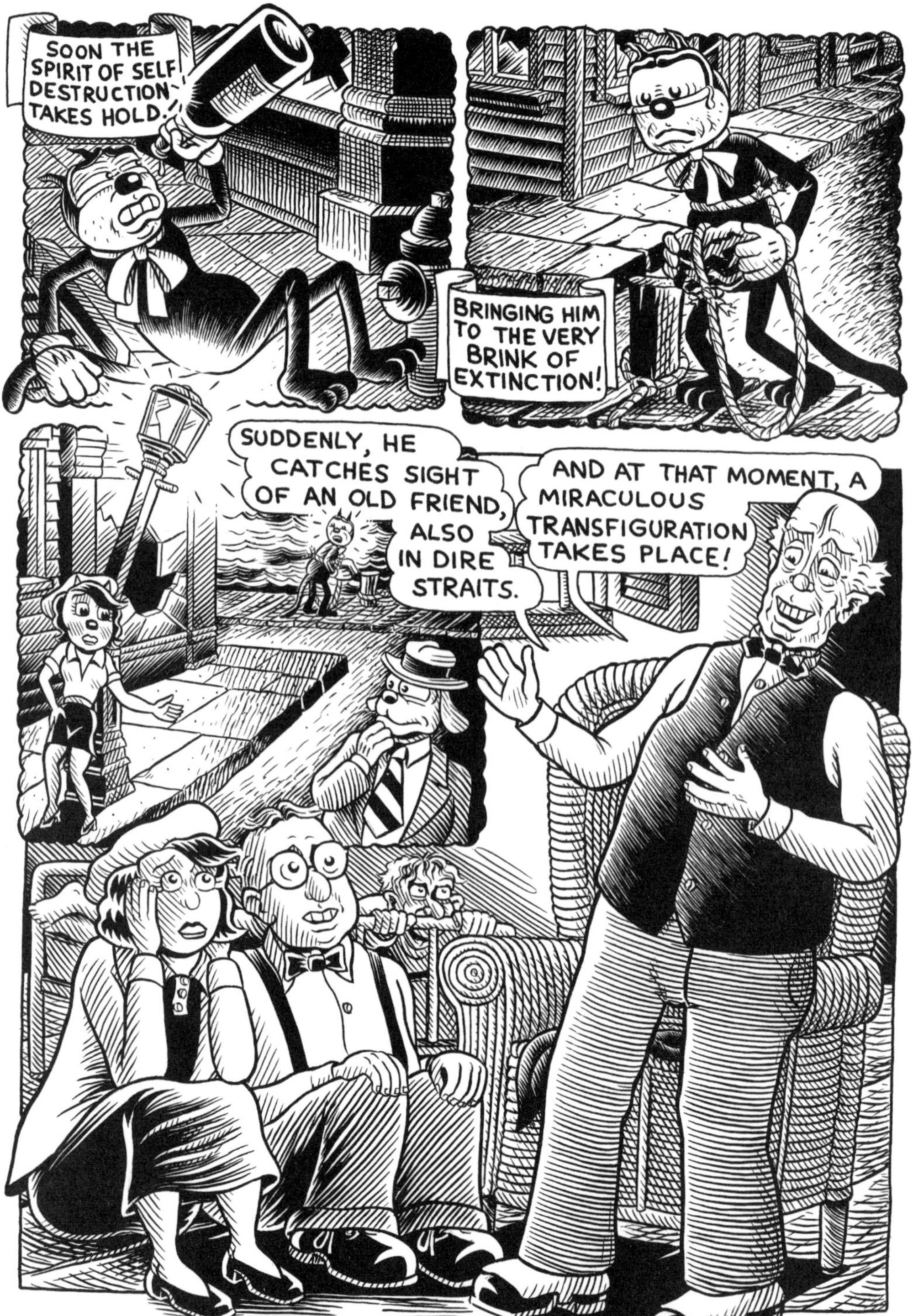
SOON THE SPIRIT OF SELF DESTRUCTION TAKES HOLD.
BRINGING HIM TO THE VERY BRINK OF EXTINCTION!
SUDDENLY, HE CATCHES SIGHT OF AN OLD FRIEND, ALSO IN DIRE STRAITS.
AND AT THAT MOMENT, A MIRACULOUS TRANSFIGURATION TAKES PLACE!

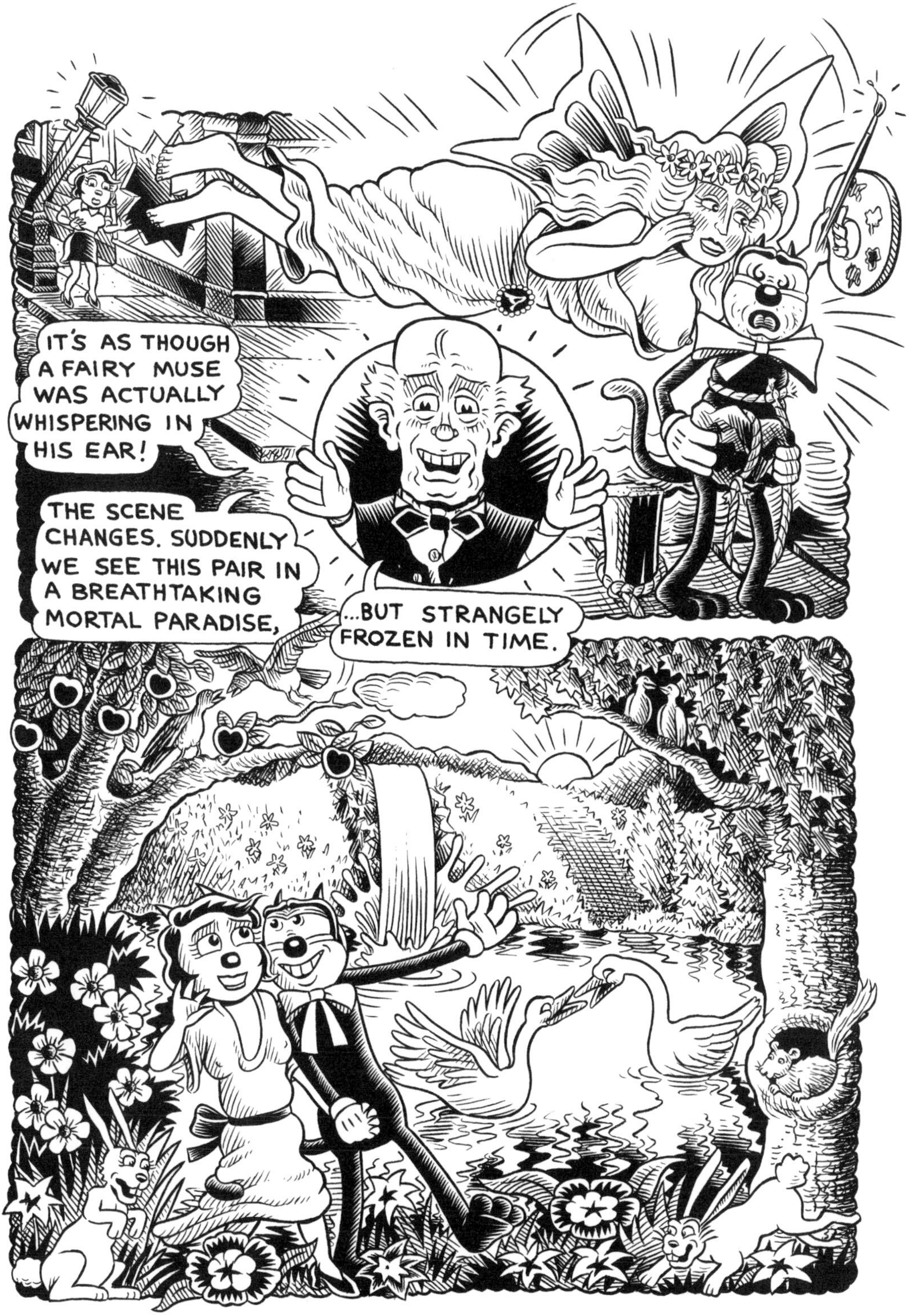
IT'S AS THOUGH A FAIRY MUSE WAS ACTUALLY WHISPERING IN HIS EAR!
THE SCENE CHANGES. SUDDENLY WE SEE THIS PAIR IN A BREATHTAKING MORTAL PARADISE,
...BUT STRANGELY FROZEN IN TIME.

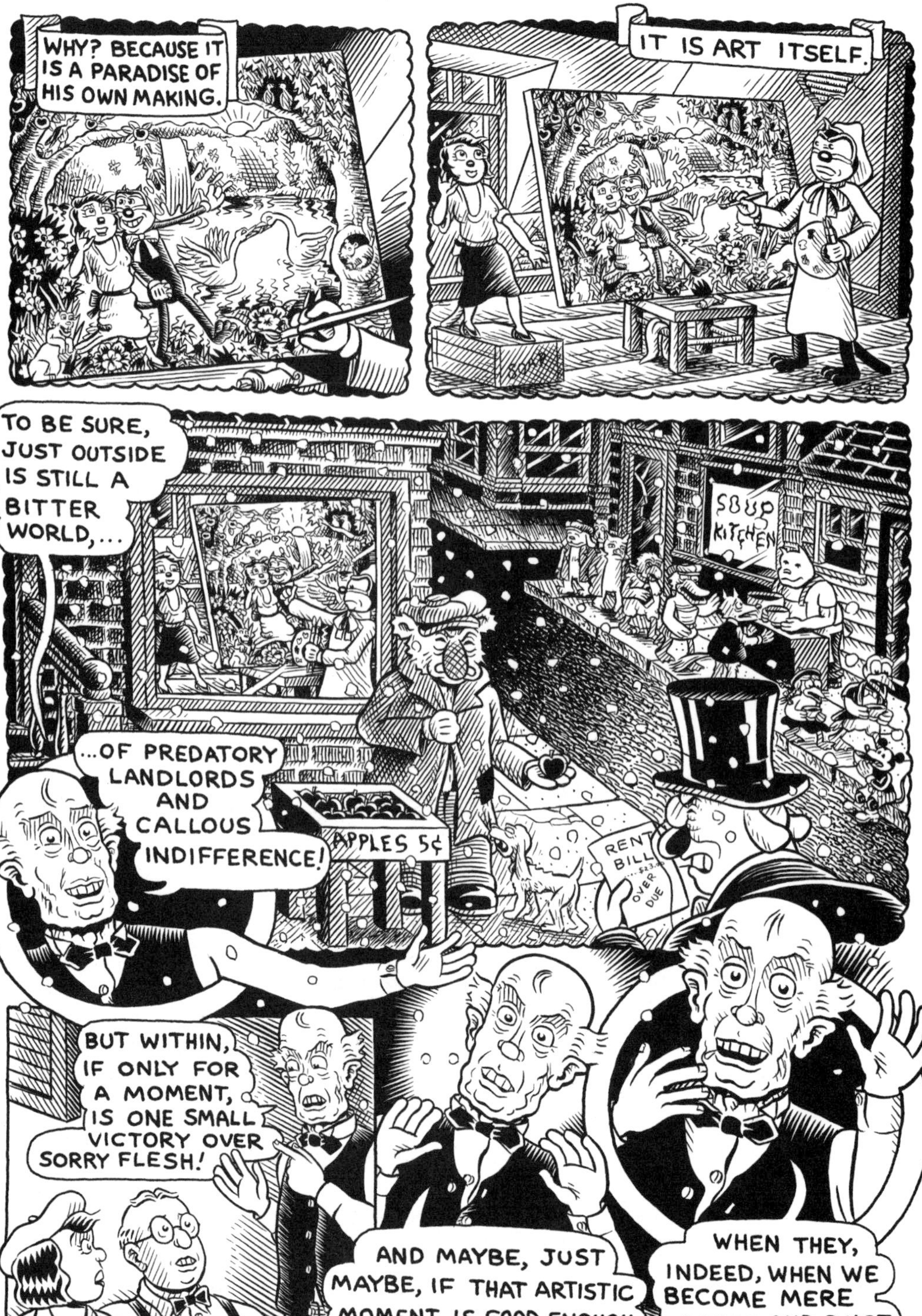

WHY? BECAUSE IT IS A PARADISE OF HIS OWN MAKING.
IT IS ART ITSELF.
TO BE SURE, JUST OUTSIDE IS STILL A BITTER WORLD, . . .
SOUP KITCHEN
...OF PREDATORY LANDLORDS AND CALLOUS INDIFFERENCE!
APPLES 5¢
RENT BILL OVER DUE
BUT WITHIN, IF ONLY FOR A MOMENT, IS ONE SMALL VICTORY OVER SORRY FLESH!
AND MAYBE, JUST MAYBE, IF THAT ARTISTIC MOMENT IS GOOD ENOUGH,
WHEN THEY, INDEED, WHEN WE BECOME MERE ASHES AND DUST,

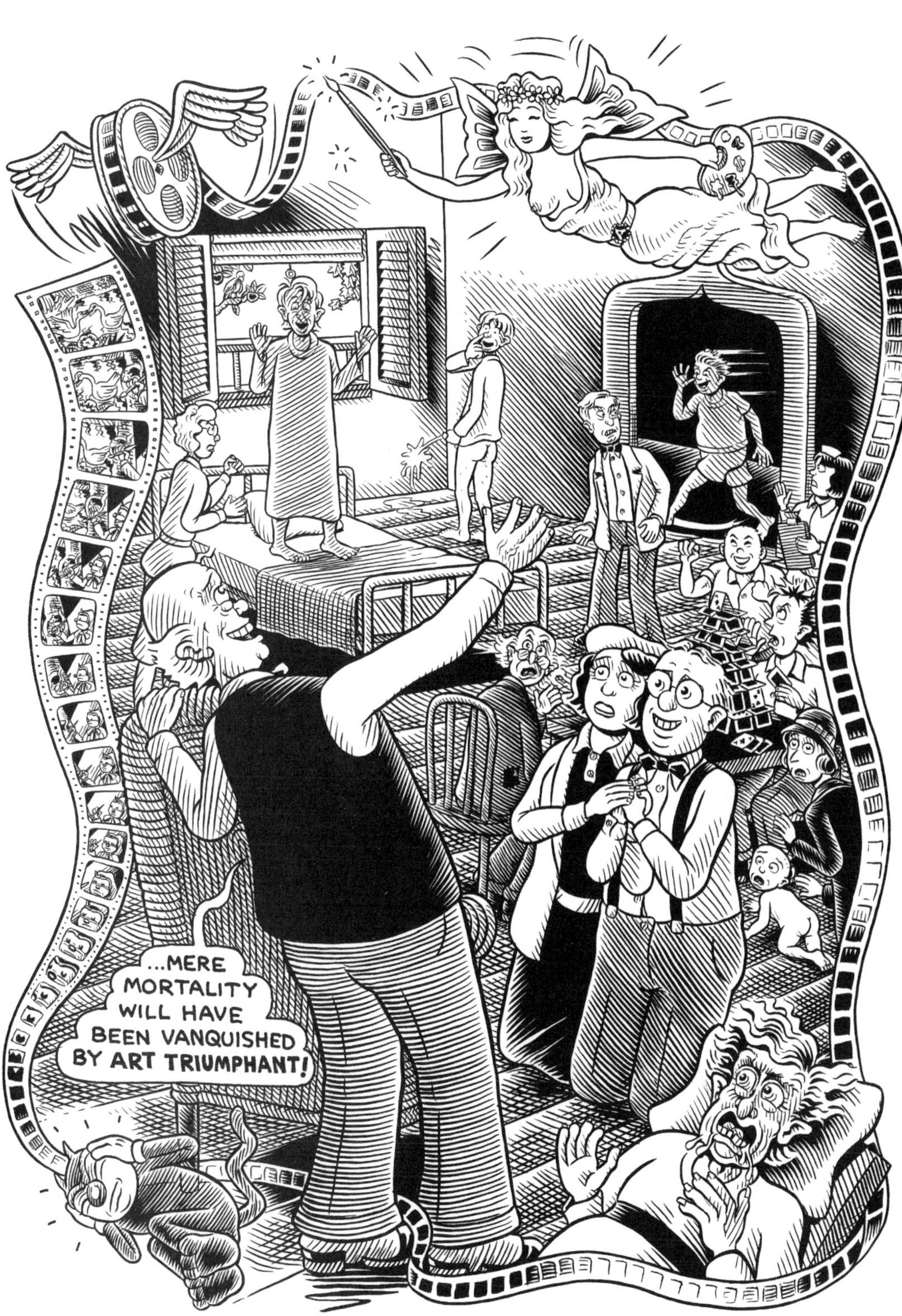
...MERE MORTALITY WILL HAVE BEEN VANQUISHED BY ART TRIUMPHANT!

EPILOGUE: GOOD NEWS.....BAD NEWS.

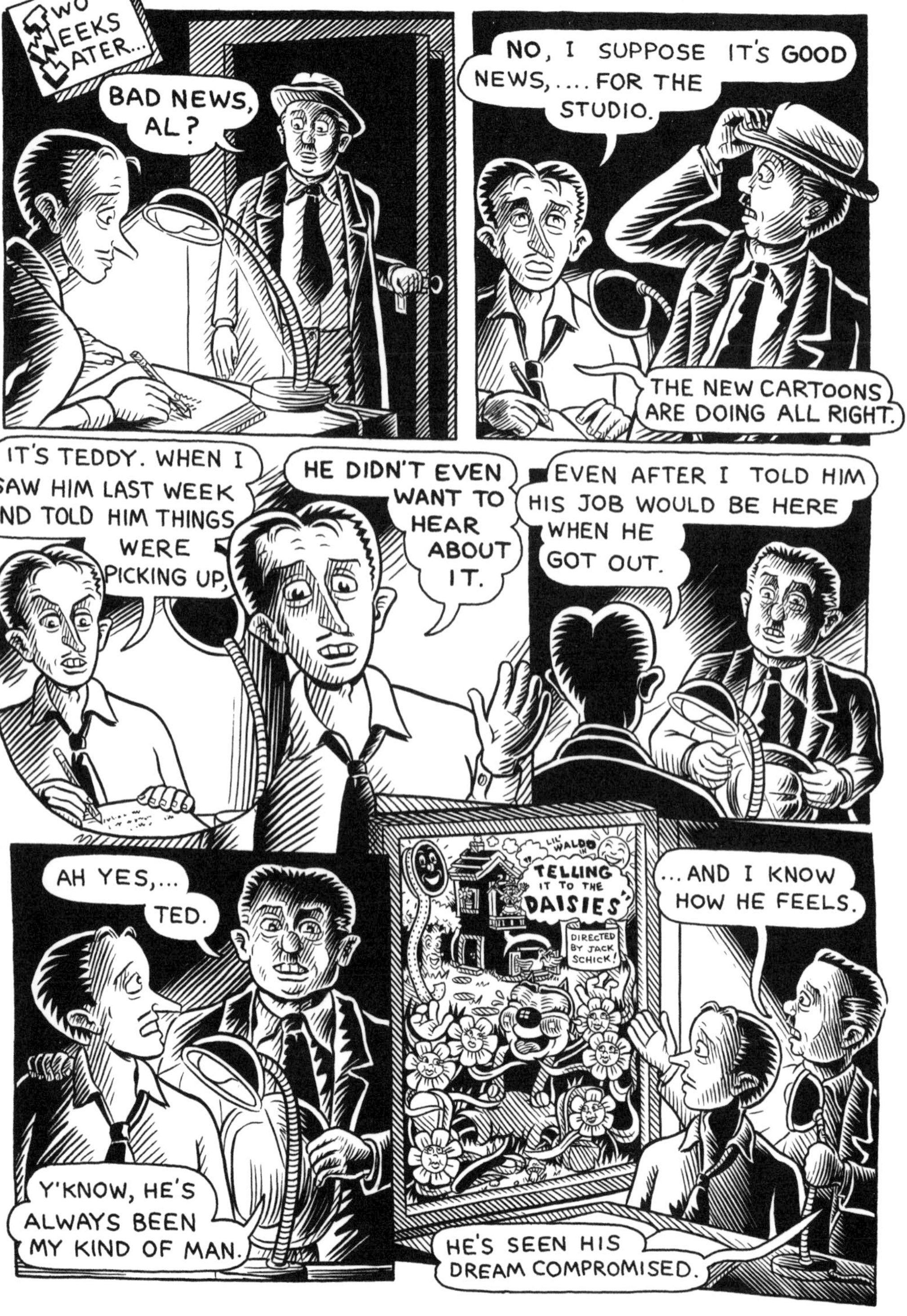
TWO WEEKS LATER...
BAD NEWS, AL?
NO, I SUPPOSE IT'S GOOD NEWS,.... FOR THE STUDIO.
THE NEW CARTOONS ARE DOING ALL RIGHT.
IT'S TEDDY. WHEN I SAW HIM LAST WEEK AND TOLD HIM THINGS WERE PICKING UP,
HE DIDN'T EVEN WANT TO HEAR ABOUT IT.
EVEN AFTER I TOLD HIM HIS JOB WOULD BE HERE WHEN HE GOT OUT.
AH YES,... TED.
Y'KNOW, HE'S ALWAYS BEEN MY KIND OF MAN.
LIL' WALDO IN "TELLING IT TO THE DAISIES"
DIRECTED BY JACK SCHICK!
...AND I KNOW HOW HE FEELS.
HE'S SEEN HIS DREAM COMPROMISED.

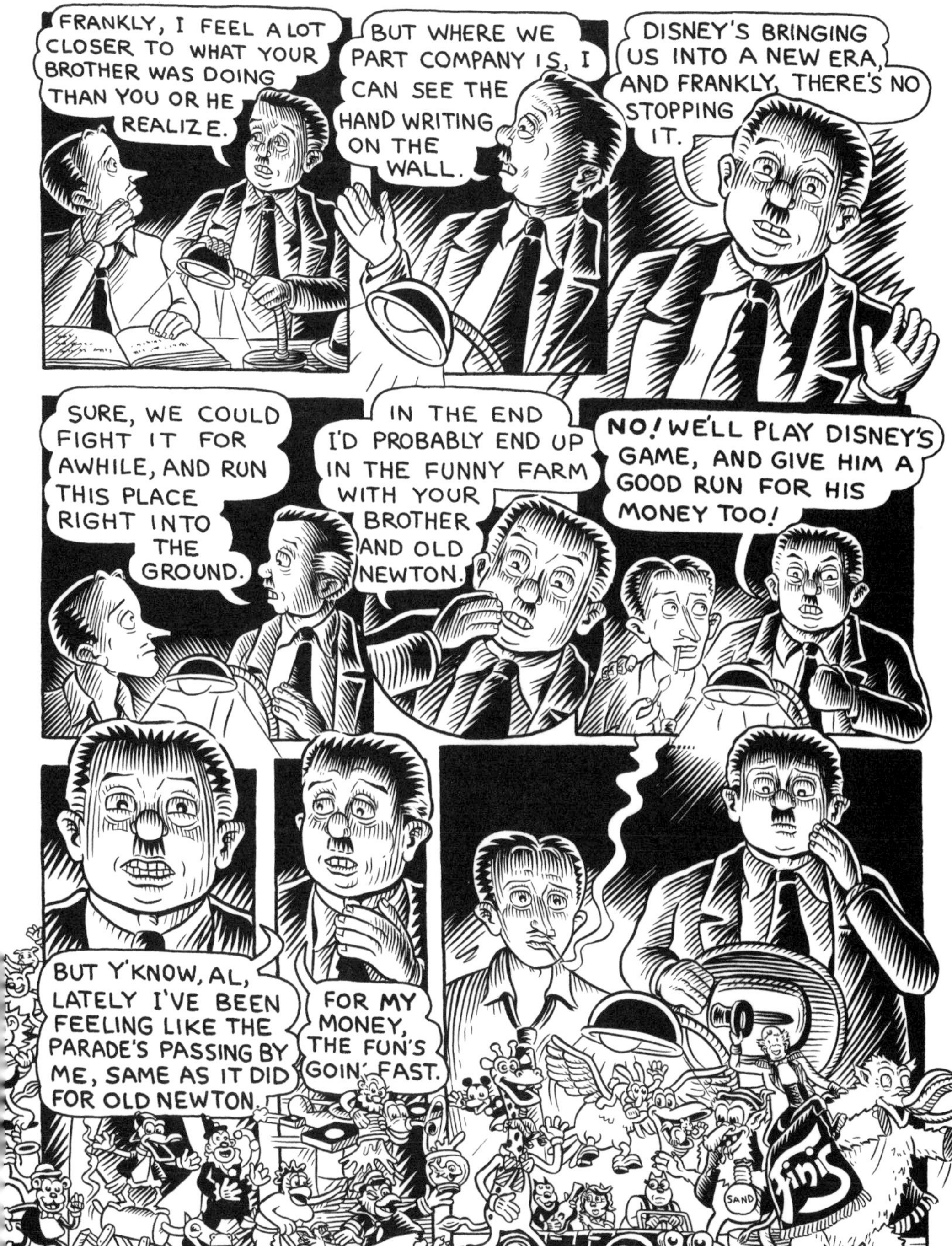

FRANKLY, I FEEL A LOT CLOSER TO WHAT YOUR BROTHER WAS DOING THAN YOU OR HE REALIZE.
BUT WHERE WE PART COMPANY IS, I CAN SEE THE HAND WRITING ON THE WALL.
DISNEY'S BRINGING US INTO A NEW ERA, AND FRANKLY, THERE'S NO STOPPING IT.
SURE, WE COULD FIGHT IT FOR AWHILE, AND RUN THIS PLACE RIGHT INTO THE GROUND.
IN THE END I'D PROBABLY END UP IN THE FUNNY FARM WITH YOUR BROTHER AND OLD NEWTON.
NO! WE'LL PLAY DISNEY'S GAME, AND GIVE HIM A GOOD RUN FOR HIS MONEY TOO!
BUT Y'KNOW, AL, LATELY I'VE BEEN FEELING LIKE THE PARADE'S PASSING BY ME, SAME AS IT DID FOR OLD NEWTON.
FOR MY MONEY, THE FUN'S GOIN' FAST.
SAND
FINIS

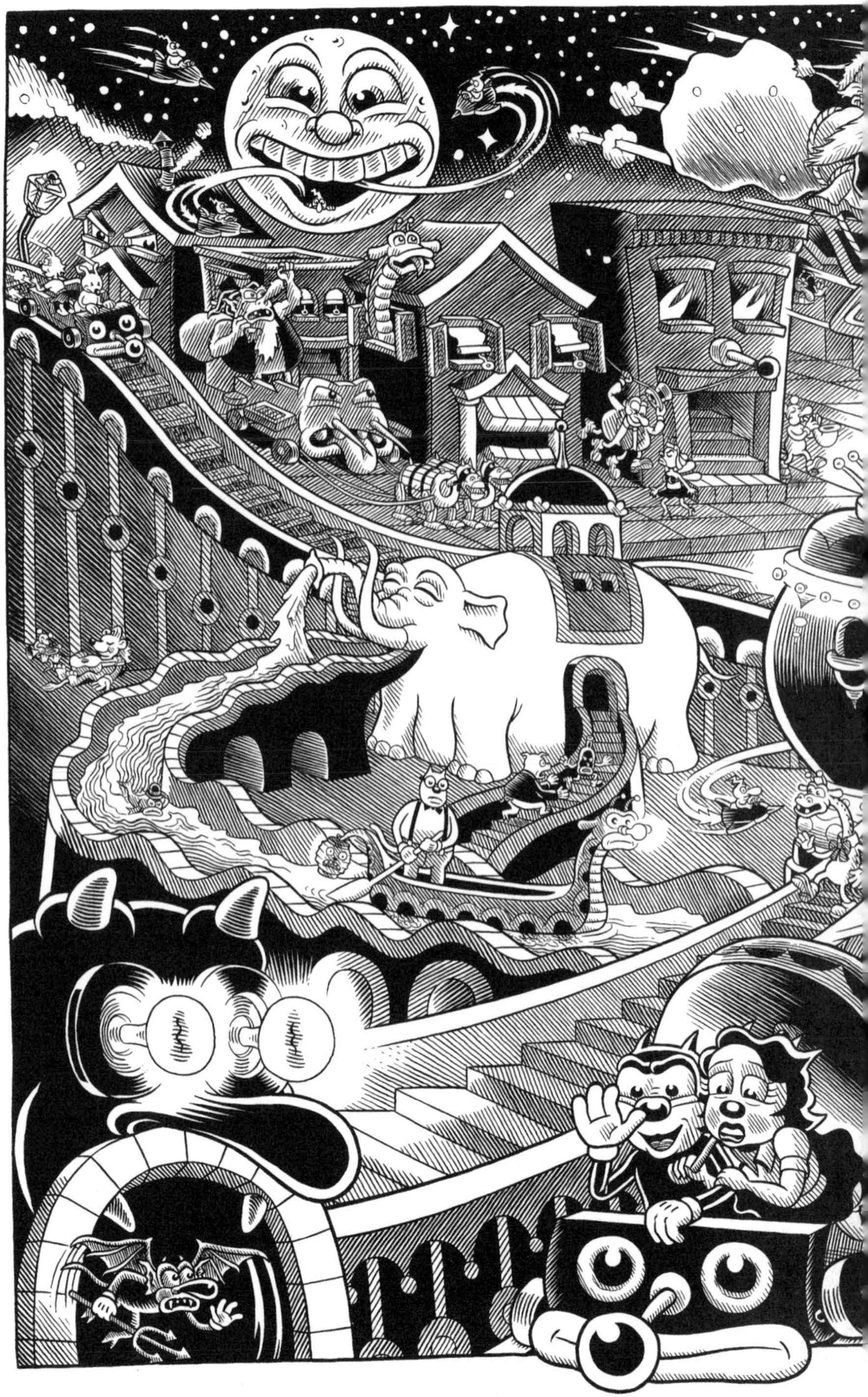

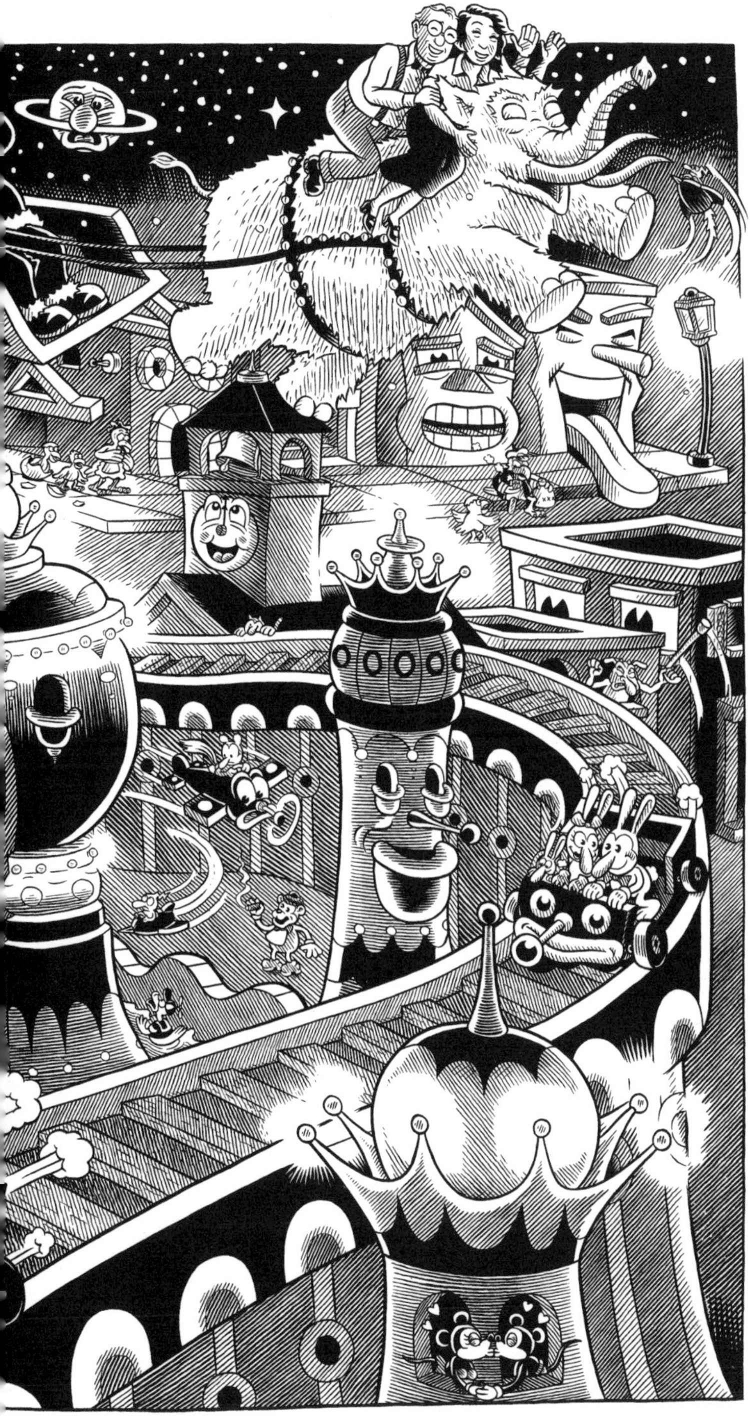

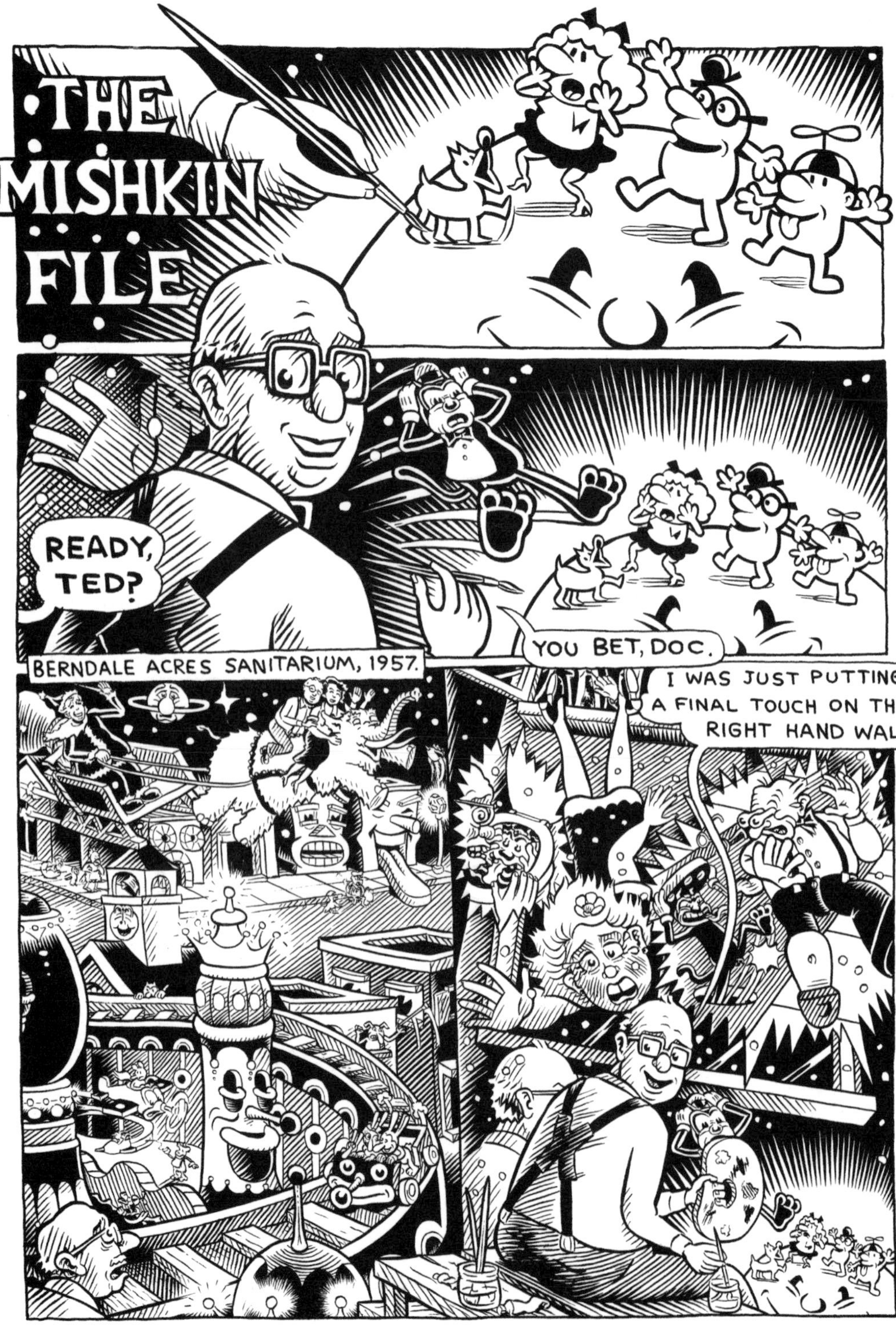
THE MISHKIN FILE
READY, TED?
YOU BET, DOC.
BERNDALE ACRES SANITARIUM, 1957.
I WAS JUST PUTTING A FINAL TOUCH ON THE RIGHT HAND WALL.

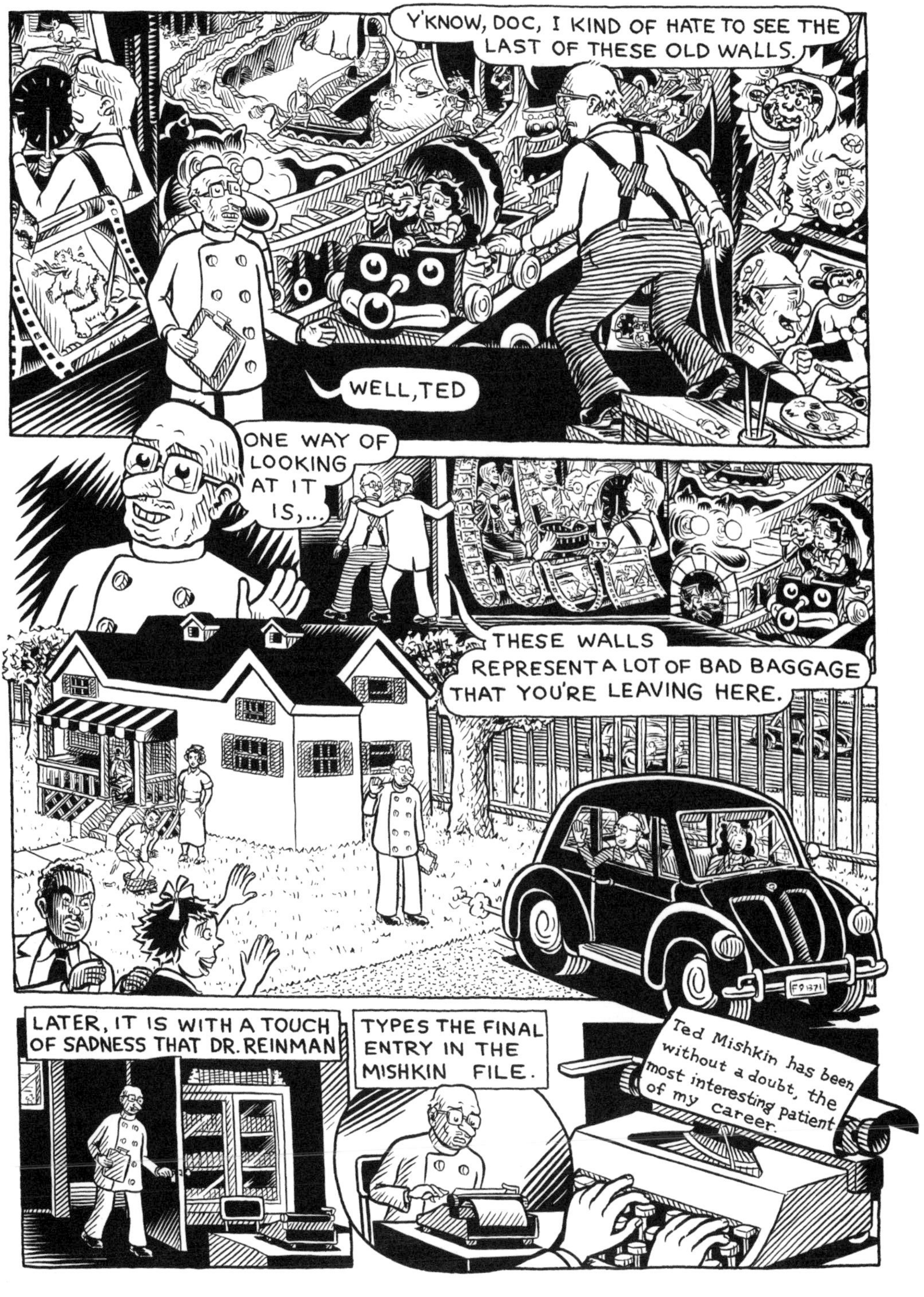
Y'KNOW, DOC, I KIND OF HATE TO SEE THE LAST OF THESE OLD WALLS.
WELL, TED
ONE WAY OF LOOKING AT IT IS,...
THESE WALLS REPRESENT A LOT OF BAD BAGGAGE THAT YOU'RE LEAVING HERE.
LATER, IT IS WITH A TOUCH OF SADNESS THAT DR. REINMAN
TYPES THE FINAL ENTRY IN THE MISHKIN FILE.
Ted Mishkin has been without a doubt, the most interesting patient of my career.

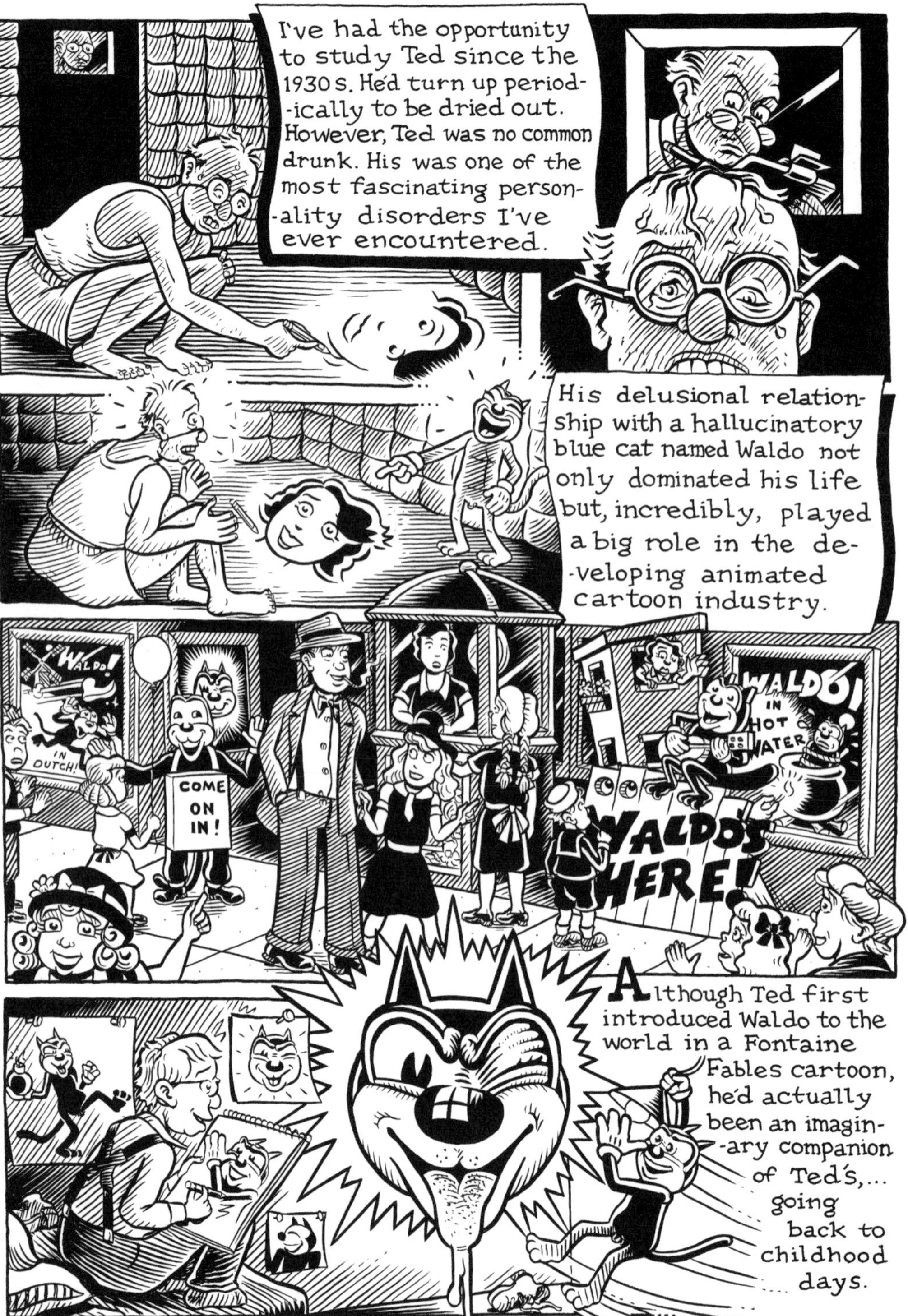
I've had the opportunity to study Ted since the 1930s. He'd turn up periodically to be dried out. However, Ted was no common drunk. His was one of the most fascinating personality disorders I've ever encountered.
His delusional relationship with a hallucinatory blue cat named Waldo not only dominated his life but, incredibly, played a big role in the developing animated cartoon industry.
WALDO!
IN DUTCH!
COME ON IN!
WALDO! IN HOT WATER
WALDO'S HERE!
Although Ted first introduced Waldo to the world in a Fontaine Fables cartoon, he'd actually been an imaginary companion of Ted's,... going back to childhood days.

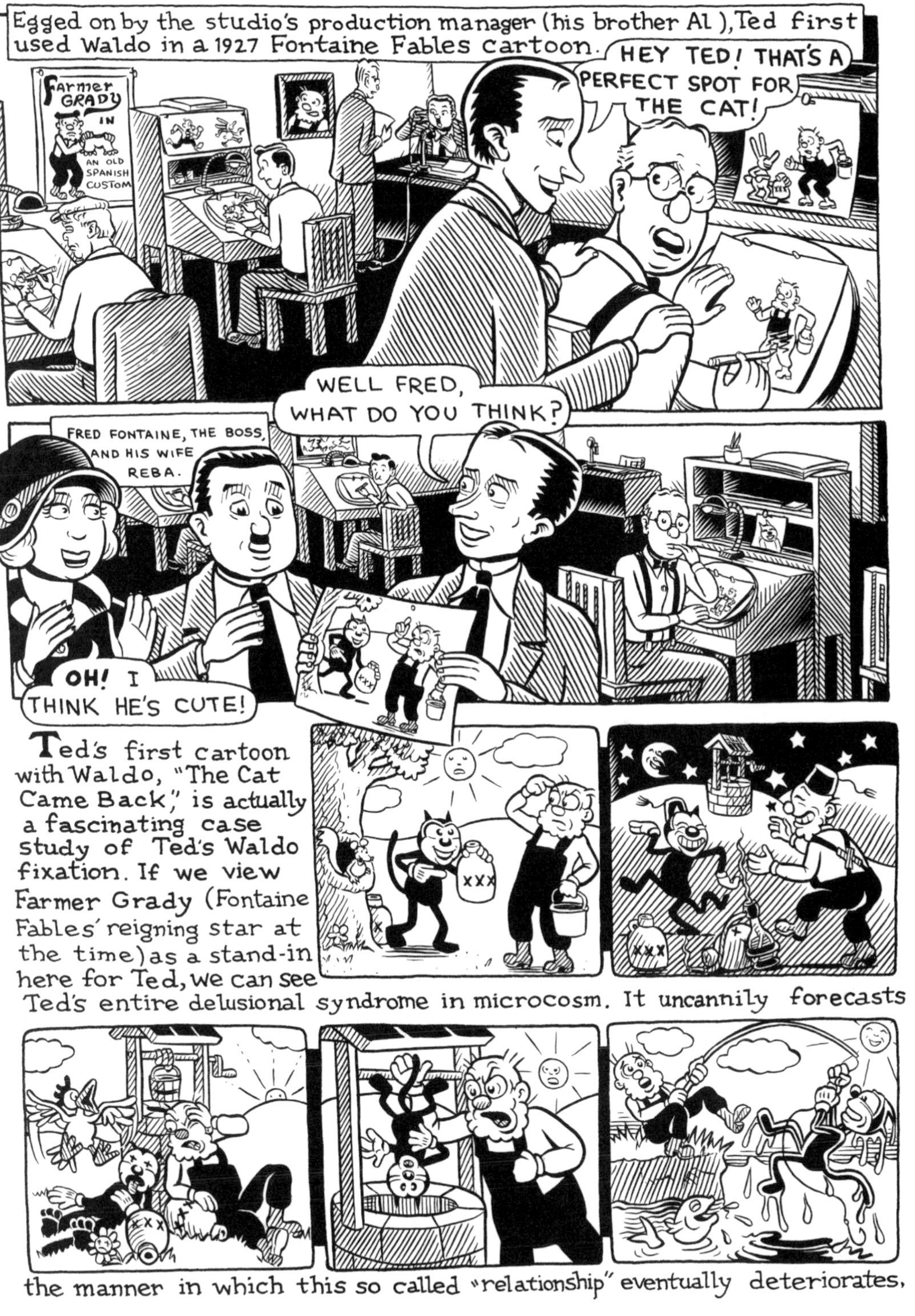
Egged on by the studio's production manager (his brother Al), Ted first used Waldo in a 1927 Fontaine Fables cartoon.
HEY TED! THAT'S A PERFECT SPOT FOR THE CAT!
Farmer GRADY IN AN OLD SPANISH CUSTOM
WELL FRED, WHAT DO YOU THINK?
FRED FONTAINE, THE BOSS, AND HIS WIFE REBA.
OH! I THINK HE'S CUTE!
Ted's first cartoon with Waldo, "The Cat Came Back," is actually a fascinating case study of Ted's Waldo fixation. If we view Farmer Grady (Fontaine Fables' reigning star at the time) as a stand-in here for Ted, we can see Ted's entire delusional syndrome in microcosm. It uncannily forecasts
XXX
XXX
XXX
the manner in which this so called "relationship" eventually deteriorates,

.......only to become a nightmare that repeatedly comes back to haunt him.

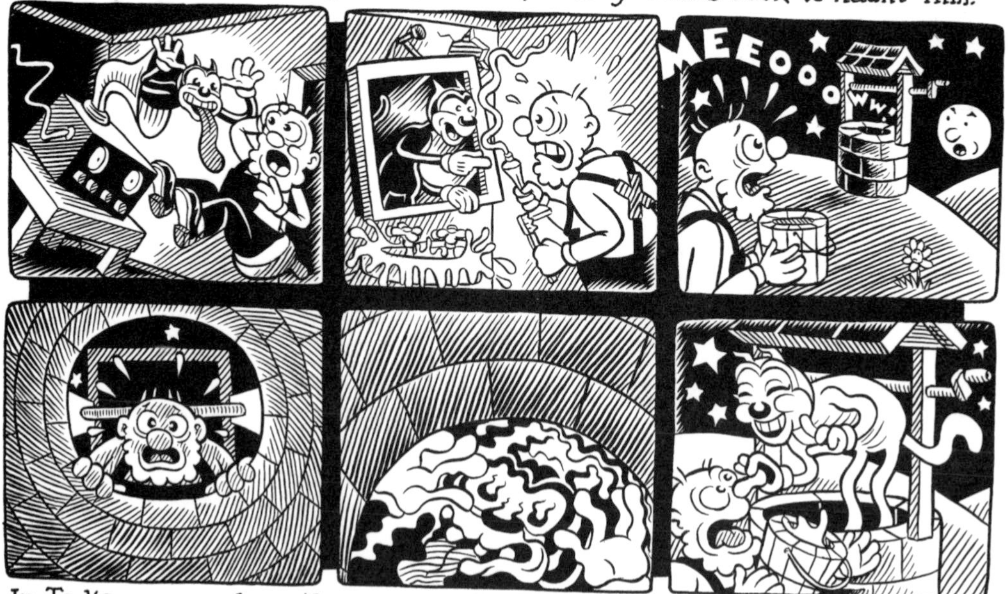
MEEOOOWW..

In Ted's case, when the Waldo cartoons became successful, his delusional relationship with Waldo went haywire.

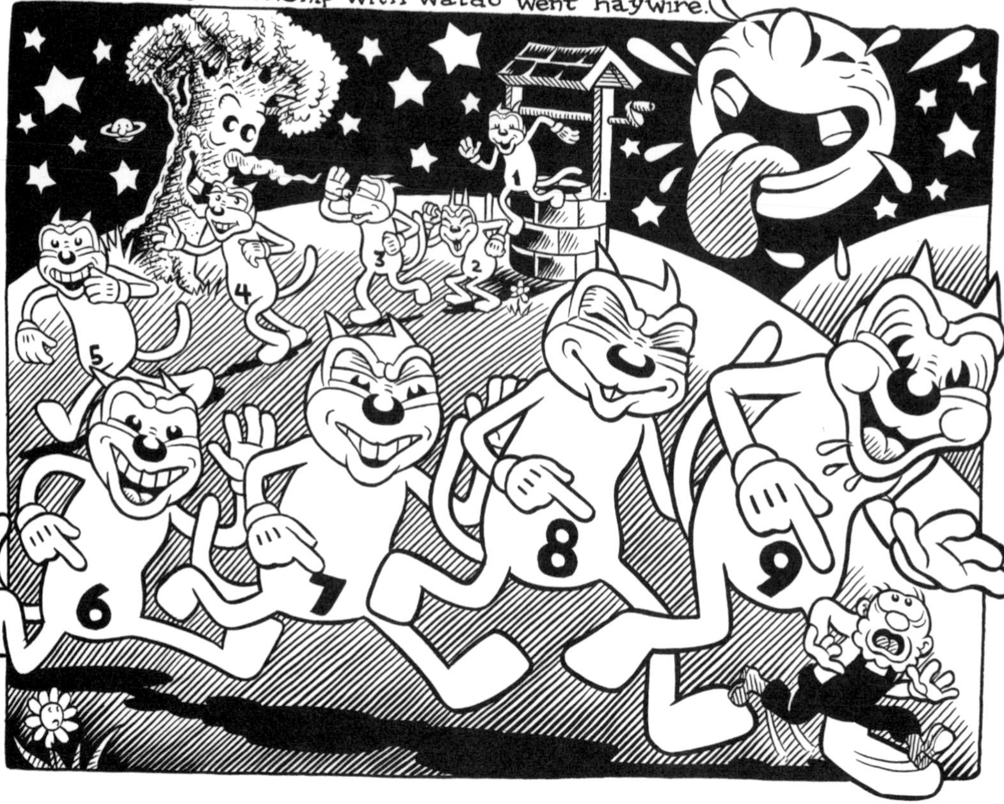
1
2
3
4
5
6
7
8
9

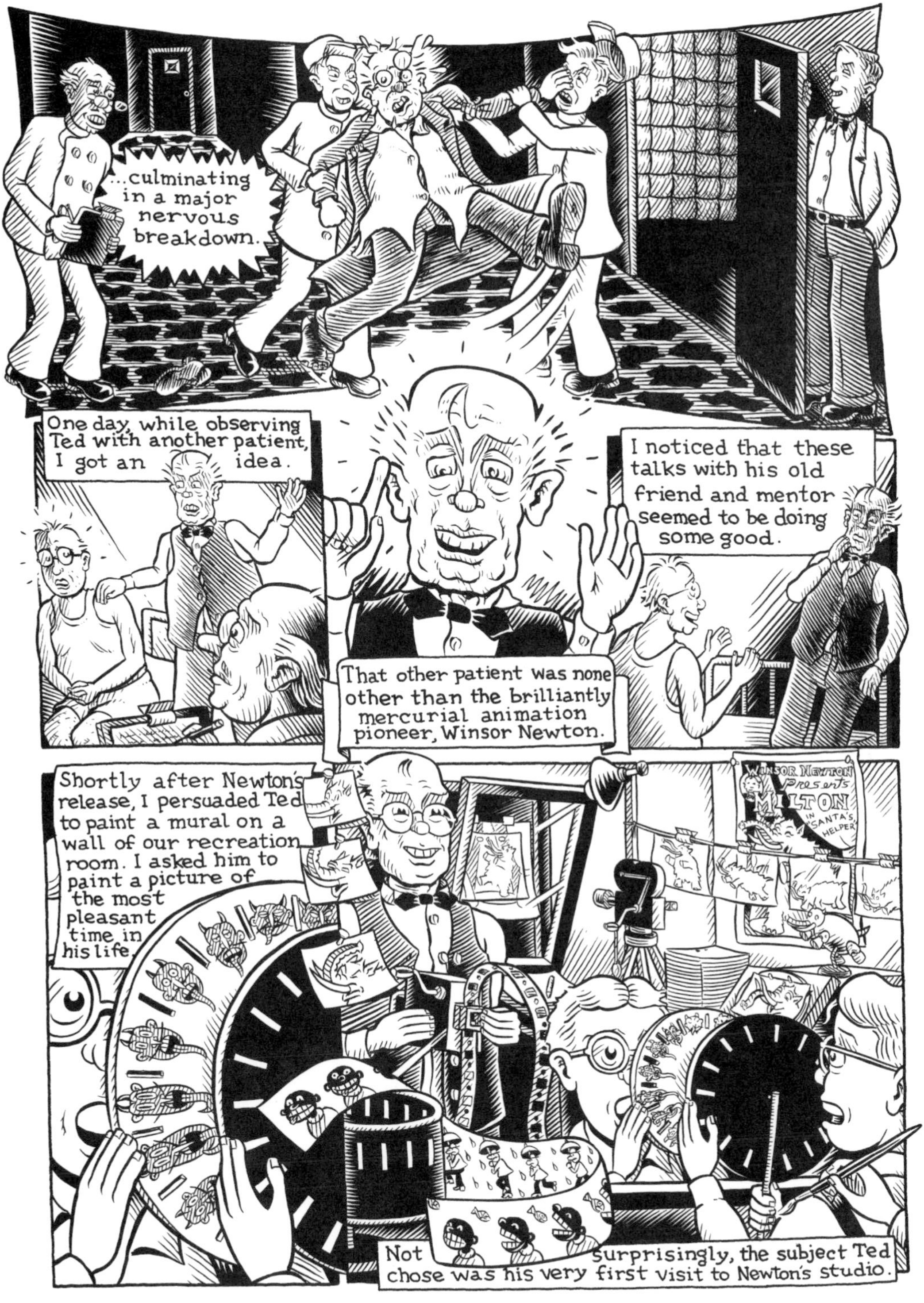
...culminating in a major nervous breakdown.
One day, while observing Ted with another patient, I got an idea.
I noticed that these talks with his old friend and mentor seemed to be doing some good.
That other patient was none other than the brilliantly mercurial animation pioneer, Winsor Newton.
Shortly after Newton's release, I persuaded Ted to paint a mural on a wall of our recreation room. I asked him to paint a picture of the most pleasant time in his life.
WINSOR NEWTON presents MILTON IN SANTA'S HELPER
Not surprisingly, the subject Ted chose was his very first visit to Newton's studio.

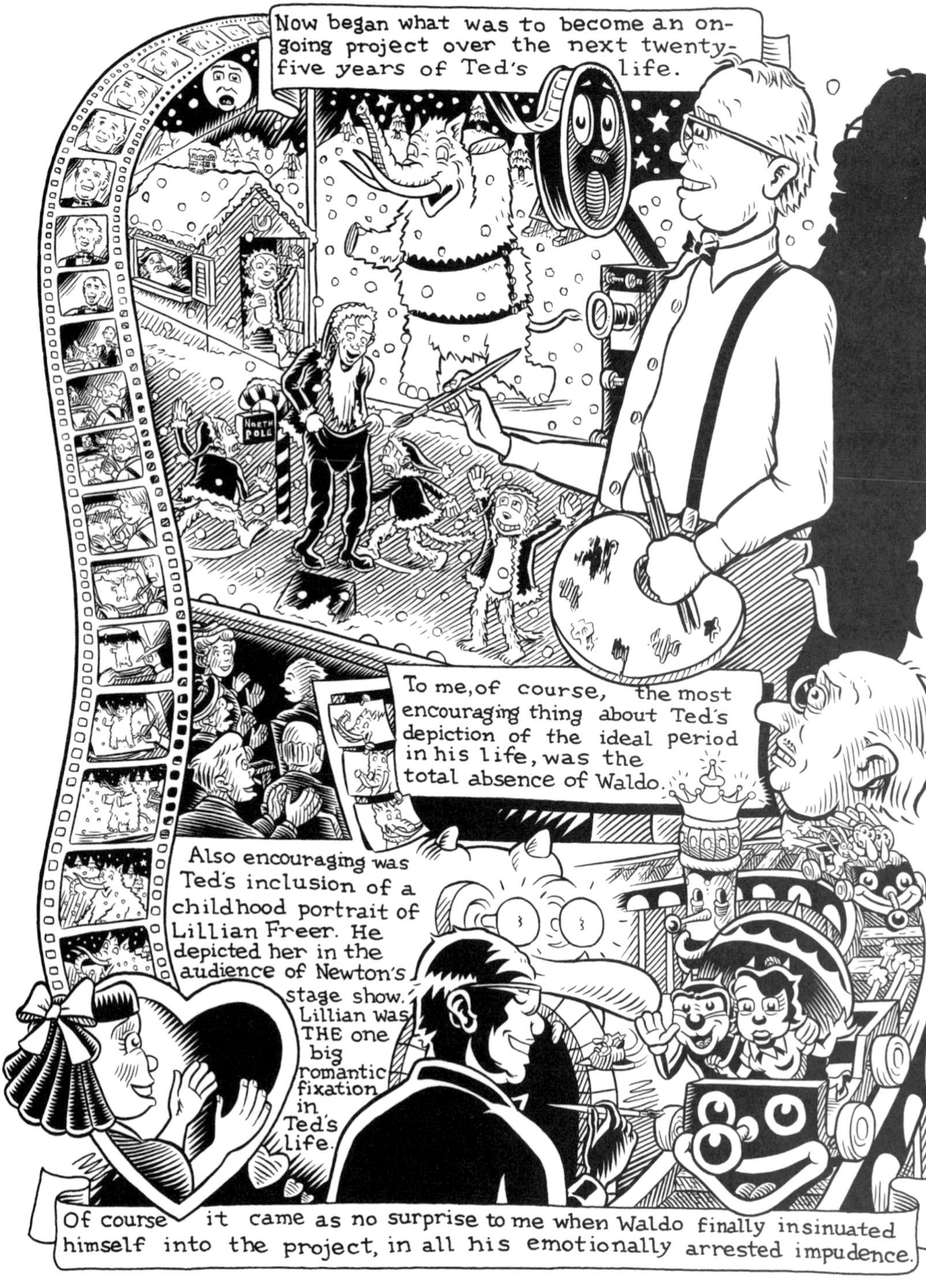
Now began what was to become an ongoing project over the next twenty-five years of Ted's life.
To me, of course, the most encouraging thing about Ted's depiction of the ideal period in his life, was the total absence of Waldo.
NORTH POLE
Also encouraging was Ted's inclusion of a childhood portrait of Lillian Freer. He depicted her in the audience of Newton's stage show. Lillian was THE one big romantic fixation in Ted's life.
Of course it came as no surprise to me when Waldo finally insinuated himself into the project, in all his emotionally arrested impudence.

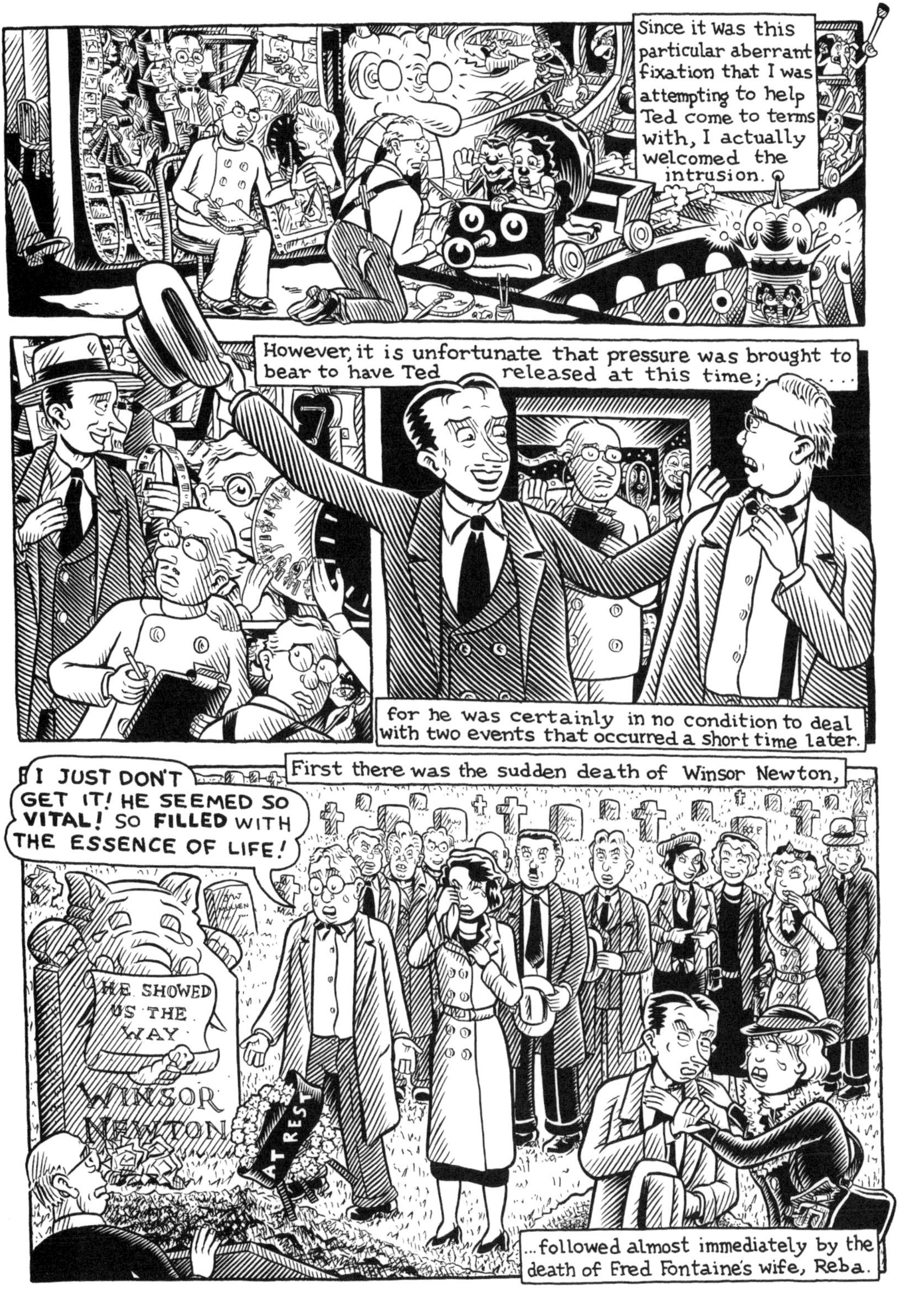
Since it was this particular aberrant fixation that I was attempting to help Ted come to terms with, I actually welcomed the intrusion.
However, it is unfortunate that pressure was brought to bear to have Ted released at this time;.......
for he was certainly in no condition to deal with two events that occurred a short time later.
First there was the sudden death of Winsor Newton,
I JUST DON'T GET IT! HE SEEMED SO VITAL! SO FILLED WITH THE ESSENCE OF LIFE!
HE SHOWED US THE WAY
WINSOR NEWTON
AT REST
...followed almost immediately by the death of Fred Fontaine's wife, Reba.

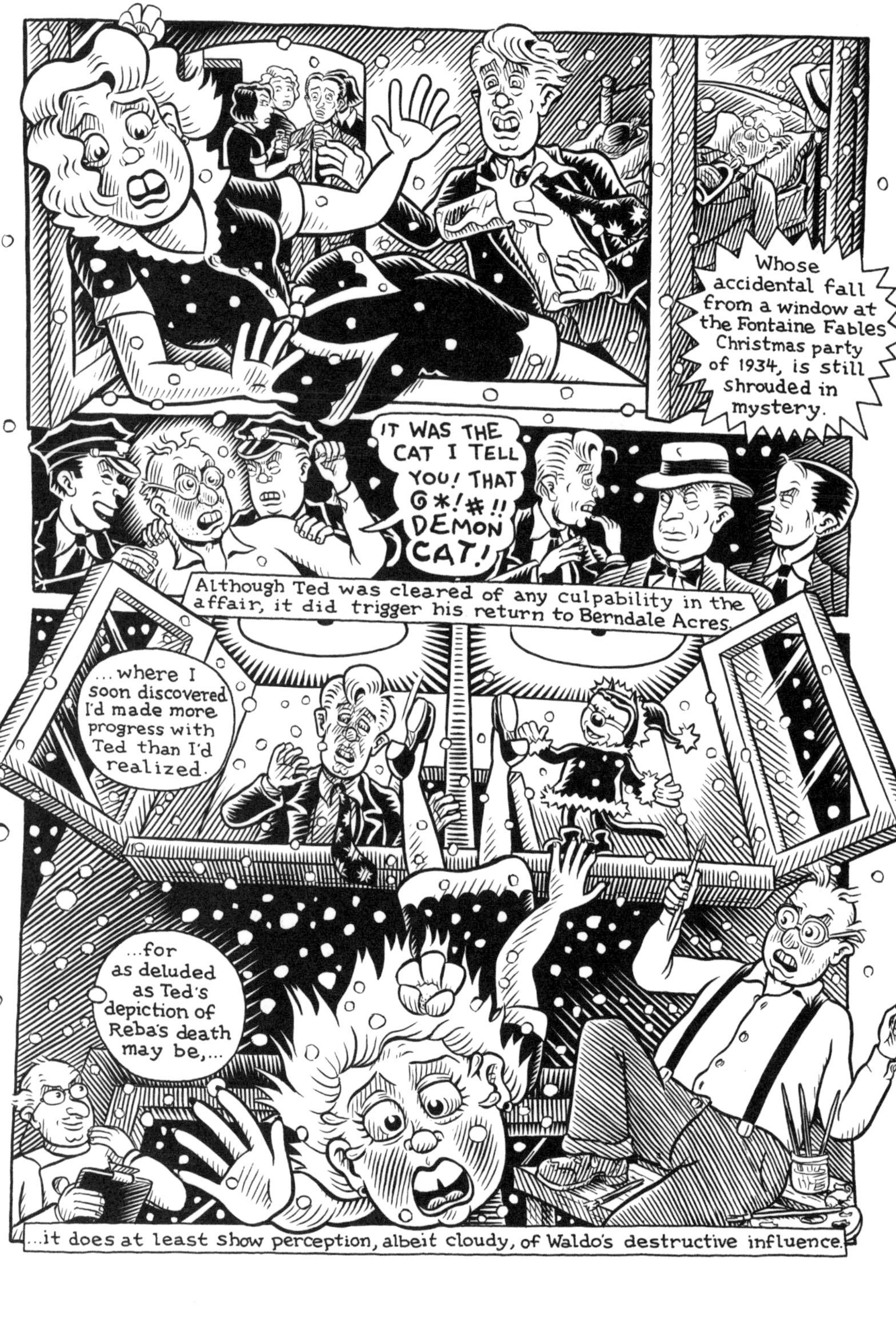
Whose accidental fall from a window at the Fontaine Fables Christmas party of 1934, is still shrouded in mystery.
IT WAS THE CAT I TELL YOU! THAT @*!#!! DEMON CAT!
Although Ted was cleared of any culpability in the affair, it did trigger his return to Berndale Acres.
...where I soon discovered I'd made more progress with Ted than I'd realized.
...for as deluded as Ted's depiction of Reba's death may be,...
...it does at least show perception, albeit cloudy, of Waldo's destructive influence.

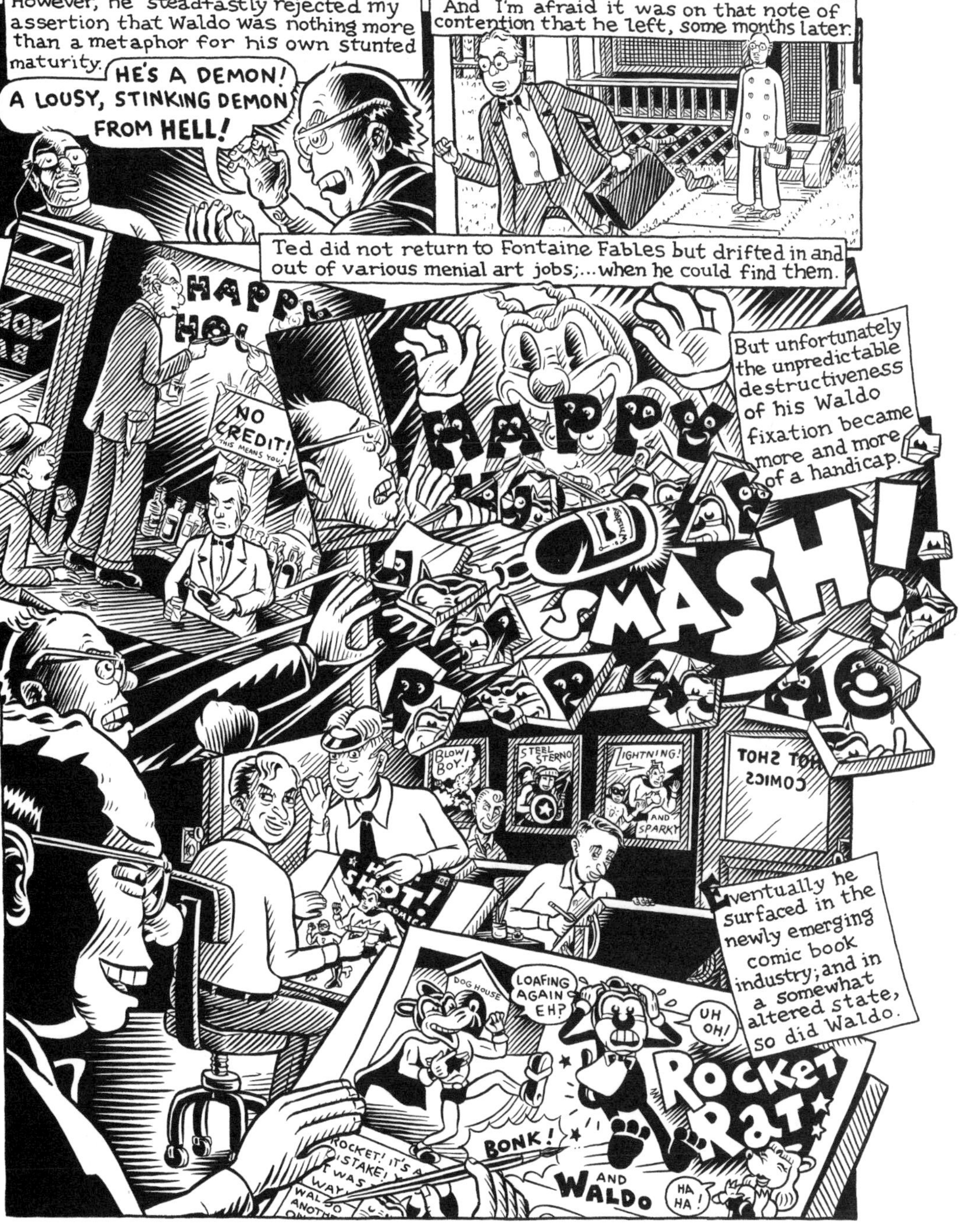
However, he steadfastly rejected my assertion that Waldo was nothing more than a metaphor for his own stunted maturity.
HE'S A DEMON! A LOUSY, STINKING DEMON FROM HELL!
And I'm afraid it was on that note of contention that he left, some months later.
Ted did not return to Fontaine Fables but drifted in and out of various menial art jobs;...when he could find them.
NO CREDIT! THIS MEANS YOU!
But unfortunately the unpredictable destructiveness of his Waldo fixation became more and more of a handicap.
HAPPY
SMASH!
BLOW BOY!
STEEL STERNO
LIGHTNING! AND SPARKY
Eventually he surfaced in the newly emerging comic book industry; and in a somewhat altered state, so did Waldo.
DOG HOUSE
LOAFING AGAIN EH?
UH OH!
ROCKET RAT
BONK!
AND WALDO
HA HA!

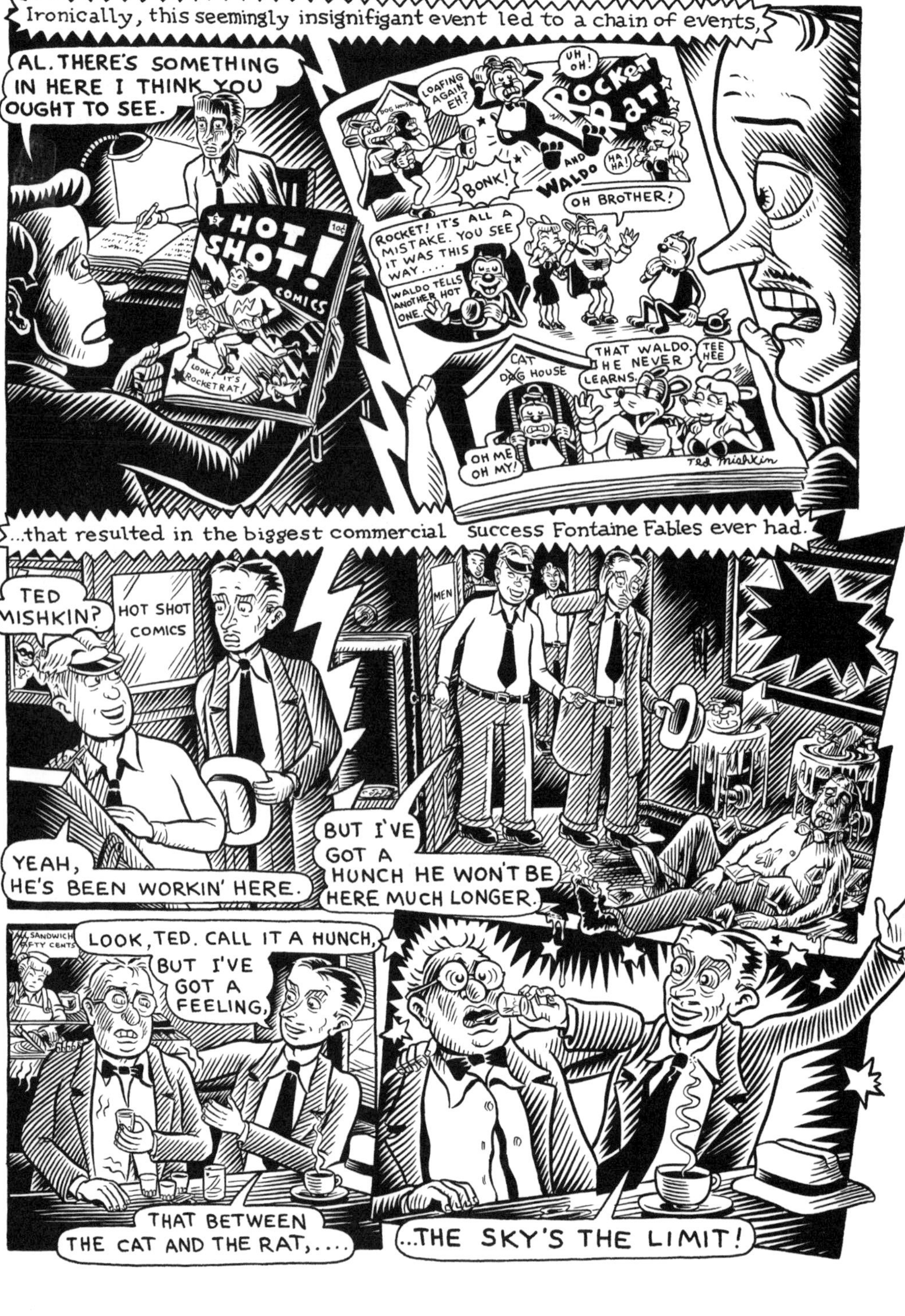

Ironically, this seemingly insignifigant event led to a chain of events,
AL. THERE'S SOMETHING IN HERE I THINK YOU OUGHT TO SEE.
HOT SHOT! COMICS
LOOK! IT'S ROCKET RAT!
ROCKET RAT
UH OH!
LOAFING AGAIN EH?
DOG HOUSE
BONK!
AND WALDO
HA HA!
OH BROTHER!
ROCKET! IT'S ALL A MISTAKE. YOU SEE IT WAS THIS WAY....
WALDO TELLS ANOTHER HOT ONE.
CAT DOG HOUSE
THAT WALDO. HE NEVER LEARNS.
TEE HEE
OH ME OH MY!
Ted Mishkin
...that resulted in the biggest commercial success Fontaine Fables ever had.
TED MISHKIN?
HOT SHOT COMICS
YEAH, HE'S BEEN WORKIN' HERE.
BUT I'VE GOT A HUNCH HE WON'T BE HERE MUCH LONGER.
MEN
ALL SANDWICH FIFTY CENTS
LOOK, TED. CALL IT A HUNCH,
BUT I'VE GOT A FEELING,
THAT BETWEEN THE CAT AND THE RAT,....
...THE SKY'S THE LIMIT!

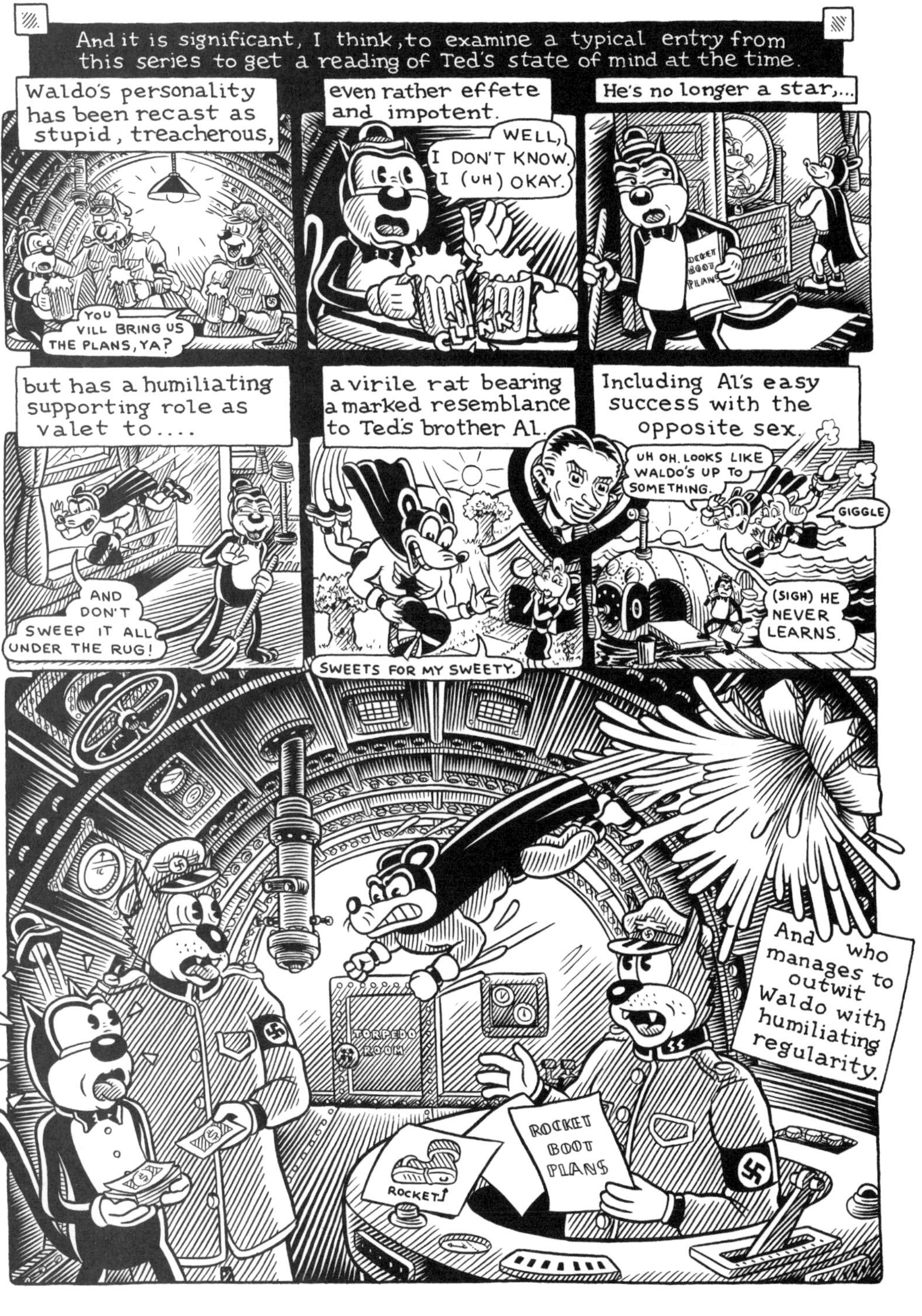
And it is significant, I think, to examine a typical entry from this series to get a reading of Ted's state of mind at the time.
Waldo's personality has been recast as stupid, treacherous,
YOU VILL BRING US THE PLANS, YA?
even rather effete and impotent.
WELL, I DON'T KNOW. I (UH) OKAY.
CLINK
He's no longer a star,...
but has a humiliating supporting role as valet to....
AND DON'T SWEEP IT ALL UNDER THE RUG!
a virile rat bearing a marked resemblance to Ted's brother Al.
SWEETS FOR MY SWEETY.
Including Al's easy success with the opposite sex.
UH OH. LOOKS LIKE WALDO'S UP TO SOMETHING.
GIGGLE
(SIGH) HE NEVER LEARNS.
TORPEDO ROOM
ROCKET BOOT PLANS
ROCKET
And who manages to outwit Waldo with humiliating regularity.

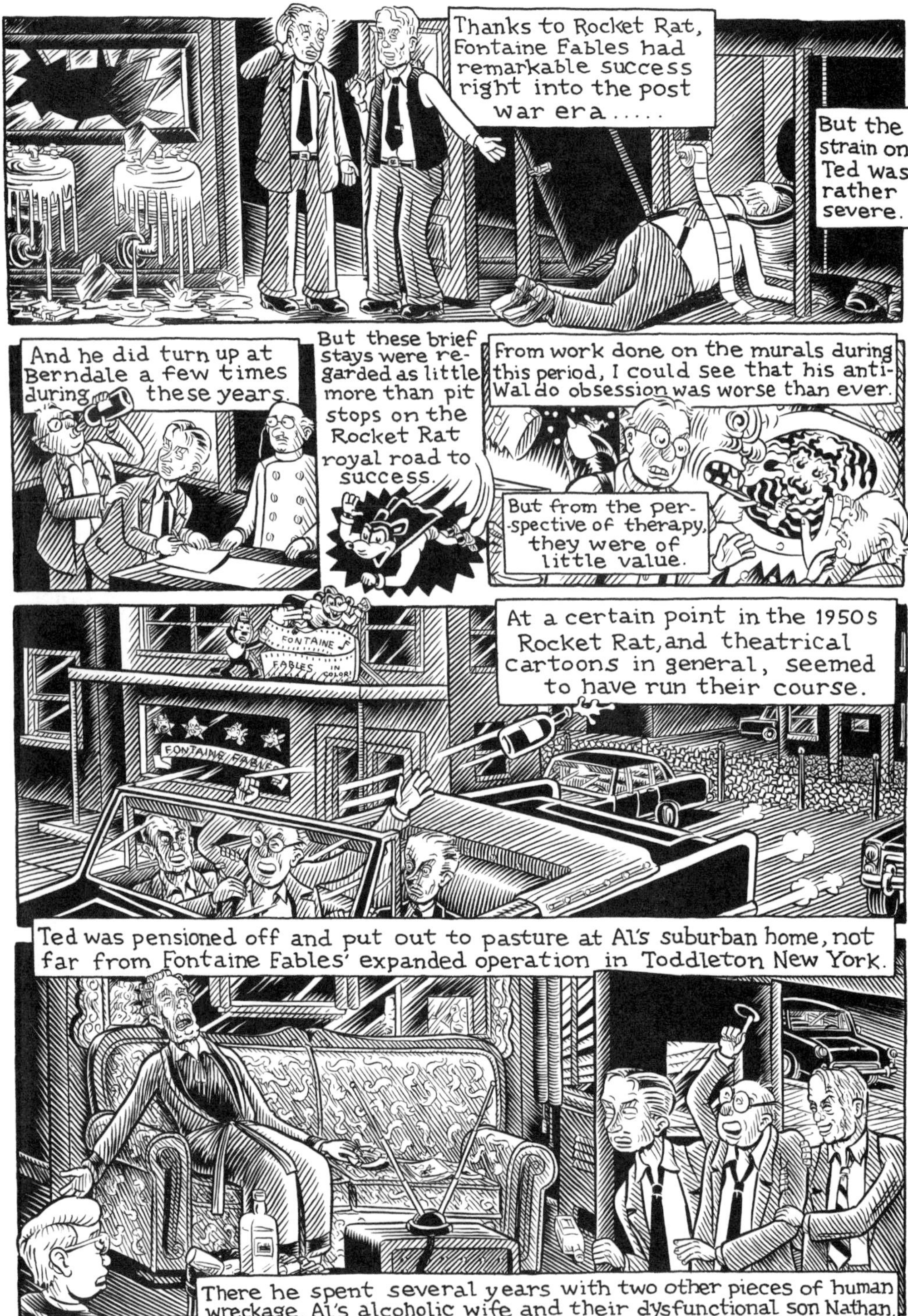
Thanks to Rocket Rat, Fontaine Fables had remarkable success right into the post war era.....
But the strain on Ted was rather severe.
And he did turn up at Berndale a few times during these years.
But these brief stays were regarded as little more than pit stops on the Rocket Rat royal road to success.
From work done on the murals during this period, I could see that his anti-Waldo obsession was worse than ever.
But from the perspective of therapy, they were of little value.
FONTAINE
FABLES IN COLOR!
FONTAINE FABLES
At a certain point in the 1950s Rocket Rat, and theatrical cartoons in general, seemed to have run their course.
Ted was pensioned off and put out to pasture at Al's suburban home, not far from Fontaine Fables' expanded operation in Toddleton New York.
There he spent several years with two other pieces of human wreckage, Al's alcoholic wife and their dysfunctional son Nathan.

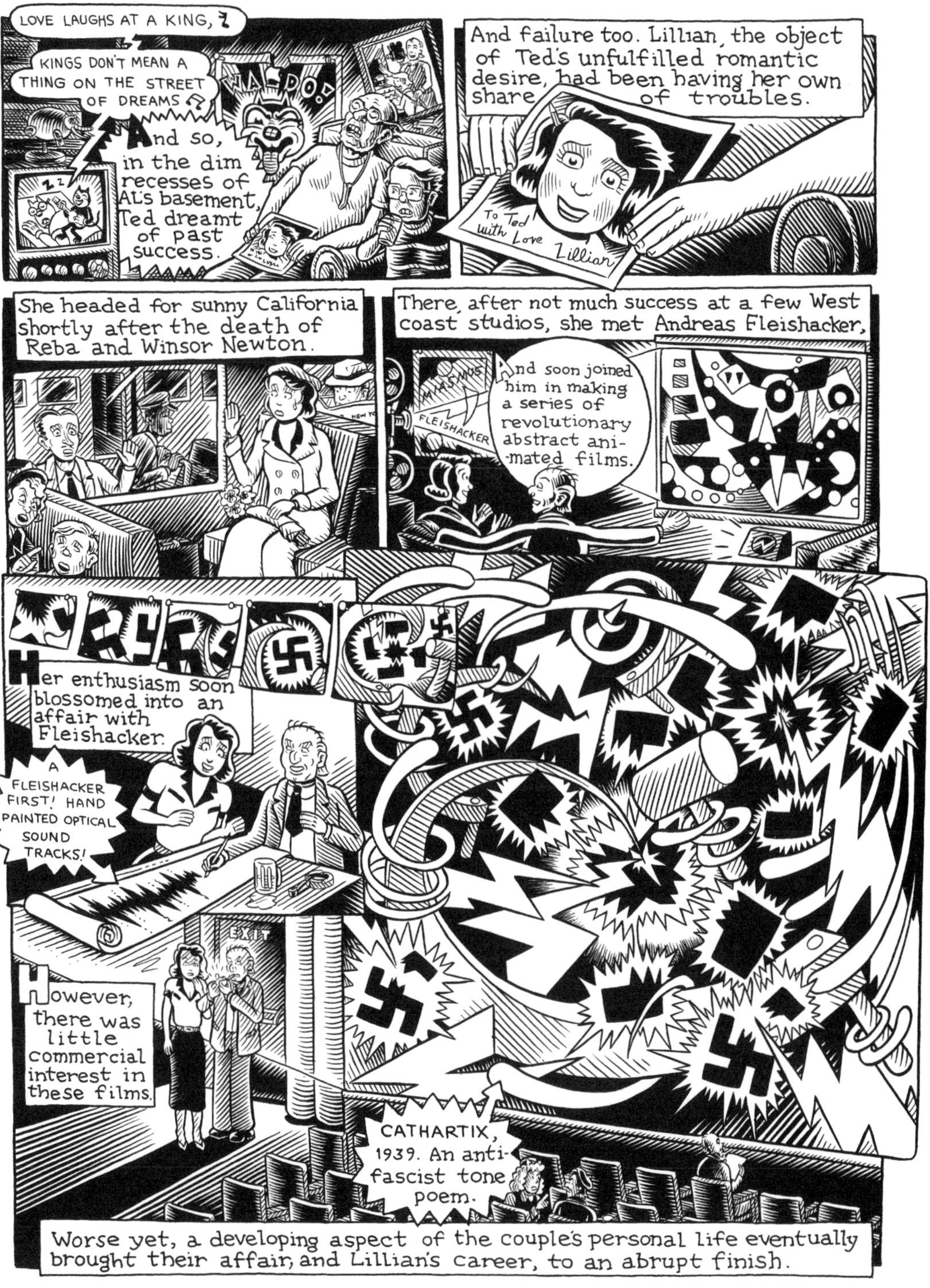
LOVE LAUGHS AT A KING,
KINGS DON'T MEAN A THING ON THE STREET OF DREAMS
WA-DO!
And so, in the dim recesses of Al's basement, Ted dreamt of past success.
And failure too. Lillian, the object of Ted's unfulfilled romantic desire, had been having her own share of troubles.
To Ted with Love Lillian
She headed for sunny California shortly after the death of Reba and Winsor Newton.
There, after not much success at a few West coast studios, she met Andreas Fleishacker,
MIASMUS
FLEISHACKER
And soon joined him in making a series of revolutionary abstract animated films.
Her enthusiasm soon blossomed into an affair with Fleishacker.
A FLEISHACKER FIRST! HAND PAINTED OPTICAL SOUND TRACKS!
EXIT
However, there was little commercial interest in these films.
CATHARTIX, 1939. An anti-fascist tone poem.
Worse yet, a developing aspect of the couple's personal life eventually brought their affair, and Lillian's career, to an abrupt finish.

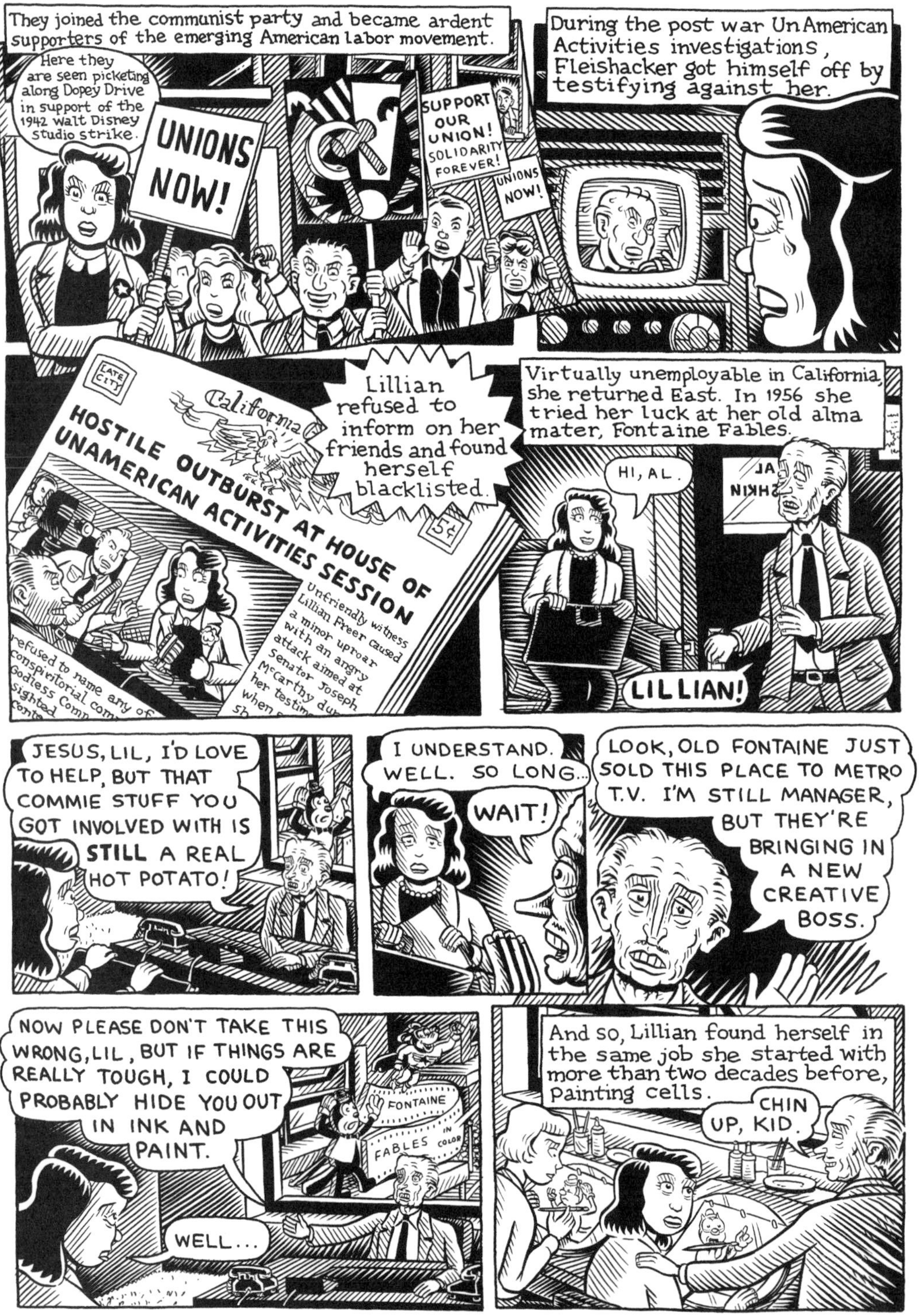
They joined the communist party and became ardent supporters of the emerging American labor movement.
Here they are seen picketing along Dopey Drive in support of the 1942 Walt Disney studio strike.
UNIONS NOW!
SUPPORT OUR UNION! SOLIDARITY FOREVER!
UNIONS NOW!
During the post war UnAmerican Activities investigations, Fleishacker got himself off by testifying against her.
LATE CITY
California
HOSTILE OUTBURST AT HOUSE OF UNAMERICAN ACTIVITIES SESSION
5¢
Unfriendly witness Lillian Freer caused a minor uproar with an angry attack aimed at Senator Joseph McCarthy
refused to name any of
Lillian refused to inform on her friends and found herself blacklisted.
Virtually unemployable in California, she returned East. In 1956 she tried her luck at her old alma mater, Fontaine Fables.
HI, AL.
LILLIAN!
JESUS, LIL, I'D LOVE TO HELP, BUT THAT COMMIE STUFF YOU GOT INVOLVED WITH IS STILL A REAL HOT POTATO!
I UNDERSTAND. WELL. SO LONG...
WAIT!
LOOK, OLD FONTAINE JUST SOLD THIS PLACE TO METRO T.V. I'M STILL MANAGER, BUT THEY'RE BRINGING IN A NEW CREATIVE BOSS.
NOW PLEASE DON'T TAKE THIS WRONG, LIL, BUT IF THINGS ARE REALLY TOUGH, I COULD PROBABLY HIDE YOU OUT IN INK AND PAINT.
FONTAINE FABLES IN COLOR
WELL...
And so, Lillian found herself in the same job she started with more than two decades before, painting cells.
CHIN UP, KID.

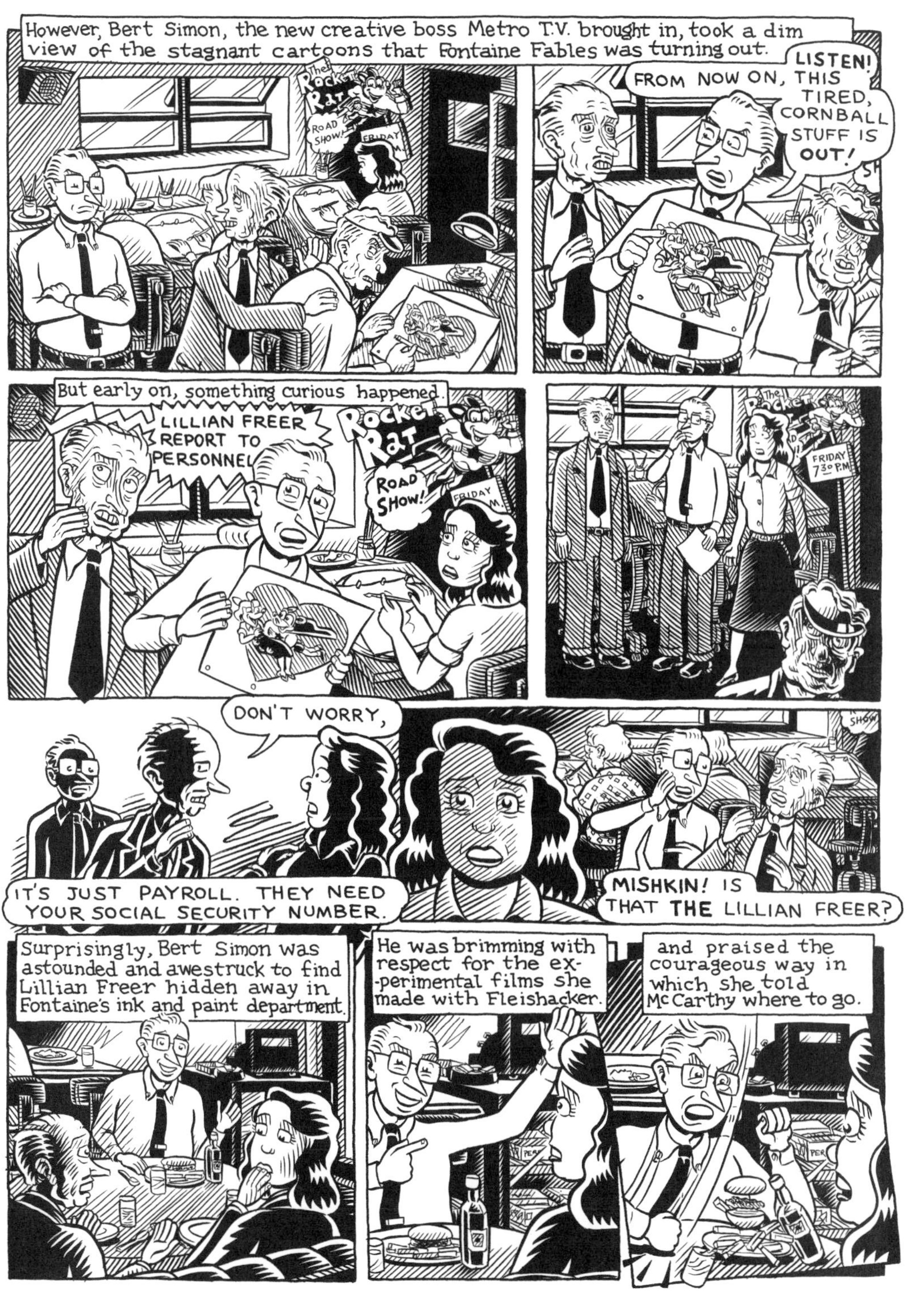
However, Bert Simon, the new creative boss Metro T.V. brought in, took a dim view of the stagnant cartoons that Fontaine Fables was turning out.
The Rocket Rat Road Show! Friday
LISTEN!
FROM NOW ON, THIS TIRED, CORNBALL STUFF IS OUT!
But early on, something curious happened.
LILLIAN FREER REPORT TO PERSONNEL
Rocket Rat Road Show! Friday
Friday 7:30 P.M.
DON'T WORRY,
IT'S JUST PAYROLL. THEY NEED YOUR SOCIAL SECURITY NUMBER.
MISHKIN! IS THAT THE LILLIAN FREER?
Surprisingly, Bert Simon was astounded and awestruck to find Lillian Freer hidden away in Fontaine's ink and paint department.
He was brimming with respect for the ex-perimental films she made with Fleishacker.
and praised the courageous way in which she told McCarthy where to go.

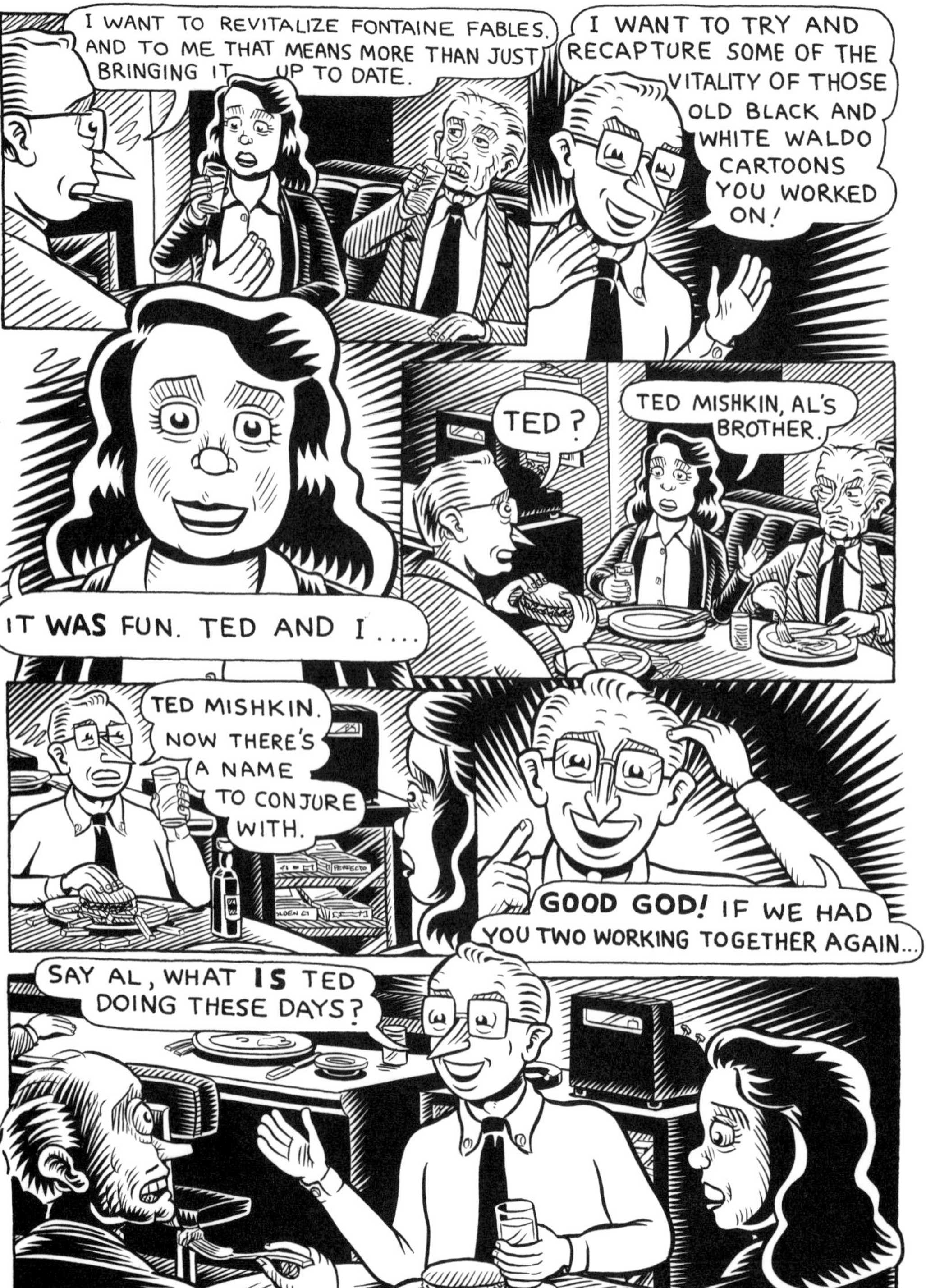
I WANT TO REVITALIZE FONTAINE FABLES. AND TO ME THAT MEANS MORE THAN JUST BRINGING IT UP TO DATE.
I WANT TO TRY AND RECAPTURE SOME OF THE VITALITY OF THOSE OLD BLACK AND WHITE WALDO CARTOONS YOU WORKED ON!
IT **WAS** FUN. TED AND I....
TED?
TED MISHKIN, AL'S BROTHER.
TED MISHKIN. NOW THERE'S A NAME TO CONJURE WITH.
GOOD GOD! IF WE HAD YOU TWO WORKING TOGETHER AGAIN...
SAY AL, WHAT **IS** TED DOING THESE DAYS?

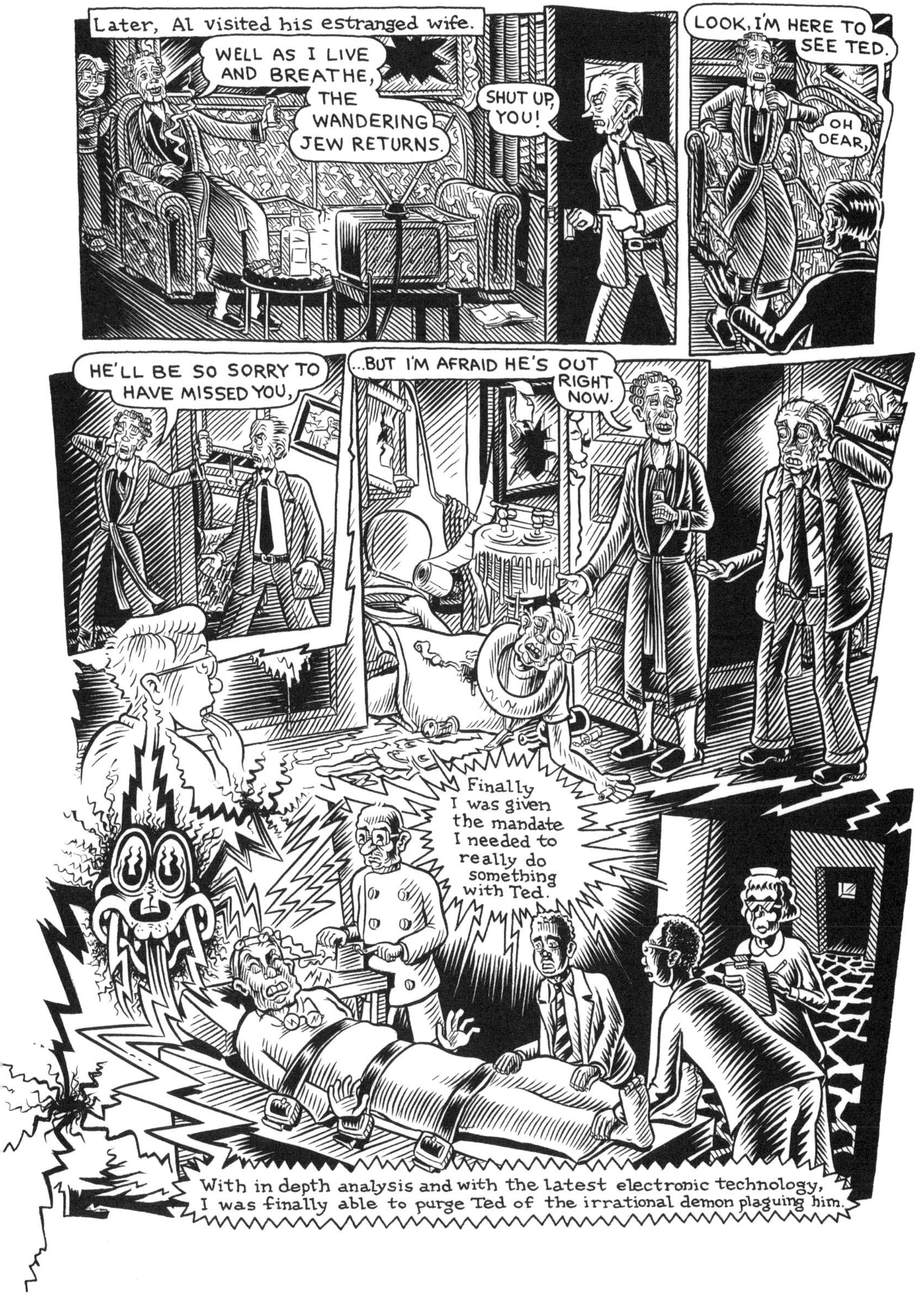

Later, Al visited his estranged wife.
WELL AS I LIVE AND BREATHE, THE WANDERING JEW RETURNS.
SHUT UP, YOU!
LOOK, I'M HERE TO SEE TED.
OH DEAR,
HE'LL BE SO SORRY TO HAVE MISSED YOU,
...BUT I'M AFRAID HE'S OUT RIGHT NOW.
Finally I was given the mandate I needed to really do something with Ted.
With in depth analysis and with the latest electronic technology, I was finally able to purge Ted of the irrational demon plaguing him.

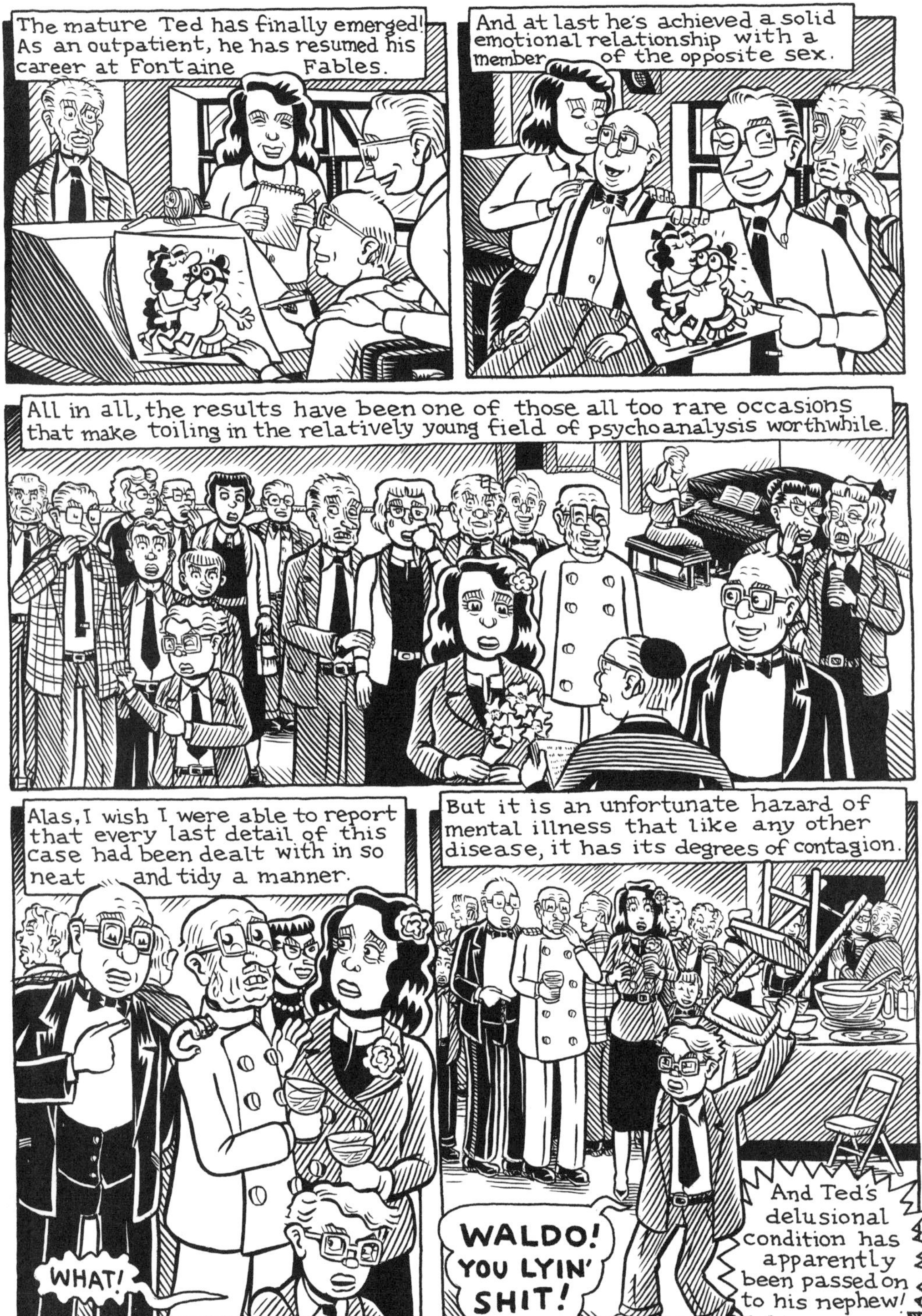
The mature Ted has finally emerged! As an outpatient, he has resumed his career at Fontaine Fables.
And at last he's achieved a solid emotional relationship with a member of the opposite sex.
All in all, the results have been one of those all too rare occasions that make toiling in the relatively young field of psychoanalysis worthwhile.
Alas, I wish I were able to report that every last detail of this case had been dealt with in so neat and tidy a manner.
WHAT!
But it is an unfortunate hazard of mental illness that like any other disease, it has its degrees of contagion.
WALDO! YOU LYIN' SHIT!
And Ted's delusional condition has apparently been passed on to his nephew!

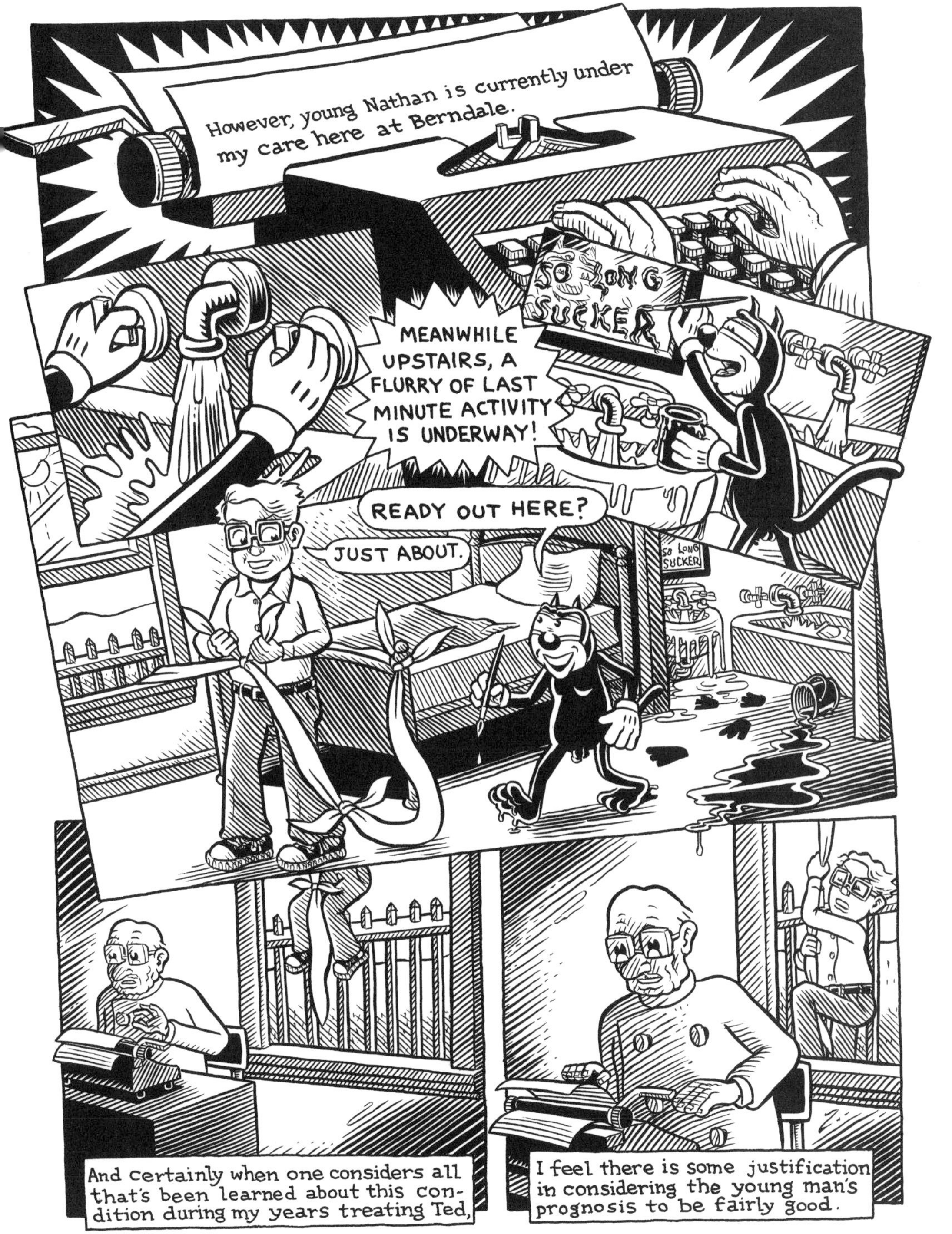
However, young Nathan is currently under my care here at Berndale.
SO LONG SUCKER
MEANWHILE UPSTAIRS, A FLURRY OF LAST MINUTE ACTIVITY IS UNDERWAY!
READY OUT HERE?
JUST ABOUT.
SO LONG SUCKER
And certainly when one considers all that's been learned about this condition during my years treating Ted,
I feel there is some justification in considering the young man's prognosis to be fairly good.

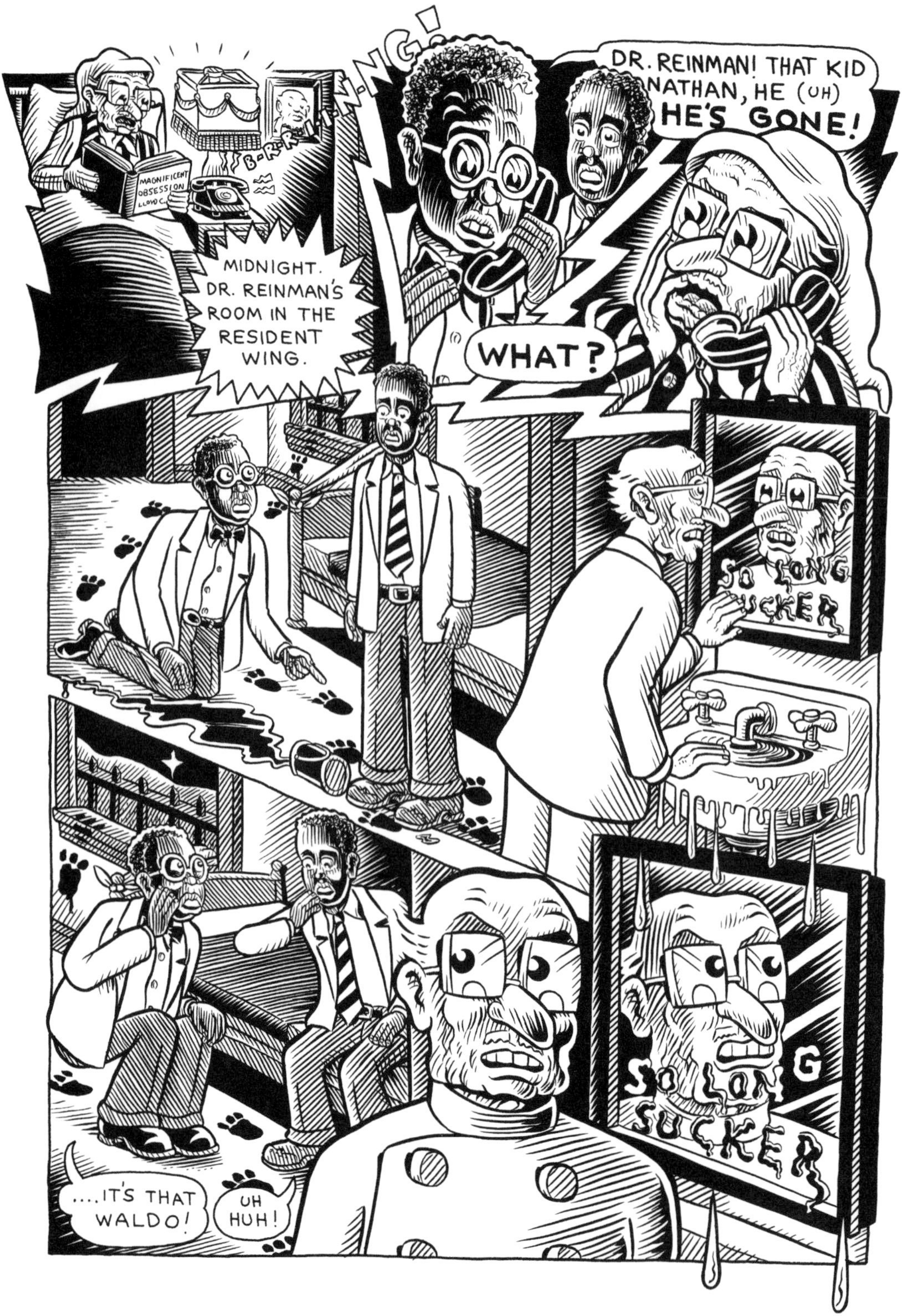
MAGNIFICENT OBSESSION LLOYD C.
B-R-R-I-N-N-NG!
MIDNIGHT. DR. REINMAN'S ROOM IN THE RESIDENT WING.
DR. REINMAN! THAT KID NATHAN, HE (UH) HE'S GONE!
WHAT?
SO LONG SUCKER
SO LONG SUCKER
....IT'S THAT WALDO!
UH HUH!

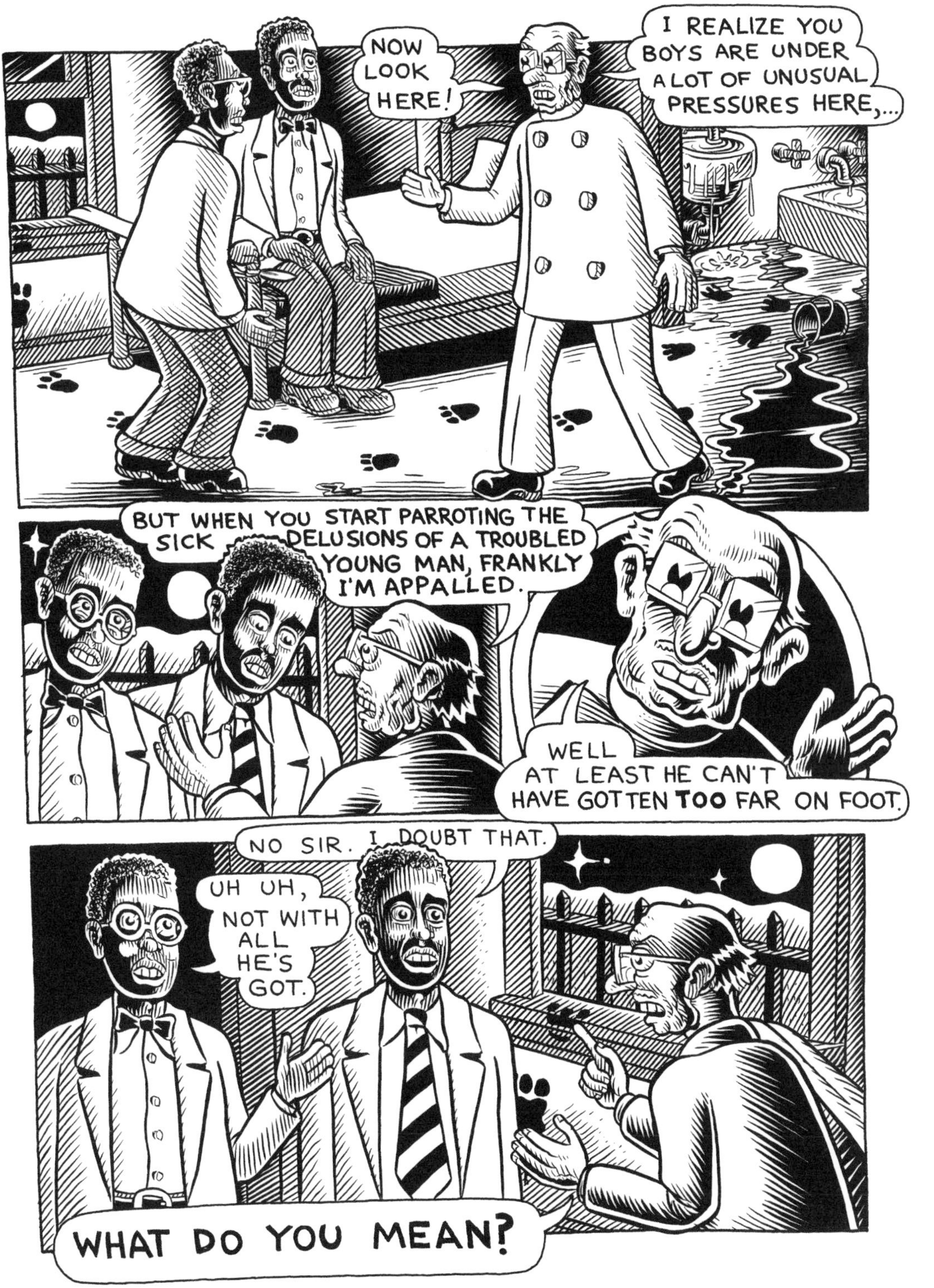
NOW LOOK HERE!
I REALIZE YOU BOYS ARE UNDER A LOT OF UNUSUAL PRESSURES HERE,...
BUT WHEN YOU START PARROTING THE SICK DELUSIONS OF A TROUBLED YOUNG MAN, FRANKLY I'M APPALLED.
WELL AT LEAST HE CAN'T HAVE GOTTEN TOO FAR ON FOOT.
NO SIR. I DOUBT THAT.
UH UH, NOT WITH ALL HE'S GOT.
WHAT DO YOU MEAN?

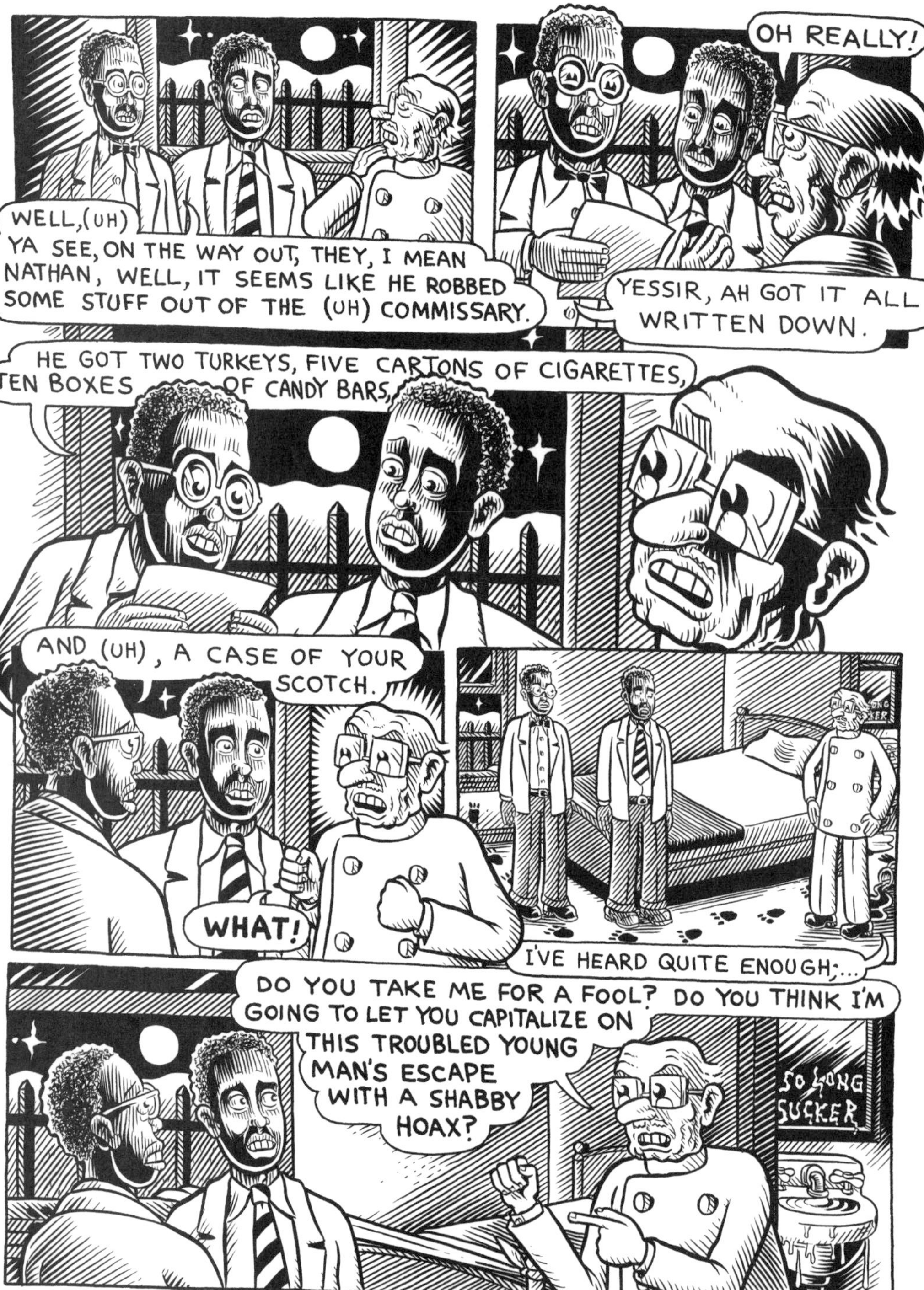

WELL, (UH)
YA SEE, ON THE WAY OUT, THEY, I MEAN NATHAN, WELL, IT SEEMS LIKE HE ROBBED SOME STUFF OUT OF THE (UH) COMMISSARY.
OH REALLY!
YESSIR, AH GOT IT ALL WRITTEN DOWN.
HE GOT TWO TURKEYS, FIVE CARTONS OF CIGARETTES, TEN BOXES OF CANDY BARS,
AND (UH), A CASE OF YOUR SCOTCH.
WHAT!
I'VE HEARD QUITE ENOUGH;...
DO YOU TAKE ME FOR A FOOL? DO YOU THINK I'M GOING TO LET YOU CAPITALIZE ON THIS TROUBLED YOUNG MAN'S ESCAPE WITH A SHABBY HOAX?
SO LONG SUCKER

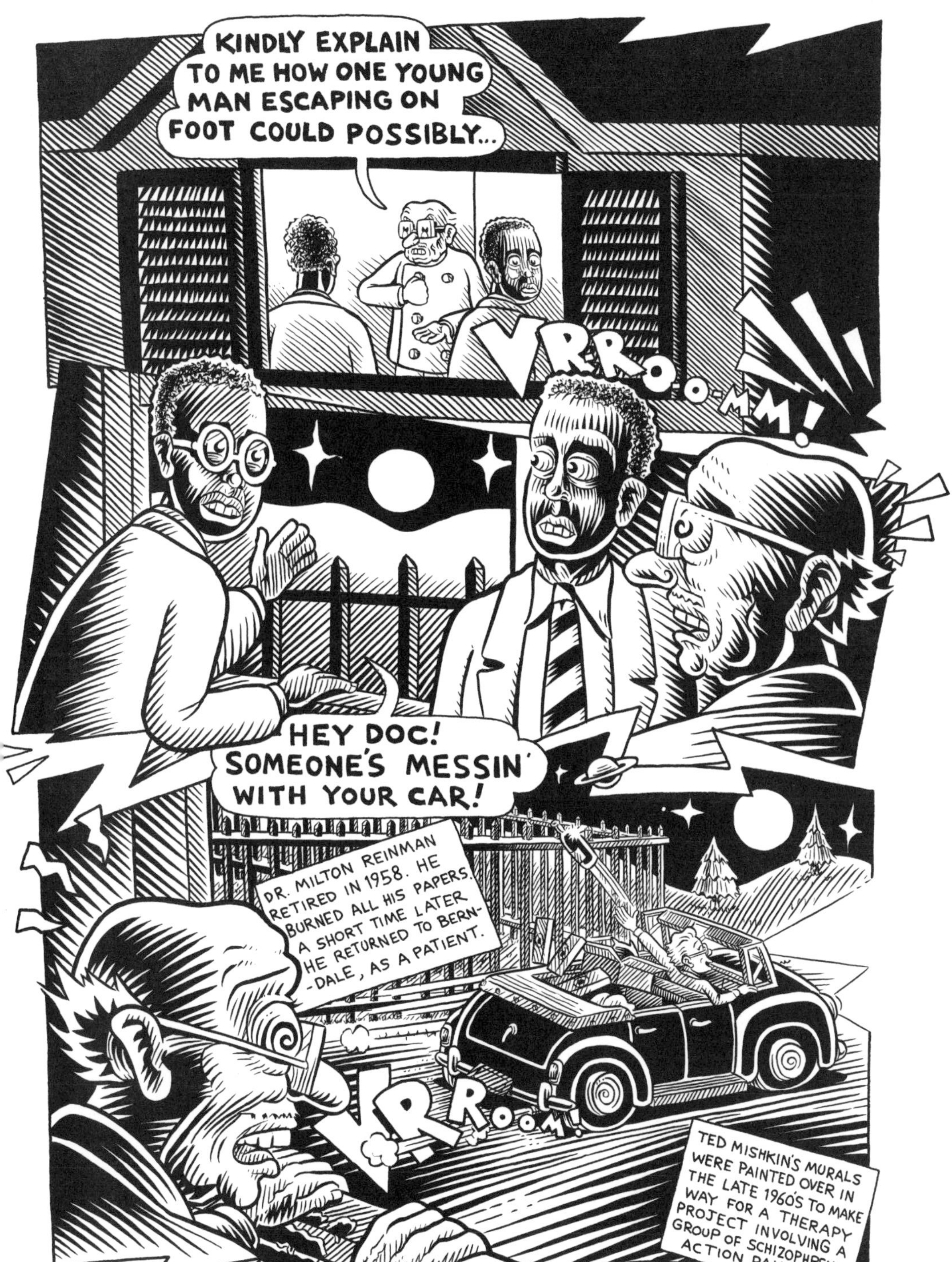
KINDLY EXPLAIN TO ME HOW ONE YOUNG MAN ESCAPING ON FOOT COULD POSSIBLY...
VRROO-OMM!
HEY DOC! SOMEONE'S MESSIN' WITH YOUR CAR!
DR. MILTON REINMAN RETIRED IN 1958. HE BURNED ALL HIS PAPERS. A SHORT TIME LATER HE RETURNED TO BERN-DALE, AS A PATIENT.
VRROOM!
TED MISHKIN'S MURALS WERE PAINTED OVER IN THE LATE 1960'S TO MAKE WAY FOR A THERAPY PROJECT INVOLVING A GROUP OF SCHIZOPHRENIC ACTION PAINTERS.

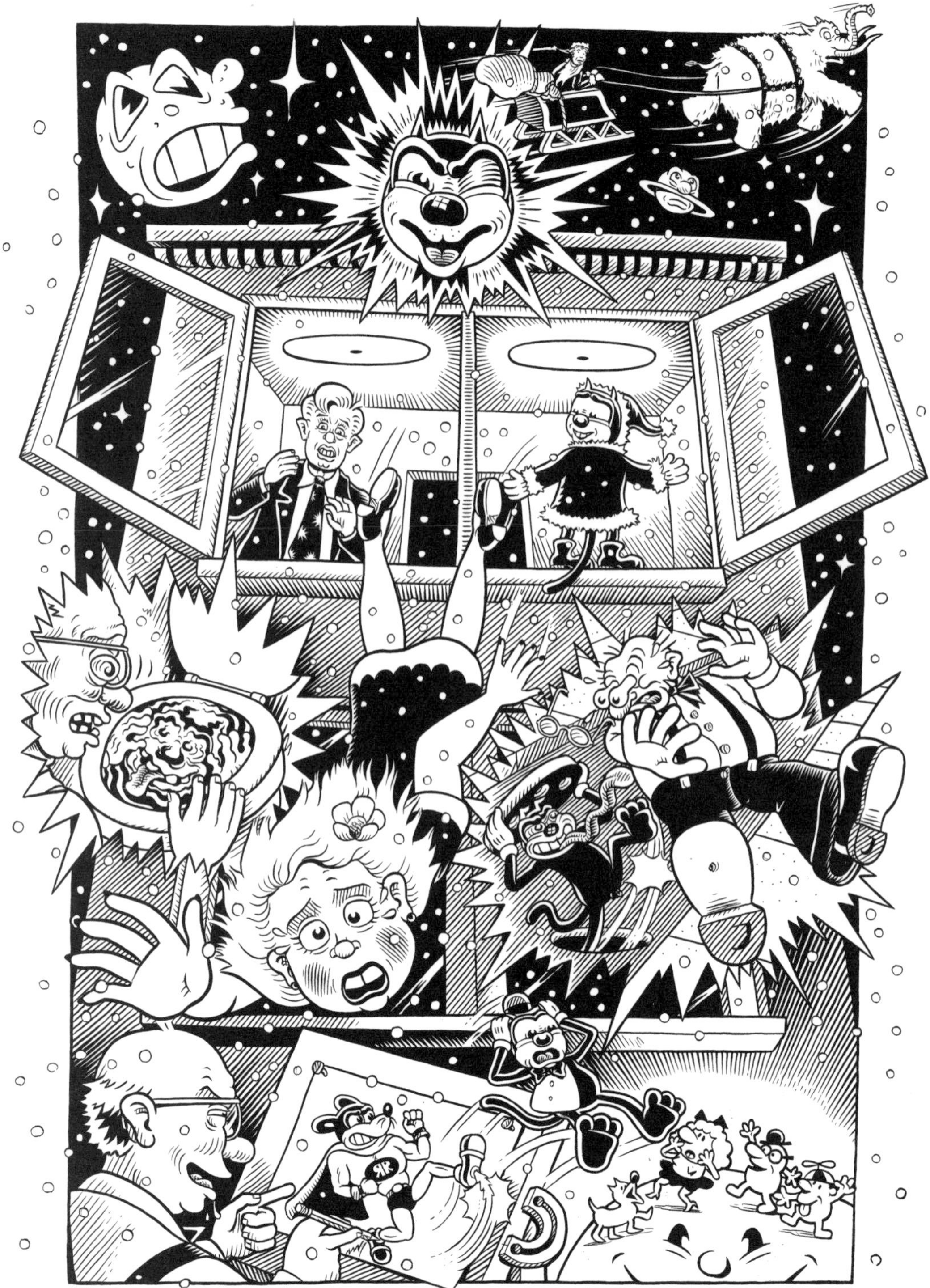

Kim Deitch

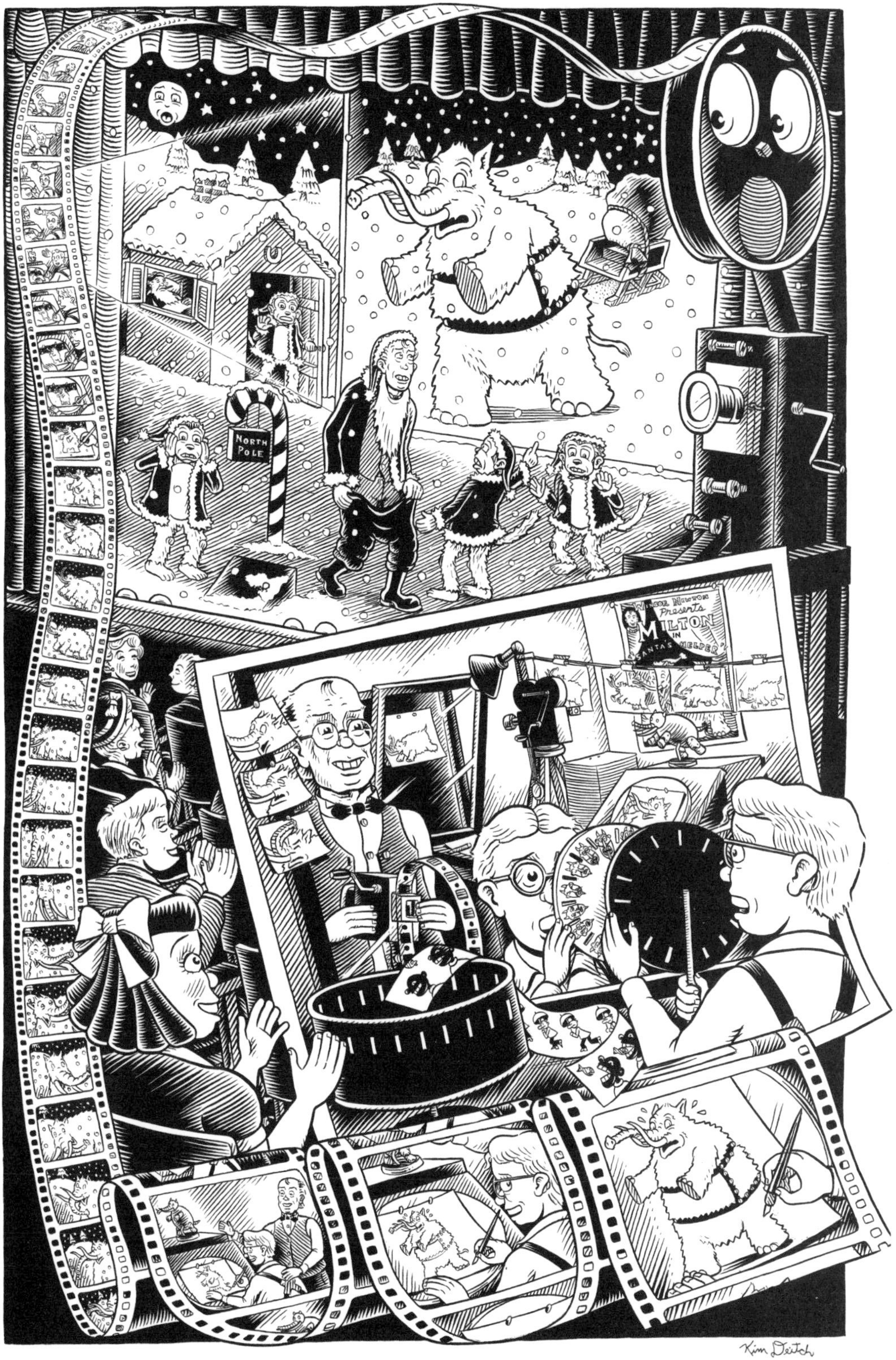
NORTH POLE
WINSOR NEWTON Presents MILTON IN 'SANTA'S HELPER'
Kim Deitch

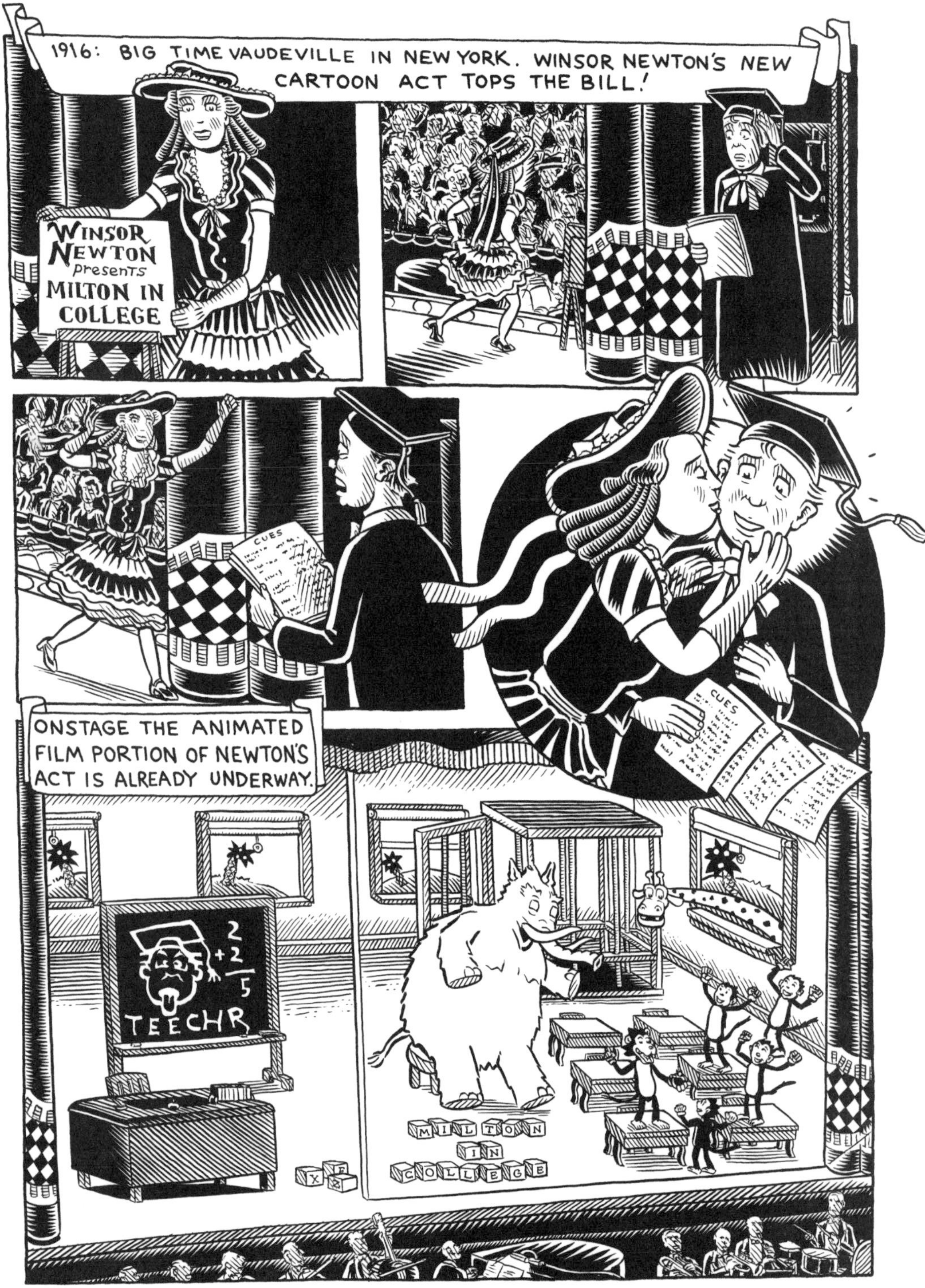
1916: BIG TIME VAUDEVILLE IN NEW YORK. WINSOR NEWTON'S NEW CARTOON ACT TOPS THE BILL!
WINSOR NEWTON presents MILTON IN COLLEGE
CUES
CUES
ONSTAGE THE ANIMATED FILM PORTION OF NEWTON'S ACT IS ALREADY UNDERWAY.
2 +2 5
TEECHR
MILTON IN COLLEGE

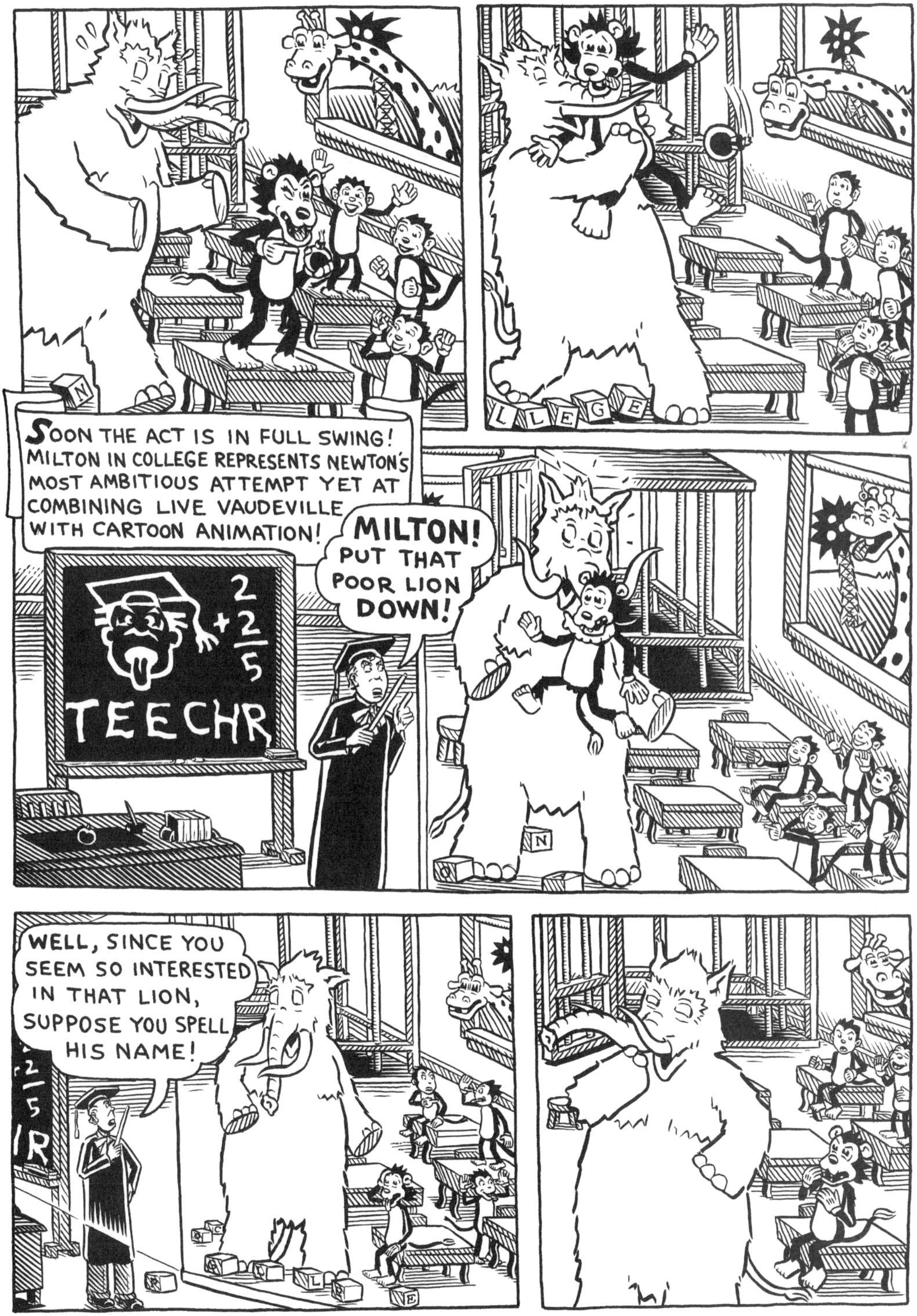

N
L L E G E
SOON THE ACT IS IN FULL SWING! MILTON IN COLLEGE REPRESENTS NEWTON'S MOST AMBITIOUS ATTEMPT YET AT COMBINING LIVE VAUDEVILLE WITH CARTOON ANIMATION!
MILTON! PUT THAT POOR LION DOWN!
2 +2/5
TEECHR
N
WELL, SINCE YOU SEEM SO INTERESTED IN THAT LION, SUPPOSE YOU SPELL HIS NAME!

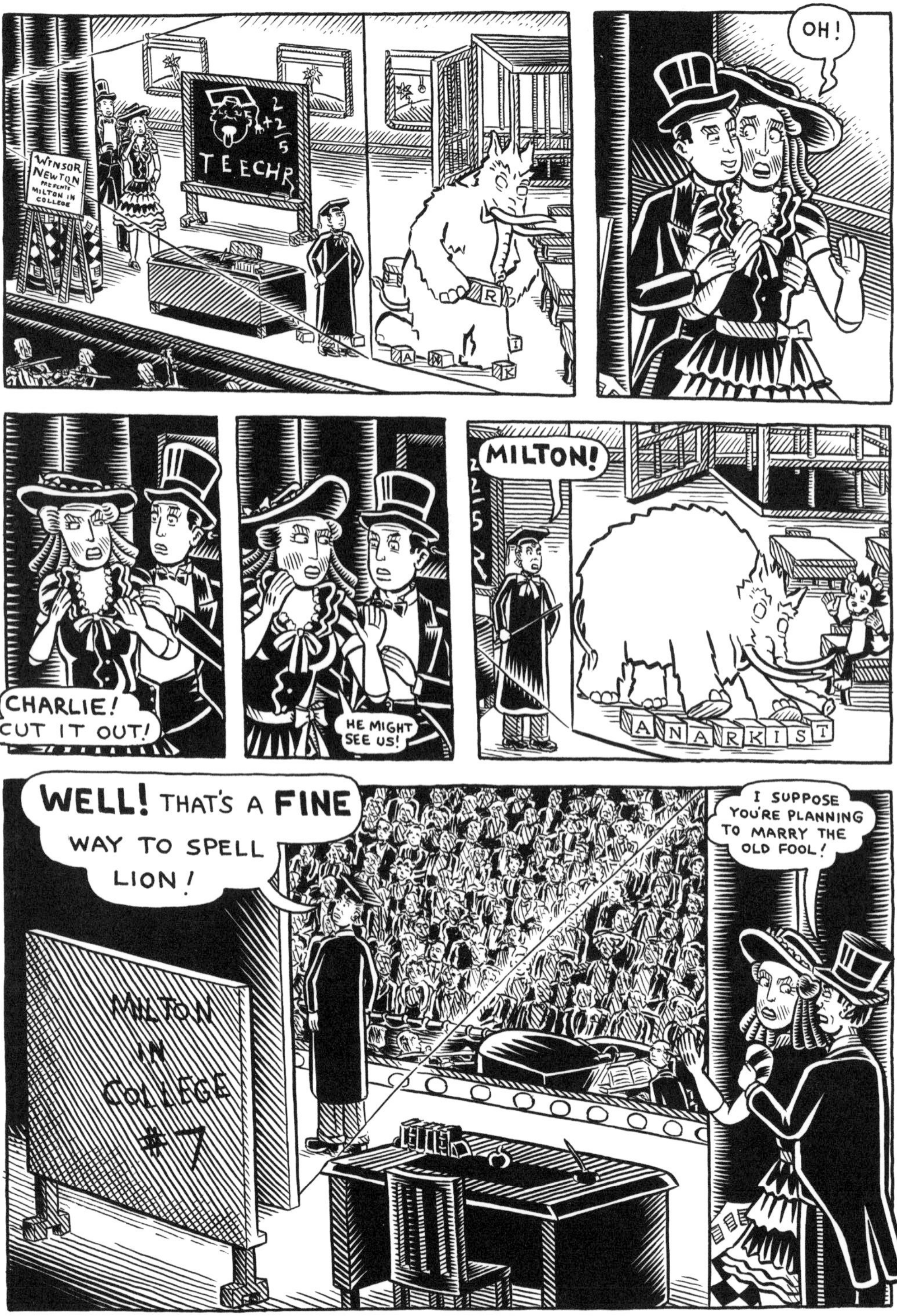
WINSOR NEWTON PRESENTS MILTON IN COLLEGE
TEECHR
OH!
CHARLIE! CUT IT OUT!
HE MIGHT SEE US!
MILTON!
ANARKIST
WELL! THAT'S A FINE WAY TO SPELL LION!
I SUPPOSE YOU'RE PLANNING TO MARRY THE OLD FOOL!
MILTON IN COLLEGE #7

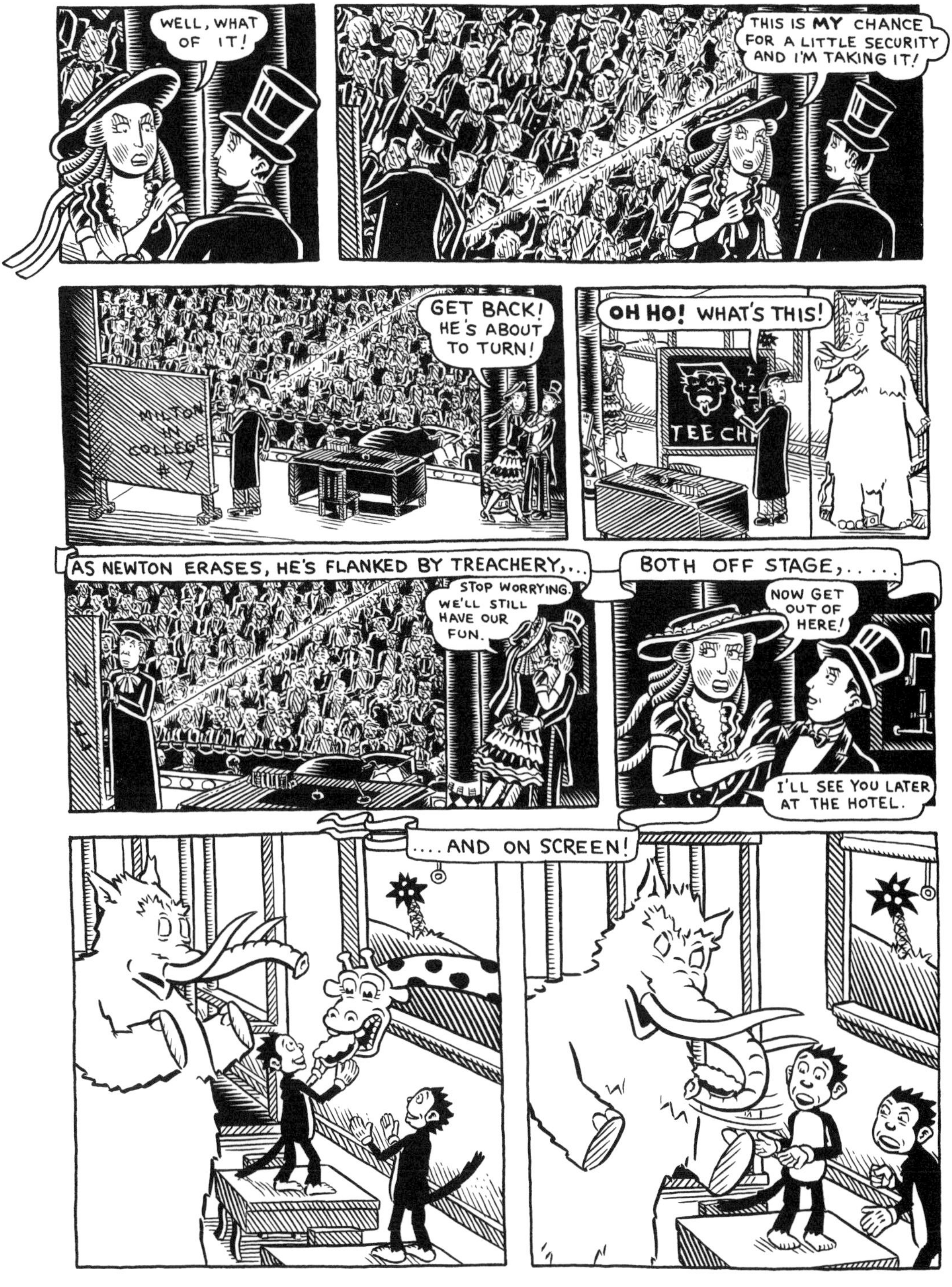
WELL, WHAT OF IT!
THIS IS MY CHANCE FOR A LITTLE SECURITY AND I'M TAKING IT!
MILTON IN COLLEGE #7
GET BACK! HE'S ABOUT TO TURN!
OH HO! WHAT'S THIS!
TEE CH
AS NEWTON ERASES, HE'S FLANKED BY TREACHERY,...
STOP WORRYING. WE'LL STILL HAVE OUR FUN.
BOTH OFF STAGE,....
NOW GET OUT OF HERE!
I'LL SEE YOU LATER AT THE HOTEL.
....AND ON SCREEN!

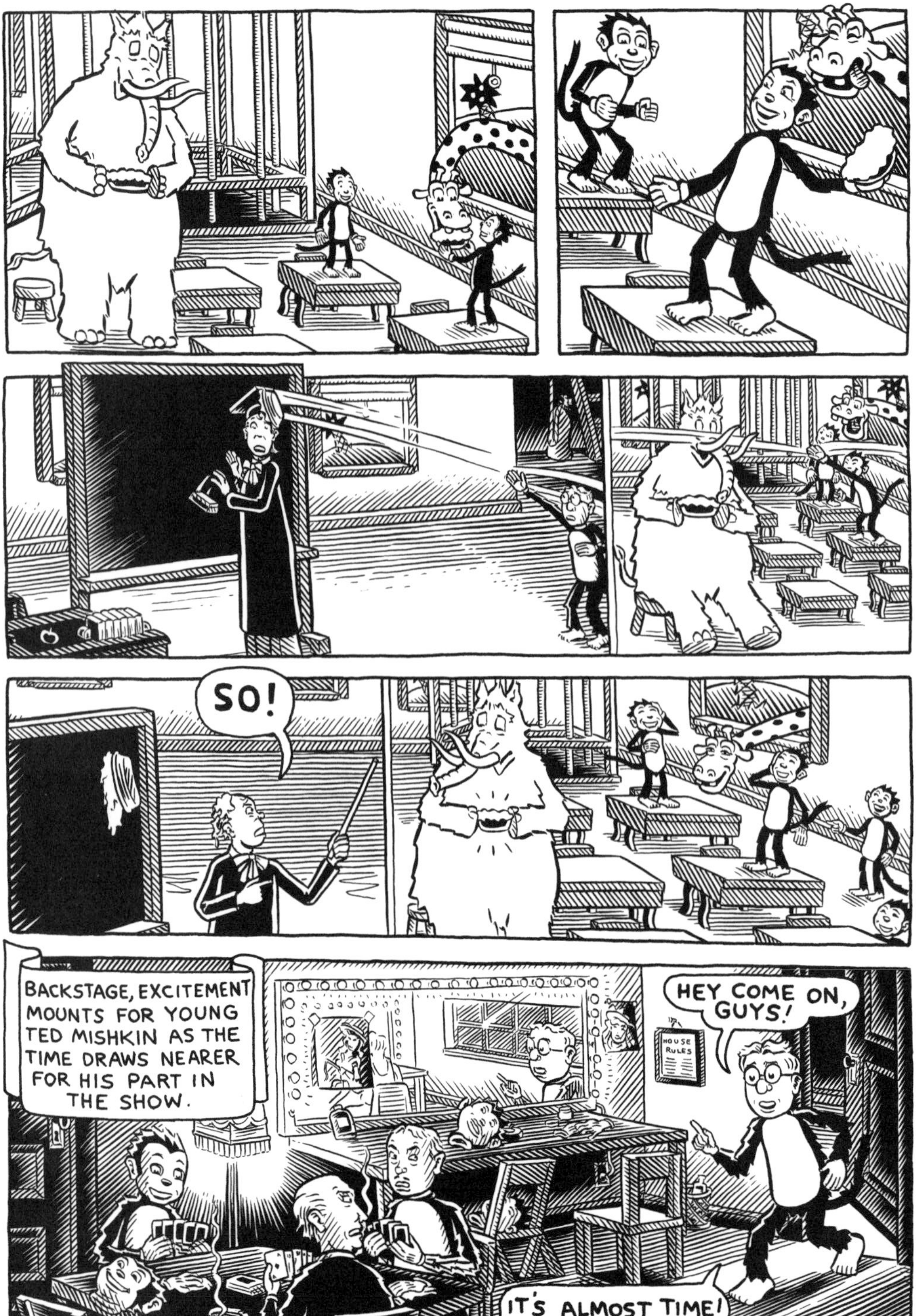
SO!
BACKSTAGE, EXCITEMENT MOUNTS FOR YOUNG TED MISHKIN AS THE TIME DRAWS NEARER FOR HIS PART IN THE SHOW.
HOUSE RULES
HEY COME ON, GUYS!
IT'S ALMOST TIME!

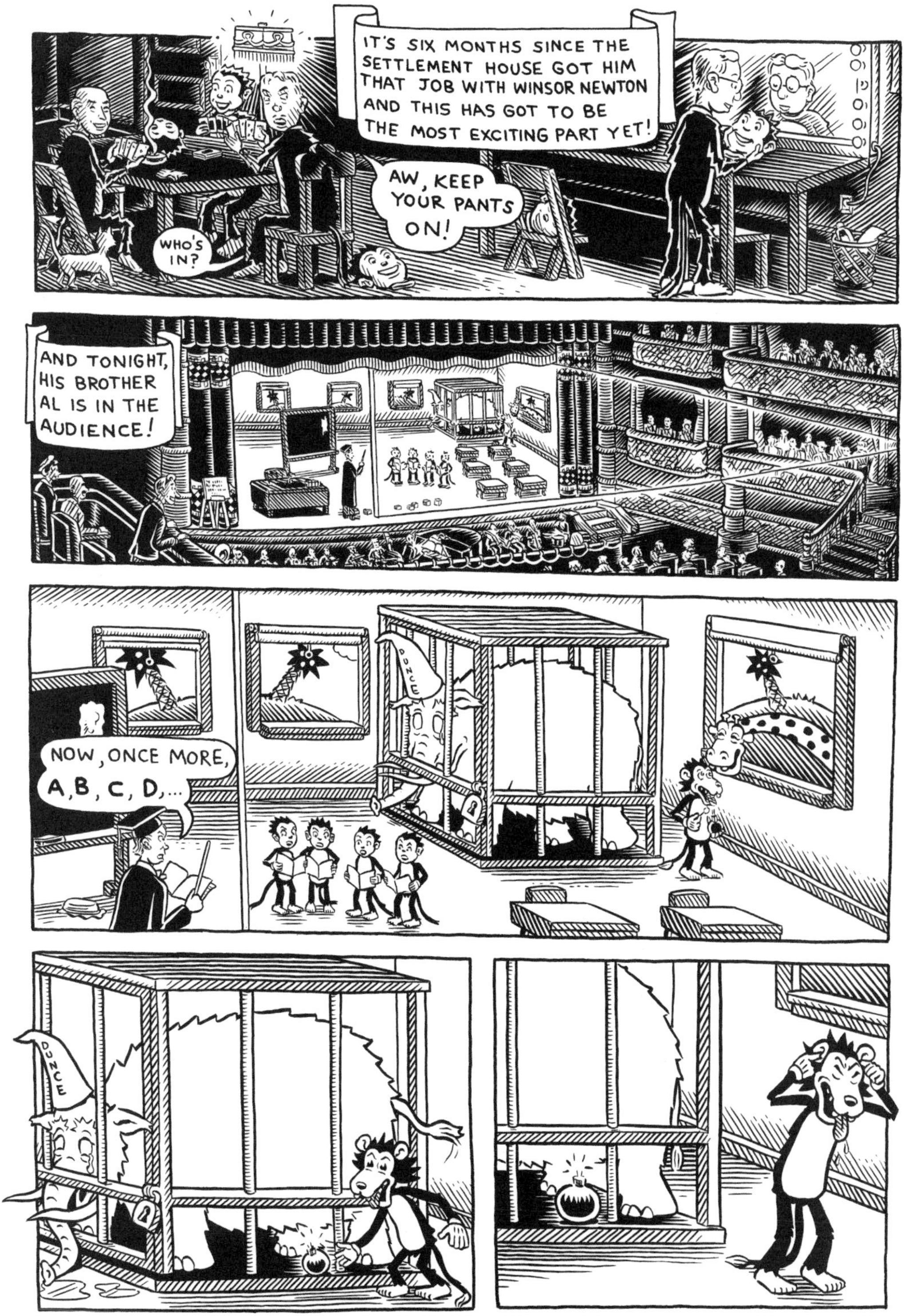
IT'S SIX MONTHS SINCE THE SETTLEMENT HOUSE GOT HIM THAT JOB WITH WINSOR NEWTON AND THIS HAS GOT TO BE THE MOST EXCITING PART YET!
AW, KEEP YOUR PANTS ON!
WHO'S IN?
AND TONIGHT, HIS BROTHER AL IS IN THE AUDIENCE!
DUNCE
NOW, ONCE MORE, A, B, C, D, ...
DUNCE

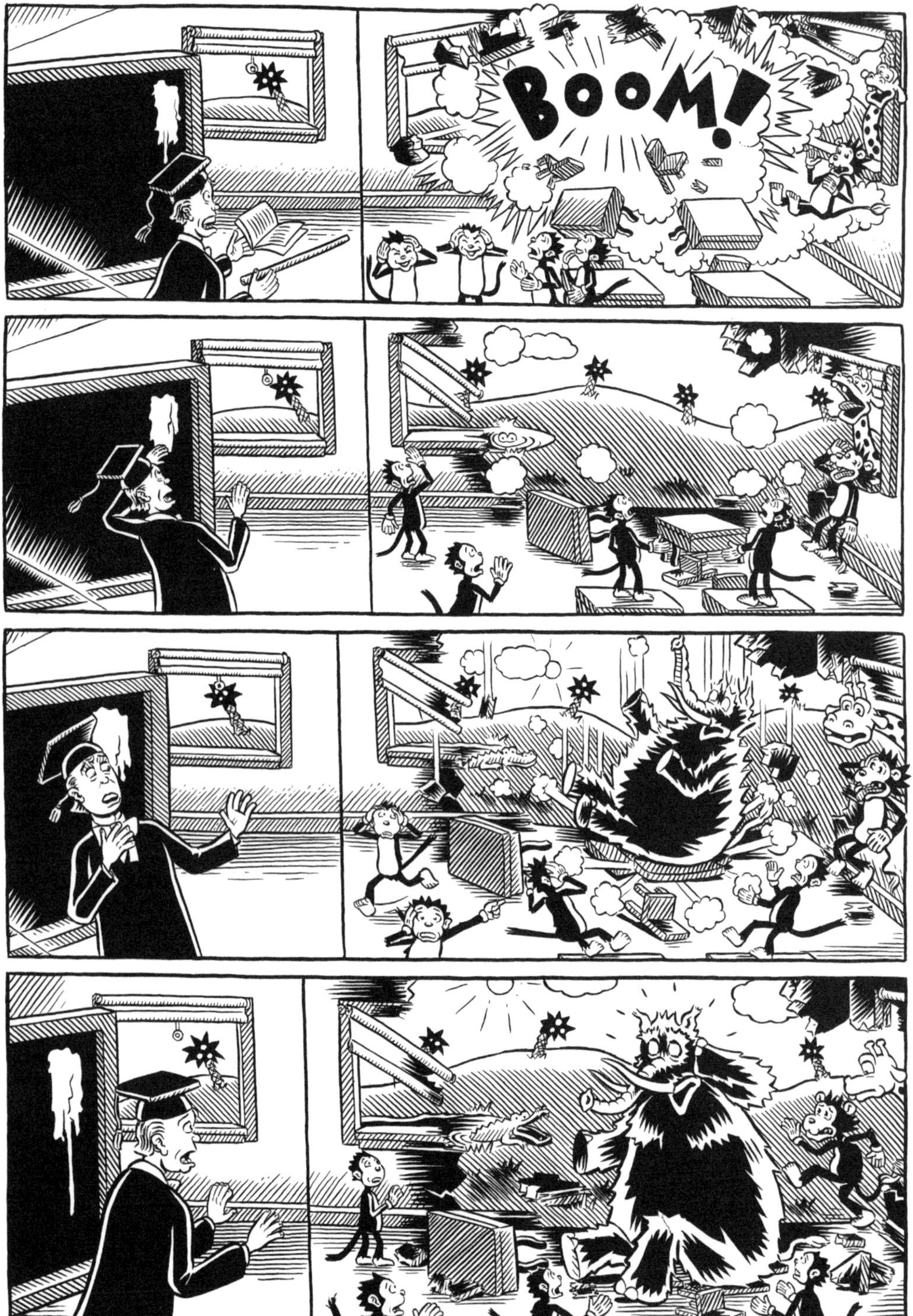
BOOM!

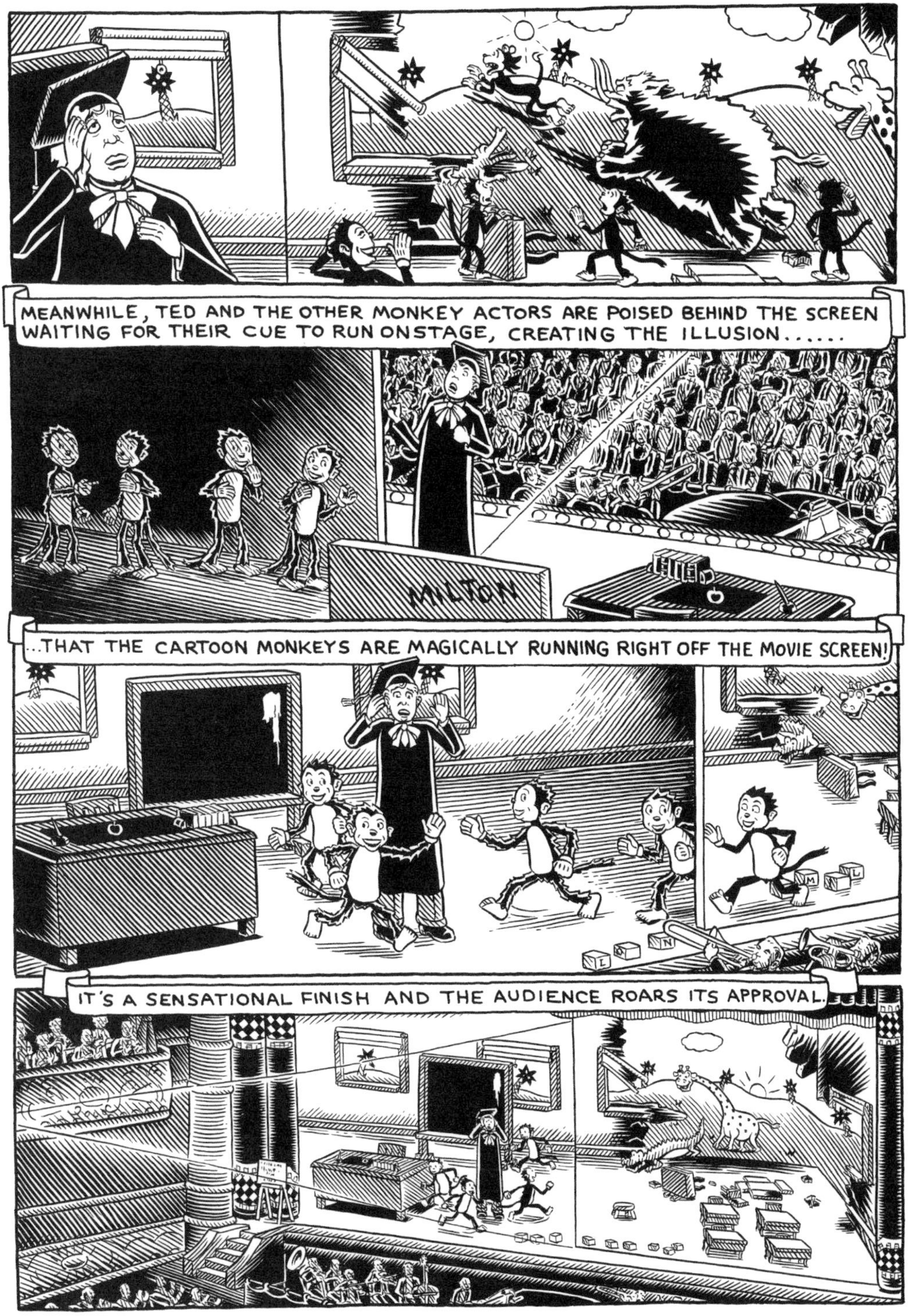
MEANWHILE, TED AND THE OTHER MONKEY ACTORS ARE POISED BEHIND THE SCREEN WAITING FOR THEIR CUE TO RUN ONSTAGE, CREATING THE ILLUSION......
MILTON
...THAT THE CARTOON MONKEYS ARE MAGICALLY RUNNING RIGHT OFF THE MOVIE SCREEN!
IT'S A SENSATIONAL FINISH AND THE AUDIENCE ROARS ITS APPROVAL.

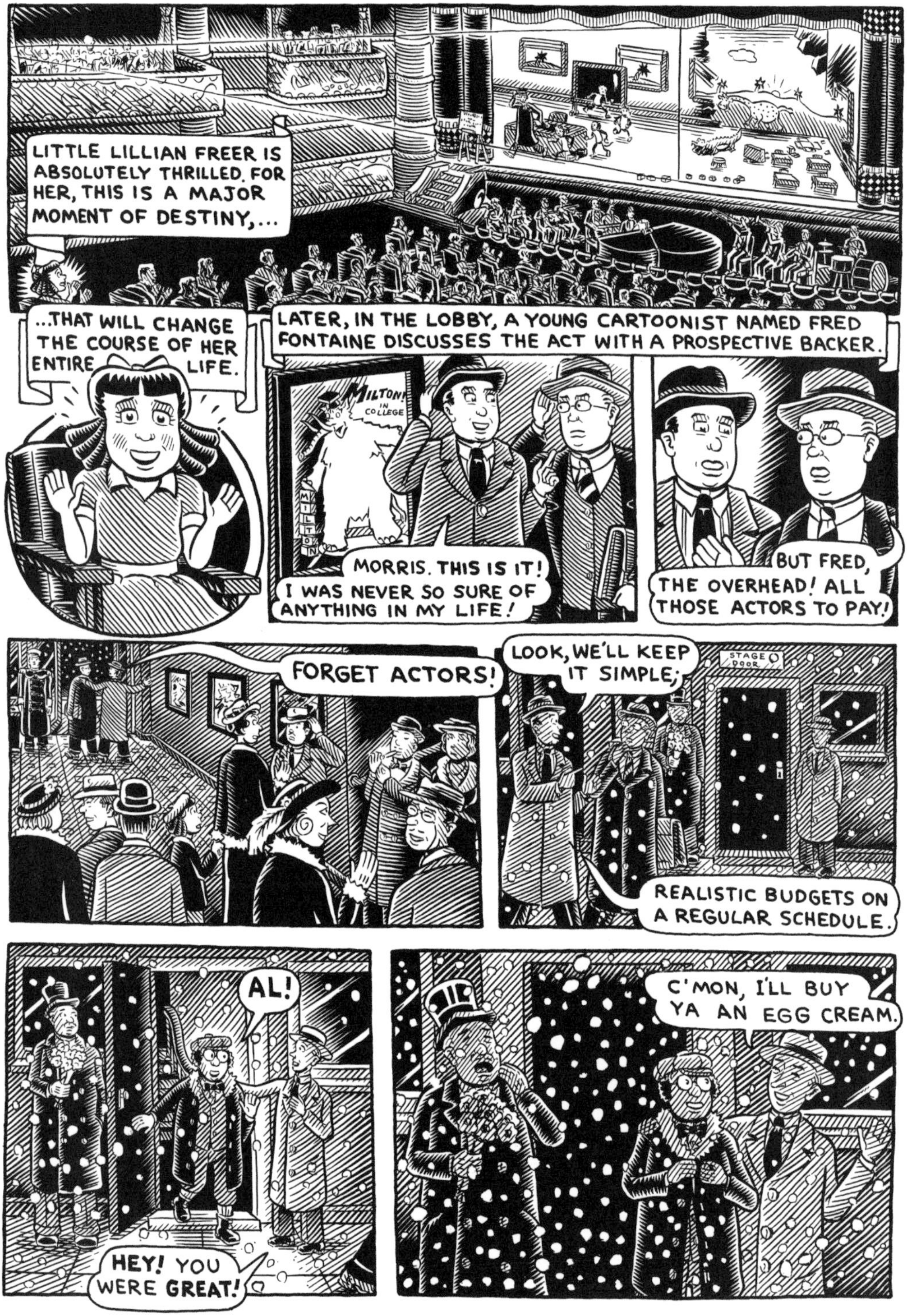
LITTLE LILLIAN FREER IS ABSOLUTELY THRILLED. FOR HER, THIS IS A MAJOR MOMENT OF DESTINY,...
...THAT WILL CHANGE THE COURSE OF HER ENTIRE LIFE.
LATER, IN THE LOBBY, A YOUNG CARTOONIST NAMED FRED FONTAINE DISCUSSES THE ACT WITH A PROSPECTIVE BACKER.
MILTON! IN COLLEGE
MORRIS. THIS IS IT! I WAS NEVER SO SURE OF ANYTHING IN MY LIFE!
BUT FRED, THE OVERHEAD! ALL THOSE ACTORS TO PAY!
FORGET ACTORS!
LOOK, WE'LL KEEP IT SIMPLE;
STAGE DOOR
REALISTIC BUDGETS ON A REGULAR SCHEDULE.
AL!
HEY! YOU WERE GREAT!
C'MON, I'LL BUY YA AN EGG CREAM.

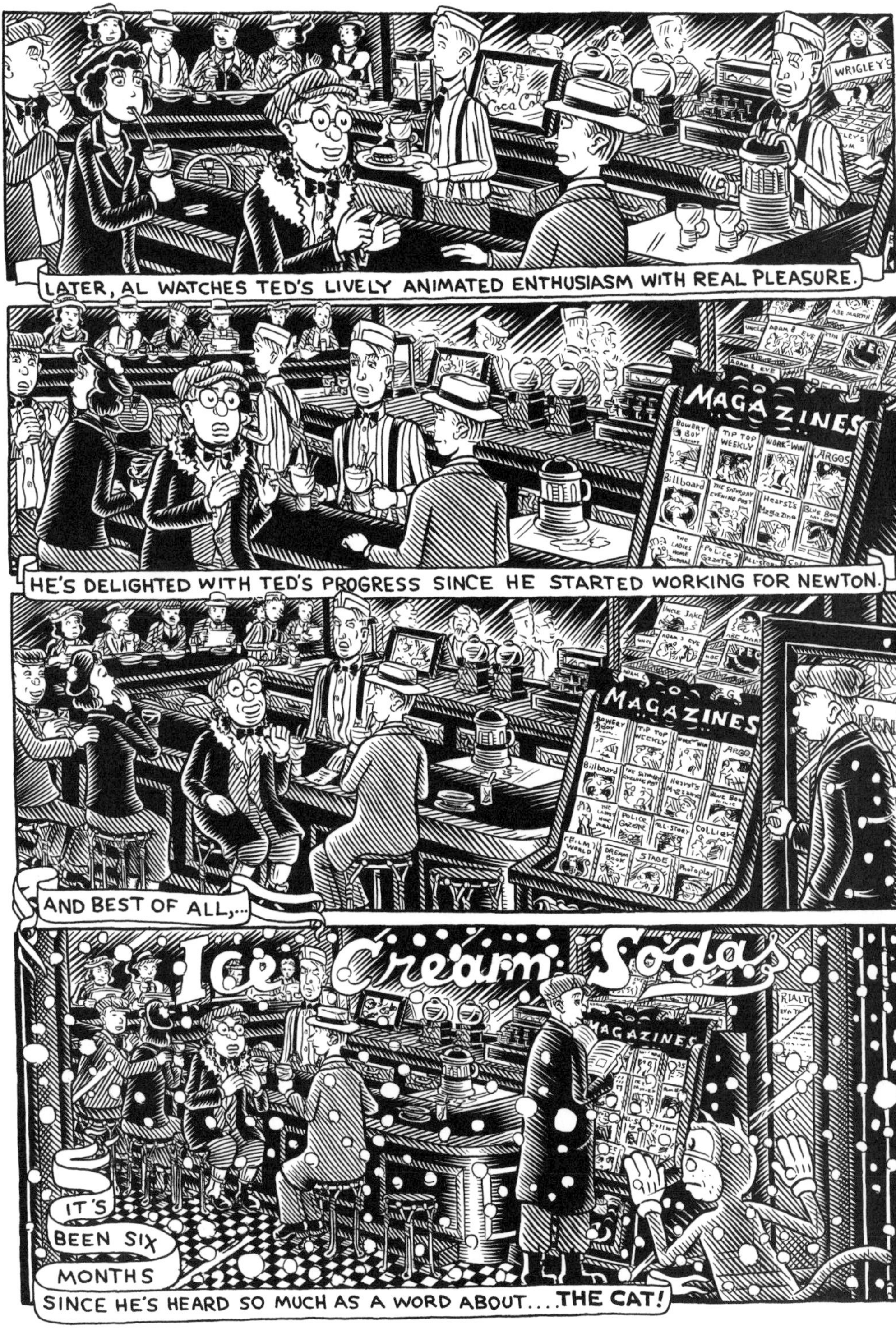
WRIGLEY'S
LATER, AL WATCHES TED'S LIVELY ANIMATED ENTHUSIASM WITH REAL PLEASURE.
MAGAZINES
TIP TOP WEEKLY
ARGOS
Billboard
THE SATURDAY EVENING POST
Hearst's Magazine
Police Gazette
HE'S DELIGHTED WITH TED'S PROGRESS SINCE HE STARTED WORKING FOR NEWTON.
MAGAZINES
Billboard
ALL-STORY
Collier's
DREAM BOOK
STAGE
AND BEST OF ALL,...
Ice Cream Sodas
MAGAZINES
IT'S BEEN SIX MONTHS
SINCE HE'S HEARD SO MUCH AS A WORD ABOUT.... THE CAT!

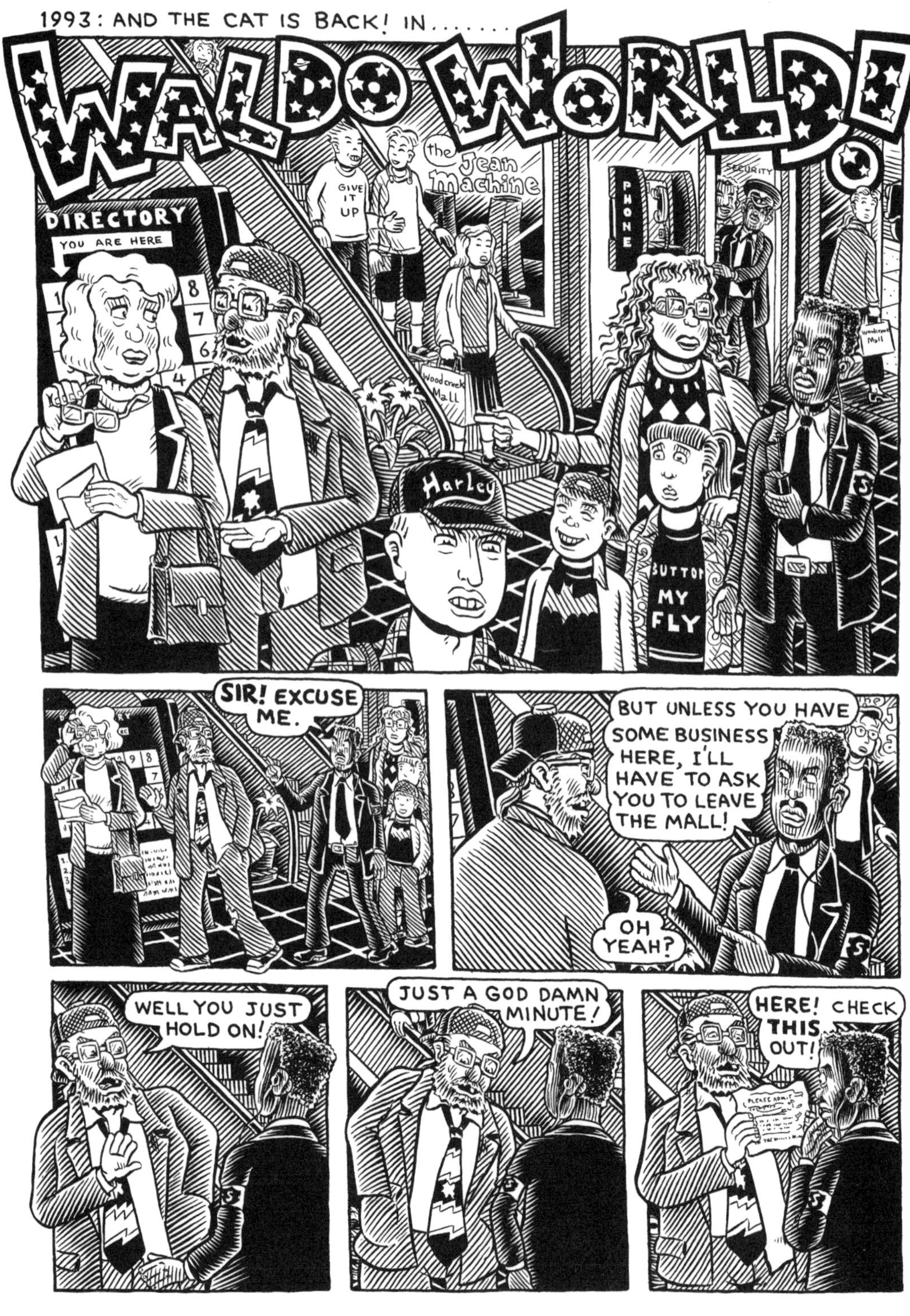
1993: AND THE CAT IS BACK! IN.......
WALDO WORLD!
DIRECTORY
YOU ARE HERE
GIVE IT UP
the Jean machine
PHONE
SECURITY
Woodcreek Mall
Harley
BUTTON MY FLY
SIR! EXCUSE ME.
BUT UNLESS YOU HAVE SOME BUSINESS HERE, I'LL HAVE TO ASK YOU TO LEAVE THE MALL!
OH YEAH?
WELL YOU JUST HOLD ON!
JUST A GOD DAMN MINUTE!
HERE! CHECK THIS OUT!

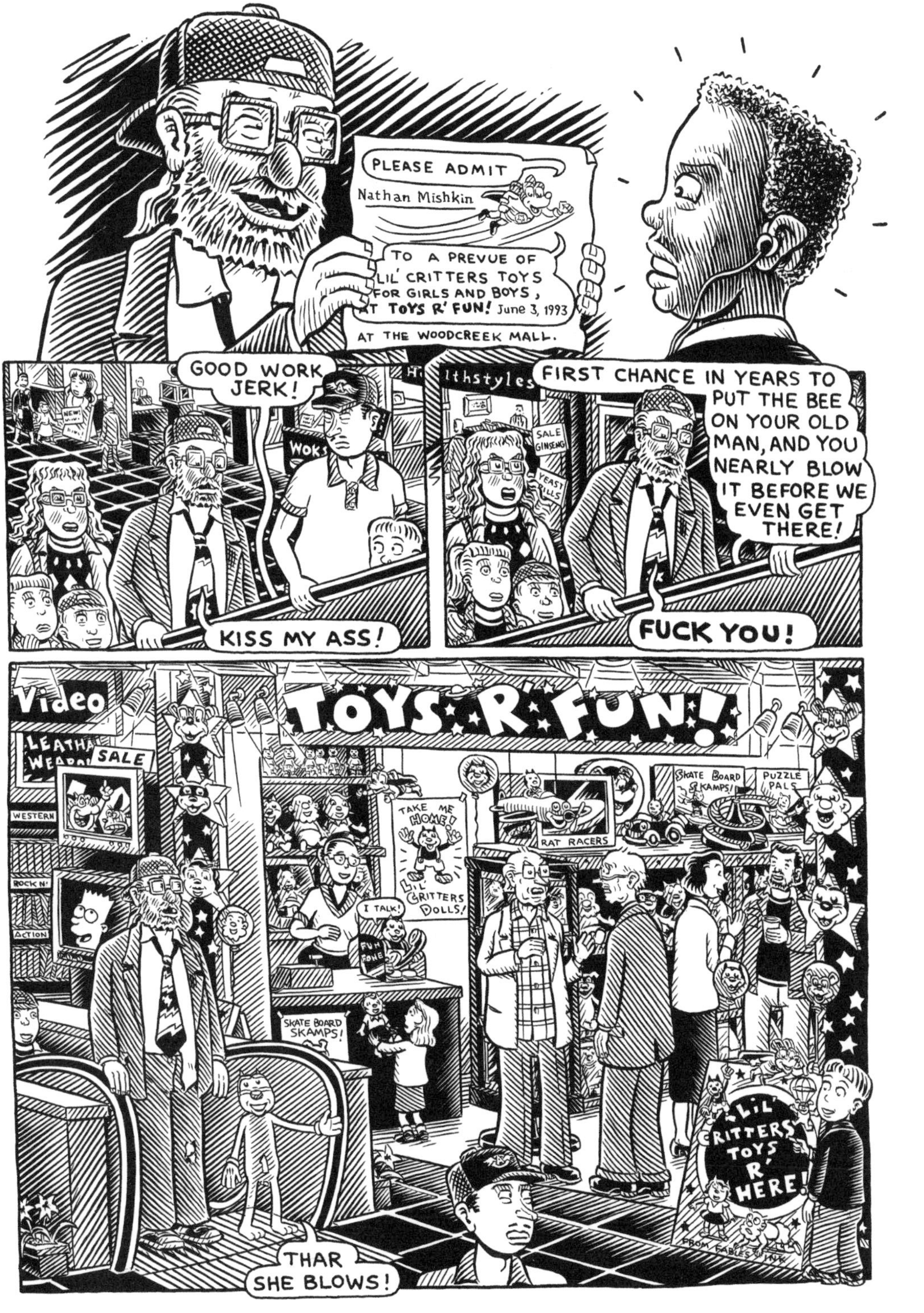
PLEASE ADMIT
Nathan Mishkin
TO A PREVUE OF LIL' CRITTERS TOYS FOR GIRLS AND BOYS, AT TOYS R' FUN! June 3, 1993
AT THE WOODCREEK MALL.
GOOD WORK JERK!
KISS MY ASS!
FIRST CHANCE IN YEARS TO PUT THE BEE ON YOUR OLD MAN, AND YOU NEARLY BLOW IT BEFORE WE EVEN GET THERE!
FUCK YOU!
WOKS
SALE GINSENG
Video
TOYS R' FUN!
SALE
WESTERN
ROCK N'
ACTION
TAKE ME HOME!
LIL' CRITTERS DOLLS!
I TALK!
FUN FONE
SKATE BOARD SKAMPS!
PUZZLE PALS
RAT RACERS
SKATE BOARD SKAMPS!
LIL' CRITTERS TOYS R' HERE!
THAR SHE BLOWS!

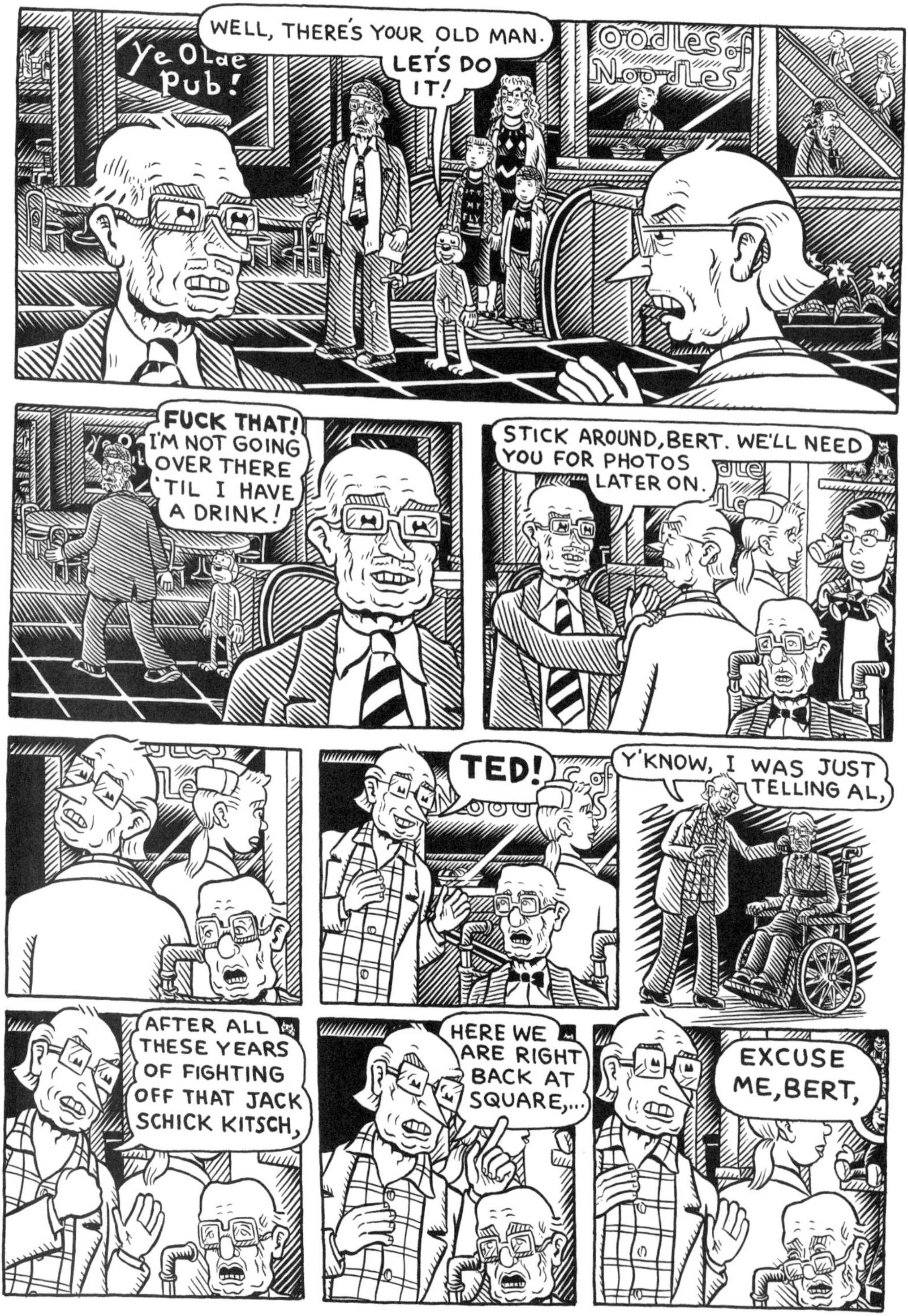
Ye Olde Pub!
WELL, THERE'S YOUR OLD MAN.
LET'S DO IT!
Oodles of Noodles
FUCK THAT! I'M NOT GOING OVER THERE 'TIL I HAVE A DRINK!
STICK AROUND, BERT. WE'LL NEED YOU FOR PHOTOS LATER ON.
TED!
Y'KNOW, I WAS JUST TELLING AL,
AFTER ALL THESE YEARS OF FIGHTING OFF THAT JACK SCHICK KITSCH,
HERE WE ARE RIGHT BACK AT SQUARE,...
EXCUSE ME, BERT,

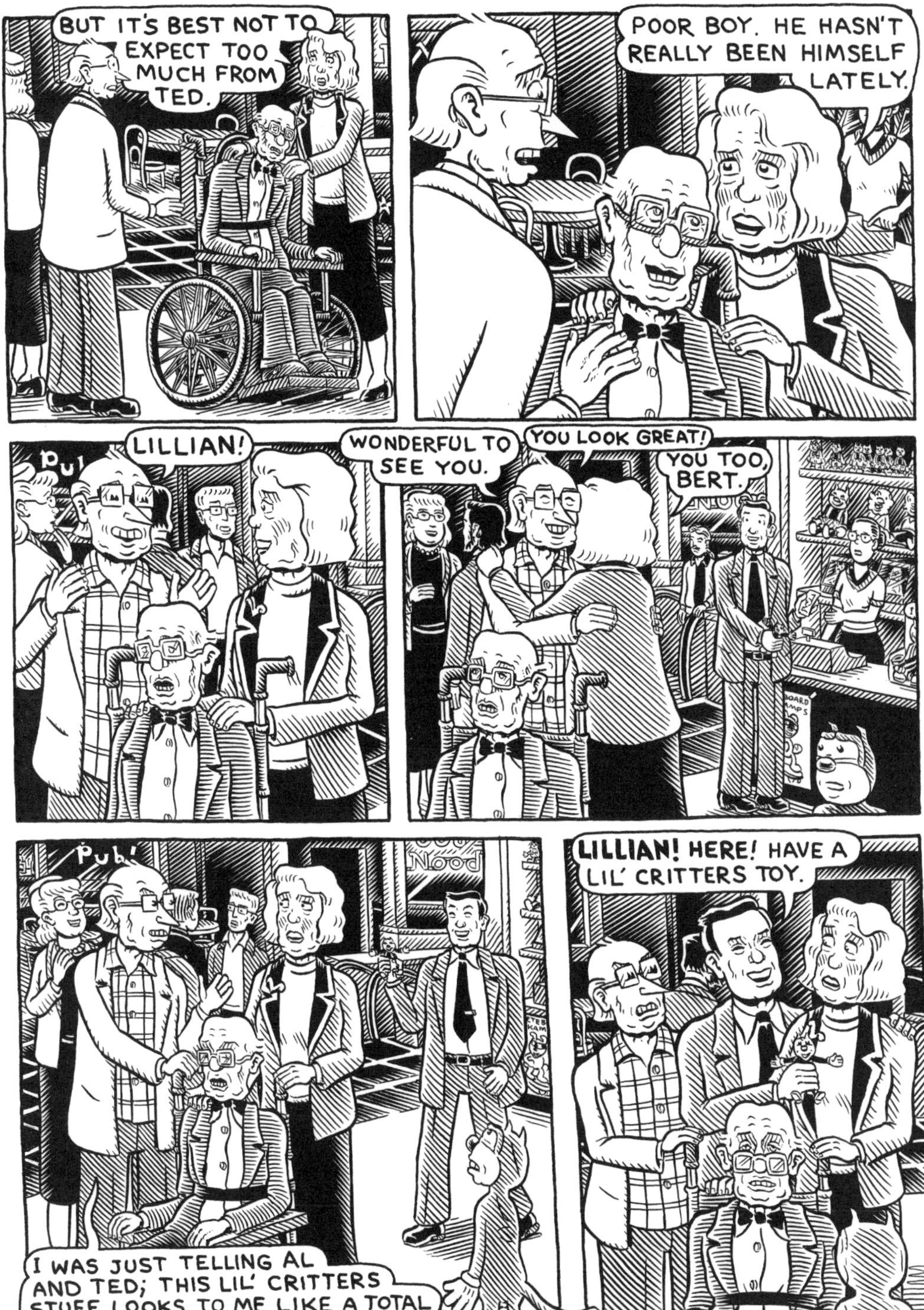
BUT IT'S BEST NOT TO EXPECT TOO MUCH FROM TED.
POOR BOY. HE HASN'T REALLY BEEN HIMSELF LATELY.
LILLIAN!
WONDERFUL TO SEE YOU.
YOU LOOK GREAT!
YOU TOO, BERT.
I WAS JUST TELLING AL AND TED; THIS LIL' CRITTERS STUFF LOOKS TO ME LIKE A TOTAL RETREAT TO THE OLD TIME SHLOCK.
LILLIAN! HERE! HAVE A LIL' CRITTERS TOY.

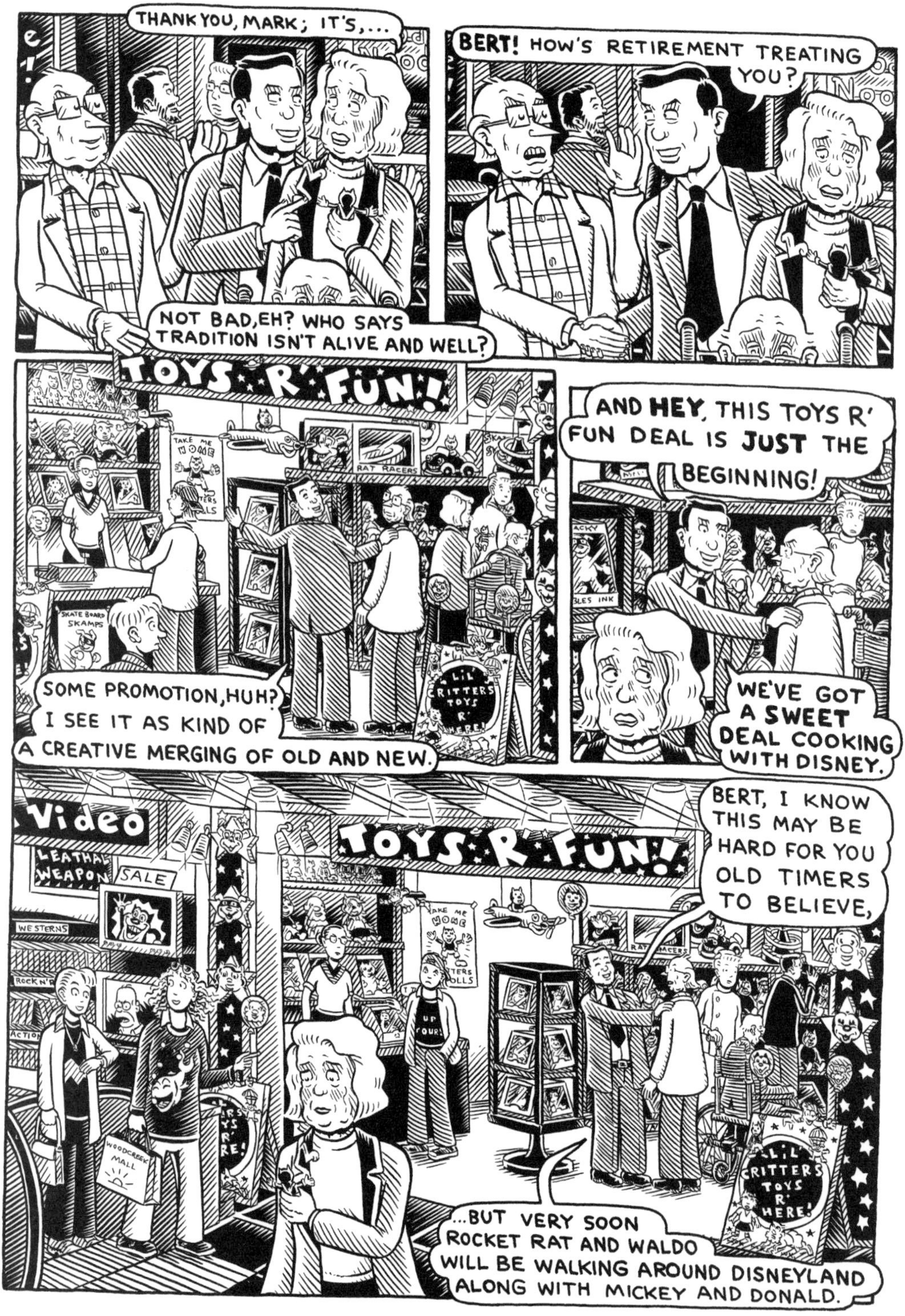

THANK YOU, MARK; IT'S,...
NOT BAD, EH? WHO SAYS TRADITION ISN'T ALIVE AND WELL?
BERT! HOW'S RETIREMENT TREATING YOU?
TOYS R' FUN!
TAKE ME HOME
RAT RACERS
SKATE BOARD SKAMPS
LI'L CRITTERS TOYS R' HERE!
SOME PROMOTION, HUH? I SEE IT AS KIND OF A CREATIVE MERGING OF OLD AND NEW.
AND HEY, THIS TOYS R' FUN DEAL IS JUST THE BEGINNING!
WE'VE GOT A SWEET DEAL COOKING WITH DISNEY.
Video
LEATHAL WEAPON
SALE
WESTERNS
TOYS R' FUN!
BERT, I KNOW THIS MAY BE HARD FOR YOU OLD TIMERS TO BELIEVE,
UP YOURS
WOODCREEK MALL
LI'L CRITTERS TOYS R' HERE!
...BUT VERY SOON ROCKET RAT AND WALDO WILL BE WALKING AROUND DISNEYLAND ALONG WITH MICKEY AND DONALD.

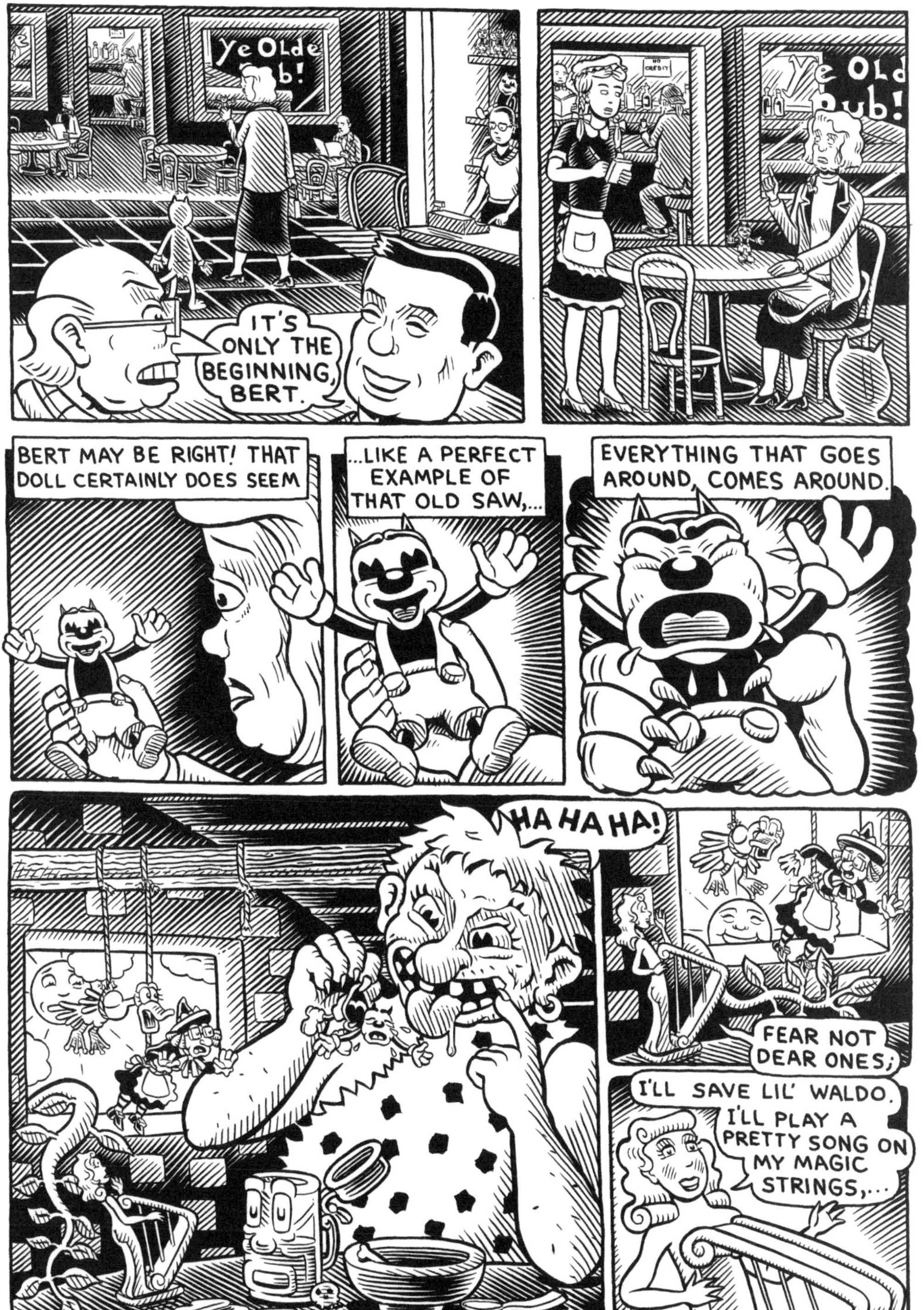
ye Olde
b!
NO CREDIT
IT'S ONLY THE BEGINNING, BERT.
Ye Old
Pub!
BERT MAY BE RIGHT! THAT DOLL CERTAINLY DOES SEEM
...LIKE A PERFECT EXAMPLE OF THAT OLD SAW,...
EVERYTHING THAT GOES AROUND, COMES AROUND.
HA HA HA!
FEAR NOT DEAR ONES;
I'LL SAVE LIL' WALDO.
I'LL PLAY A PRETTY SONG ON MY MAGIC STRINGS,...

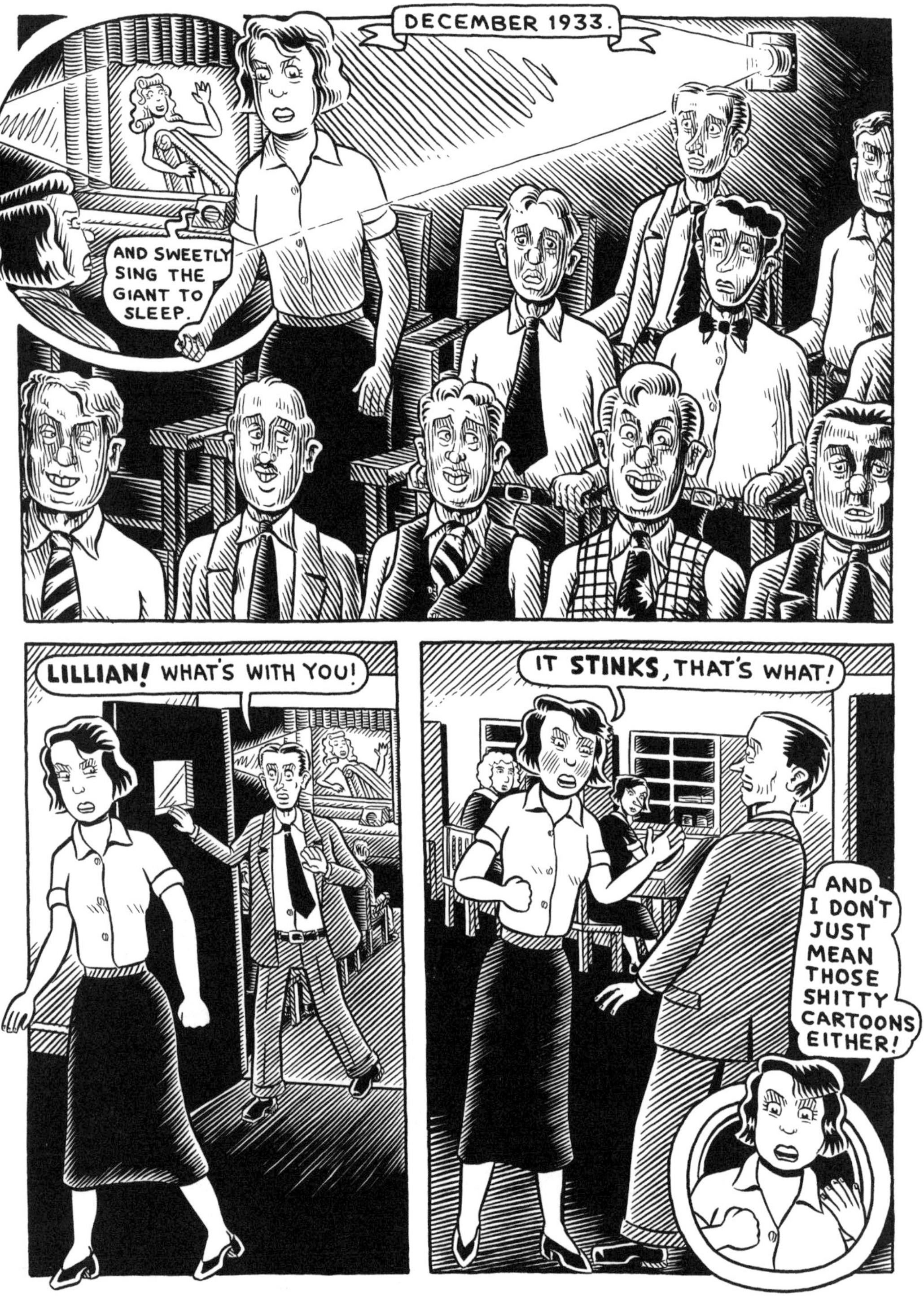
DECEMBER 1933.
AND SWEETLY SING THE GIANT TO SLEEP.
LILLIAN! WHAT'S WITH YOU!
IT STINKS, THAT'S WHAT!
AND I DON'T JUST MEAN THOSE SHITTY CARTOONS EITHER!

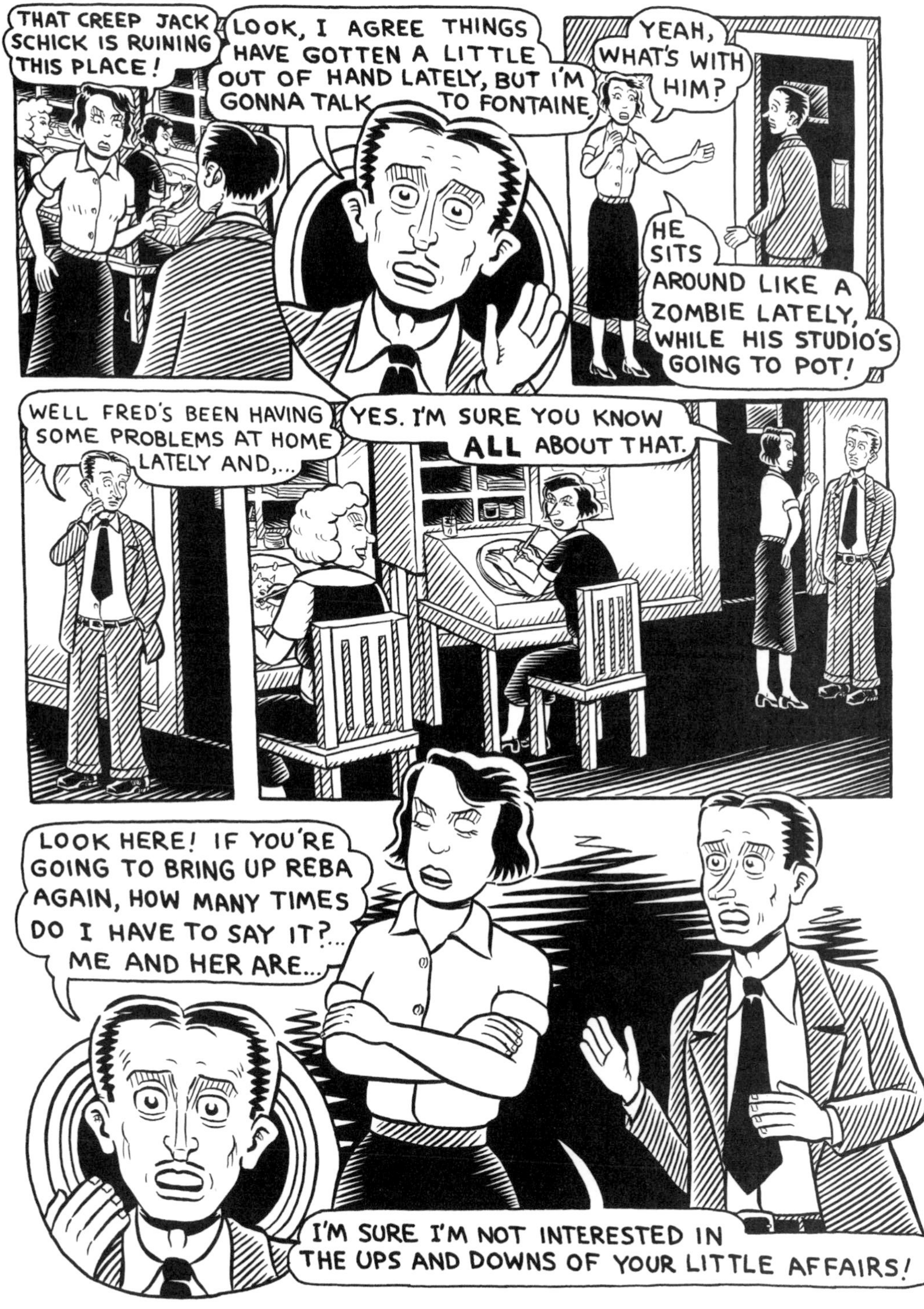
THAT CREEP JACK SCHICK IS RUINING THIS PLACE!
LOOK, I AGREE THINGS HAVE GOTTEN A LITTLE OUT OF HAND LATELY, BUT I'M GONNA TALK TO FONTAINE.
YEAH, WHAT'S WITH HIM?
HE SITS AROUND LIKE A ZOMBIE LATELY, WHILE HIS STUDIO'S GOING TO POT!
WELL FRED'S BEEN HAVING SOME PROBLEMS AT HOME LATELY AND,...
YES. I'M SURE YOU KNOW ALL ABOUT THAT.
LOOK HERE! IF YOU'RE GOING TO BRING UP REBA AGAIN, HOW MANY TIMES DO I HAVE TO SAY IT?... ME AND HER ARE...
I'M SURE I'M NOT INTERESTED IN THE UPS AND DOWNS OF YOUR LITTLE AFFAIRS!

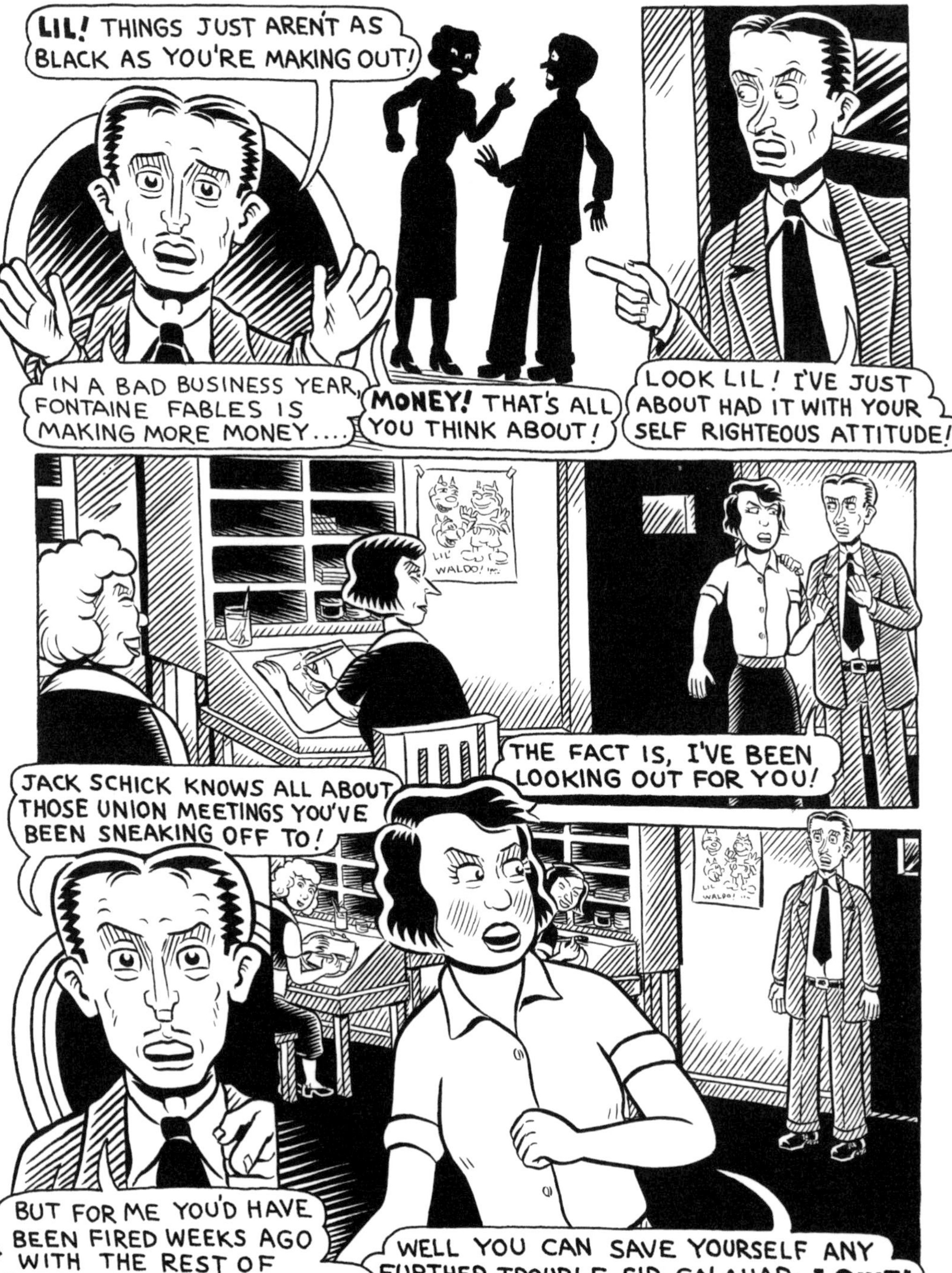
LIL! THINGS JUST AREN'T AS BLACK AS YOU'RE MAKING OUT!
IN A BAD BUSINESS YEAR, FONTAINE FABLES IS MAKING MORE MONEY....
MONEY! THAT'S ALL YOU THINK ABOUT!
LOOK LIL! I'VE JUST ABOUT HAD IT WITH YOUR SELF RIGHTEOUS ATTITUDE!
LIL' WALDO!
THE FACT IS, I'VE BEEN LOOKING OUT FOR YOU!
JACK SCHICK KNOWS ALL ABOUT THOSE UNION MEETINGS YOU'VE BEEN SNEAKING OFF TO!
BUT FOR ME YOU'D HAVE BEEN FIRED WEEKS AGO WITH THE REST OF THOSE TROUBLE MAKING REDS!
WELL YOU CAN SAVE YOURSELF ANY FURTHER TROUBLE, SIR GALAHAD; I QUIT!

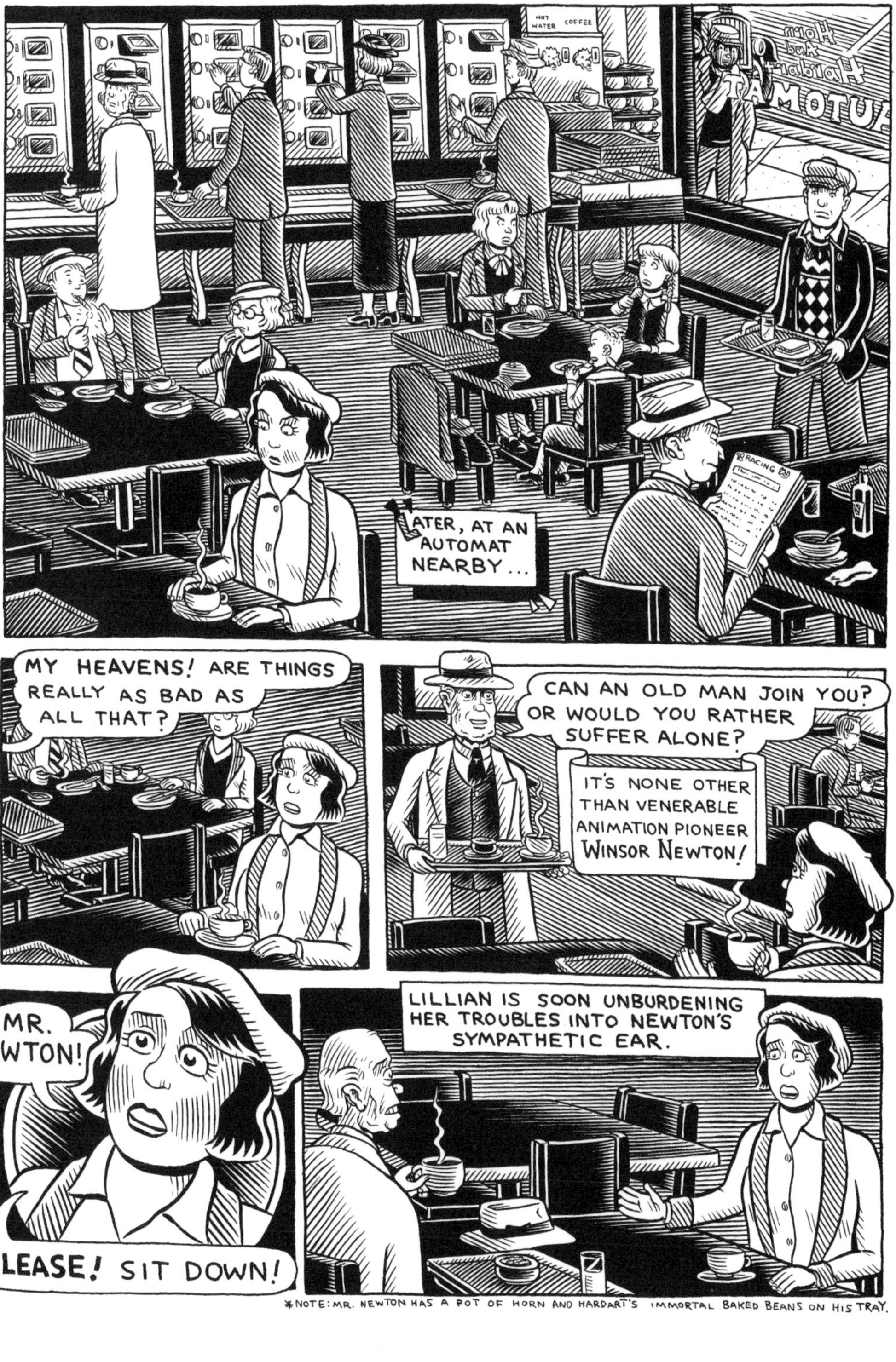
HOT WATER
COFFEE
RACING
LATER, AT AN AUTOMAT NEARBY...
MY HEAVENS! ARE THINGS REALLY AS BAD AS ALL THAT?
CAN AN OLD MAN JOIN YOU? OR WOULD YOU RATHER SUFFER ALONE?
IT'S NONE OTHER THAN VENERABLE ANIMATION PIONEER WINSOR NEWTON!
MR. NEWTON!
PLEASE! SIT DOWN!
LILLIAN IS SOON UNBURDENING HER TROUBLES INTO NEWTON'S SYMPATHETIC EAR.

*NOTE: MR. NEWTON HAS A POT OF HORN AND HARDART'S IMMORTAL BAKED BEANS ON HIS TRAY.

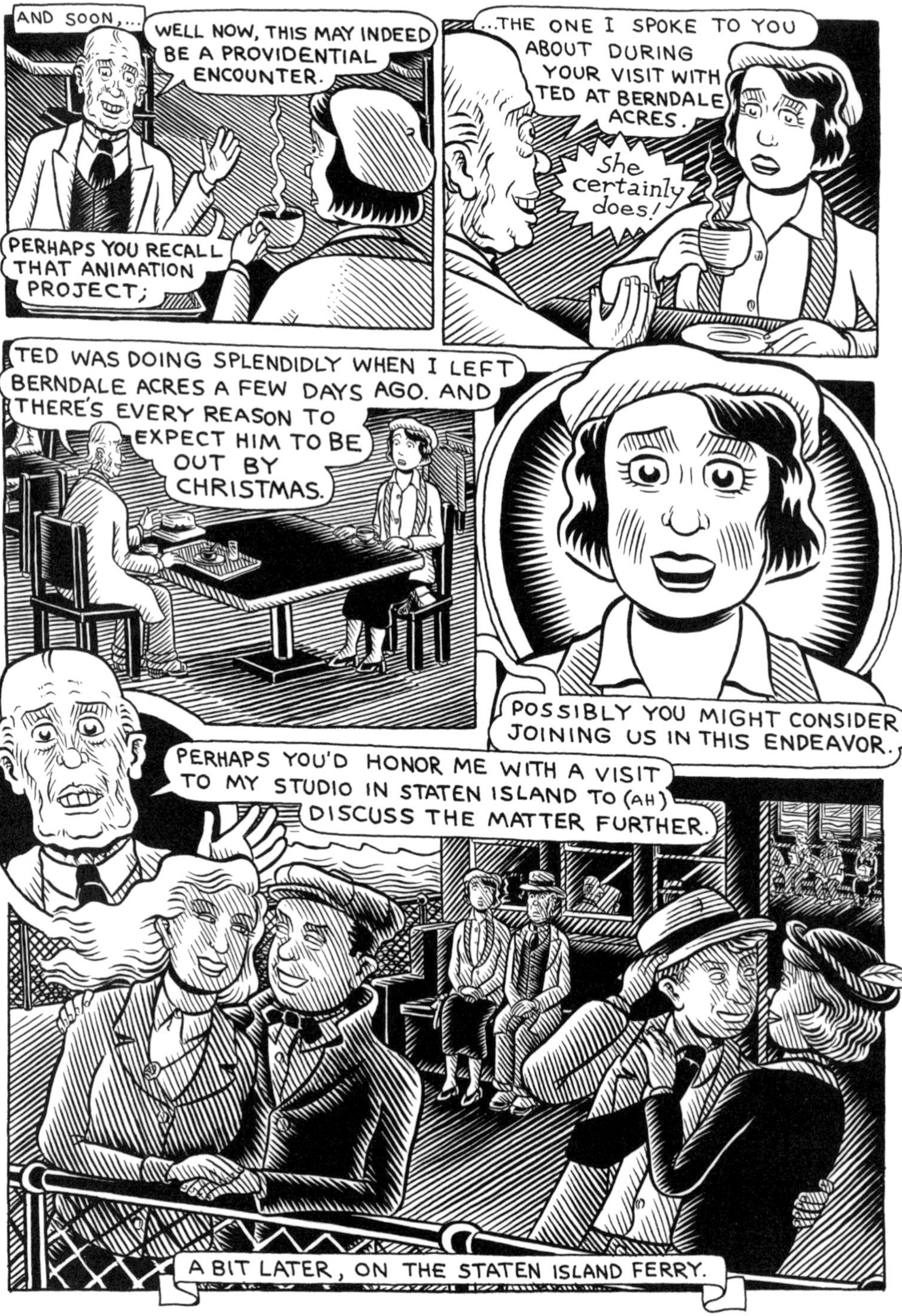
AND SOON,...
WELL NOW, THIS MAY INDEED BE A PROVIDENTIAL ENCOUNTER.
PERHAPS YOU RECALL THAT ANIMATION PROJECT;
...THE ONE I SPOKE TO YOU ABOUT DURING YOUR VISIT WITH TED AT BERNDALE ACRES.
She certainly does!
TED WAS DOING SPLENDIDLY WHEN I LEFT BERNDALE ACRES A FEW DAYS AGO. AND THERE'S EVERY REASON TO EXPECT HIM TO BE OUT BY CHRISTMAS.
POSSIBLY YOU MIGHT CONSIDER JOINING US IN THIS ENDEAVOR.
PERHAPS YOU'D HONOR ME WITH A VISIT TO MY STUDIO IN STATEN ISLAND TO (AH) DISCUSS THE MATTER FURTHER.
A BIT LATER, ON THE STATEN ISLAND FERRY.

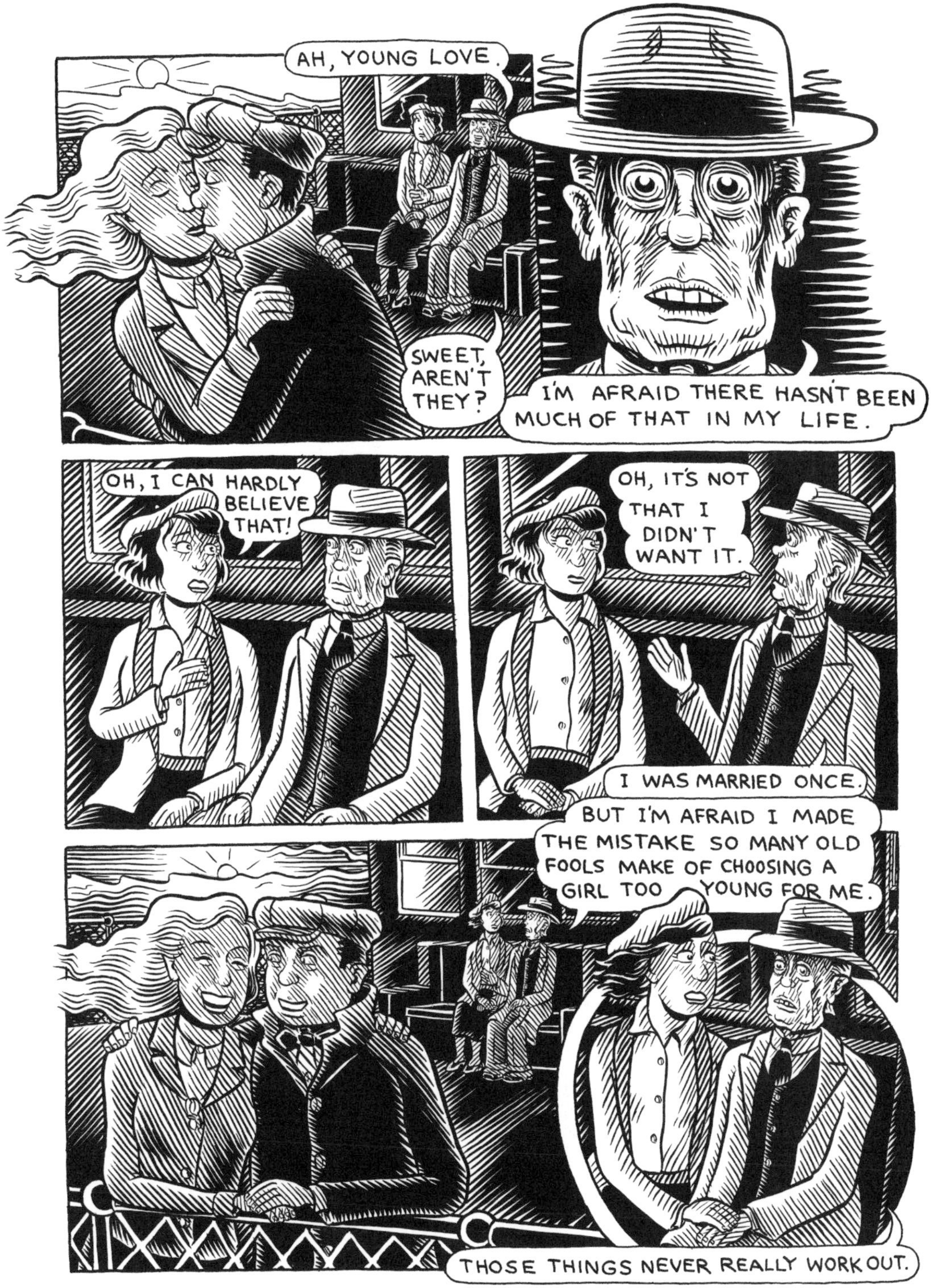

AH, YOUNG LOVE.
SWEET, AREN'T THEY?
I'M AFRAID THERE HASN'T BEEN MUCH OF THAT IN MY LIFE.
OH, I CAN HARDLY BELIEVE THAT!
OH, IT'S NOT THAT I DIDN'T WANT IT.
I WAS MARRIED ONCE.
BUT I'M AFRAID I MADE THE MISTAKE SO MANY OLD FOOLS MAKE OF CHOOSING A GIRL TOO YOUNG FOR ME.
THOSE THINGS NEVER REALLY WORK OUT.

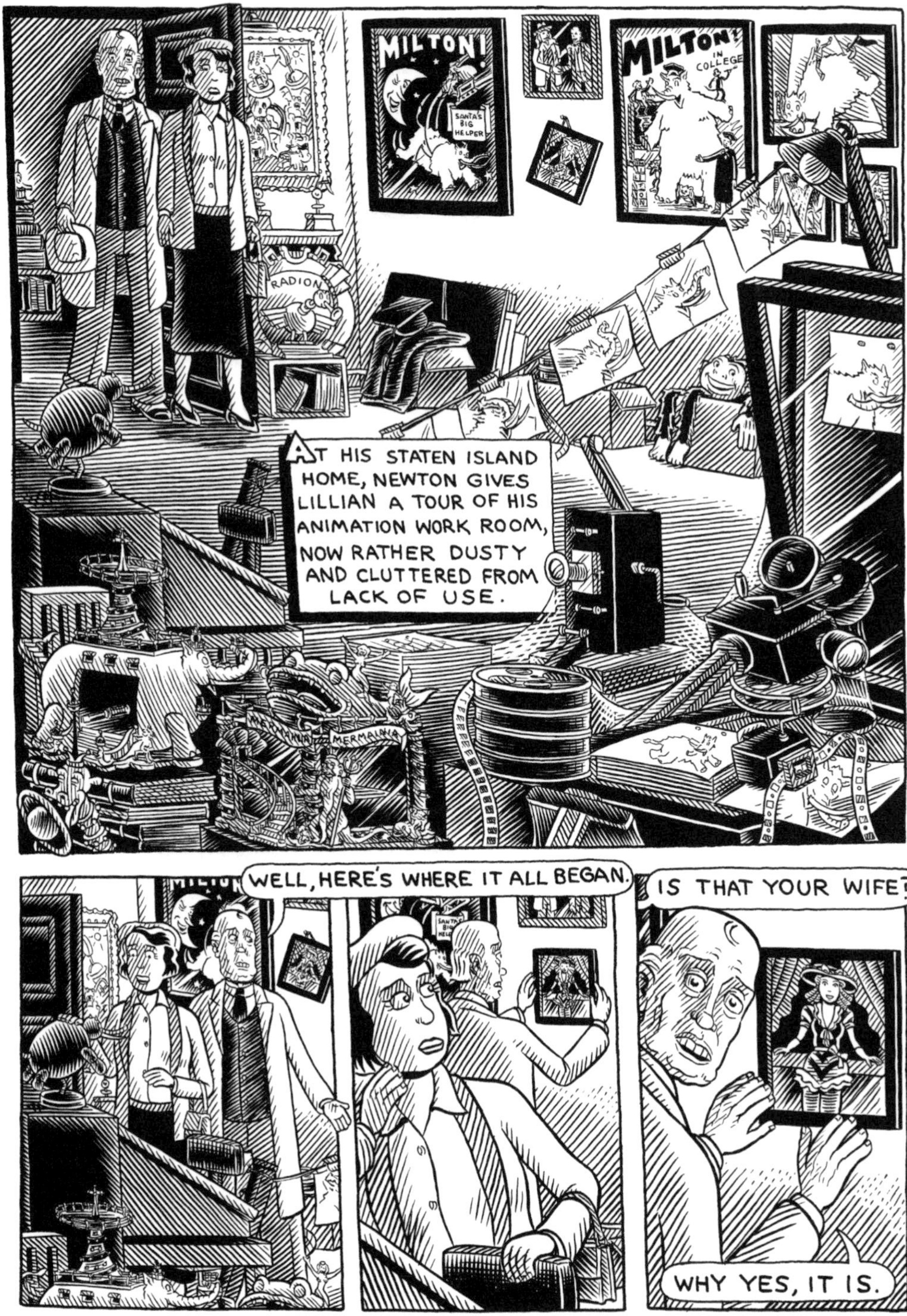
MILTON!
SANTA'S BIG HELPER
MILTON! IN COLLEGE
RADION
AT HIS STATEN ISLAND HOME, NEWTON GIVES LILLIAN A TOUR OF HIS ANIMATION WORK ROOM, NOW RATHER DUSTY AND CLUTTERED FROM LACK OF USE.
MERMAINIA
MERMAINIA
WELL, HERE'S WHERE IT ALL BEGAN.
IS THAT YOUR WIFE?
WHY YES, IT IS.

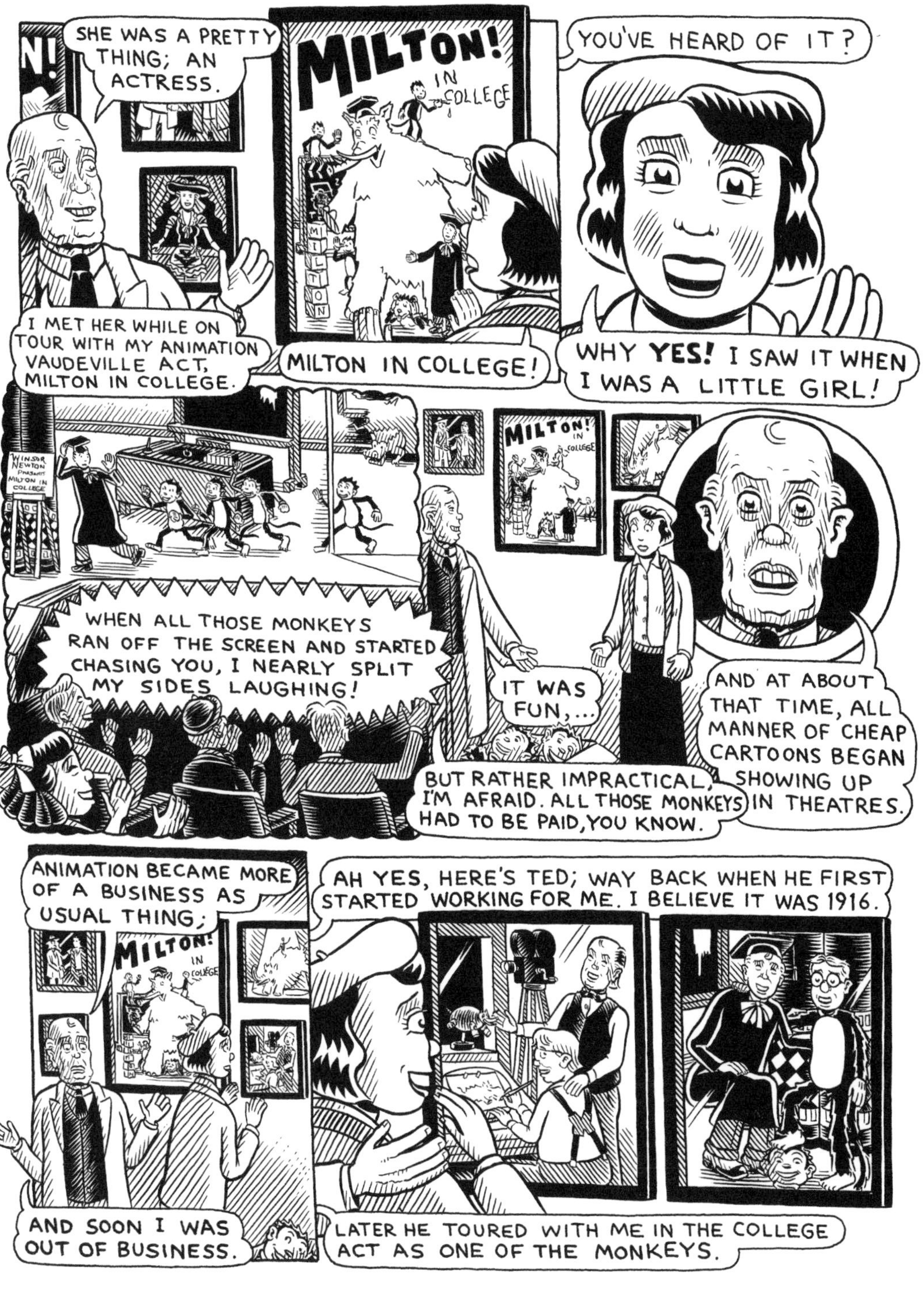
SHE WAS A PRETTY THING; AN ACTRESS.
I MET HER WHILE ON TOUR WITH MY ANIMATION VAUDEVILLE ACT, MILTON IN COLLEGE.
MILTON! IN COLLEGE
MILTON IN COLLEGE!
YOU'VE HEARD OF IT?
WHY YES! I SAW IT WHEN I WAS A LITTLE GIRL!
WINSOR NEWTON PRESENTS MILTON IN COLLEGE
WHEN ALL THOSE MONKEYS RAN OFF THE SCREEN AND STARTED CHASING YOU, I NEARLY SPLIT MY SIDES LAUGHING!
MILTON! IN COLLEGE
IT WAS FUN, ...
BUT RATHER IMPRACTICAL, I'M AFRAID. ALL THOSE MONKEYS HAD TO BE PAID, YOU KNOW.
AND AT ABOUT THAT TIME, ALL MANNER OF CHEAP CARTOONS BEGAN SHOWING UP IN THEATRES.
ANIMATION BECAME MORE OF A BUSINESS AS USUAL THING;
MILTON! IN COLLEGE
AND SOON I WAS OUT OF BUSINESS.
AH YES, HERE'S TED; WAY BACK WHEN HE FIRST STARTED WORKING FOR ME. I BELIEVE IT WAS 1916.
LATER HE TOURED WITH ME IN THE COLLEGE ACT AS ONE OF THE MONKEYS.

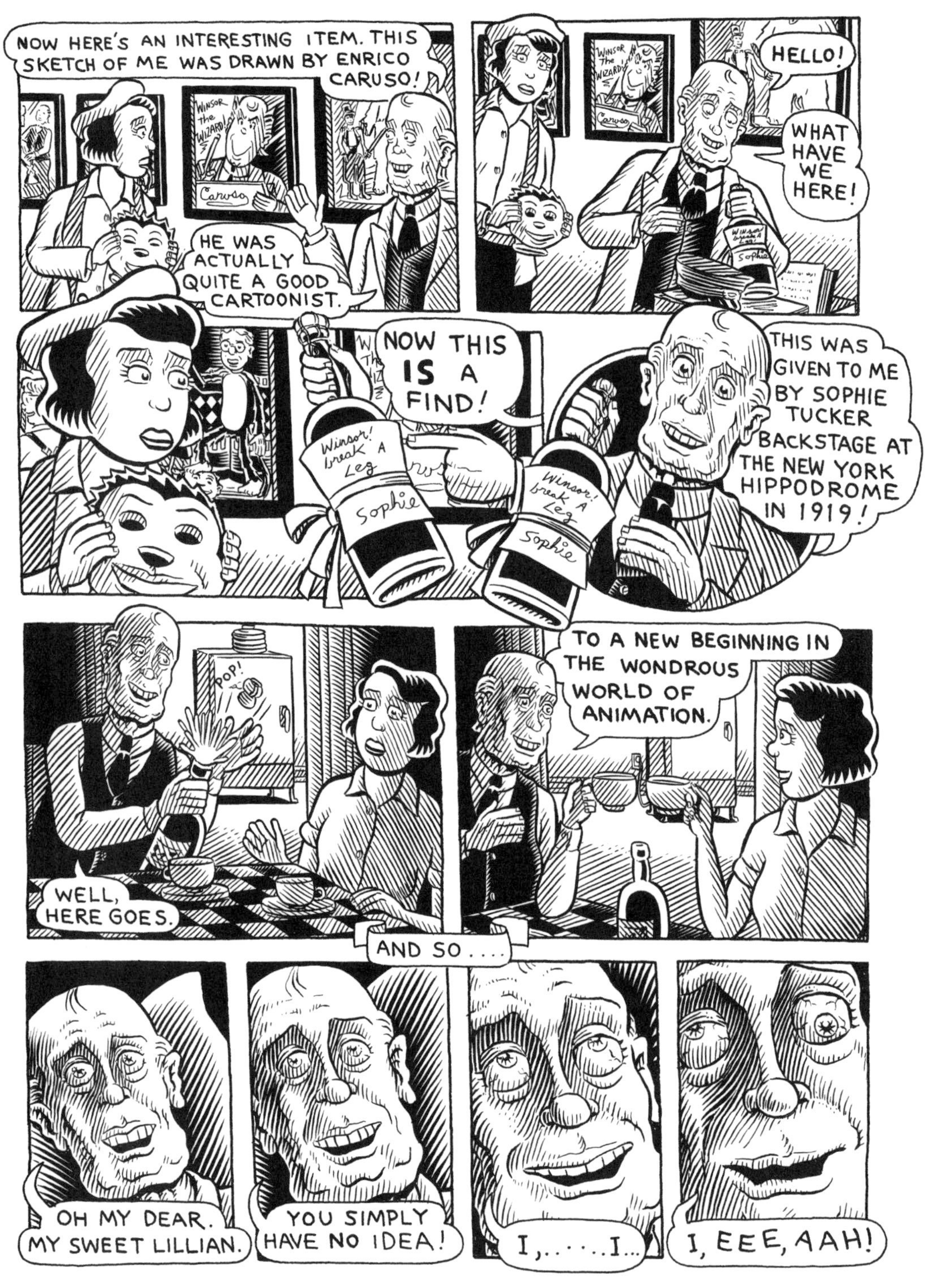
NOW HERE'S AN INTERESTING ITEM. THIS SKETCH OF ME WAS DRAWN BY ENRICO CARUSO!
WINSOR the WIZARD!
CARUSO
HE WAS ACTUALLY QUITE A GOOD CARTOONIST.
HELLO!
WHAT HAVE WE HERE!
NOW THIS **IS** A FIND!
Winsor! break A Leg
Sophie
THIS WAS GIVEN TO ME BY SOPHIE TUCKER BACKSTAGE AT THE NEW YORK HIPPODROME IN 1919!
POP!
WELL, HERE GOES.
TO A NEW BEGINNING IN THE WONDROUS WORLD OF ANIMATION.
AND SO....
OH MY DEAR. MY SWEET LILLIAN.
YOU SIMPLY HAVE NO IDEA!
I,.....I...
I, EEE, AAH!

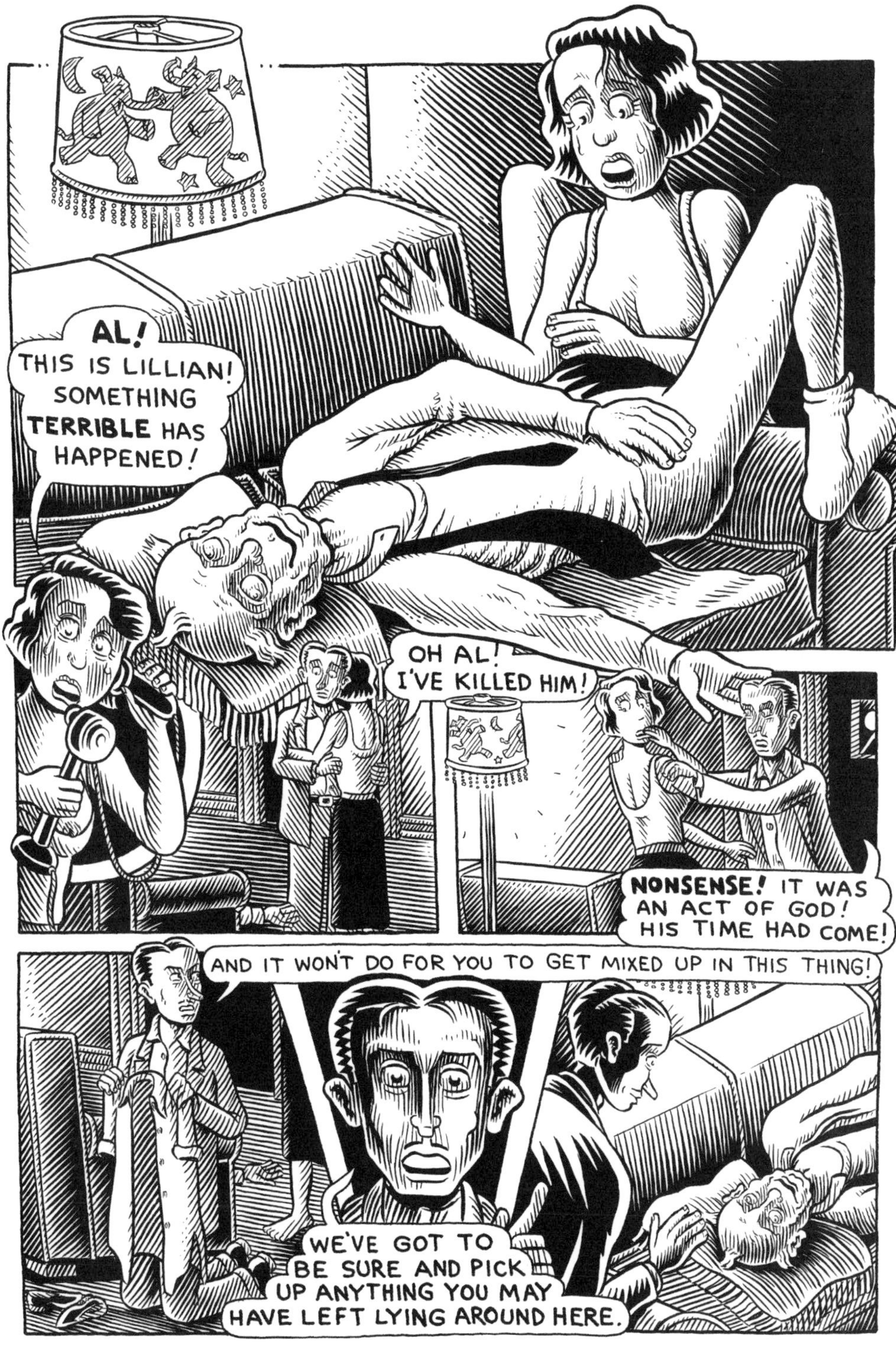
AL! THIS IS LILLIAN! SOMETHING TERRIBLE HAS HAPPENED!
OH AL! I'VE KILLED HIM!
NONSENSE! IT WAS AN ACT OF GOD! HIS TIME HAD COME!
AND IT WON'T DO FOR YOU TO GET MIXED UP IN THIS THING!
WE'VE GOT TO BE SURE AND PICK UP ANYTHING YOU MAY HAVE LEFT LYING AROUND HERE.

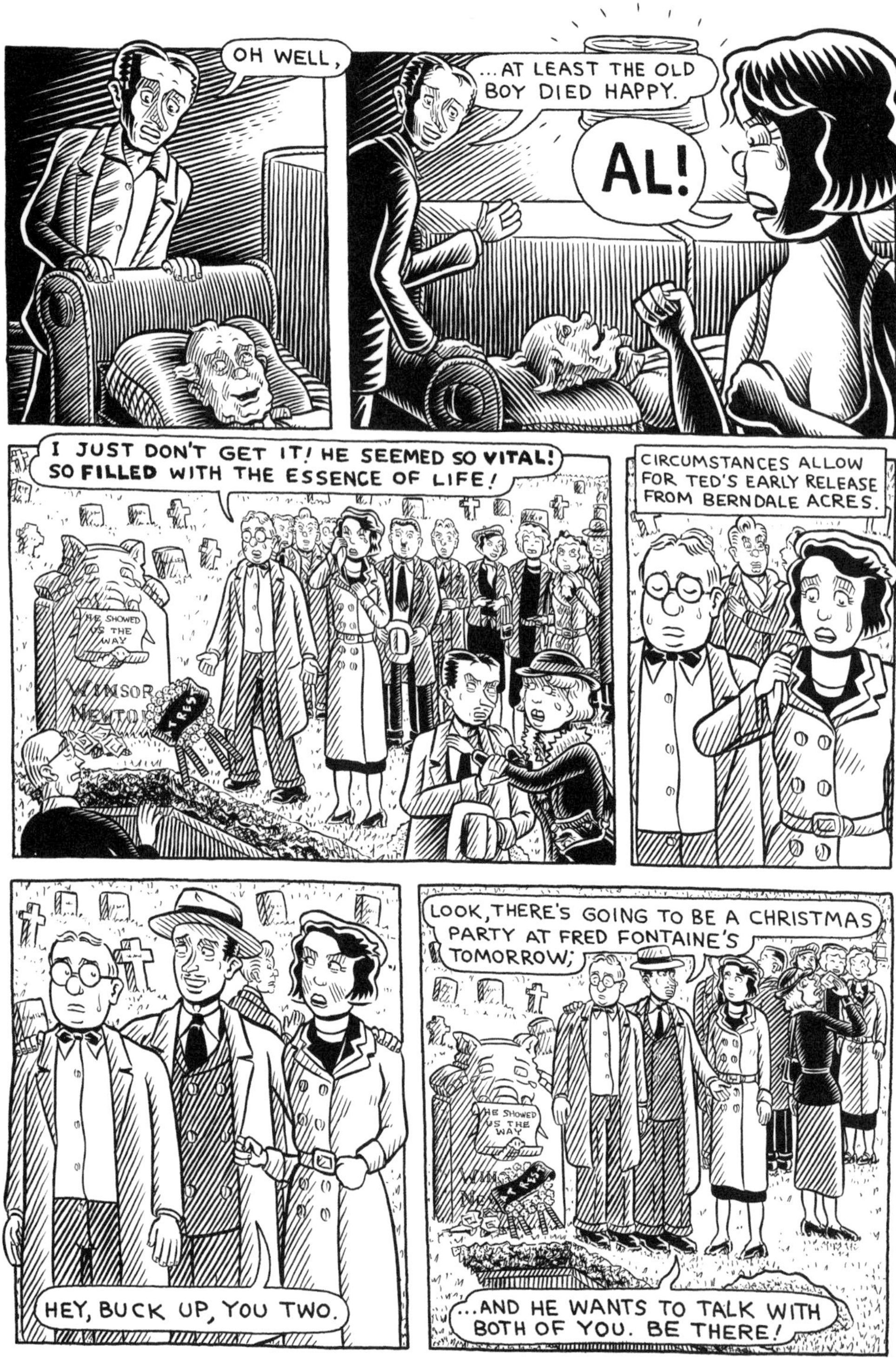
OH WELL,
...AT LEAST THE OLD BOY DIED HAPPY.
AL!
I JUST DON'T GET IT! HE SEEMED SO VITAL! SO FILLED WITH THE ESSENCE OF LIFE!
HE SHOWED US THE WAY
WINSOR NEWTON
TRES
CIRCUMSTANCES ALLOW FOR TED'S EARLY RELEASE FROM BERNDALE ACRES.
HEY, BUCK UP, YOU TWO.
LOOK, THERE'S GOING TO BE A CHRISTMAS PARTY AT FRED FONTAINE'S TOMORROW;
...AND HE WANTS TO TALK WITH BOTH OF YOU. BE THERE!

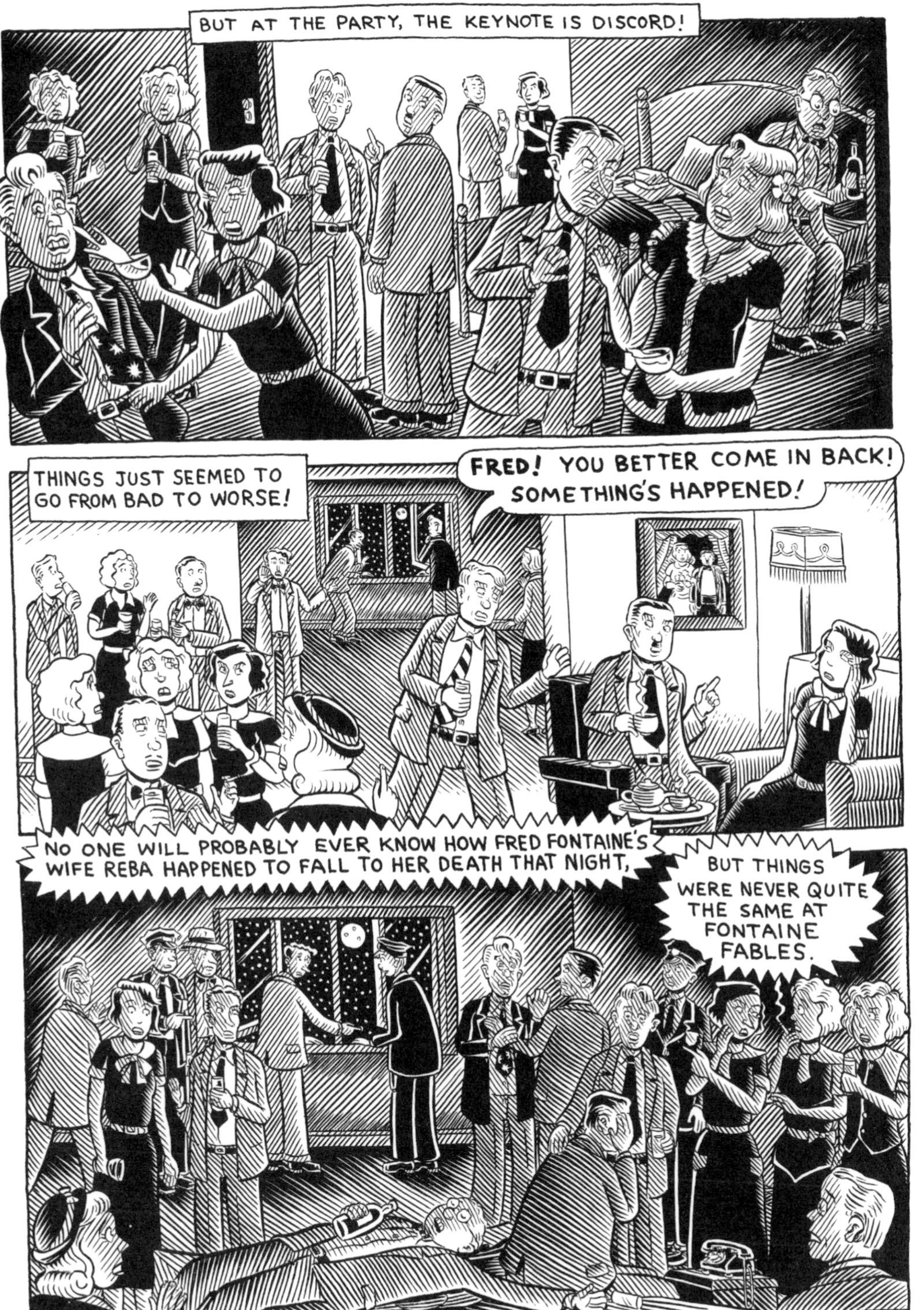
BUT AT THE PARTY, THE KEYNOTE IS DISCORD!
THINGS JUST SEEMED TO GO FROM BAD TO WORSE!
FRED! YOU BETTER COME IN BACK! SOMETHING'S HAPPENED!
NO ONE WILL PROBABLY EVER KNOW HOW FRED FONTAINE'S WIFE REBA HAPPENED TO FALL TO HER DEATH THAT NIGHT,
BUT THINGS WERE NEVER QUITE THE SAME AT FONTAINE FABLES.

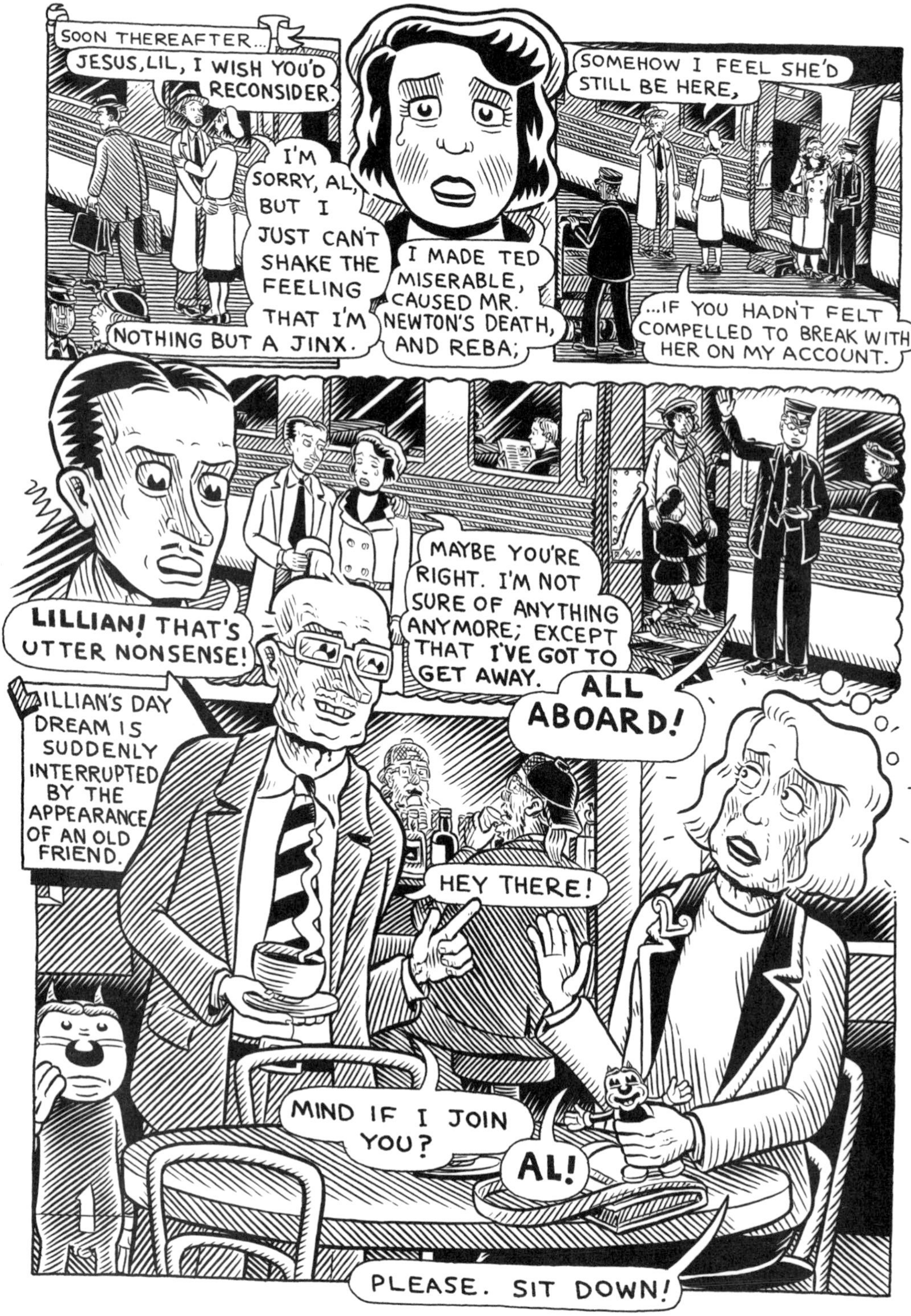
SOON THEREAFTER...
JESUS, LIL, I WISH YOU'D RECONSIDER.
I'M SORRY, AL, BUT I JUST CAN'T SHAKE THE FEELING THAT I'M NOTHING BUT A JINX.
I MADE TED MISERABLE, CAUSED MR. NEWTON'S DEATH, AND REBA;
SOMEHOW I FEEL SHE'D STILL BE HERE,
...IF YOU HADN'T FELT COMPELLED TO BREAK WITH HER ON MY ACCOUNT.
LILLIAN! THAT'S UTTER NONSENSE!
MAYBE YOU'RE RIGHT. I'M NOT SURE OF ANYTHING ANYMORE; EXCEPT THAT I'VE GOT TO GET AWAY.
ALL ABOARD!
LILLIAN'S DAY DREAM IS SUDDENLY INTERRUPTED BY THE APPEARANCE OF AN OLD FRIEND.
HEY THERE!
MIND IF I JOIN YOU?
AL!
PLEASE. SIT DOWN!

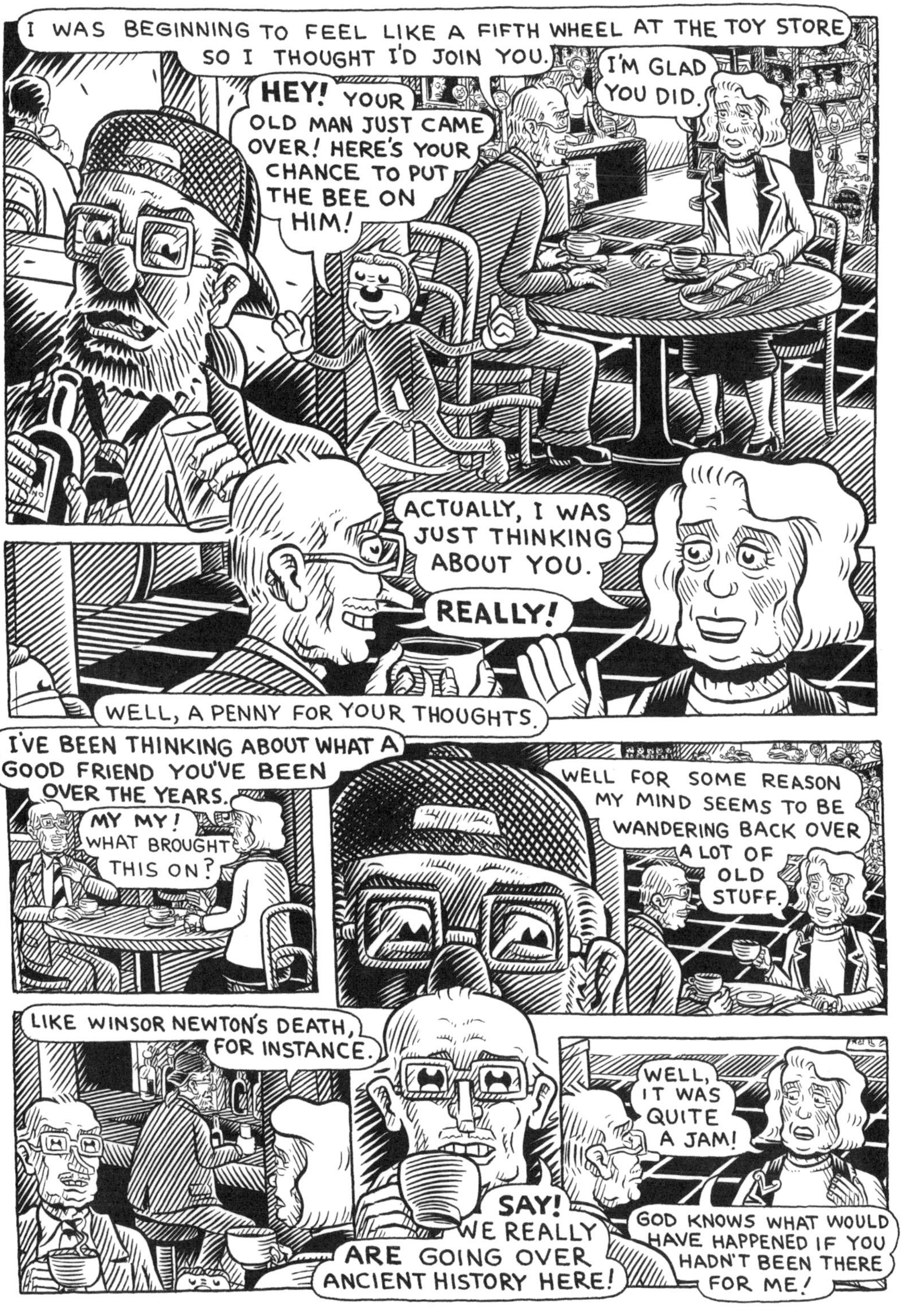
I WAS BEGINNING TO FEEL LIKE A FIFTH WHEEL AT THE TOY STORE SO I THOUGHT I'D JOIN YOU.
I'M GLAD YOU DID.
HEY! YOUR OLD MAN JUST CAME OVER! HERE'S YOUR CHANCE TO PUT THE BEE ON HIM!
ACTUALLY, I WAS JUST THINKING ABOUT YOU.
REALLY!
WELL, A PENNY FOR YOUR THOUGHTS.
I'VE BEEN THINKING ABOUT WHAT A GOOD FRIEND YOU'VE BEEN OVER THE YEARS.
MY MY! WHAT BROUGHT THIS ON?
WELL FOR SOME REASON MY MIND SEEMS TO BE WANDERING BACK OVER A LOT OF OLD STUFF.
LIKE WINSOR NEWTON'S DEATH, FOR INSTANCE.
WELL, IT WAS QUITE A JAM!
GOD KNOWS WHAT WOULD HAVE HAPPENED IF YOU HADN'T BEEN THERE FOR ME!
SAY! WE REALLY ARE GOING OVER ANCIENT HISTORY HERE!

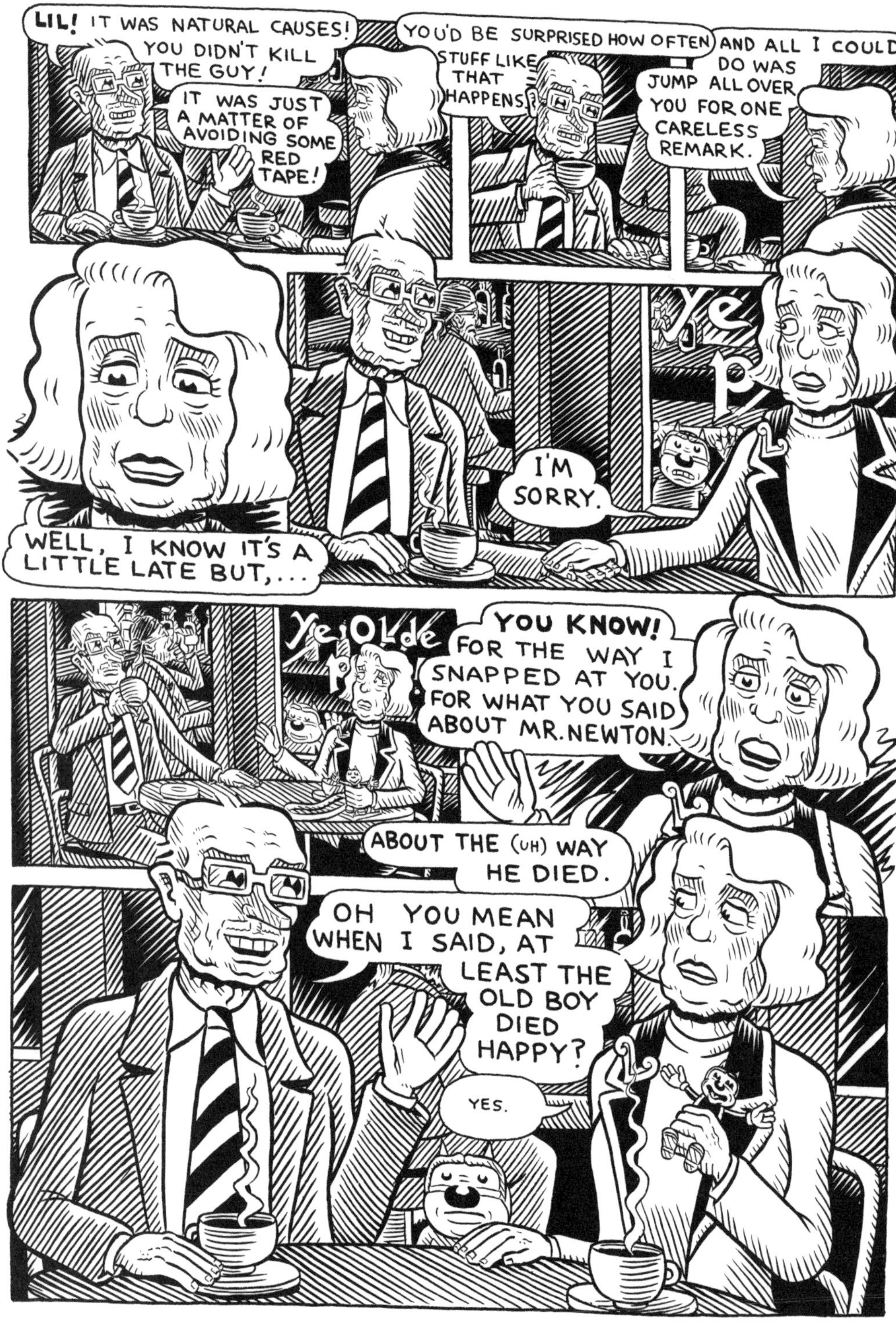
LIL! IT WAS NATURAL CAUSES! YOU DIDN'T KILL THE GUY!
IT WAS JUST A MATTER OF AVOIDING SOME RED TAPE!
YOU'D BE SURPRISED HOW OFTEN STUFF LIKE THAT HAPPENS.
AND ALL I COULD DO WAS JUMP ALL OVER YOU FOR ONE CARELESS REMARK.
WELL, I KNOW IT'S A LITTLE LATE BUT,...
I'M SORRY.
Ye Olde
YOU KNOW! FOR THE WAY I SNAPPED AT YOU. FOR WHAT YOU SAID ABOUT MR. NEWTON.
ABOUT THE (UH) WAY HE DIED.
OH YOU MEAN WHEN I SAID, AT LEAST THE OLD BOY DIED HAPPY?
YES.

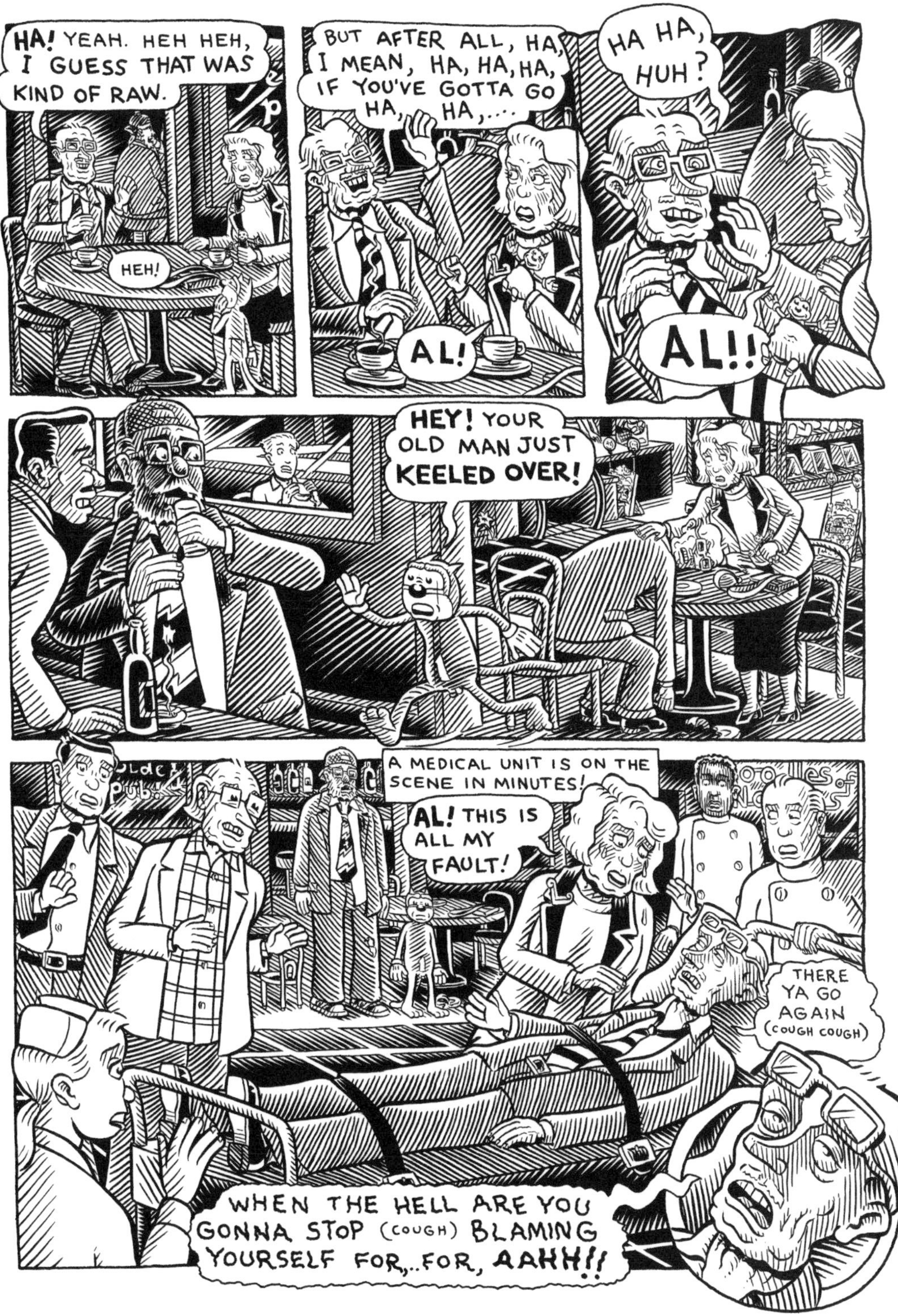
HA! YEAH. HEH HEH, I GUESS THAT WAS KIND OF RAW.
HEH!
BUT AFTER ALL, HA, I MEAN, HA, HA, HA, IF YOU'VE GOTTA GO HA, HA, ...
AL!
HA HA, HUH?
AL!!
HEY! YOUR OLD MAN JUST KEELED OVER!
A MEDICAL UNIT IS ON THE SCENE IN MINUTES!
AL! THIS IS ALL MY FAULT!
THERE YA GO AGAIN (COUGH COUGH)
WHEN THE HELL ARE YOU GONNA STOP (COUGH) BLAMING YOURSELF FOR,..FOR, AAHH!!

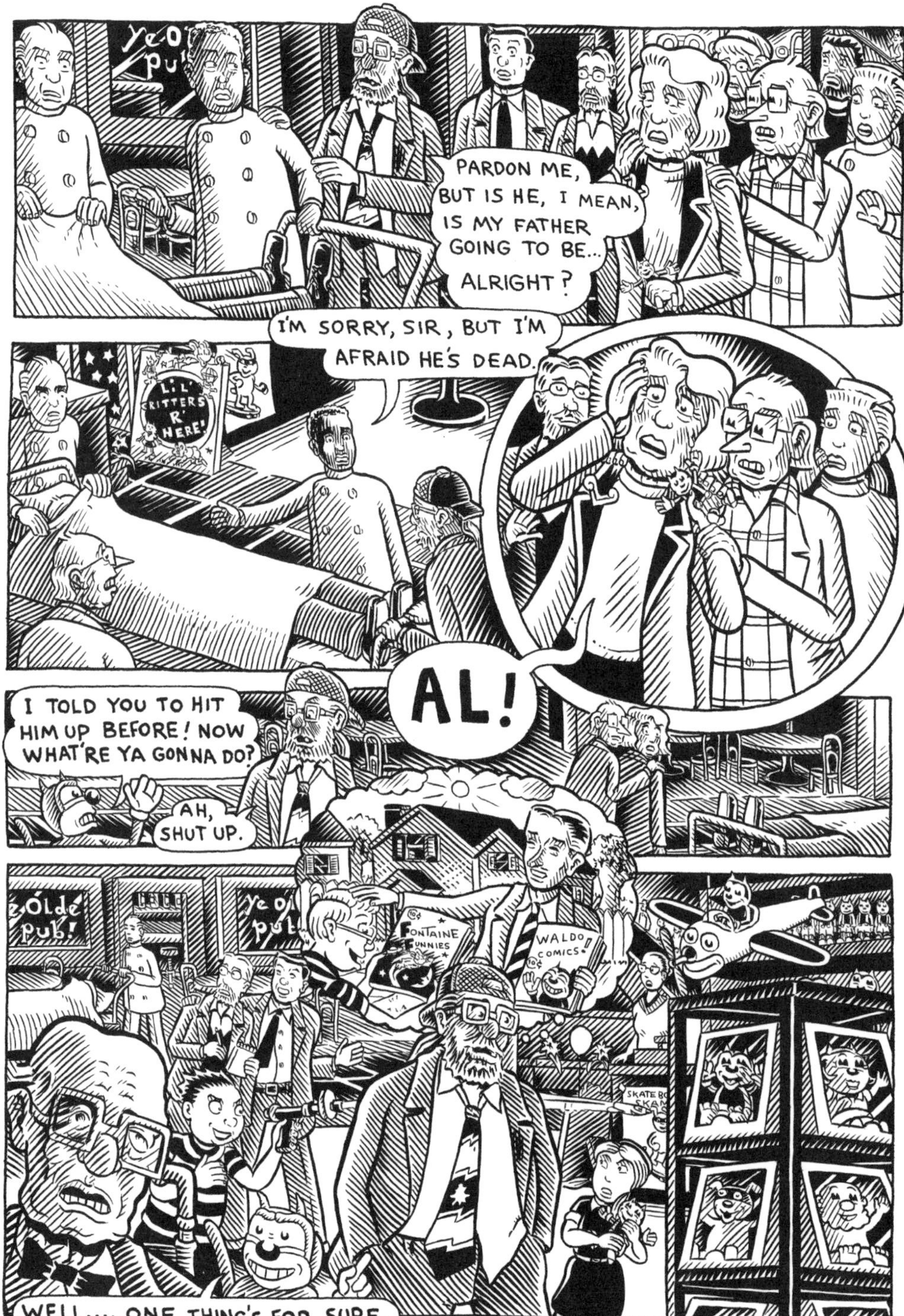

ye Olde pub
PARDON ME, BUT IS HE, I MEAN, IS MY FATHER GOING TO BE... ALRIGHT?
I'M SORRY, SIR, BUT I'M AFRAID HE'S DEAD.
LI'L CRITTERS R' HERE!
AL!
I TOLD YOU TO HIT HIM UP BEFORE! NOW WHAT'RE YA GONNA DO?
AH, SHUT UP.
ye Olde pub!
FONTAINE FUNNIES
WALDO COMICS!
WELL,.... ONE THING'S FOR SURE,

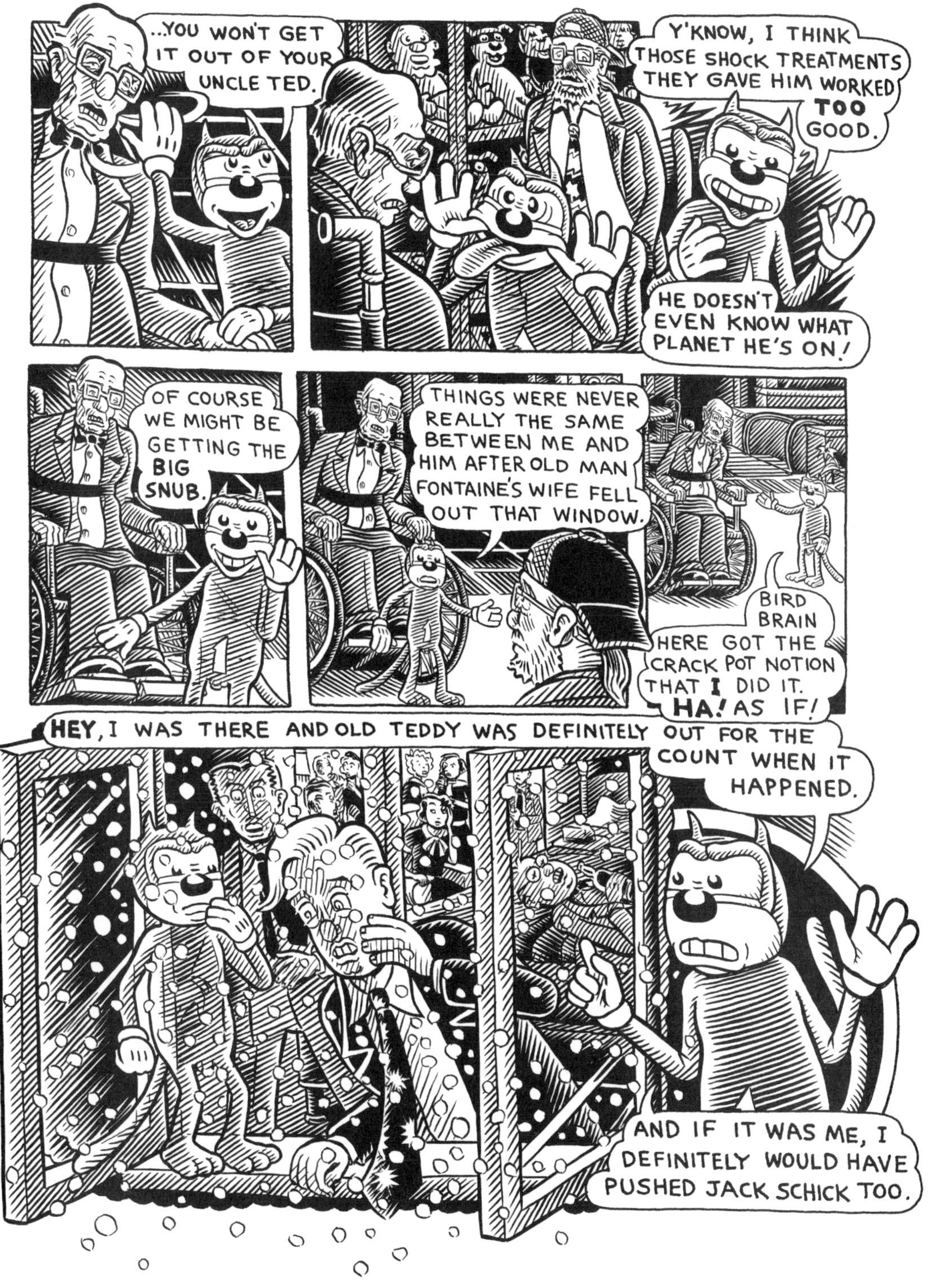
...YOU WON'T GET IT OUT OF YOUR UNCLE TED.
Y'KNOW, I THINK THOSE SHOCK TREATMENTS THEY GAVE HIM WORKED **TOO** GOOD.
HE DOESN'T EVEN KNOW WHAT PLANET HE'S ON!
OF COURSE WE MIGHT BE GETTING THE **BIG** SNUB.
THINGS WERE NEVER REALLY THE SAME BETWEEN ME AND HIM AFTER OLD MAN FONTAINE'S WIFE FELL OUT THAT WINDOW.
BIRD BRAIN HERE GOT THE CRACK POT NOTION THAT **I** DID IT. **HA!** AS IF!
HEY, I WAS THERE AND OLD TEDDY WAS DEFINITELY OUT FOR THE COUNT WHEN IT HAPPENED.
AND IF IT WAS ME, I DEFINITELY WOULD HAVE PUSHED JACK SCHICK TOO.

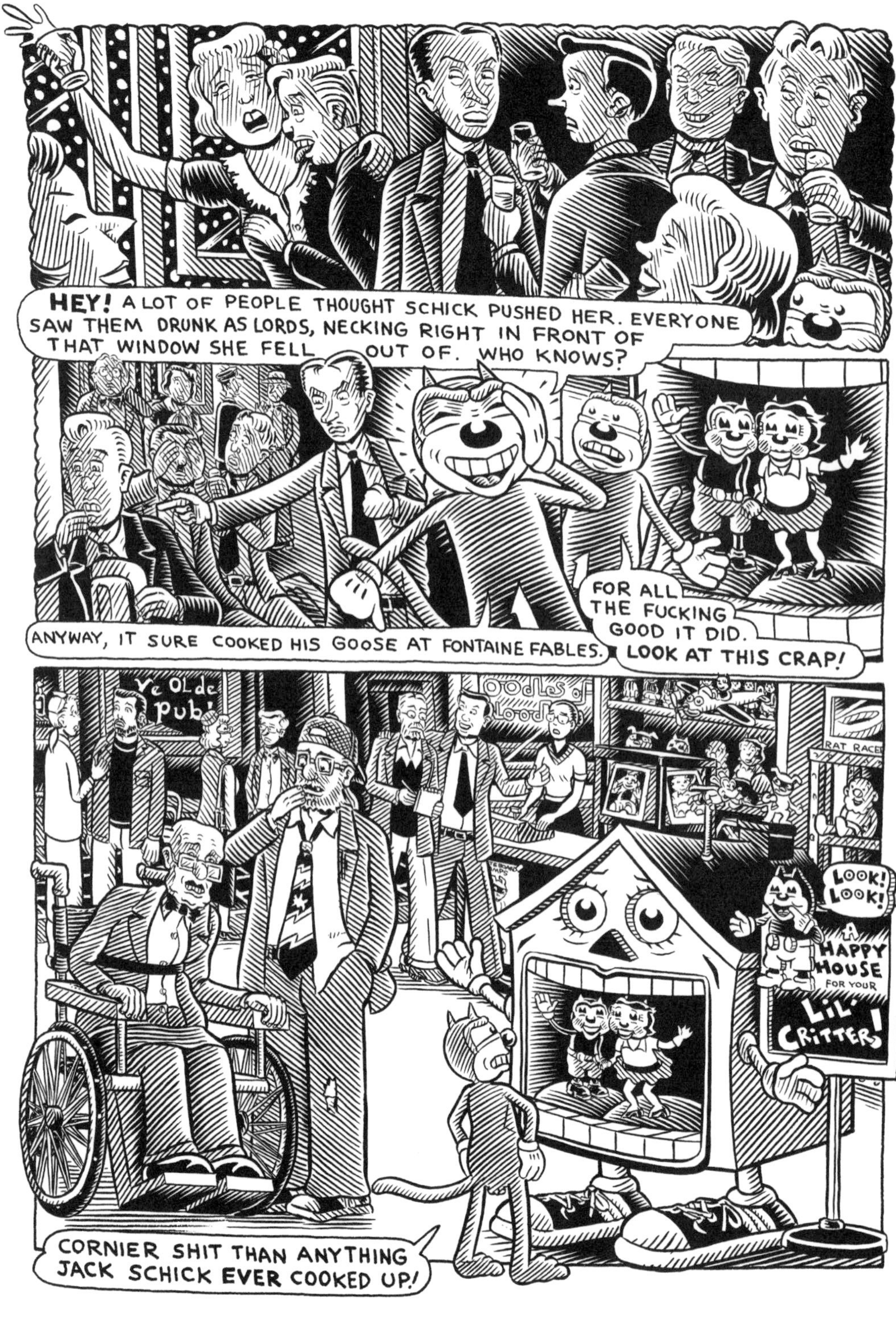
HEY! A LOT OF PEOPLE THOUGHT SCHICK PUSHED HER. EVERYONE SAW THEM DRUNK AS LORDS, NECKING RIGHT IN FRONT OF THAT WINDOW SHE FELL OUT OF. WHO KNOWS?
ANYWAY, IT SURE COOKED HIS GOOSE AT FONTAINE FABLES.
FOR ALL THE FUCKING GOOD IT DID. LOOK AT THIS CRAP!
Ye OLde Pub
RAT RACE
LOOK! LOOK!
A HAPPY HOUSE FOR YOUR LIL' CRITTER!
CORNIER SHIT THAN ANYTHING JACK SCHICK EVER COOKED UP!

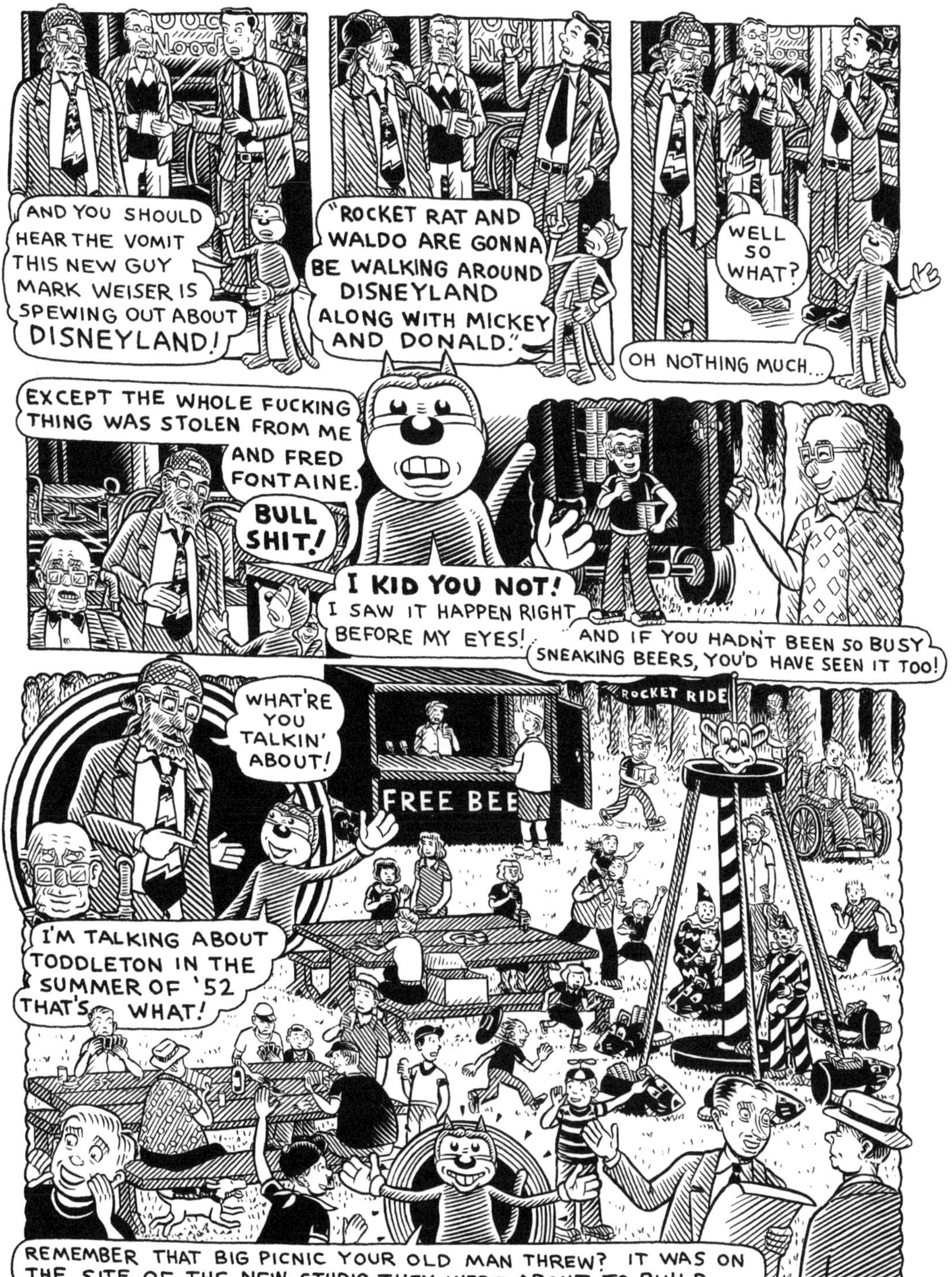
AND YOU SHOULD HEAR THE VOMIT THIS NEW GUY MARK WEISER IS SPEWING OUT ABOUT DISNEYLAND!
"ROCKET RAT AND WALDO ARE GONNA BE WALKING AROUND DISNEYLAND ALONG WITH MICKEY AND DONALD."
WELL SO WHAT?
OH NOTHING MUCH...
EXCEPT THE WHOLE FUCKING THING WAS STOLEN FROM ME AND FRED FONTAINE.
BULL SHIT!
I KID YOU NOT! I SAW IT HAPPEN RIGHT BEFORE MY EYES!...
...AND IF YOU HADN'T BEEN SO BUSY SNEAKING BEERS, YOU'D HAVE SEEN IT TOO!
WHAT'RE YOU TALKIN' ABOUT!
FREE BEE
ROCKET RIDE
I'M TALKING ABOUT TODDLETON IN THE SUMMER OF '52 THAT'S WHAT!
REMEMBER THAT BIG PICNIC YOUR OLD MAN THREW? IT WAS ON THE SITE OF THE NEW STUDIO THEY WERE ABOUT TO BUILD.

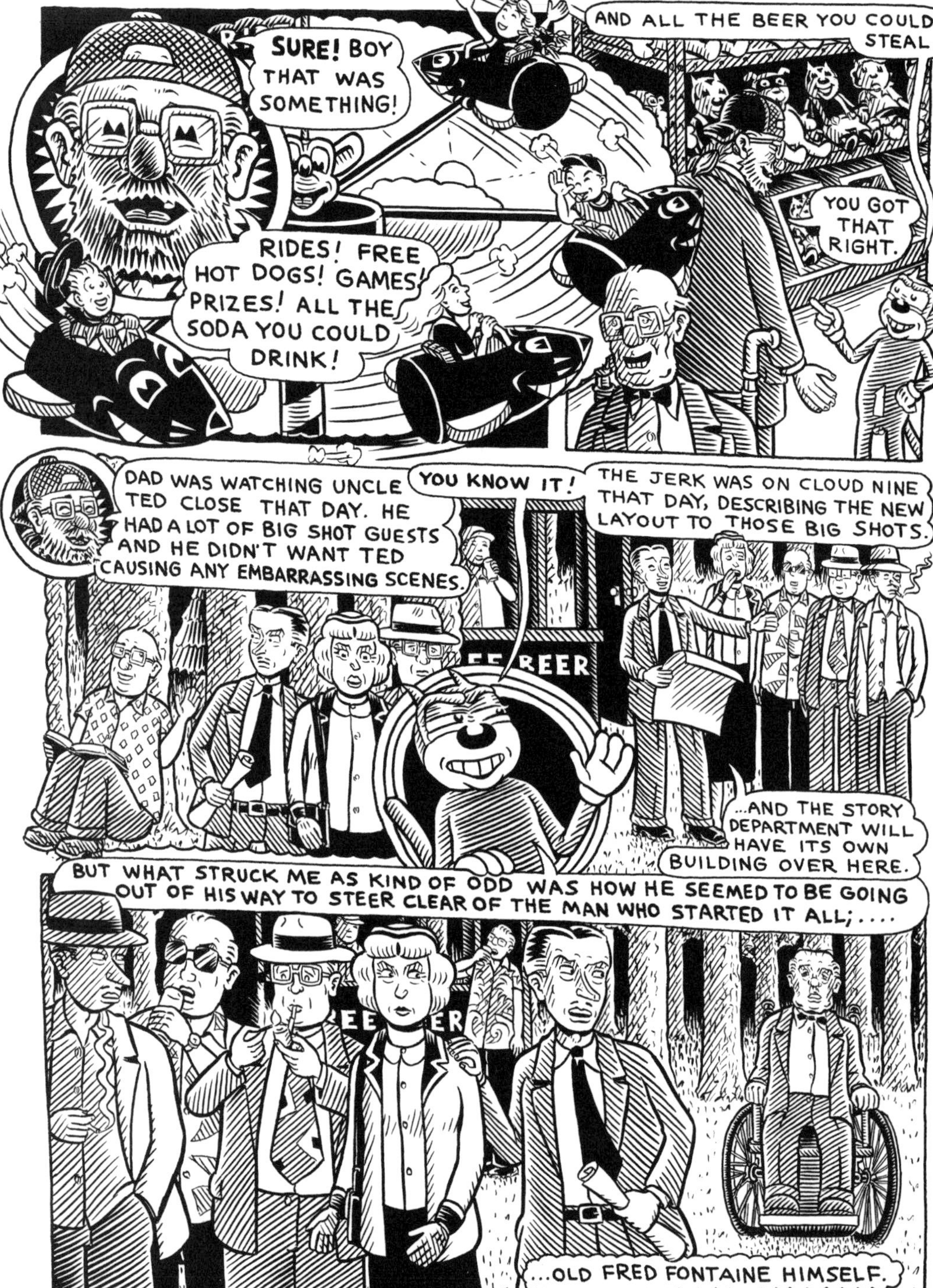
SURE! BOY THAT WAS SOMETHING!
RIDES! FREE HOT DOGS! GAMES! PRIZES! ALL THE SODA YOU COULD DRINK!
AND ALL THE BEER YOU COULD STEAL.
YOU GOT THAT RIGHT.
DAD WAS WATCHING UNCLE TED CLOSE THAT DAY. HE HAD A LOT OF BIG SHOT GUESTS AND HE DIDN'T WANT TED CAUSING ANY EMBARRASSING SCENES.
YOU KNOW IT!
THE JERK WAS ON CLOUD NINE THAT DAY, DESCRIBING THE NEW LAYOUT TO THOSE BIG SHOTS.
BEER
...AND THE STORY DEPARTMENT WILL HAVE ITS OWN BUILDING OVER HERE.
BUT WHAT STRUCK ME AS KIND OF ODD WAS HOW HE SEEMED TO BE GOING OUT OF HIS WAY TO STEER CLEAR OF THE MAN WHO STARTED IT ALL; . . . .
...OLD FRED FONTAINE HIMSELF.

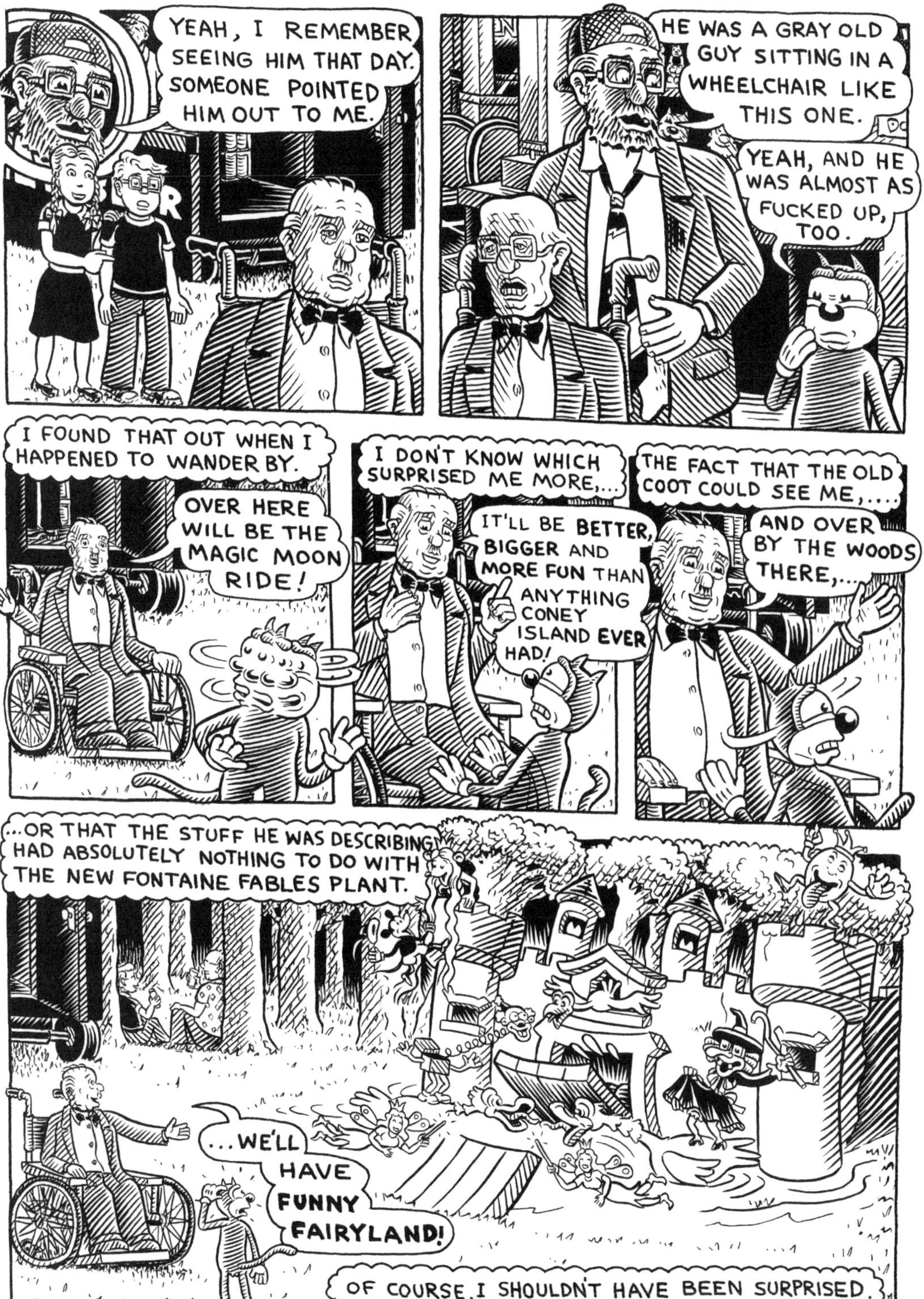
YEAH, I REMEMBER SEEING HIM THAT DAY. SOMEONE POINTED HIM OUT TO ME.
HE WAS A GRAY OLD GUY SITTING IN A WHEELCHAIR LIKE THIS ONE.
YEAH, AND HE WAS ALMOST AS FUCKED UP, TOO.
I FOUND THAT OUT WHEN I HAPPENED TO WANDER BY.
OVER HERE WILL BE THE MAGIC MOON RIDE!
I DON'T KNOW WHICH SURPRISED ME MORE,...
IT'LL BE BETTER, BIGGER AND MORE FUN THAN ANYTHING CONEY ISLAND EVER HAD!
THE FACT THAT THE OLD COOT COULD SEE ME,...
AND OVER BY THE WOODS THERE,...
...OR THAT THE STUFF HE WAS DESCRIBING HAD ABSOLUTELY NOTHING TO DO WITH THE NEW FONTAINE FABLES PLANT.
...WE'LL HAVE FUNNY FAIRYLAND!
OF COURSE, I SHOULDN'T HAVE BEEN SURPRISED.

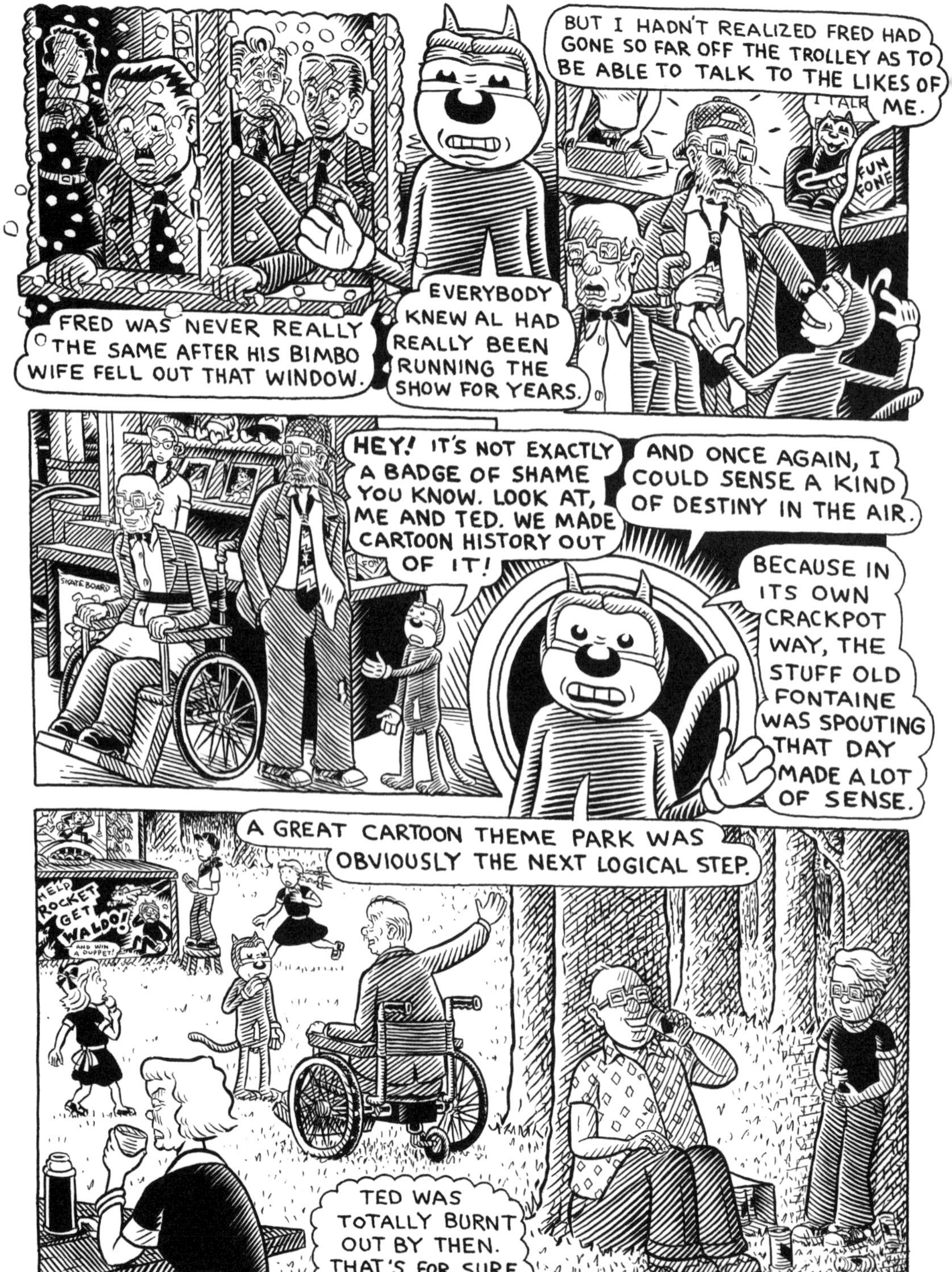
FRED WAS NEVER REALLY THE SAME AFTER HIS BIMBO WIFE FELL OUT THAT WINDOW.
EVERYBODY KNEW AL HAD REALLY BEEN RUNNING THE SHOW FOR YEARS.
BUT I HADN'T REALIZED FRED HAD GONE SO FAR OFF THE TROLLEY AS TO BE ABLE TO TALK TO THE LIKES OF ME.
FUN FONE
HEY! IT'S NOT EXACTLY A BADGE OF SHAME YOU KNOW. LOOK AT, ME AND TED. WE MADE CARTOON HISTORY OUT OF IT!
AND ONCE AGAIN, I COULD SENSE A KIND OF DESTINY IN THE AIR.
BECAUSE IN ITS OWN CRACKPOT WAY, THE STUFF OLD FONTAINE WAS SPOUTING THAT DAY MADE A LOT OF SENSE.
A GREAT CARTOON THEME PARK WAS OBVIOUSLY THE NEXT LOGICAL STEP.
HELP ROCKET GET WALDO!
AND WIN A PUPPET!
TED WAS TOTALLY BURNT OUT BY THEN. THAT'S FOR SURE.

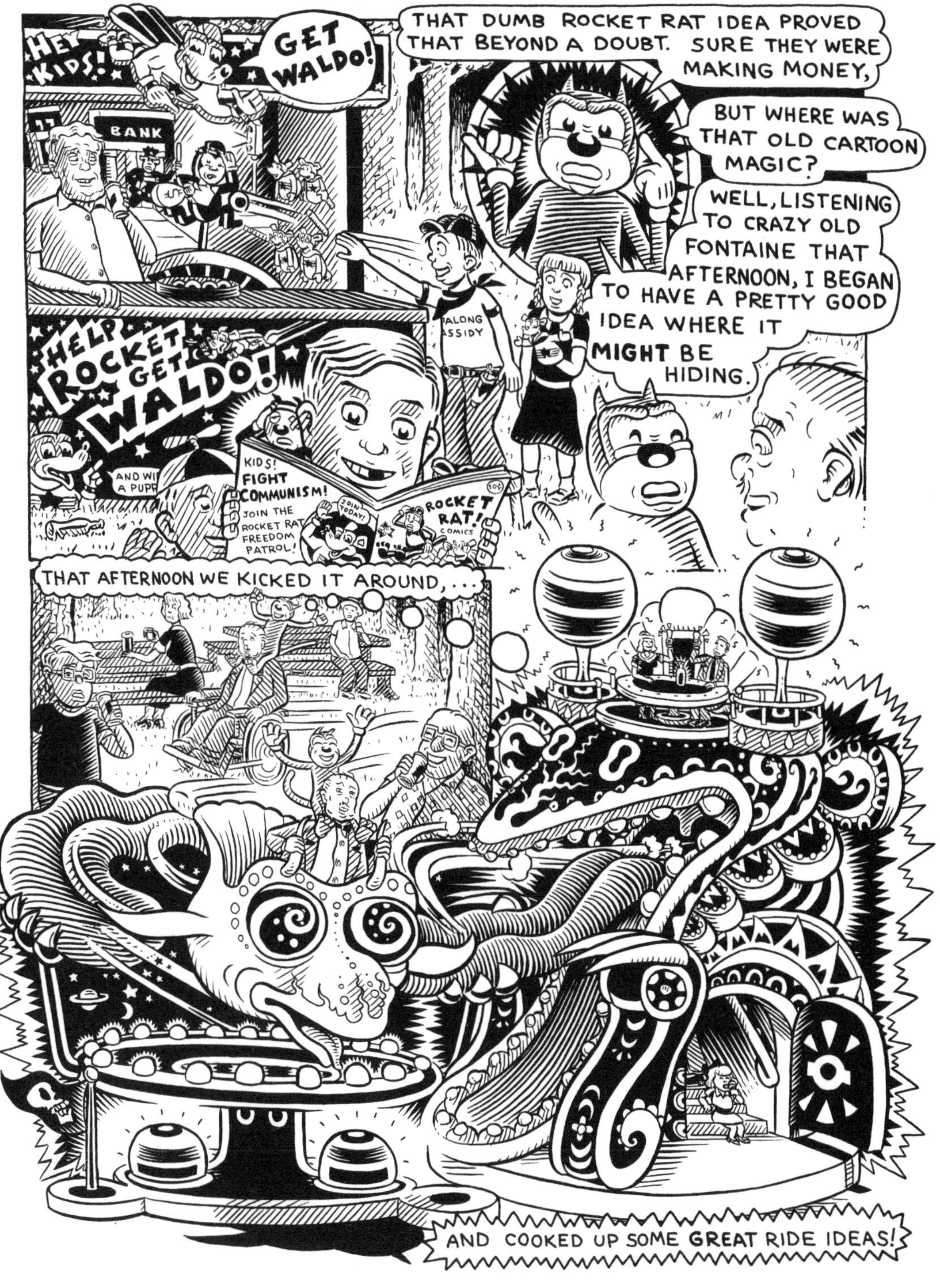
HEY KIDS!
GET WALDO!
BANK
THAT DUMB ROCKET RAT IDEA PROVED THAT BEYOND A DOUBT. SURE THEY WERE MAKING MONEY,
BUT WHERE WAS THAT OLD CARTOON MAGIC?
WELL, LISTENING TO CRAZY OLD FONTAINE THAT AFTERNOON, I BEGAN TO HAVE A PRETTY GOOD IDEA WHERE IT MIGHT BE HIDING.
HELP ROCKET GET WALDO!
KIDS! FIGHT COMMUNISM! JOIN THE ROCKET RAT FREEDOM PATROL!
JOIN TODAY!
ROCKET RAT! COMICS
10¢
THAT AFTERNOON WE KICKED IT AROUND, . . .
AND COOKED UP SOME GREAT RIDE IDEAS!

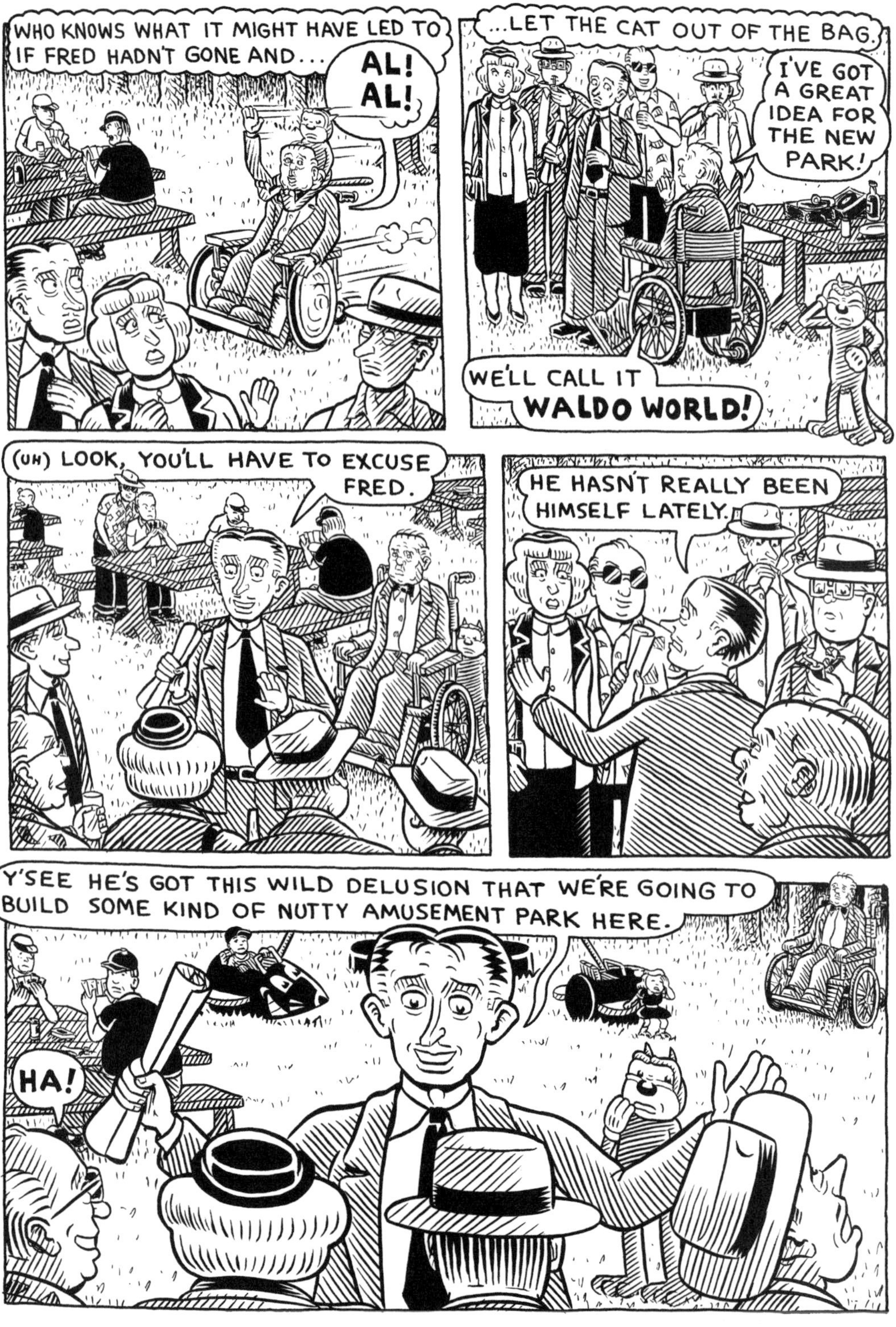
WHO KNOWS WHAT IT MIGHT HAVE LED TO IF FRED HADN'T GONE AND...
AL! AL!
...LET THE CAT OUT OF THE BAG.
I'VE GOT A GREAT IDEA FOR THE NEW PARK!
WE'LL CALL IT WALDO WORLD!
(UH) LOOK, YOU'LL HAVE TO EXCUSE FRED.
HE HASN'T REALLY BEEN HIMSELF LATELY.
Y'SEE HE'S GOT THIS WILD DELUSION THAT WE'RE GOING TO BUILD SOME KIND OF NUTTY AMUSEMENT PARK HERE.
HA!

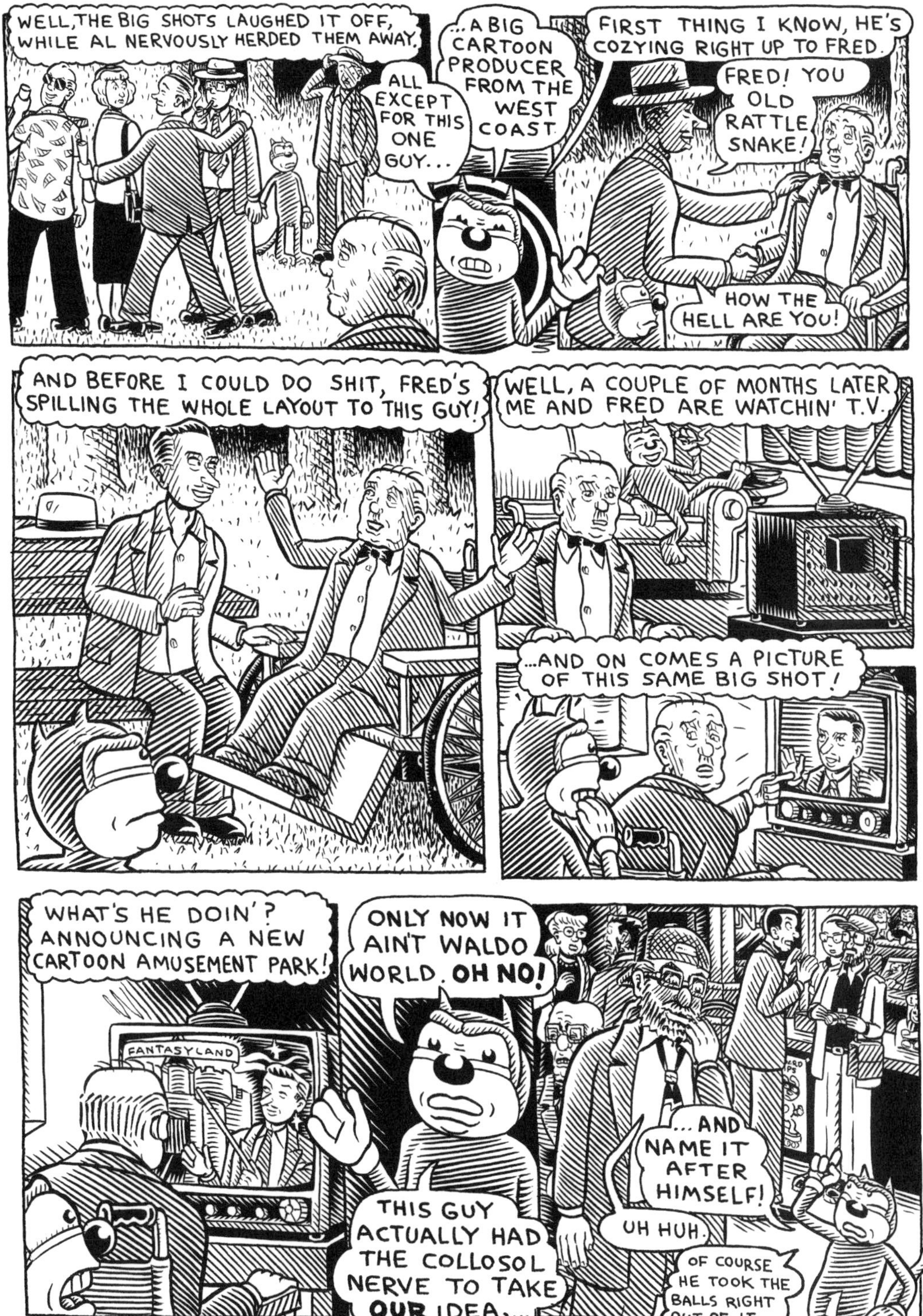
WELL, THE BIG SHOTS LAUGHED IT OFF, WHILE AL NERVOUSLY HERDED THEM AWAY.
ALL EXCEPT FOR THIS ONE GUY...
...A BIG CARTOON PRODUCER FROM THE WEST COAST.
FIRST THING I KNOW, HE'S COZYING RIGHT UP TO FRED.
FRED! YOU OLD RATTLE SNAKE!
HOW THE HELL ARE YOU!
AND BEFORE I COULD DO SHIT, FRED'S SPILLING THE WHOLE LAYOUT TO THIS GUY!
WELL, A COUPLE OF MONTHS LATER ME AND FRED ARE WATCHIN' T.V.
...AND ON COMES A PICTURE OF THIS SAME BIG SHOT!
WHAT'S HE DOIN'? ANNOUNCING A NEW CARTOON AMUSEMENT PARK!
FANTASYLAND
ONLY NOW IT AIN'T WALDO WORLD. OH NO!
THIS GUY ACTUALLY HAD THE COLLOSOL NERVE TO TAKE OUR IDEA,...
...AND NAME IT AFTER HIMSELF!
UH HUH.
OF COURSE HE TOOK THE BALLS RIGHT OUT OF IT.

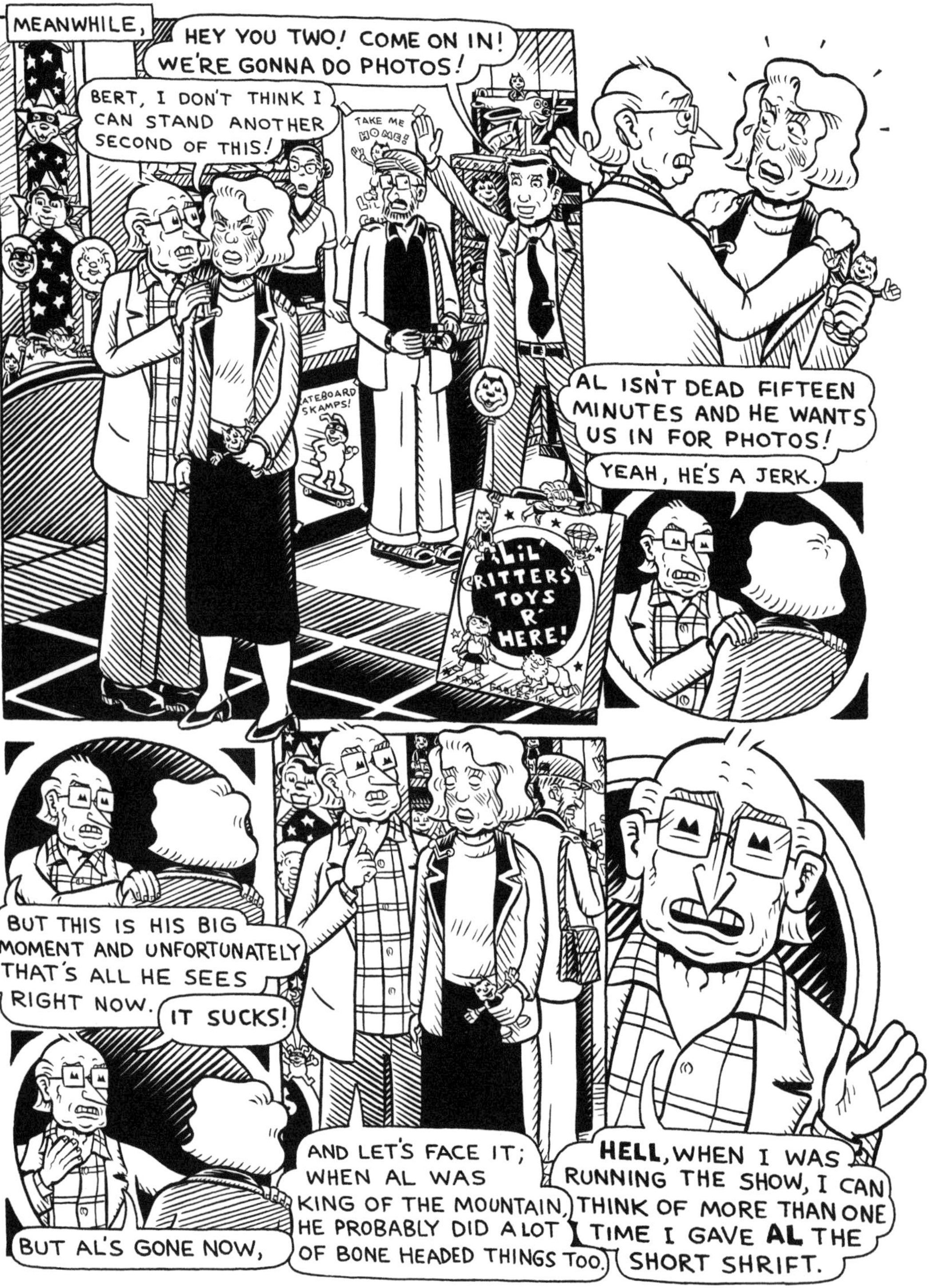
MEANWHILE,
HEY YOU TWO! COME ON IN! WE'RE GONNA DO PHOTOS!
BERT, I DON'T THINK I CAN STAND ANOTHER SECOND OF THIS!
TAKE ME HOME!
SKATEBOARD SKAMPS!
LIL' RITTERS TOYS R' HERE!
FROM FABLES INK
AL ISN'T DEAD FIFTEEN MINUTES AND HE WANTS US IN FOR PHOTOS!
YEAH, HE'S A JERK.
BUT THIS IS HIS BIG MOMENT AND UNFORTUNATELY THAT'S ALL HE SEES RIGHT NOW.
IT SUCKS!
BUT AL'S GONE NOW,
AND LET'S FACE IT; WHEN AL WAS KING OF THE MOUNTAIN, HE PROBABLY DID A LOT OF BONE HEADED THINGS TOO.
HELL, WHEN I WAS RUNNING THE SHOW, I CAN THINK OF MORE THAN ONE TIME I GAVE **AL** THE SHORT SHRIFT.

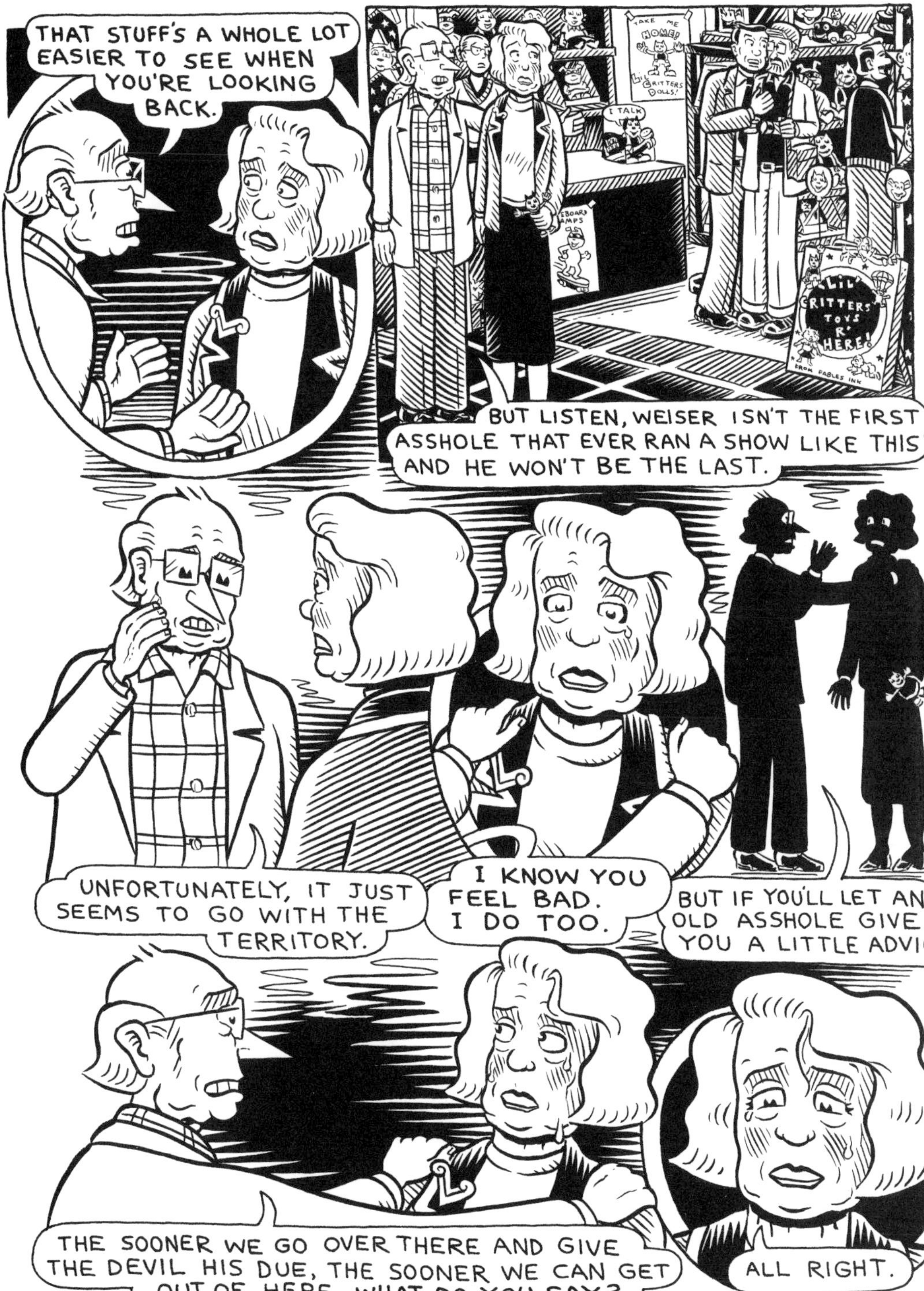
THAT STUFF'S A WHOLE LOT EASIER TO SEE WHEN YOU'RE LOOKING BACK.
TAKE ME HOME! LIL' CRITTERS DOLLS!
I TALK
LIL' CRITTERS TOYS R' HERE!
FROM FABLES INK
BUT LISTEN, WEISER ISN'T THE FIRST ASSHOLE THAT EVER RAN A SHOW LIKE THIS AND HE WON'T BE THE LAST.
UNFORTUNATELY, IT JUST SEEMS TO GO WITH THE TERRITORY.
I KNOW YOU FEEL BAD. I DO TOO.
BUT IF YOU'LL LET AN OLD ASSHOLE GIVE YOU A LITTLE ADVICE,
THE SOONER WE GO OVER THERE AND GIVE THE DEVIL HIS DUE, THE SOONER WE CAN GET OUT OF HERE. WHAT DO YOU SAY?
ALL RIGHT.

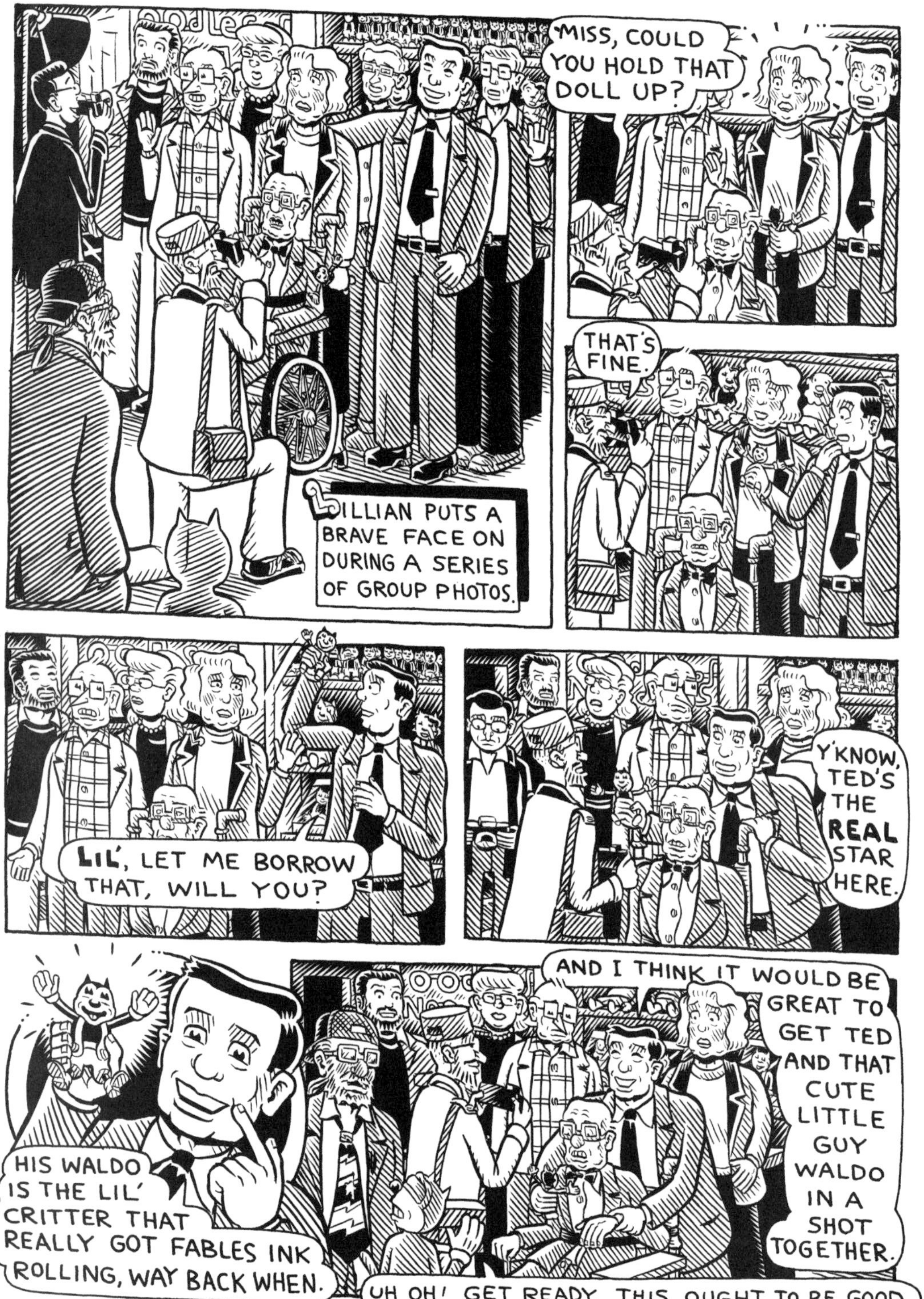
LILLIAN PUTS A BRAVE FACE ON DURING A SERIES OF GROUP PHOTOS.
MISS, COULD YOU HOLD THAT DOLL UP?
THAT'S FINE.
LIL', LET ME BORROW THAT, WILL YOU?
Y'KNOW, TED'S THE REAL STAR HERE.
HIS WALDO IS THE LIL' CRITTER THAT REALLY GOT FABLES INK ROLLING, WAY BACK WHEN.
AND I THINK IT WOULD BE GREAT TO GET TED AND THAT CUTE LITTLE GUY WALDO IN A SHOT TOGETHER.
UH OH! GET READY, THIS OUGHT TO BE GOOD.

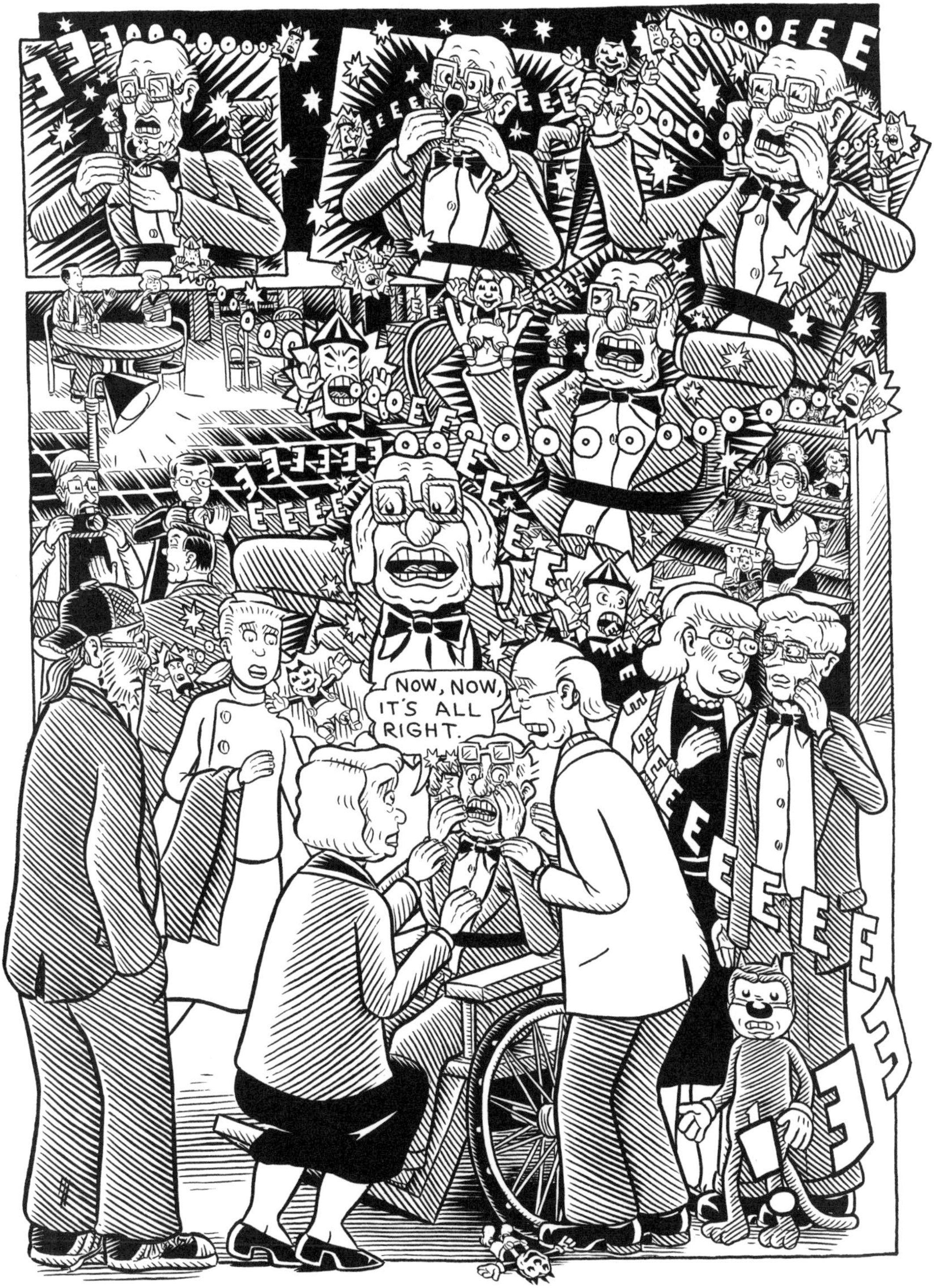
I TALK
NOW, NOW, IT'S ALL RIGHT.

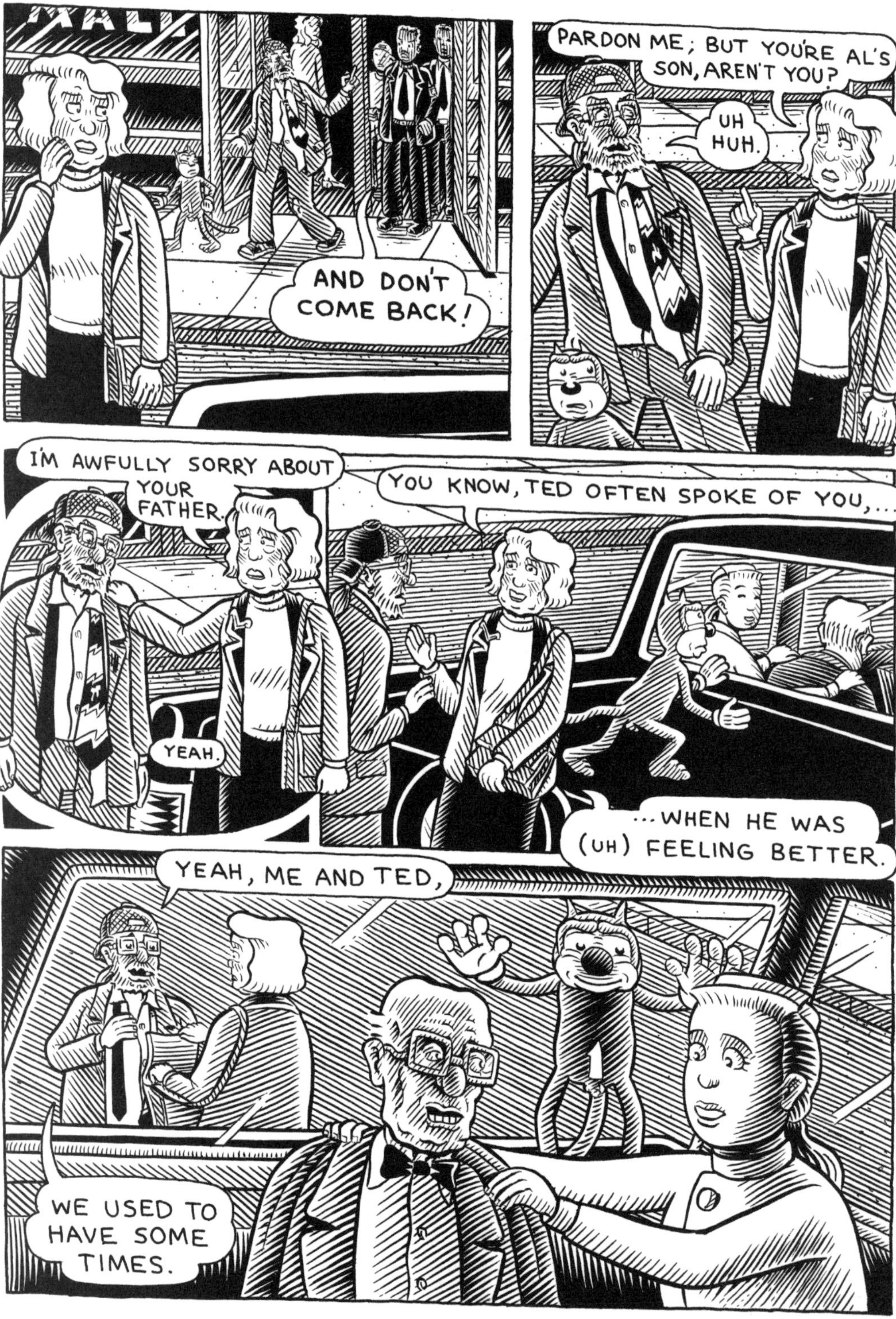
AND DON'T COME BACK!
PARDON ME; BUT YOU'RE AL'S SON, AREN'T YOU?
UH HUH.
I'M AWFULLY SORRY ABOUT YOUR FATHER.
YEAH.
YOU KNOW, TED OFTEN SPOKE OF YOU,...
...WHEN HE WAS (UH) FEELING BETTER.
YEAH, ME AND TED,
WE USED TO HAVE SOME TIMES.

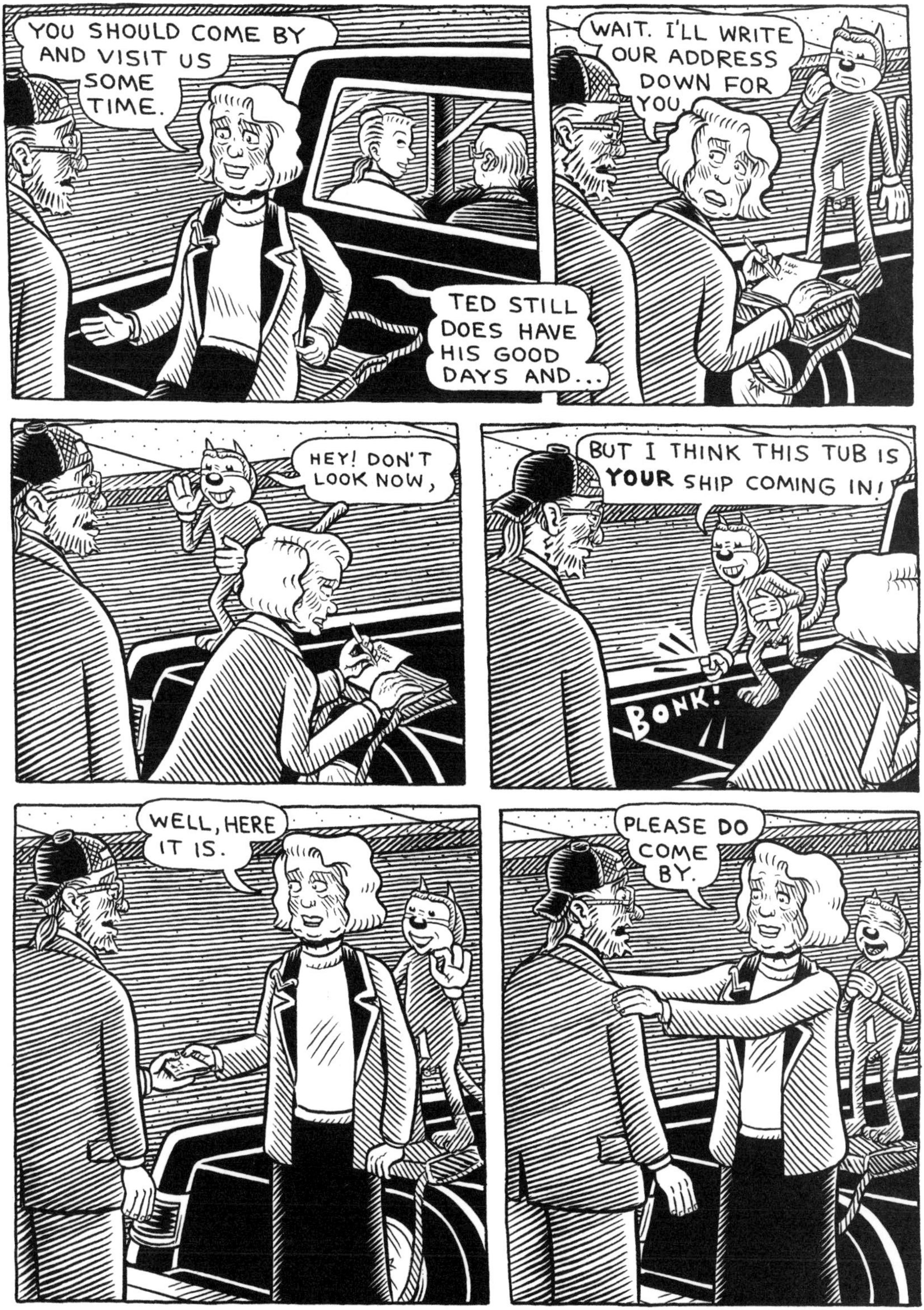
YOU SHOULD COME BY AND VISIT US SOME TIME.
TED STILL DOES HAVE HIS GOOD DAYS AND...
WAIT. I'LL WRITE OUR ADDRESS DOWN FOR YOU.
HEY! DON'T LOOK NOW,
BUT I THINK THIS TUB IS **YOUR** SHIP COMING IN!
BONK!
WELL, HERE IT IS.
PLEASE DO COME BY.

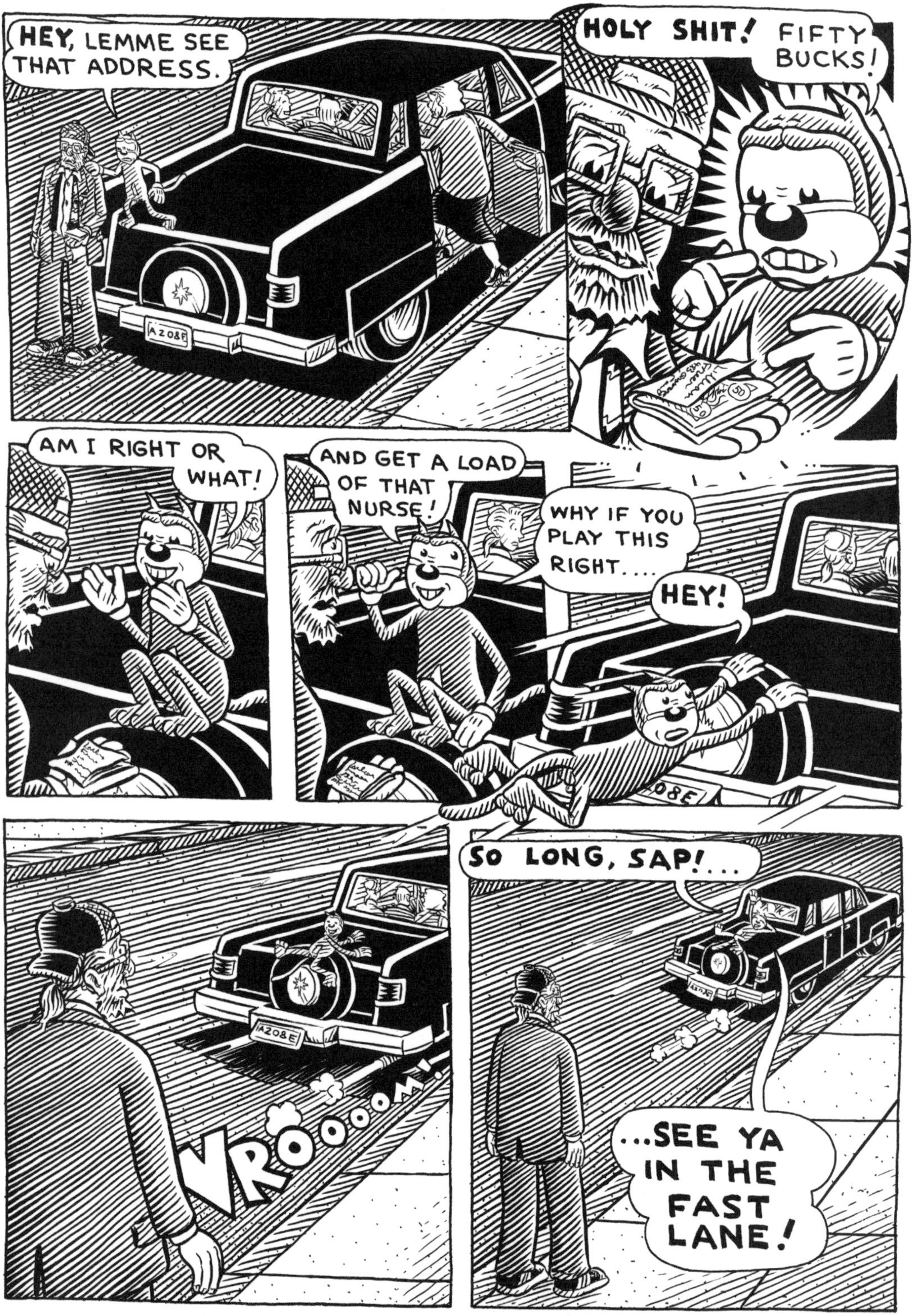
HEY, LEMME SEE THAT ADDRESS.
HOLY SHIT! FIFTY BUCKS!
AM I RIGHT OR WHAT!
AND GET A LOAD OF THAT NURSE!
WHY IF YOU PLAY THIS RIGHT....
HEY!
VROOOOOM!
SO LONG, SAP!...
...SEE YA IN THE FAST LANE!

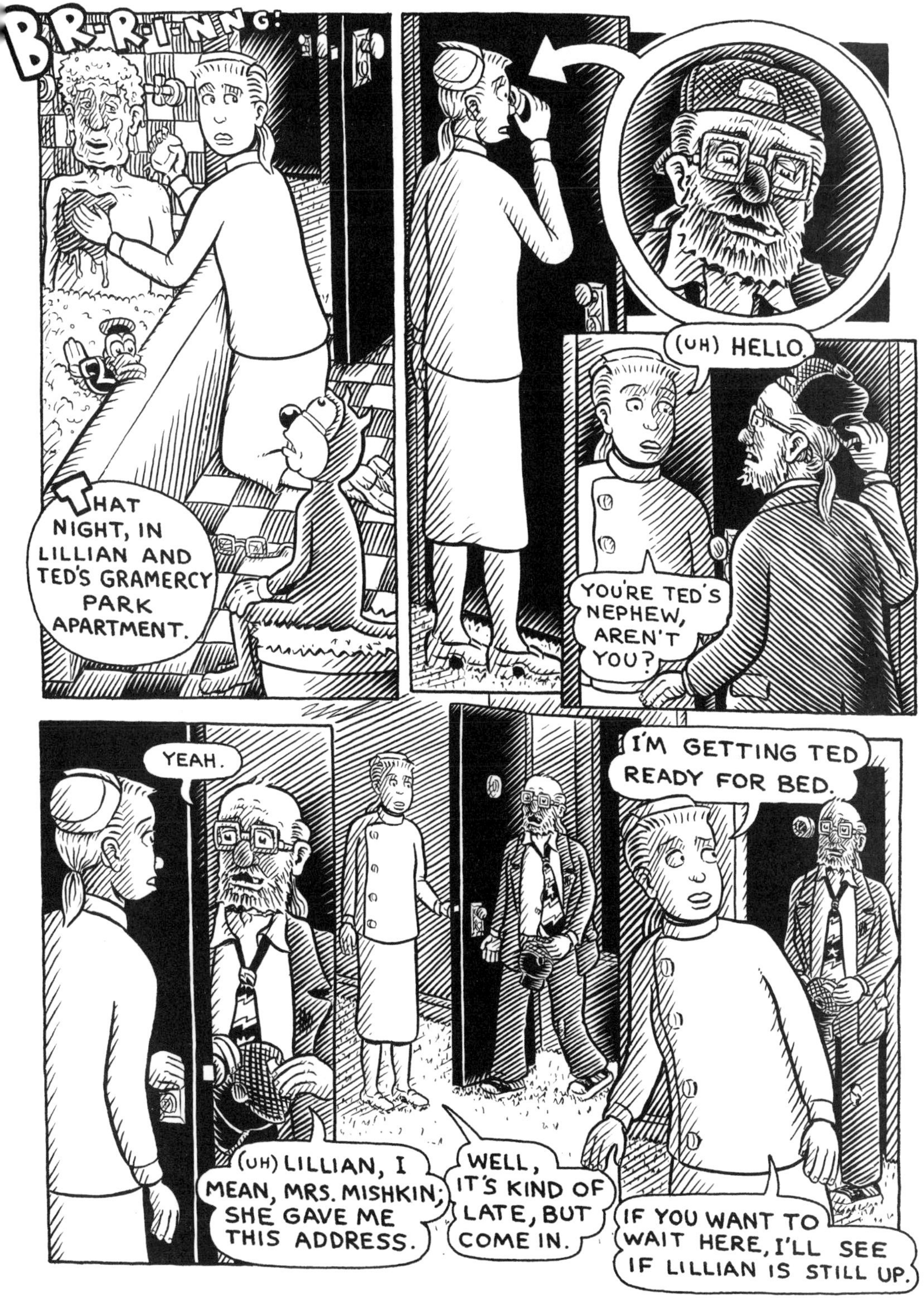
B-R-R-I-N-N-G!
THAT NIGHT, IN LILLIAN AND TED'S GRAMERCY PARK APARTMENT.
(UH) HELLO.
YOU'RE TED'S NEPHEW, AREN'T YOU?
YEAH.
(UH) LILLIAN, I MEAN, MRS. MISHKIN; SHE GAVE ME THIS ADDRESS.
WELL, IT'S KIND OF LATE, BUT COME IN.
I'M GETTING TED READY FOR BED.
IF YOU WANT TO WAIT HERE, I'LL SEE IF LILLIAN IS STILL UP.

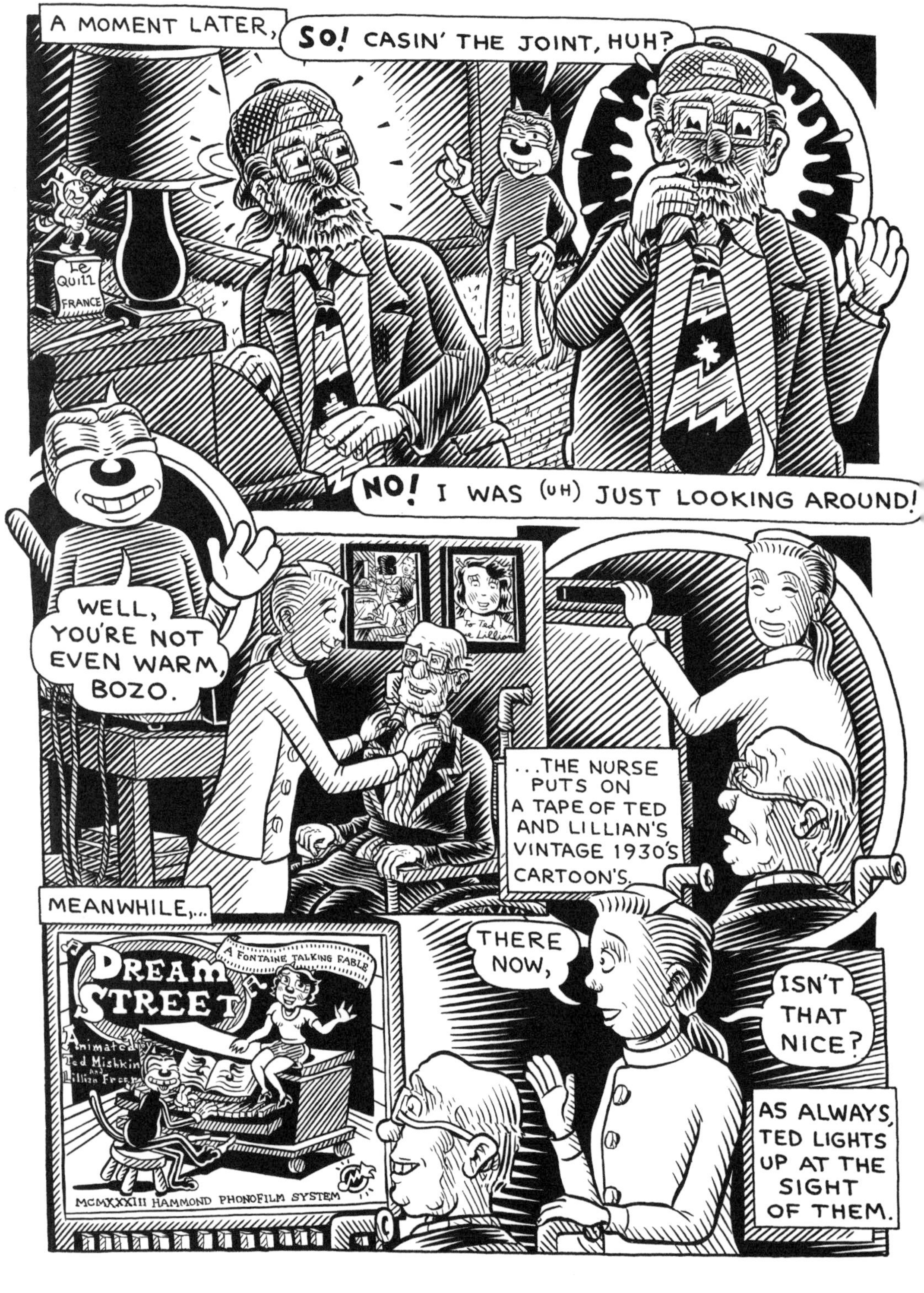
A MOMENT LATER,
SO! CASIN' THE JOINT, HUH?
LE QUILL FRANCE
NO! I WAS (UH) JUST LOOKING AROUND!
WELL, YOU'RE NOT EVEN WARM, BOZO.
...THE NURSE PUTS ON A TAPE OF TED AND LILLIAN'S VINTAGE 1930'S CARTOON'S.
MEANWHILE,...
A FONTAINE TALKING FABLE
DREAM STREET
MCMXXXIII HAMMOND PHONOFILM SYSTEM
THERE NOW,
ISN'T THAT NICE?
AS ALWAYS, TED LIGHTS UP AT THE SIGHT OF THEM.

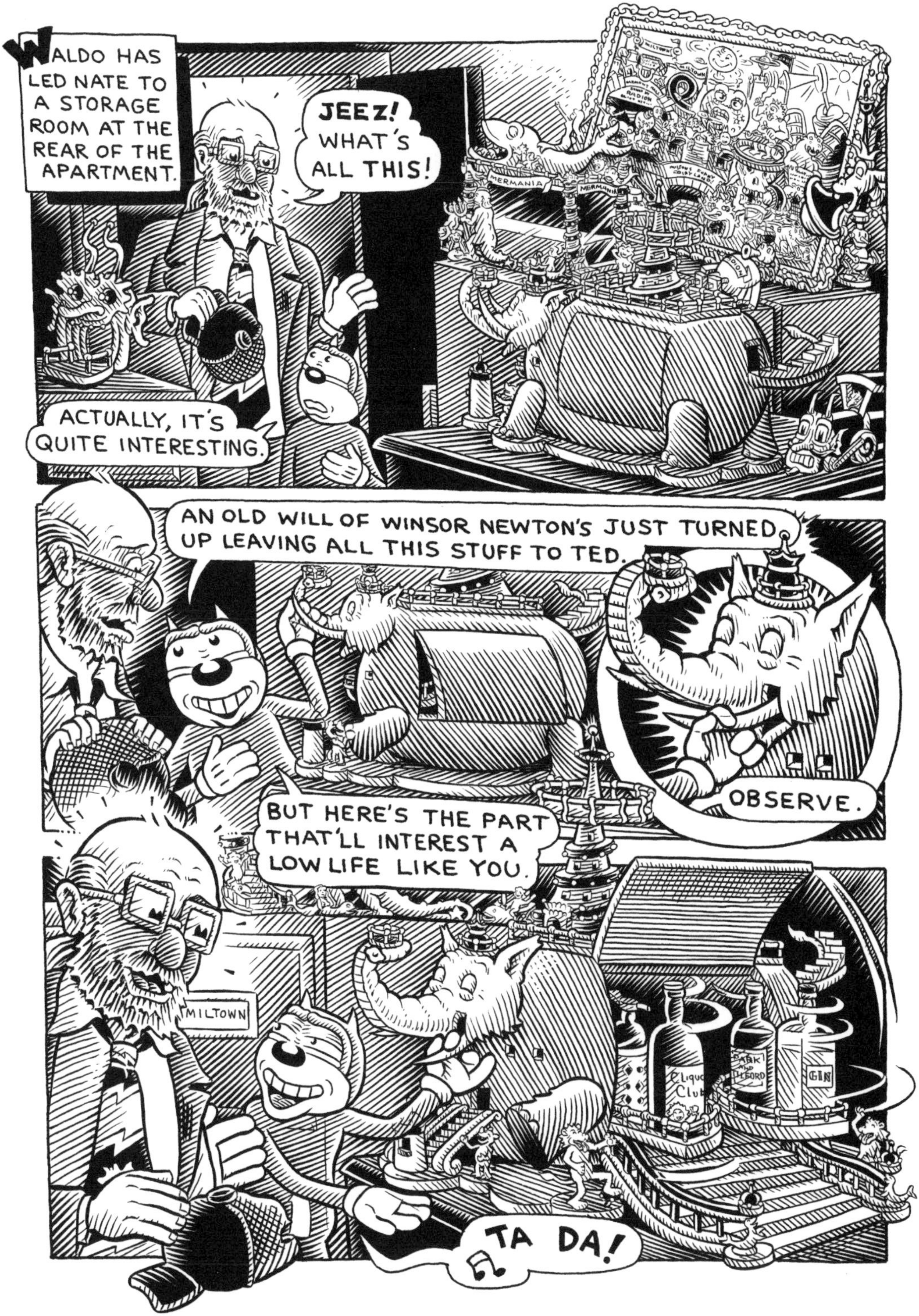
WALDO HAS LED NATE TO A STORAGE ROOM AT THE REAR OF THE APARTMENT.
JEEZ! WHAT'S ALL THIS!
ACTUALLY, IT'S QUITE INTERESTING.
MERMANIA
MERMANIA
AN OLD WILL OF WINSOR NEWTON'S JUST TURNED UP LEAVING ALL THIS STUFF TO TED.
OBSERVE.
BUT HERE'S THE PART THAT'LL INTEREST A LOW LIFE LIKE YOU.
MILTOWN
GIN
TA DA!

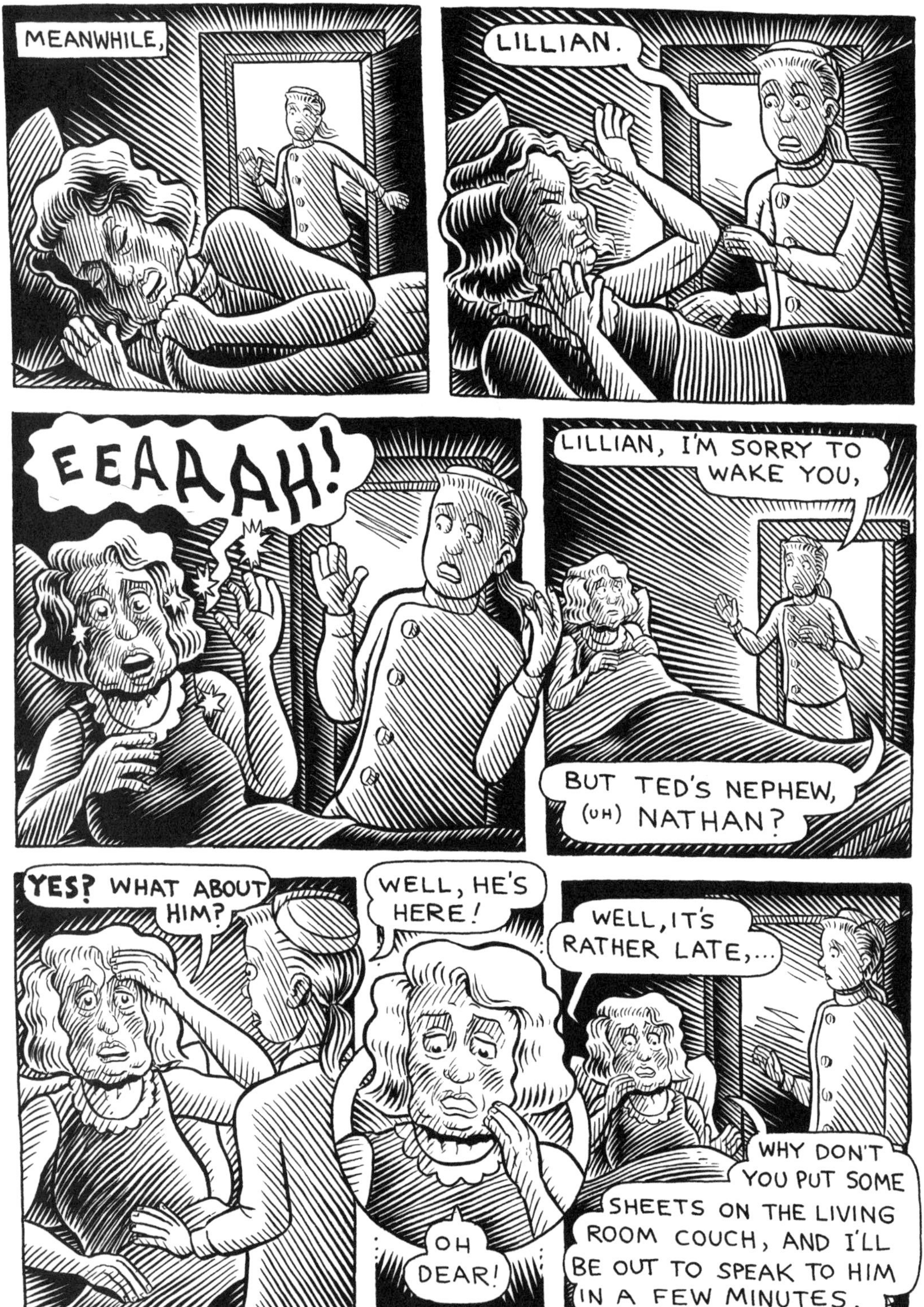
MEANWHILE,
LILLIAN.
EEAAAH!
LILLIAN, I'M SORRY TO WAKE YOU,
BUT TED'S NEPHEW, (UH) NATHAN?
YES? WHAT ABOUT HIM?
WELL, HE'S HERE!
OH DEAR!
WELL, IT'S RATHER LATE,...
WHY DON'T YOU PUT SOME SHEETS ON THE LIVING ROOM COUCH, AND I'LL BE OUT TO SPEAK TO HIM IN A FEW MINUTES.

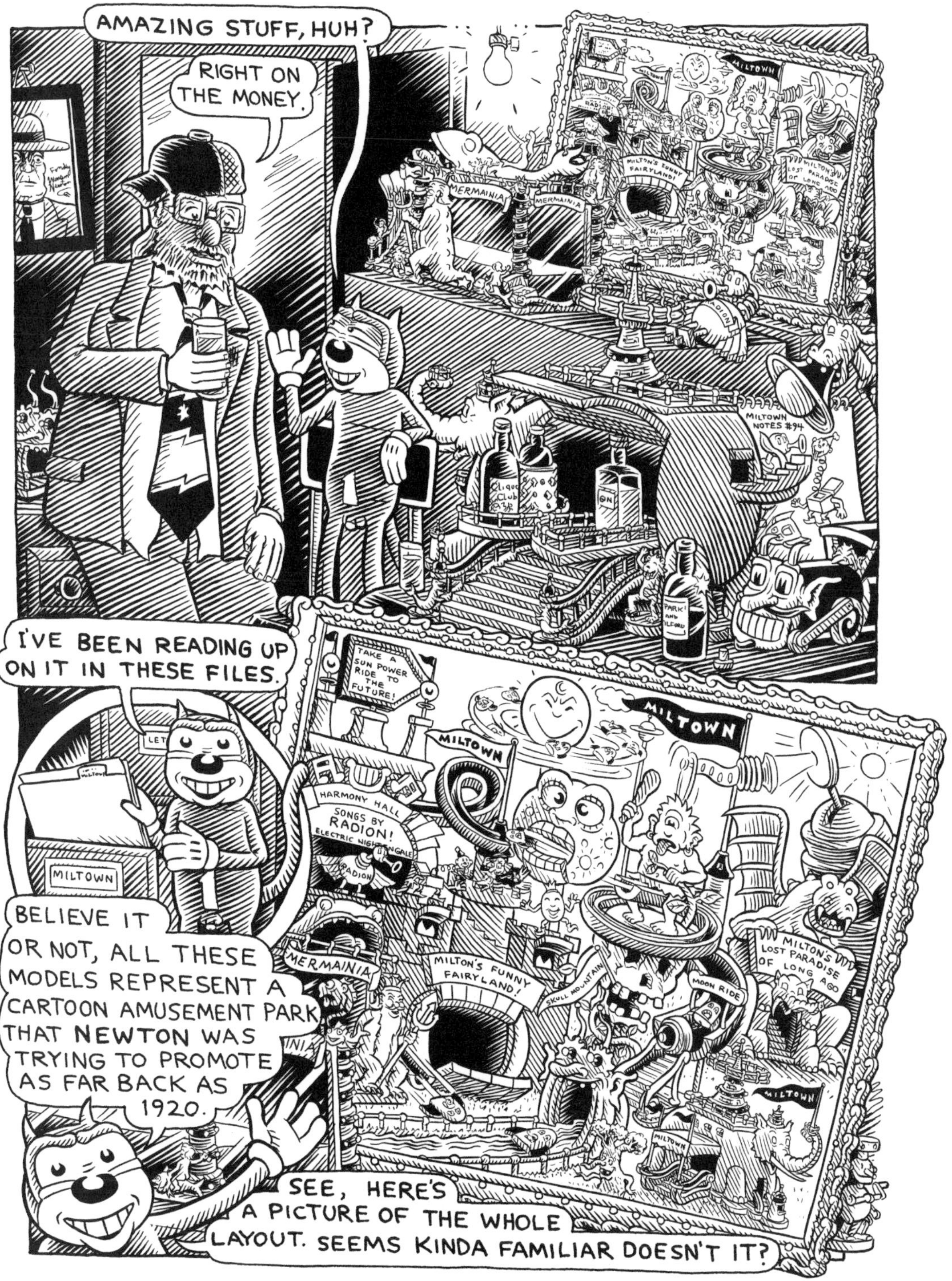
AMAZING STUFF, HUH?
RIGHT ON THE MONEY.
MERMAINIA
MILTOWN
MILTON'S FUNNY FAIRYLAND!
MILTOWN NOTES #94
GIN
I'VE BEEN READING UP ON IT IN THESE FILES.
MILTOWN
BELIEVE IT OR NOT, ALL THESE MODELS REPRESENT A CARTOON AMUSEMENT PARK THAT NEWTON WAS TRYING TO PROMOTE AS FAR BACK AS 1920.
TAKE A SUN POWER RIDE TO THE FUTURE!
MILTOWN
MILTOWN
HARMONY HALL
SONGS BY RADION! ELECTRIC NIGHTINGALE
RADION
MERMAINIA
MILTON'S FUNNY FAIRYLAND!
SKULL MOUNTAIN
MOON RIDE
MILTON'S LOST PARADISE OF LONG AGO
MILTOWN
SEE, HERE'S A PICTURE OF THE WHOLE LAYOUT. SEEMS KINDA FAMILIAR DOESN'T IT?

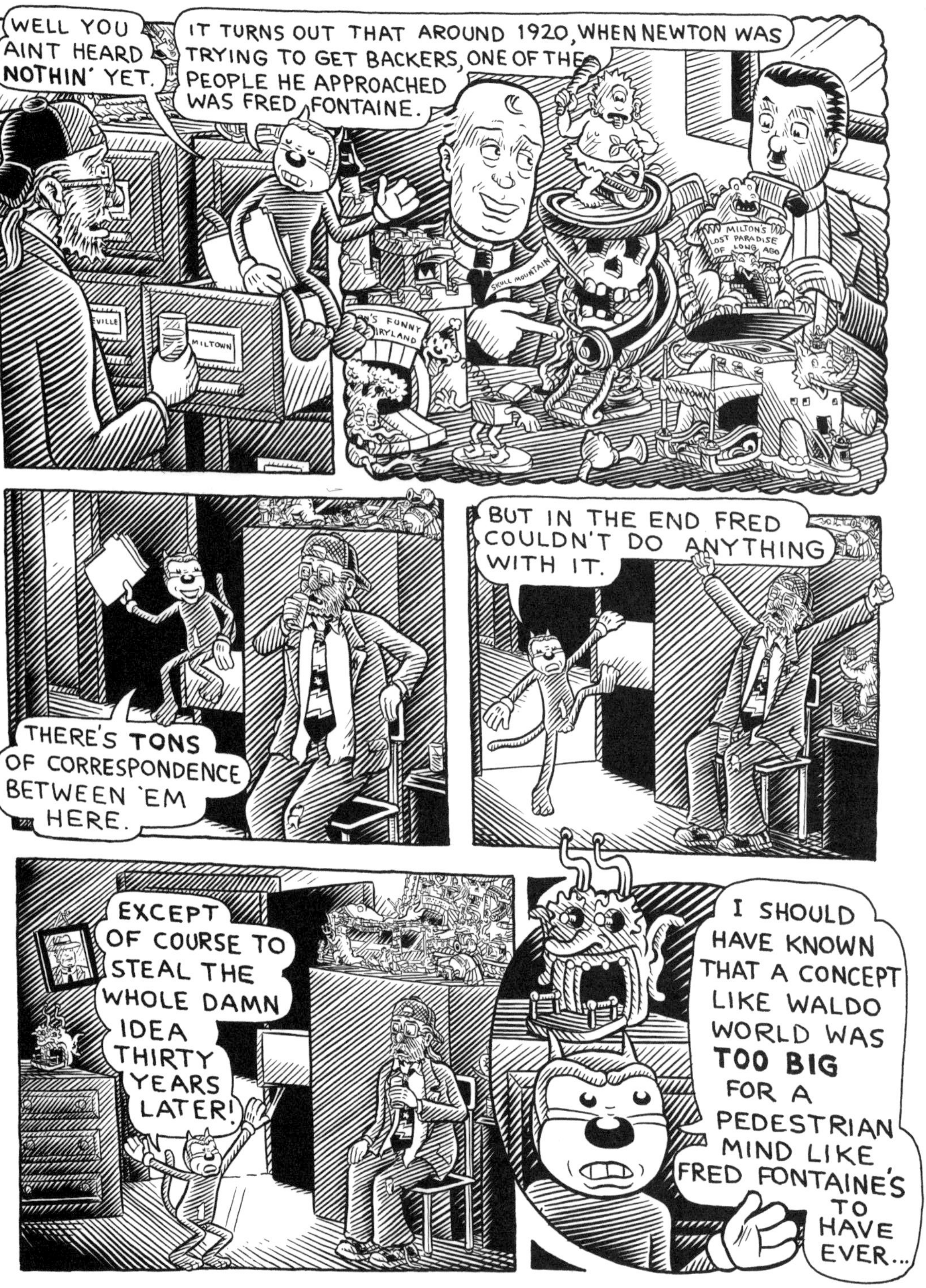
WELL YOU AINT HEARD **NOTHIN'** YET.
IT TURNS OUT THAT AROUND 1920, WHEN NEWTON WAS TRYING TO GET BACKERS, ONE OF THE PEOPLE HE APPROACHED WAS FRED FONTAINE.
MILTOWN
SKULL MOUNTAIN
MILTON'S LOST PARADISE OF LONG AGO
THERE'S **TONS** OF CORRESPONDENCE BETWEEN 'EM HERE.
BUT IN THE END FRED COULDN'T DO ANYTHING WITH IT.
EXCEPT OF COURSE TO STEAL THE WHOLE DAMN IDEA THIRTY YEARS LATER!
I SHOULD HAVE KNOWN THAT A CONCEPT LIKE WALDO WORLD WAS **TOO BIG** FOR A PEDESTRIAN MIND LIKE FRED FONTAINE'S TO HAVE EVER...

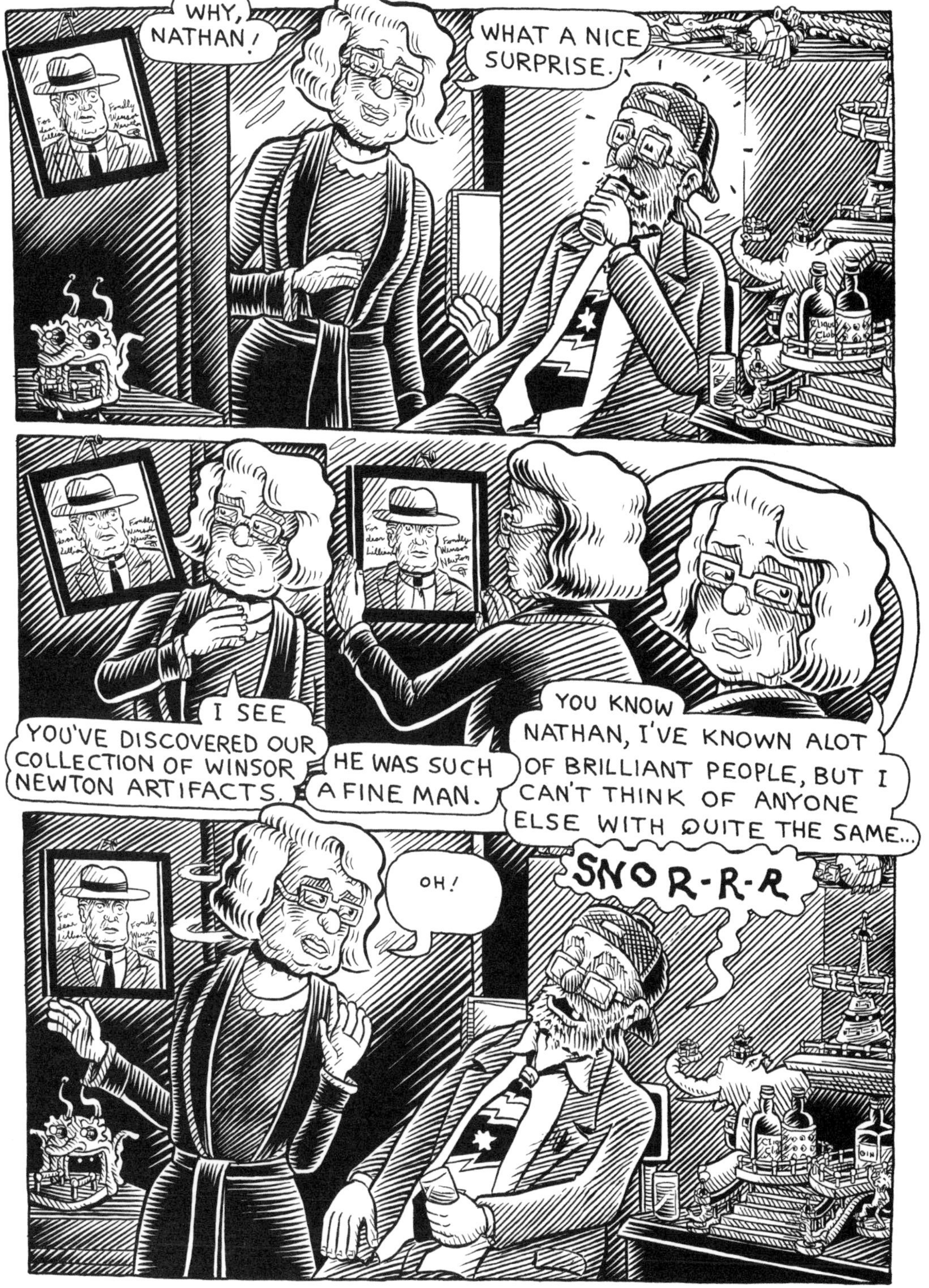
WHY, NATHAN!
WHAT A NICE SURPRISE.
For dear Lillian
Fondly Winsor Newton
Cliquot Club
I SEE YOU'VE DISCOVERED OUR COLLECTION OF WINSOR NEWTON ARTIFACTS.
HE WAS SUCH A FINE MAN.
YOU KNOW NATHAN, I'VE KNOWN ALOT OF BRILLIANT PEOPLE, BUT I CAN'T THINK OF ANYONE ELSE WITH QUITE THE SAME...
SNOR-R-R
OH!
GIN

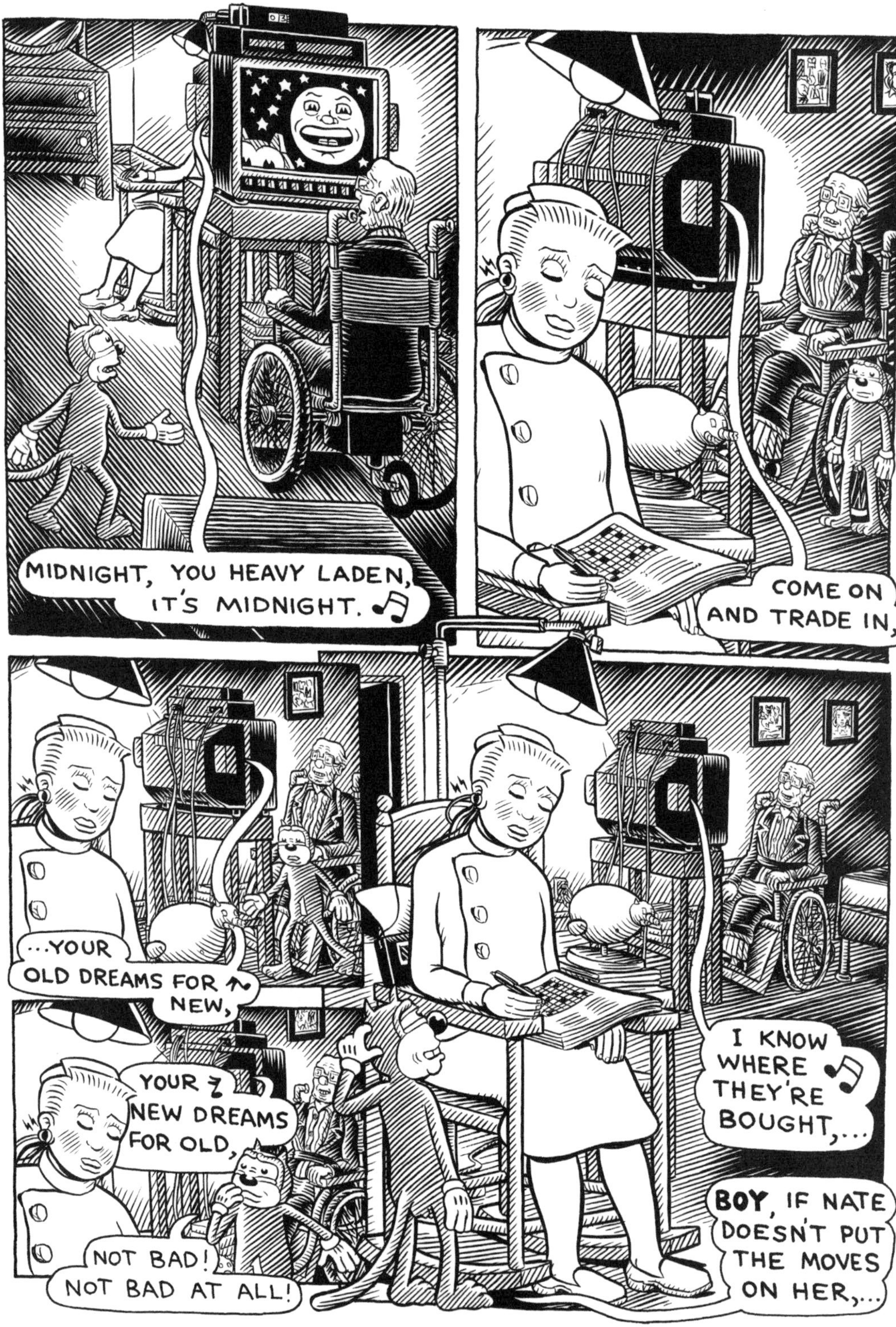
MIDNIGHT, YOU HEAVY LADEN, IT'S MIDNIGHT.
COME ON AND TRADE IN,
...YOUR OLD DREAMS FOR NEW,
YOUR NEW DREAMS FOR OLD,
I KNOW WHERE THEY'RE BOUGHT,...
NOT BAD! NOT BAD AT ALL!
BOY, IF NATE DOESN'T PUT THE MOVES ON HER,...

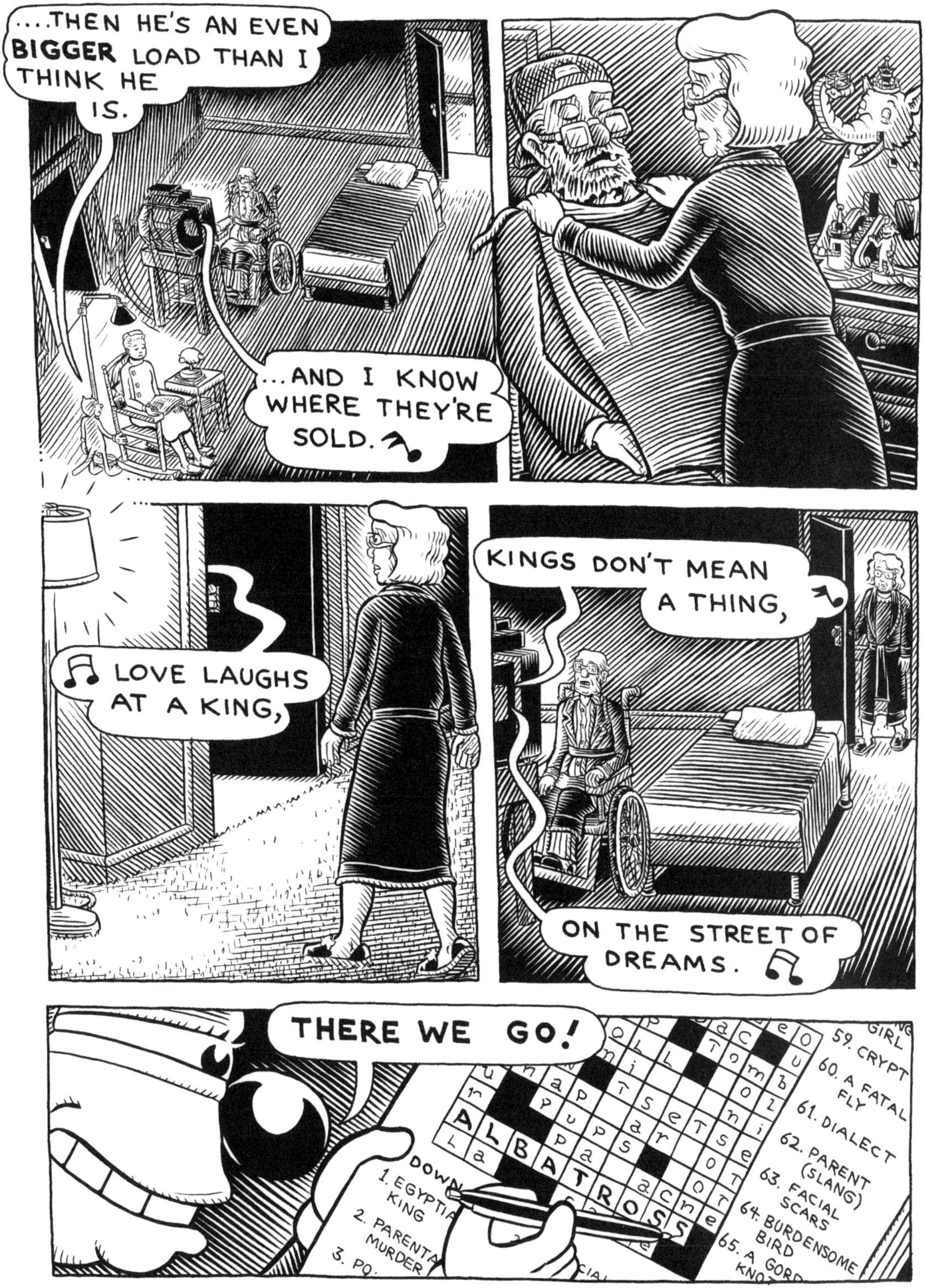
....THEN HE'S AN EVEN **BIGGER** LOAD THAN I THINK HE IS.
...AND I KNOW WHERE THEY'RE SOLD.
LOVE LAUGHS AT A KING,
KINGS DON'T MEAN A THING,
ON THE STREET OF DREAMS.
THERE WE GO!
ALBATROSS
DOWN
1. EGYPTIA KING
2. PARENTA MURDER
3. PO
59. CRYPT
60. A FATAL FLY
61. DIALECT
62. PARENT (SLANG)
63. FACIAL SCARS
64. BURDENSOME BIRD
65. A GORD KNOT

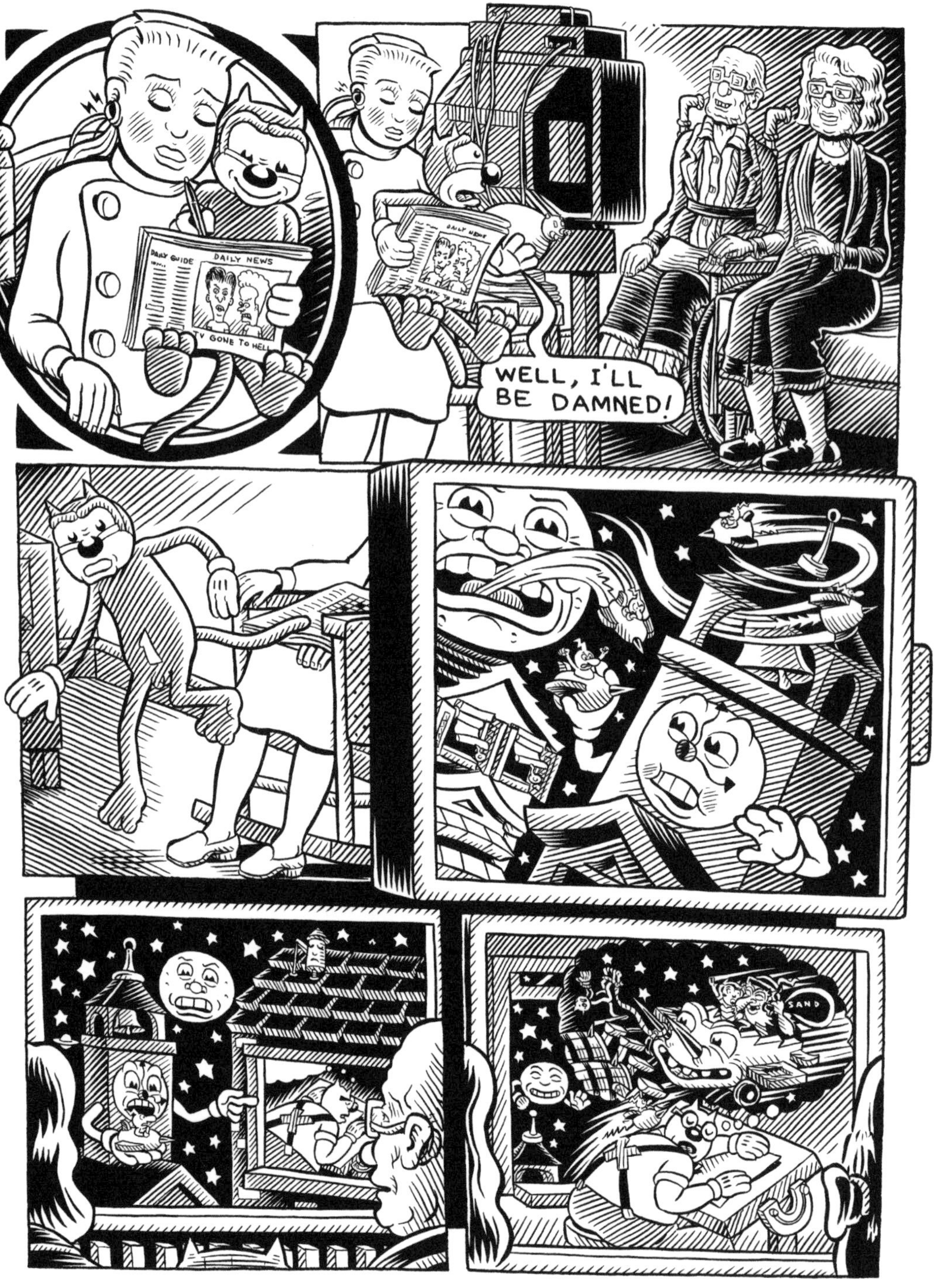
DAILY GUIDE
DAILY NEWS
TV GONE TO HELL
WELL, I'LL BE DAMNED!
SAND

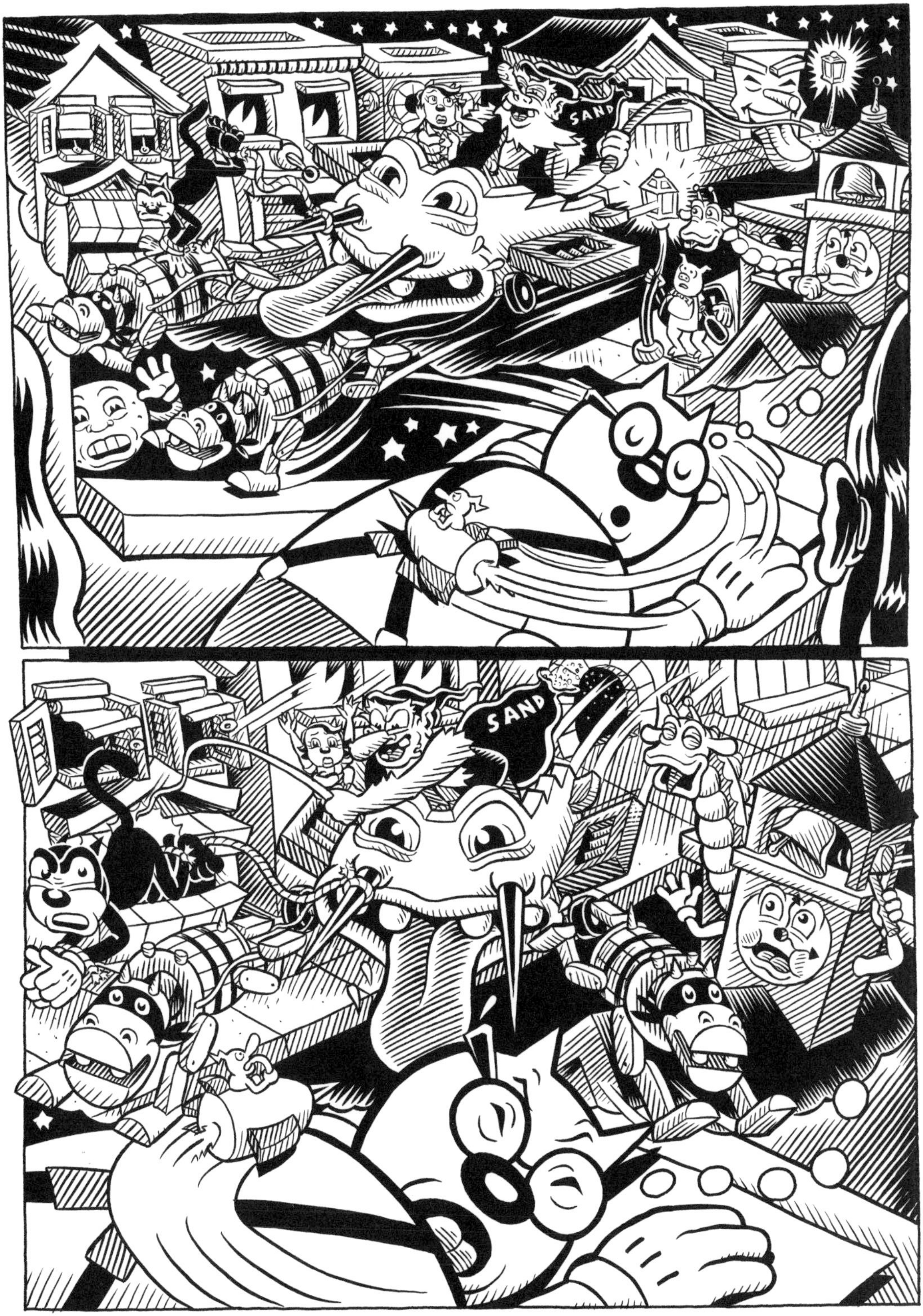
SAND
SAND

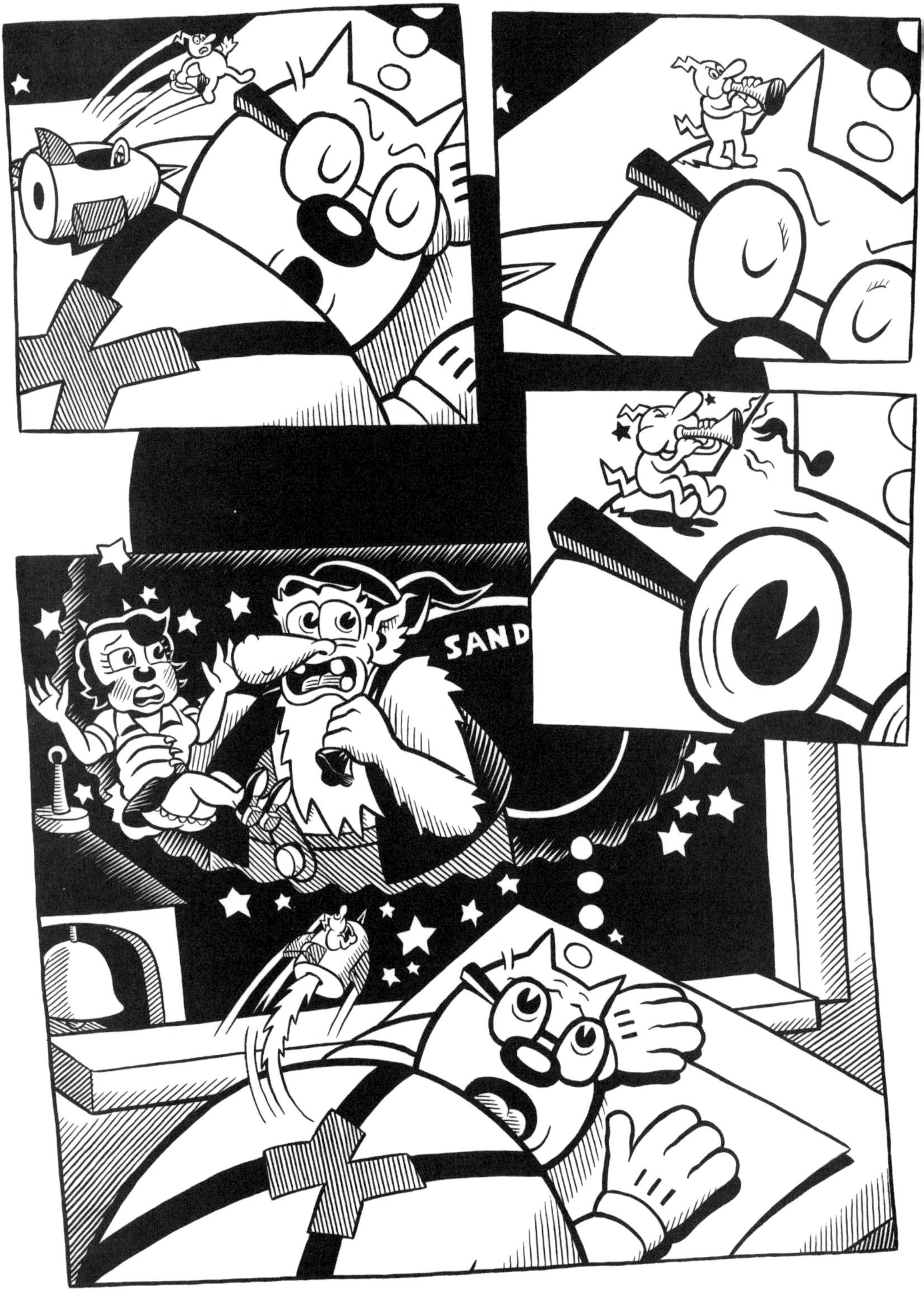
SAND

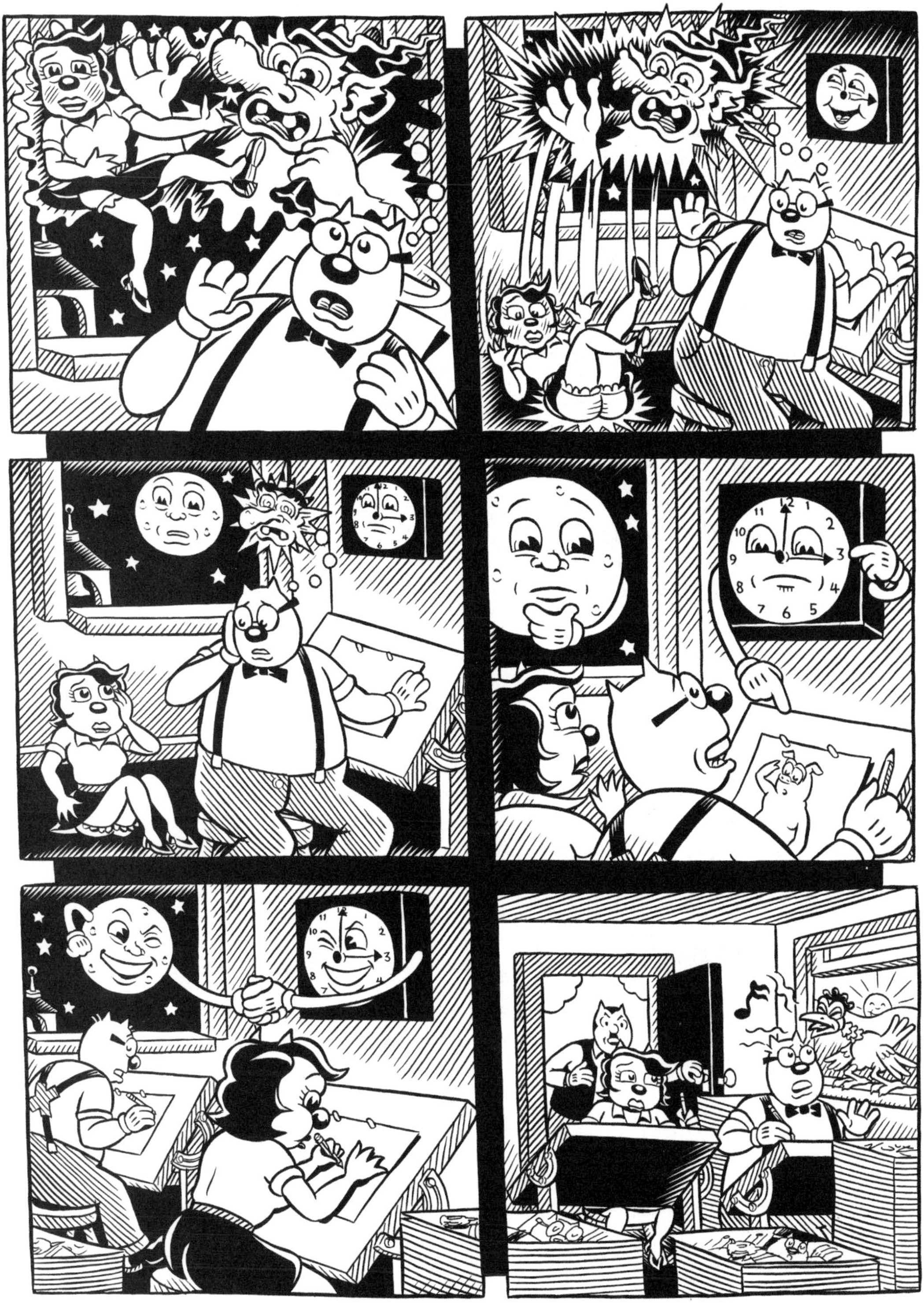

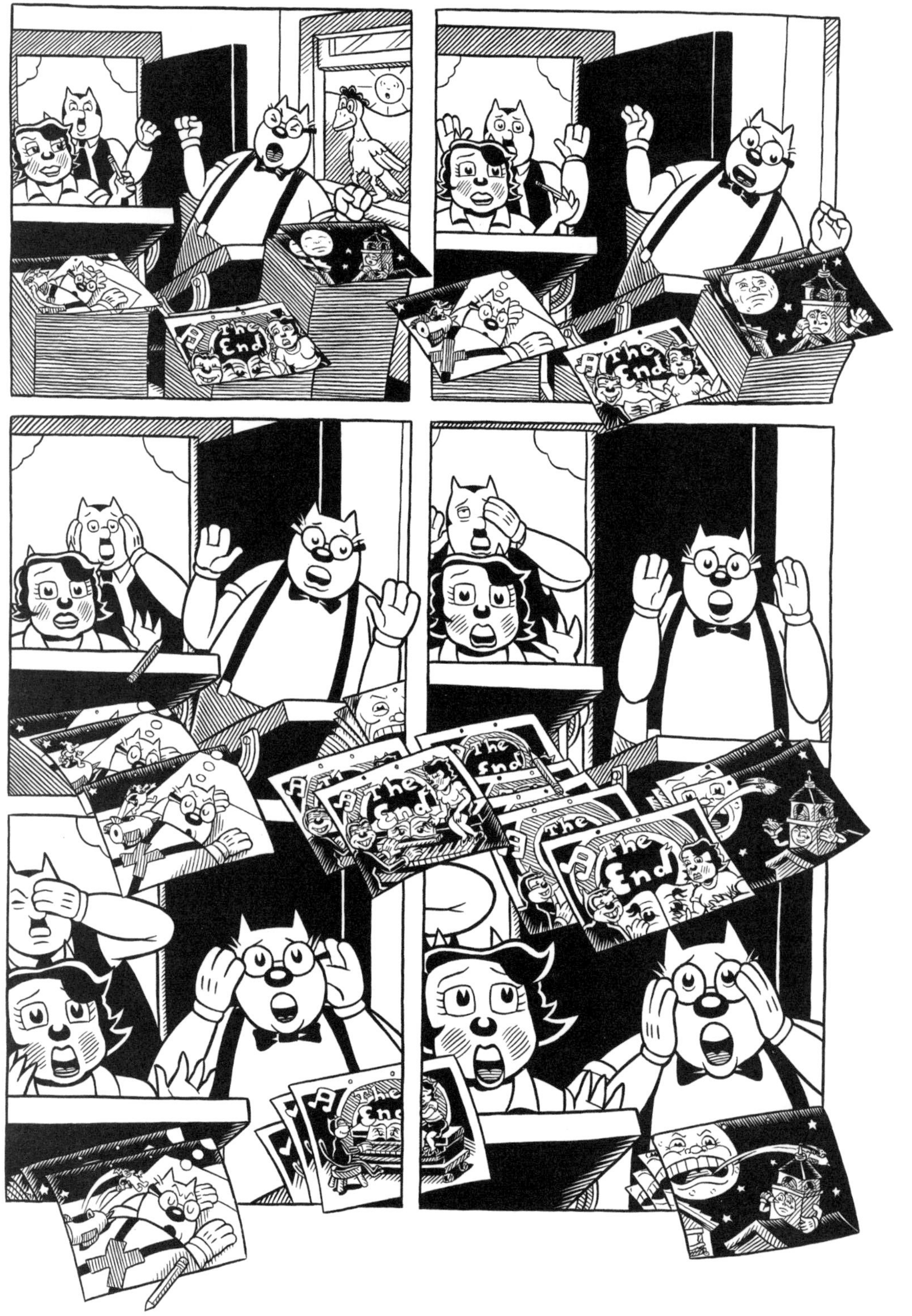
The End

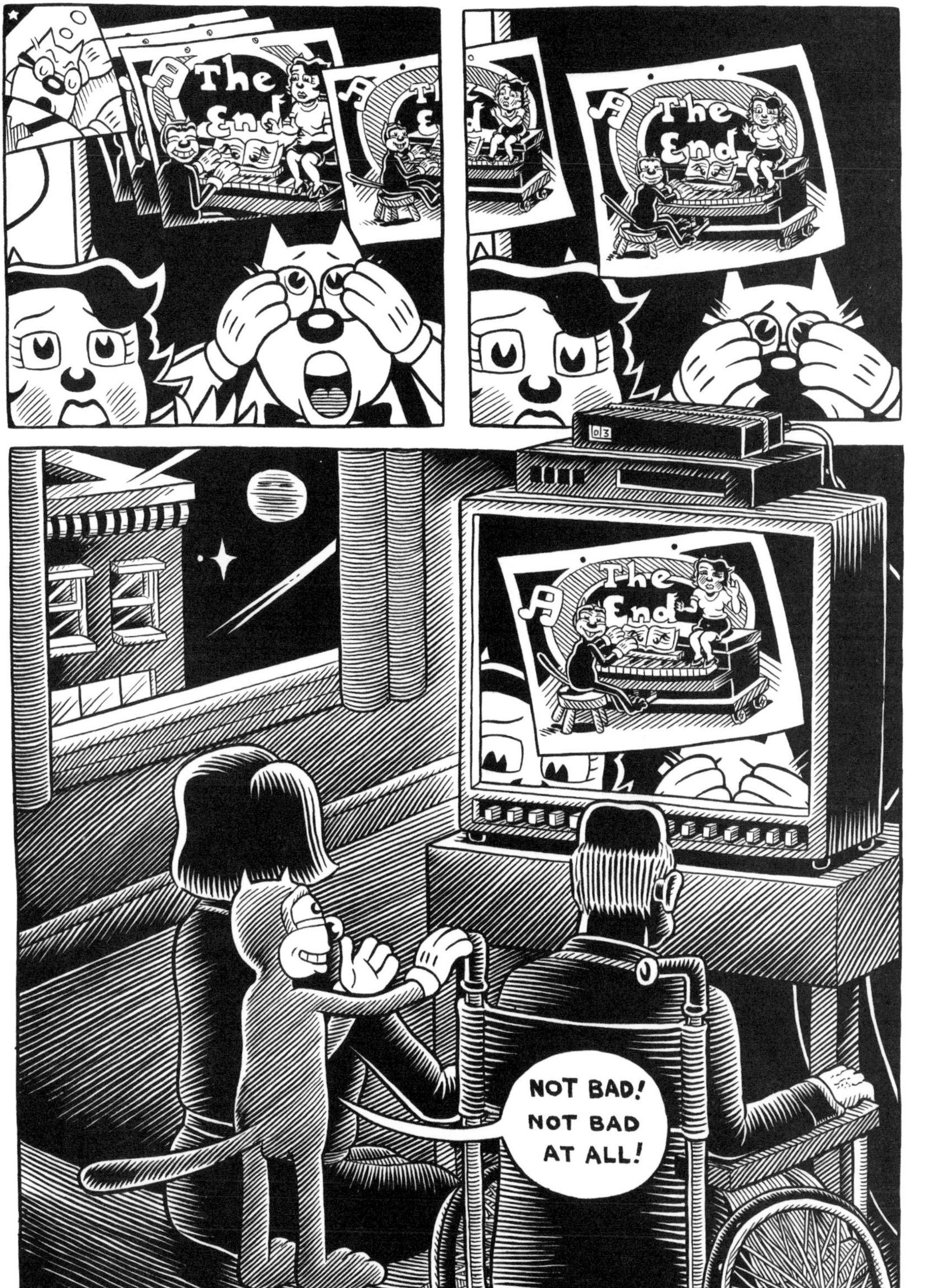
The End
03
NOT BAD! NOT BAD AT ALL!

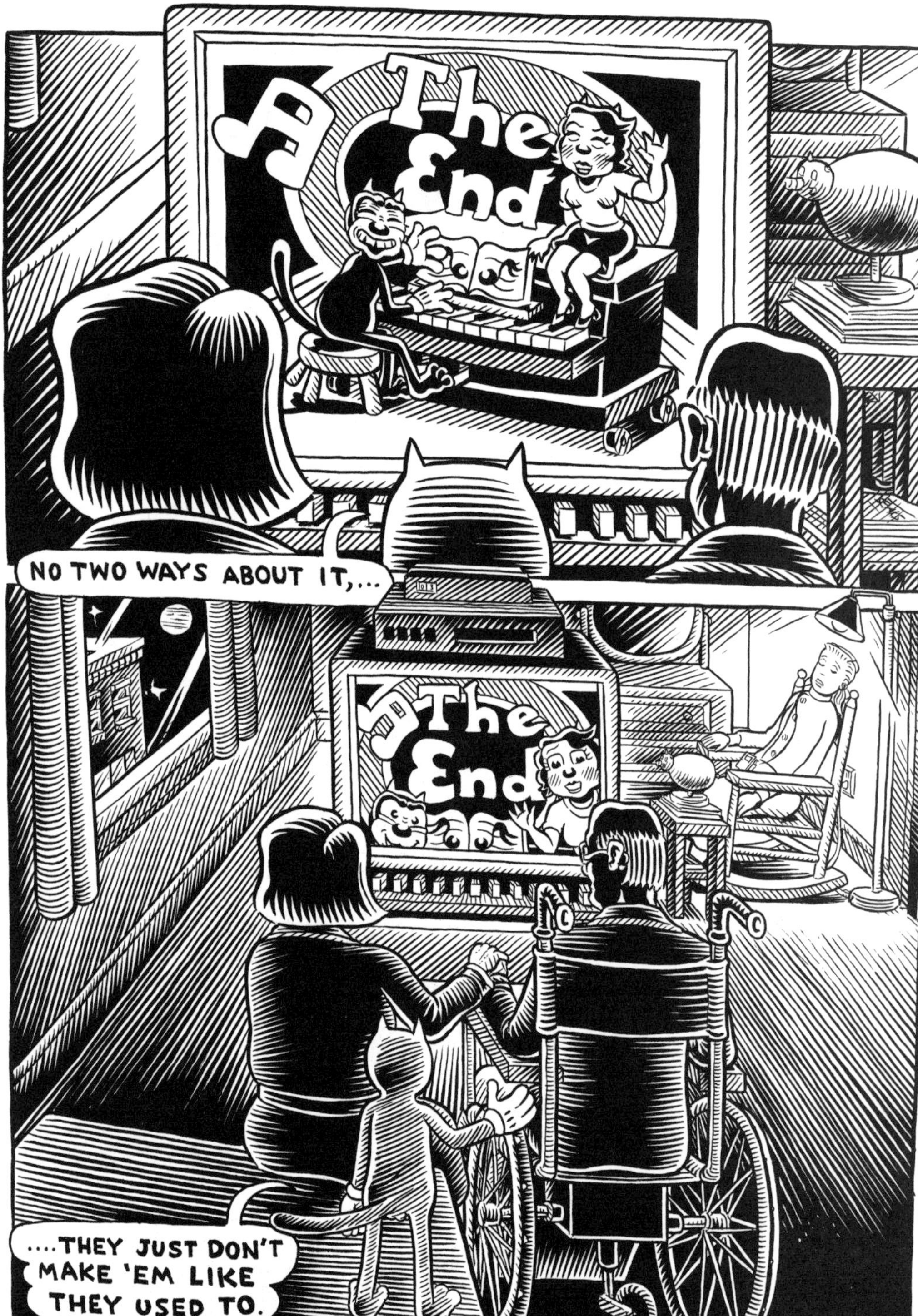
The End
NO TWO WAYS ABOUT IT,...
The End
....THEY JUST DON'T MAKE 'EM LIKE THEY USED TO.

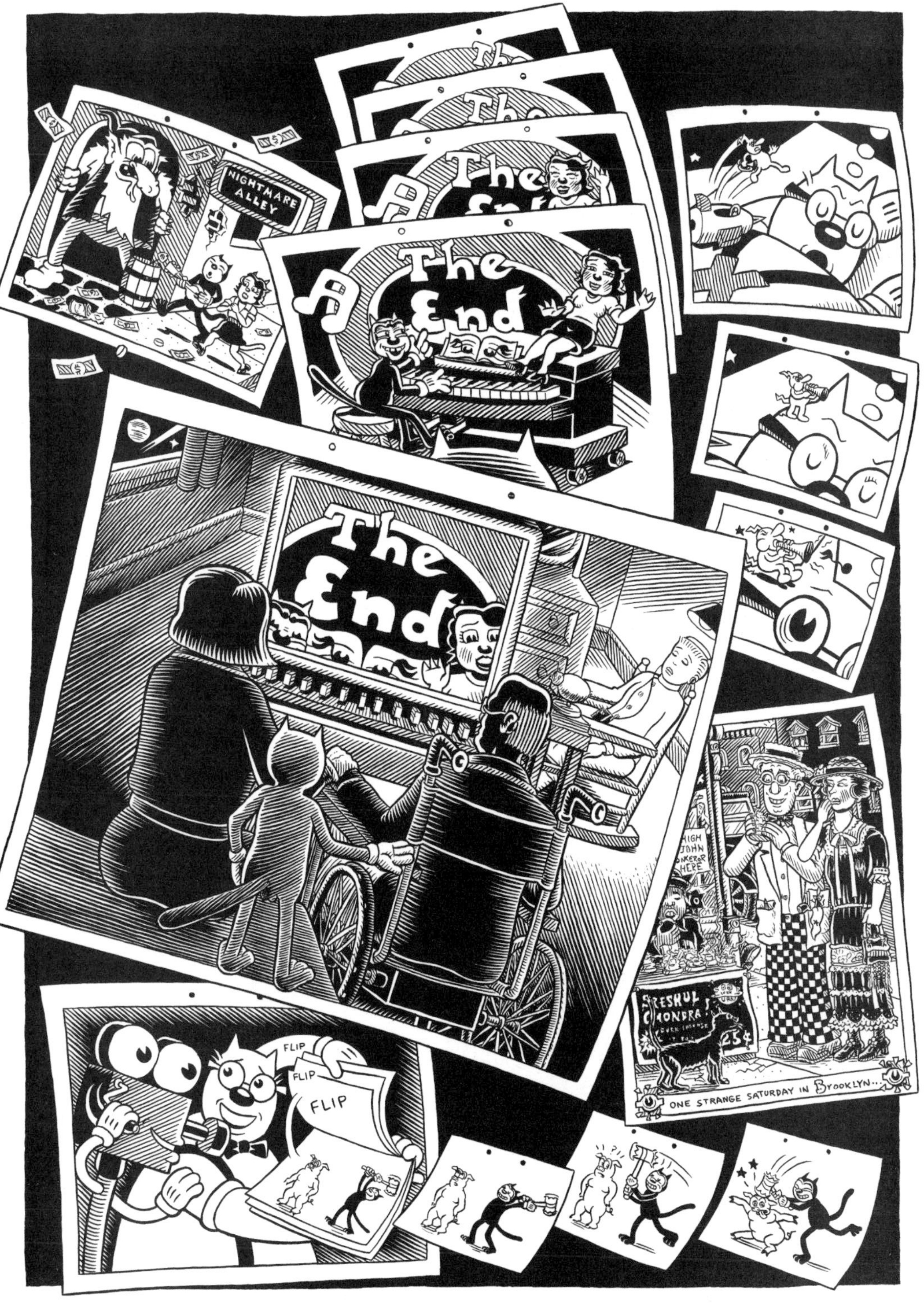
NIGHTMARE ALLEY
The End
The End
HIGH JOHN CONKER OR HERE
SPESHUL CHONDRA
25¢
ONE STRANGE SATURDAY IN BROOKLYN...
FLIP
FLIP
FLIP

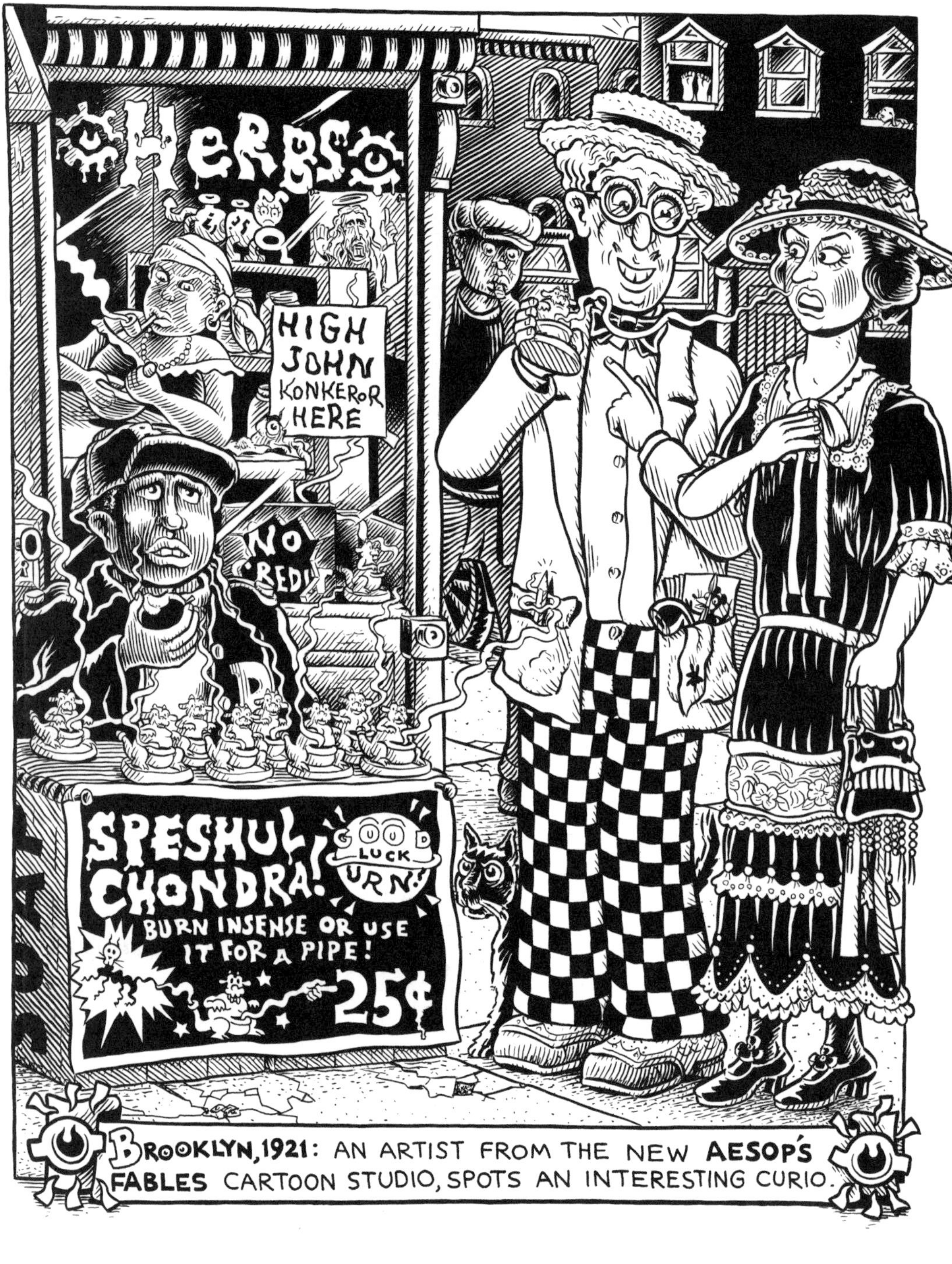
HERBS
HIGH JOHN KONKEROR HERE
SPESHUL CHONDRA!
GOOD LUCK URN!
BURN INSENSE OR USE IT FOR A PIPE!
25¢
BROOKLYN, 1921: AN ARTIST FROM THE NEW AESOP'S FABLES CARTOON STUDIO, SPOTS AN INTERESTING CURIO.

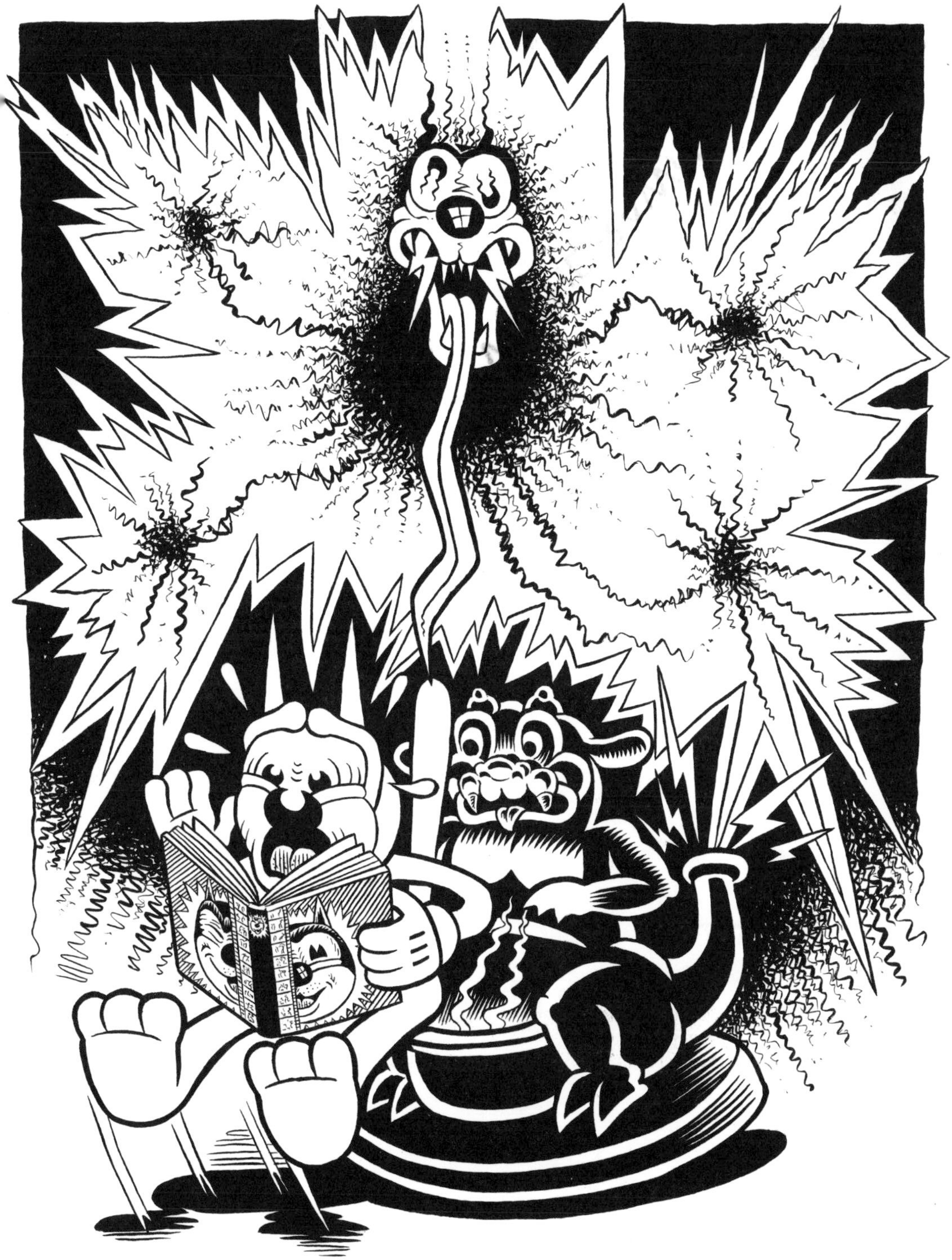

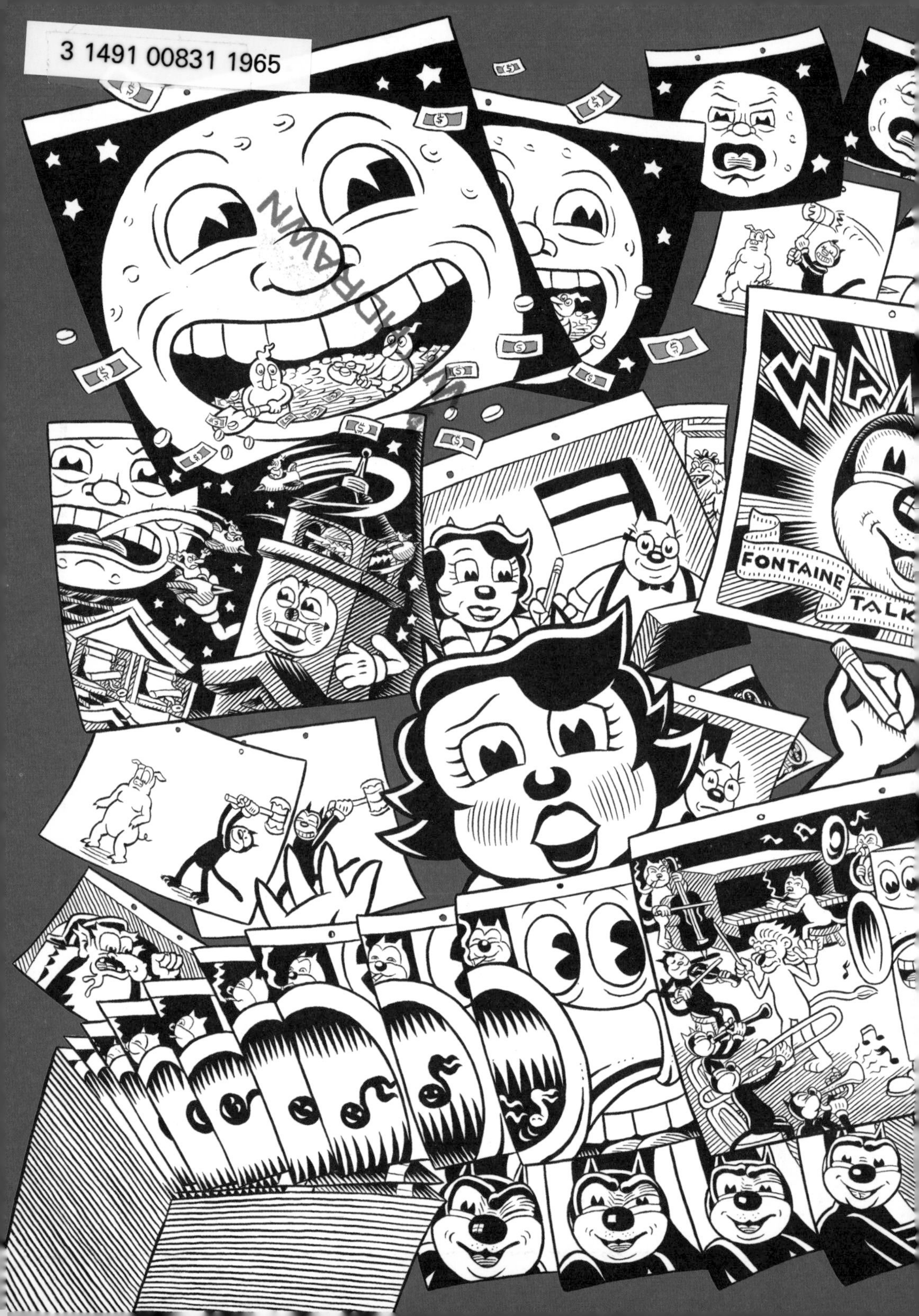

FONTAINE
TALK